P9-DMS-577

BY THE
KING'S DESIGN

Books by Christine Trent

By the King's Design

A Royal Likeness

The Queen's Dollmaker

BY THE
KING'S DESIGN

CHRISTINE TRENT

KENSINGTON BOOKS
www.kensingtonbooks.com

BUNCOMBE COUNTY PUBLIC LIBRARIES

KENSINGTON BOOKS are published by

Kensington Publishing Corp.
119 West 40th Street
New York, NY 10018

Copyright © 2012 by Christine Trent

All rights reserved. No part of this book may be reproduced in any form or by any means without the prior written consent of the Publisher, excepting brief quotes used in reviews.

All Kensington titles, imprints, and distributed lines are available at special quantity discounts for bulk purchases for sales promotion, premiums, fund-raising, educational or institutional use.

Special book excerpts or customized printings can also be created to fit specific needs. For details, write or phone the office of the Kensington Special Sales Manager: Kensington Publishing Corp., 119 West 40th Street, New York, NY 10018. Attn. Special Sales Department. Phone: 1-800-221-2647.

Kensington and the K logo Reg. U.S. Pat. & TM Off.

ISBN-13: 978-0-7582-6590-6
ISBN-10: 0-7582-6590-5

First Kensington Trade Paperback Printing: February 2012
10 9 8 7 6 5 4 3 2 1

Printed in the United States of America

For my husband, Jon,
my very own master cabinetmaker

and

For Georgia Carpenter—
mother, editor, friend

ACKNOWLEDGMENTS

No novel can come into existence without plenty of research, and it's especially true for historical fiction. My sincere thanks go to the craftsmen at the Colonial Williamsburg cabinetmaker's shop, who spent a few hours on a warm spring day entertaining all of my pesky questions about the similarities between cabinetmaking in early nineteenth-century England versus colonial America. Cabinetmakers Bill Pavlak, Kaare Loftheim, and Edward Wright all had a vast knowledge of the tools, techniques, and living conditions of their counterparts from two centuries ago.

Thanks are also due to my agent, Helen Breitwieser, who is a simply wonderful combination of coach and teammate over my career, as well as to my editor, Audrey LaFehr, who gives me freedom to write stories the way I want.

I am perpetually indebted to my mother, Georgia, and friend Diane Townsend, who continue to diligently read my manuscripts and pluck out all of my errors, as well as listen to a writer's self-doubt. My brother, Tony, ripped my characters to shreds and helped me put them back together again. *Dude.*

This writer's days are perked up by Leslie Carroll, fellow novelist and friend, with whom I spent entirely too many hours e-mailing about the minutiae of life instead of working on my manuscript.

Jackie and Hayley at The Hair Company make my three hours each month pure bliss with their pampering while I occupy a chair, scribbling away. Jackie, I may still one day take you up on that offer for a permanent writing chair!

I cannot overstate my gratitude to the online historical fiction blogging world for their enthusiasm for the genre and their warm welcome of new novelists into their world. Any readers seeking good recommendations for books can do no better than to visit blogs such as All Things Historical Fiction, Tea at Trianon, Confessions and Ramblings of a Muse in the Fog, Enchanted by

Josephine, Historical Tapestry, Obsessed With Books, Passages to the Past, and Tanzanite's Shelf and Stuff. There are many more bloggers out there, as well, who devote many hours to reading and reporting on books.

In particular, my thanks for their fabulously coordinated blog tours go to Liz at Historically Obsessed, Heather at The Maiden's Court, Allie at Hist-Fic Chick, and Arleigh at Historical-Fiction.com. You're a warm, wonderfully supportive group of bloggers!

Finally, and most important, my love and high regard go to my husband, Jon, who brainstorms plots with me, champions me to the finish line and, in the case of this book, advised me step-by-step on woodworking tools and techniques. I would be utterly unable to complete a book without this extraordinary man.

Laus Deo.

PROLOGUE

I do of my own free will and accord to hereby promise and swear that I will never reveal any of the names of any one of this secret committee under the penalty of being sent out of this world by the first brother that may meet me.

—From the 1812 Luddite Oath, "Twisting In"

April 1812
In a field near Rawfold's Mill, Brighouse, Yorkshire

"Remember what I told you, brothers. Leave the machines, but shoot the masters." George Mellor pulled his mask back over his face, leaving only his blue eyes blazing out from atop the soiled kerchief. His large, brawny presence belied his age of two and twenty.

Dozens of men imitated him in silence, the rustling of their masks the only sound in the growing twilight. The remainder of Mellor's straggling army had foregone masks and blackened their faces. The malodor of his mask made Mellor wish he'd done the same.

He shook his head in wonder at the few who had adopted a strange uniform, an ill-fitting woman's dress over homespun trousers. He, like most of the men, wore his cropping apron, used to protect his clothing from loose fibers as he used huge, weighty shears with curved blades to cut away the nap of recently woven and pounded fabric. This slow and laborious work resulted in cloth with a smooth and even surface. The croppers' work was the final stage of manufacture before fabric was sent to market.

The average cropper had bulging arms, carved and toned from years of handling his forty-pound cropping blades. But these talented craftsmen, whose work was so highly prized that they typically earned three times the pay of mere wool spinners, were this night planning to use their strength for more nefarious purposes.

"I'll personally smash in Cartwright's head!" bellowed a man in the crowd, holding up a smithy hammer with a nasty iron head.

"Quiet, fool!" Mellor hissed. "Can't have anyone noticing us before we even get started."

The men jostled restlessly, and an "Ow!" from the direction of the shouter told Mellor that someone had swiftly applied an elbow to his side to shut him up.

Mellor crouched down to wait until it was dark enough to complete the march to Rawfold's Mill. Tonight they were going to teach William Cartwright a lesson. The man had brazenly used new cloth-finishing machinery for the past year, putting many honest, competent men out of work and ruining the trade by producing inferior fabrics, stockings, and lace. Nothing exceeded what a Yorkshire man could do with a pair of cropping shears.

It could be tolerated no longer.

Known affectionately as "King Ludd" by the other croppers, in honor of Ned Ludd, who had initially started the rebellion against machinery in Nottinghamshire, Mellor had steadfastly tried to be precise in his attacks, directing men to smash only the offending pieces of equipment and not to molest buildings or mill families. After all, he wasn't a murderer, he was only trying to protect a generations-old way of life for thousands of people.

But Cartwright's arrogance had driven Mellor insane with fury.

First, the mill owner had sent derisive responses to Mellor's letters instructing him to remove the new mechanized cropping frames and gig mills. Then, to make matters worse, rumors reached Mellor's ears that Cartwright was reinforcing his mill, trying to turn it into a fortress against him. Even the smaller outbuildings of the mill complex had supposedly been fortified. Doors strengthened, spikes set on stairwells, and men poised on the roof with acid carboys ready to be poured on any attackers.

It was insufferable. Not that Mellor believed the bit about the acid.

And so Mellor changed his policy of protecting the mill owners. Tonight, Cartwright would pay the ultimate price.

Mellor gave a hand gesture, which was repeated throughout the crowd, signaling that it was time to begin their three-mile walk to the mill. Along the way, they converged with a Luddite group from Leeds, and now marched as a strong, three-hundred-man army to Rawfold's. Each man armed himself in his own way, with either hammer, sword, or pistol. Mellor smiled grimly at the terrifying sight they must be.

It was completely dark as they approached the five-story mill and its thatched outbuildings. Mellor spread word that all but a few torches were to be extinguished.

All was quiet and still at Cartwright's place, with just a lone lamp burning in an upper-story window. Probably left behind by one of those witless new machine operators.

Mellor signaled again, and his men silently began fanning themselves around the main building. This was the moment that always thrilled Mellor the most. Those last ninety seconds before he and his fellow Luddites rampaged into a mill. The smell of fear and excitement blended into an energizing intoxicant, and he could feel his own power oozing from his pores, knowing that no one would raise a pike, stick, or hammer without his say-so.

He paused to let a light breeze pass over him. He closed his eyes, and breathed deep of the crisp night air. Their cause was just and they were fearless to a man.

It was time.

"Now, boys, now!" he shouted. Who cared if any of Cartwright's people heard him at this point? Mellor's men were too numerous and too keyed up to be stopped.

The men began whooping and brandishing their weapons as they ran closer, intending to both smash windows and batter down doors in their effort to get to Cartwright.

From his peripheral vision, Mellor saw the upstairs lamp go out. Just as suddenly, lamps were lit along the roofs of all the mill buildings, illuminating their defenses.

Mellor gasped. It was true. Cartwright really did have acid vessels. The Luddite leader shouted for everyone to hold, to pull back, but it was too late. The men were in a frenzy and could neither hear him nor pay attention to the cauldrons being tipped over.

And then windows began creaking open all over, and the sound of pistols being loaded, fired, and reloaded soon overcame the deafening screams of his men being drenched in skin-flaying acid.

George Mellor froze in his vantage point. His raids had always been successful before, with little or no resistance by mill owners.

But this night he had miscalculated badly.

❧ 1 ❧

Come Cropper lads of high renown,
Who love to drink strong ale that's brown.
And strike each haughty tyrant down
With hatchet, pike and gun

—From "The Croppers Song," 1812

April 1812
Leeds, Yorkshire

Annabelle Stirling reached out a hand to reverently stroke her shop's new gig mill, which would mechanize the raise of a fabric's nap. She'd scrimped from the shop's profits for over a year to afford it, and it was finally here. The shop had been chaotic and disorganized during the three days it took for the workmen to set it up, but it was surely worth it.

She frowned. All of the shop's workers, and half the village, were here to see it in operation for the first time. But where was Wesley?

"May I try it, Miss Stirling?" Henry asked. He was the first cropper they'd hired when deciding to expand from merely being cloth merchants to also taking rough cloth and doing the final finishing work on it. Since bringing on Henry, they—well, Belle—had hired three more croppers.

"Of course, it's only right that you should try it. You'll be the one in charge of it," she said.

Henry looked tentatively at the enormous piece of machinery, which looked like a large drum in the middle of a letter C. Fabric would be fed in at the top of the C, and fed around the spine and over the drum, straightening and stretching through a set of rollers, then would be gathered in soft folds at the bottom of the C. Henry stood facing the inside of the C, which towered at least two feet over his head, his foot poised over a foot pedal.

"When you're ready," she said quietly.

Henry began pumping his foot pedal, and a combination of gears and belts attached at various points to the mill screeched and protested loudly. Sweat was already pouring down the man's face as the drum began rotating slowly. He reached up and pulled the edge of the long length of fabric over the top of the C and into the first roller above the drum, feeding it in and out of the rollers that would automatically smooth the cloth, removing the nap in a consistent and reliable manner.

His audience stood breathlessly, Belle included, to see the finished product. After Henry had fed about ten yards of cloth through the machine, he stopped pedaling to examine the cloth. He furrowed his brow as he pinched a section of fabric and ran his thumb over it. He looked up at Belle.

"Miss Stirling, I don't know. Not as good as I could do myself."

Belle lifted a section of cloth that had been cropped and deposited in the bottom of the C. Henry was right. The finishing wasn't quite as fine as what he did. But she looked at the quantity of fabric that had been finished in record time and announced, "Henry, nothing could possibly replace your hands on a set of shears. But look at how much you've accomplished already this morning. I say the gig mill is a success."

And with that, everyone who had crowded inside the room ran forward to touch the fabric and form their own opinion on its quality.

Late in the day, after nearly everyone in their village near Leeds had come forward to handle the newly processed cloth and then gone off to gossip about it in the coffee shop, Henry came to her, hat in hand.

"I dunno, Miss Stirling, how we can 'spec to compete with merchants selling hand-finished cloth. My own work is much better, and I surely don't mind goin' back to it."

"Yes, your handwork is better, but you saw how much fabric you were able to finish in just a short amount of time."

He twisted his hat through his fingers. "Yes, ma'am. But it's your reputation I'm worried about. If you start selling poor-quality cloth and all."

She smiled. "Henry, your job is secure. I couldn't possibly do without you. I'm just glad you'll be able to accomplish so much more each day."

"Yes, ma'am." He continued to stand there, looking nervously from side to side.

"Is there more?"

"I was just wondering, er, whether Mr. Stirling was pleased about the new gig mill. I noticed he wasn't here when we started it up. Just thought he might have his own opinion."

"I'm not quite sure where Mr. Stirling is today. I know, though, that he will be quite delighted when he sees its remarkable potential for the shop."

Which wasn't entirely true, but enough to satisfy Henry and send him on his way back to his family for the night.

Where *was* Wesley today? He knew the gig mill was being installed and would be in operation for the first time this morning. Belle sighed. Although her brother, Wesley Stirling, had inherited the shop after both their parents had been swept away in a fever epidemic that had run through the area nearly five years ago, it was Belle who had taken responsibility for the small shop and its workers. Her parents ran it as merely a cloth merchant's shop, but Belle saw the benefit in bringing in pre-finished cloth and having it finished herself before sending it on its way downriver via the River Aire to land transport for eventual arrival and sale in London and beyond.

By establishing her own dressing shop and having fabric finished on the premises, she could control the final quality of what was sold and thereby manage the shop's growing reputation. The new gig mill didn't produce as fine a finish, but, oh, the output.

Not that Wesley had much interest. Much to their father's despair, her brother, older by two years, had run off to India with a local village girl, Alice Treadle, in some kind of business prospect that he never quite explained. When he was called back after their parents took ill, he never explained why Alice didn't accompany him on his return.

Wesley's presence was largely unnecessary, since he merely signed or approved whatever Belle wanted, leaving management of the shop to her and spending days—and sometimes nights—at undisclosed locations.

It had been this way for as long as she could remember. Her father—Fafa, as she always called him—had tried to encourage Wesley's interest in the business, but he was always more concerned with playing in the woods, or chasing birds, or, later, pursuing comely girls he fancied.

So when Belle first reached out a hand to stroke a piece of fabric and cooed about its softness, Fafa turned his attentions to his younger child. He and Belle would ride over to farms so she could stroke the backs of sheep, cattle, and goats, and Fafa would explain to her how wool, leather, and cashmere came from each animal, respectively, and why the animals must be husbanded properly for not only meat but skin and hair.

They visited fields together, where he would pick stalks of flax and place them in her hands. "This will become a linen fabric one day, Belle," he said, much to her amazement. How could a plant with sweet, pale blue flowers turn into lengths of linen, damask, and cambric?

"It can become fabric and more. Cabinetmakers turn its seed into an oil to finish wood. It's also used for medicine. But I'll show you how it becomes cloth."

They went to a heckling shop, where Fafa lifted her onto his shoulders to watch workers preparing dried flax fibers that had already had their seeds threshed and straw scutched, or separated, from the fibers. Belle was entranced as she watched workers drawing the flax stalks through what Fafa called heckling combs, each a bed of long iron pins driven into a wooden block. The shop contained various sizes of these combs.

"Why are they different?" she asked.

"Depends on what they're making," Fafa said. "The finer the combs, the finer the yarn spun from the flax will be."

The workers carefully drew the processed fibers through the nails, leaving behind more straw and even some of the fiber. The dust produced was stifling and the smell odious, but Belle was too spellbound in the rhythmic pulling and gathering to care.

Fafa pointed. "See the fiber left behind? It will be used to make rope. Practically every bit of the flax plant can be consumed for various purposes. The better fibers will be spun into yarns, and from there woven into different linen fabrics. The croppers will perform the final finishing on the fabric."

"But how does the yellow fiber become different colors?"

Fafa laughed at her enthusiasm. "Ah, Daughter, that's the dyeing and printing process. You have much to learn."

Belle was never sure what she loved more: learning about the cloth trade or spending so much time with her father. Eventually the two became one in her mind.

Fafa gave her simple tasks in the shop, such as sweeping scraps from the floor, and later taught her how to measure and cut. But she was also spending more and more time at his knee, learning.

As she grew older and could recognize various fabrics on sight, Fafa tested her in many ways. He would have her close her eyes, then place pieces of cloth in her hands, asking her to identify them by touch.

Sometimes he would randomly ask her questions. "I am a customer who needs to have a shirt made. What fabrics would you recommend for me?"

"For everyday wear or a dress occasion?"

"Everyday wear."

"For warm days or cool?" she asked.

"Warm."

"Are you working class or an aristocrat?"

"Let's say I am an architect with aristocratic clients. More highly esteemed than, say, a butcher, but no hope of a title."

Ah, Fafa was trying to confuse her. "Then I would suggest our gray broadcloth for you, sir. Although it's a wool, it hangs lightly and will be comfortable on summer days. You will look elegant enough before your clients, but the pale color will prevent you overstepping your bounds as a tradesman and offending them."

Her father clasped her in his arms. "Ah, Belle, you are my clever girl. Your mother and I will be proud to watch you grow into a respected draper one day."

She basked in this kind of praise.

One day, Fafa presented her with a badge that he told her came from the Worshipful Company of Drapers in London. It signified that she was an honorary member of this guild. Her heart nearly swelled to bursting over the badge, which she wore pinned to every dress she had until the badge was nearly in tatters. Later she realized that her father had made the badge himself, but she loved him the more for it. She still kept the badge's remnant as a reminder of Fafa's faith in her talent.

Belle knew she was becoming the son and heir Fafa wanted. Papa's loving but resigned eyes acknowledged it. And Wesley's resentment reflected it.

The day Fafa said cryptically, "The future of the family is solely in your hands, Belle," she knew he intended the shop for her, not Wesley, even though her brother would be the official heir.

And so it happened. Belle learned more, Wesley cared less, and Fafa gradually turned responsibilities over to his teenage daughter. By the time Wesley returned from India following their parents' deaths, Belle was the de facto owner of the Stirling Draper Shop.

Belle shook her head. Well, it was better this way, for there was nothing more satisfying than being in the shop, *her* shop, rolling the long bolts of fabric after the croppers—now the gig mill—had done their work for the day. Even more, she enjoyed using cloth samples to show how they might cover plump pillows, or turn a drab settee into a striking centerpiece for a parlor. She perpetually kept an ever-changing tableau or two at the front of the shop to show local customers the latest fabric styles and how they could improve even the simplest home into one that was warm and inviting.

Many cloth merchants, Fafa included, were concerned about selling fabrics to dressmakers. Belle cared about getting her cloth turned into draperies, chair cushions, and sometimes even wall coverings. She wondered what Fafa would think now of the new mechanization taking place, and her interest in interiors.

The jangling of the doorbell broke her reverie. Hurrying out to the front of the shop, she greeted her customer warmly.

"Amelia! Have you come to see our new mill? I noticed you weren't here this morning."

"And from what I hear, I was the only person in Leeds who wasn't here. How fares the beast?"

"Come see." Belle led her friend to the room containing the gig mill, now stilled in the waning hours of daylight. She and Amelia Wood had been friends for as long as Belle could remember, although her own boisterous personality had overshadowed Amelia's shy, thoughtful nature. Belle remembered running into the rectory like a hoyden when she was around ten years old, a bundle of stinking, freshly shorn sheep's wool in her arms, picked up during a visit to a new weaver from whom Fafa was considering a purchase.

The vicar had shooed the two girls into the yard behind the rectory, and Belle spent the afternoon draping and rearranging the wool over Amelia's shoulders, finally convincing her friend that she'd made her a royal mantle. Amelia's patience for Belle's frolics was never ending, and Belle always tried to drag her friend out of her timidity. She was usually unsuccessful.

Amelia kept her hands behind her back while owlishly inspecting the machinery from behind her wire-rimmed glasses, as though afraid it might reach out and grab her. "It's quite . . . immense," she finally proclaimed.

Belle laughed. "It is! And it will help me keep up with the other cloth manufacturers who can now supply far greater quantities to their London distributors. But enough about the shop; how's the vicar?"

"Papa's fine. He says it's high time we took you away from your servitude in the shop and had you up for tea. Come tomorrow?"

"Gladly."

The following day, Belle was admitted to the rectory. Mr. Wood and Amelia greeted her and ushered her into their small parlor to wait for a tea tray. Mrs. Wood had died the year before Belle's parents, ensuring the two girls became close, different as they were.

And despite Belle having her brother to look after her, Mr. Wood had stepped in as a sort of peevish uncle, determined to watch over her even if he didn't wholly approve of her taking over her parents' trade.

The tea was served scalding hot, exactly how Belle liked it. She blew gently on her cup while looking around the room.

"Belle, I see you're noticing our new portrait. A woman gave it to Papa as payment for officiating at her brother's funeral over in Huddersfield a few weeks ago."

The small painting was a religious allegory and appeared to be quite old.

"It's beautiful, but may I make a recommendation?" Belle said over the rim of her teacup.

Amelia leaned forward. "Of course," she said, pushing her glasses back against her face. Her glasses had been loose for some time, but despite Belle's urging, Amelia refused to see the optics man to have them fixed.

Belle put her cup down. "It's just that the portrait hangs too high upon the wall. It should come further down, like this." She stood next to the portrait and gestured to show that the subject's eyes should be nearly level with the viewer's.

Mr. Wood nodded his head seriously. "I see. And what of the rest of the room? Have we put everything in good order?"

The draperies are too heavy and dark. "Everything looks charming," she said, sitting down again. "This pound cake is delicious, Amelia. Do I taste Madeira in it? You've outdone yourself."

Her friend demurred graciously, willing to allow the subject change, but the vicar wasn't so pliable.

Shaking his head, Mr. Wood said, "Miss Stirling, you remind me more and more of your father each day. How proud—and yet exceedingly exasperated—he would be to see you now."

"I think he would be proud of the new gig mill. Did Amelia tell you about it?"

He turned to his daughter with a look that sent Amelia to fiddling with a basket of sewing next to her chair. "Indeed she did not," he said. "I suppose I'll have to take a walk down and admire it myself. Tell me, what has been the local reaction?"

"Approving, I think. Henry was an expert on it in no time, although he thinks it produces a poorer-quality product than what he can do with his hands. He's right, but it's foolish for me to have small batches of cloth finished by hand when I can have twice as much done in half the time."

"Then I suppose you heard about what just happened over in Brighouse?" Mr. Wood's voice was even, but Belle sensed an underlying tension now between herself and the vicar. Amelia looked worriedly between her father and friend.

"Brighouse? No, why?"

"A horde of Luddites descended on the cloth mill of a man named William Cartwright. Cartwright had also installed some of that new cloth-finishing machinery. Some croppers, led by a devil named George Mellor, set out to destroy the mill and kill Cartwright." Mr. Wood let his words hang in the air.

"Were they successful?" Belle asked.

"No. But only because Cartwright was ready for them. He garrisoned his mill with local militia and some of his own trusted workers, and had everything from pistols to acid ready to unleash on the gang. It was the first time the Luddites got a taste of their own medicine. Two of them were killed, Cartwright was unharmed."

"Do you mean to say that they escaped from their crime?"

"Hardly. They attacked another large mill, and this time a hundred of them were rounded up. They sit awaiting trial now, but there can be no doubt of the outcome. As there can be no doubt of what will happen to you, Belle, if you insist on keeping that newfangled machinery in your shop."

"But you said yourself that they're jailed. They can't do anything to me. To us."

"Annabelle Stirling, that's just George Mellor and his mob that were caught. Think you that they are the only Luddites on the prowl right now?"

"Father, I'm sure Wesley will protect the shop," Amelia ventured carefully.

"Wesley!" her father exploded. "You couldn't rely on Wesley to protect a hare from a three-legged fox. No, better to get rid of that machinery, young lady. You'll come to no good end with it."

Belle choked down more tea to refrain from telling the vicar her opinion of his advice. How dare he instruct her in her shop's workings? Or suggest that her management of it was deficient in some way? Besides, Belle kept a pair of flintlock pistols hidden behind the counter, although she'd only practiced loading them on one occasion. Nevertheless, no ruffians would have an easy time of it if they broke into her shop. She'd see to it personally.

Taking Belle's silence for agreement, Mr. Wood pushed further. "And anyway, once you and Mr. Pryce are married, you'll have no need for the shop's income. He'll take care of you. An honest, respectable man Mr. Pryce is. You could not do better."

Belle continued to bristle silently. The thought came unbidden to her mind that should she need protection, she was probably a better shot than Clive Pryce was, but she instantly chastised herself for such a thought about her betrothed. Certainly Clive was a good man. More important, he was her brother's most cherished friend, making him a welcome, if unexciting, addition to her life.

As welcome as he was, she had no intention of giving up the shop. It was the pride of Fafa's existence, and her own joy now. With her parents gone, she'd filled in whatever gaps in her knowledge she'd needed, and today there was almost nothing she didn't know about cloth. Consequently, Wesley was content to let her continue as she had, confident in her abilities to keep the shop profitable. And she'd done so, even coming up with her own plans for expansion and growth. Like with the new gig mill.

So now, five years later, what else was there to Annabelle Stirling's life but linen, wool, silk, and cotton?

She didn't mind that Wesley wasn't as interested in the shop as she was, for it allowed her an independence that she wouldn't otherwise have if he truly wanted to run things. But to what good purpose would she argue with a man who was not only the vicar but her best friend's father?

"Yes, Mr. Wood, I'm sure you're right about everything," she said, putting down her cup to end this line of conversation.

He beamed broadly at Belle. "Of course I am, my dear. I am.

I'm always telling Amelia that I know what's best for my women-folk. And I do consider you under my care, Belle."

Belle muttered her thanks and moved on to more innocuous topics to pass the time until she felt she'd stayed an acceptable amount of time.

Amelia followed her to the front door of the rectory to escort her out while Mr. Wood retreated to his study to work on that week's sermon.

"I'm sorry, Belle. Papa does mean well." Amelia pushed her glasses back along the ridge of her nose again.

"I suppose he does." She kissed her friend's cheek. "As enamored as he is of Clive, I think your father would rather have him as your husband than mine."

Amelia flushed. "Oh no, I'm sure he thinks no such thing."

"Amelia! I'm just teasing you." She tweaked the other girl's nose, resulting in her wire frames slipping again. "Oh, sorry."

"I don't mind." Up they went again. "I should probably have them seen to, shouldn't I? Oh, I forgot to show you the dress I'm making to attend you at the church. Papa even said he would buy me a bonnet to go with it. Would you like to see it?"

"My apologies, but I need to get back to the shop. Maybe another time." Belle hugged her friend warmly and said good-bye, pretending not to notice her friend's questioning look.

She decided to check the afternoon's progress on the new mill. While walking back to the shop through Upperhead Row, a formerly decrepit section of the town now being replaced with handsome new buildings and a wider street, all welcome improvements in Belle's mind, she thought that it was probably time she talked to Clive, to be sure he understood what she intended. A wife she would be. A cloth merchant she *must* be.

May 1812

Wesley Stirling was satisfied with his day.

First was his great success at ninepins in the alley behind the Pack Horse Inn. A group of about twenty spectators had gathered in the cobbled courtyard between the inn and its outbuildings: the kitchen, stable, laundry house, and necessary. This last building was particularly odiferous on such a warm day, but it was of no moment, for he'd collected a nice pouch of coins from those who foolishly bet he couldn't strike all the pins from forty feet away. Even Clive had bet against him.

Well, Clive was lighter by a penny or two now, wasn't he?

The two men had gone back to the cloth shop afterwards, because Wesley had promised Belle he'd take a load of cloth to Leeds Bridge for loading on a ship bound for London. Or was it Norwich? No matter. After Clive had finished flirting with Belle— who, Wesley had to say, was in an ill temper on such a beautiful day—the men had scurried back to the Pack Horse for a darts competition.

Their game resulted in more success when Wesley was able to hit the center of the painted barrel bottom hung on the wall with his back turned, throwing the dart over his shoulder. Even Phyllis Roland, who'd been little impressed with Wesley's recent attempts to astonish her with his feats of strength and cleverness, had finally taken notice of him when he'd carelessly tossed the dart behind him and struck the center of the red circle painted on the barrel. And who knew where her interest might lead?

He pushed away his empty plate, leaned back in his chair, and crossed his ankles in contentment, sipping from his tankard. Yes, today had been profitable in more ways than one.

His winnings from the day were mostly spent buying rounds of ale for his friends. But he still had a crown left. He contemplated what to do with it. Belle had been grousing lately about the shop needing a bigger window cut into the front, to make her silly little arrangements more visible. Perhaps he should turn everything over to her.

Or not.

He was distracted from his thoughts by Clive's good-natured kick on his shin.

"Blast you, Pryce. What are you about?" Wesley said.

"Time to wake up. There's still more to be done today."

"What do you mean? My belly's full"—Wesley patted it for emphasis—"and so are my pockets. Well, they're not quite as full, but I'm in good comfort and cheer. I've no intention of doing anything else today."

"We need to do something for Belle."

"I already carted off a load of cloth for her today. Isn't that enough?"

"No. I had a ring made for her and I need to pick it up."

"What kind of ring?"

"It's silver, with a locket on top to hold a clipping of my hair. My mother is braiding it for me. What?"

Wesley grinned. "Nothing, nothing. I do believe you've gone completely soft over my sister. I don't think you've figured out yet what a harridan you're getting."

"If she's a harridan, it's only because you've never used a firm hand with her since your parents died. She'll be different once we're married."

"Undoubtedly."

"You won't tell her about the ring? It's a surprise."

"I'll be silent as the grave."

Clive scowled at him, but wasn't so irritated as to give up the topic.

"My mother has written to all of her cousins to invite them to the wedding breakfast. It will be a locust plague to put Pharaoh's to shame."

"I guess I'll have to provide extra barrels of buttered ale to wash everything down, then, won't I? When will banns be read?"

"Starting the first Sunday in June for three weeks. Hasn't Belle told you this? Has she even been talking about our wedding?"

"My sister? You must be joking. She's far more concerned with the cut of the latest printed damask for a sofa than a silk for her dress. Don't know that she's even started making it."

Clive frowned again. "She isn't pleased to become my wife and keep house for me?"

"What? Of course she is. You're my best chap. She'd be a lunatic of the first order not to be happy about keeping our merry little band together."

"She said so?"

"Well, I don't quite remember. Something like that. Actually, yes, I'm sure she said so. That her marriage to you seemed the natural progression of things given our friendship. You know how high-handed she talks."

"Hmm." Clive changed the subject. "So, what do you think about what happened in Brighouse last month?"

"The Luddite attack? I s'pose they got what they deserved for attacking an innocent shop owner. That's what Belle says."

"But what do *you* say, Wesley? The workers say Parliament isn't protecting their jobs. Don't you think those bigger mill owners are taking away the livelihoods of good men who have given dedicated service?"

"I don't know. Maybe."

"And don't you think your own shop runs the risk of being attacked? What if Belle is there alone when it happens?"

"Cartwright's mill was much bigger and well-known. She doesn't think the shop is in any danger from installing one simple gig mill."

"There are many who wouldn't call it 'simple.' It would be a shame if something happened to it because of her disregard."

Wesley shrugged. "She doesn't listen to me, anyway."

"You seem to forget the shop is yours, Wesley, not Belle's. And once she becomes my wife, she won't have time for it anymore. You're her elder brother. Tell her you're taking command of the shop now that she's to be married."

Wesley muttered something unintelligible into his tankard before finishing off the contents.

"Well, I love her and I don't want to see a mob carting her off to Sherwood Forest, so something must be done." And with that, Clive slapped his knees and rose, signaling the end of the discussion. "Let's go get the ring."

And because the only person in the world Wesley listened to more than Belle was Clive, he obediently rose and followed his friend out.

Arthur Thistlewood was a discontented man.

It seemed as though the world worked against people like him. Against visionary men with purpose and great ideas.

Thistlewood removed his muddied boots and laid them outside the door before entering the rented house he shared with his wife, Susan. No need to get her tail feathers ruffled over a bit of mud dragged inside.

She'd been carping incessantly since they left their failed farm in Horncastle last year to come to London. The woman thought a man like Arthur Thistlewood should be content to follow in her father's footsteps and be a butcher. He'd refused that and gone into the army, where he'd been part of many an exploit in France.

Ah, Paris. He reflected wistfully on that exciting, dangerous period of revolution there not so many years ago, when speakers and verse-writers like Maximilien Robespierre and Louis Saint-Just were swaying crowds with their brilliant oratory about royal despotism and the right to freedom for all people. It was all heady and intoxicating.

And it was Truth. Why shouldn't a man be able to enjoy success without a monarch to steal away the fruits of his labors? For that was surely why his farm failed. And why he'd never been properly promoted in the army. Now that he thought about it, it was the root of his bad fortune as a land surveyor prior to his marriage. He suspected that oppression was somehow at the root of his miserable marriage, too, but he couldn't quite put his finger on why.

The trouble in France began when the heads of Louis XVI and his wife, Marie Antoinette, tumbled off the guillotine and into the history book of martyrs. Unfortunate, that. But what men like Robespierre and Saint-Just foresaw with clarity was that in order to effect true change to society, one must punish not only the traitors but also those who are indifferent. Those who are passive were the real threat to society.

Arthur Thistlewood couldn't agree more. That's why he'd had such high hopes for Mellor's attack on Cartwright's mill. It would have been a turning point on these Luddite attacks, increasing their violence and bloodthirstiness to effect change more quickly.

Thistlewood went to his washbasin. Susan had already filled it in anticipation of his arrival home from his gathering. He splashed water on his face as he thought about the stroke of great fortune it had been to meet Thomas Spence, a former schoolteacher who had watched the Revolution in France through newspapers. For twenty years, Spence had been in and out of prison for selling radical books, pamphlets, and newspapers. But the man's commitment was such that he never stopped his activities, so great was his belief in his cause. No failure was too great for Spence to brush off as a mere fly on a horse's tail.

Thistlewood was drawn to such a selfless, heroic man who shared his feelings about change.

At tonight's meeting of like-minded men, though, everyone was still dejected about Mellor's unsuccessful foray against an oppressor. Should they have lent him arms, money, and men? Should they have more vocally supported the Luddites' efforts in the streets and in their broadsheets?

Impossible to know. Yet Thistlewood did know that Thomas Spence's mind would continue to whirl and click until he developed an idea to further the work done by Mellor and other Luddites.

He looked forward to seeing it all unfold.

June 1812

Belle and Wesley dined together at Abbey Inn, a few miles from their shop and far away from the bustle of the growing city center of Leeds. Belle loved this old establishment, in its picturesque setting near the River Aire. It was so named for a supposed tunnel that once linked the building to the Kirkstall Abbey a distance away down the valley.

Belle liked to imagine that Charles II's royalist soldiers sought refuge in the old stone abbey, then escaped occupied Leeds by following the tunnel to the inn in the middle of the night and mounting waiting horses to carry them off to more sympathetic parts of the country where they would survive to fight another day. Of course, the royalists eventually took and held Leeds, so perhaps they were parliamentary soldiers seeking sanctuary. Either way, she admired the daring and courage involved.

Wesley had suggested they dine at her favorite place, so they were enjoying a late-afternoon meal of curried rabbit soup, along-side jugged steak with potatoes. It had been months since she'd had this layered dish of pounded meat and sliced potatoes. She'd never learned how to wield a mallet well enough to beat the steaks thin enough to make it, so it was always a treat to have it here at Abbey Inn.

Wesley, however, wasn't taking pleasure in his meal as much as he was enjoying his port. Was that his third glass? She sighed inwardly. Well, he'd been very helpful last week with getting that load of cloth sent out, and he'd promised to help her tomorrow with rolling some newly finished fabric bolts, so perhaps he deserved a night of revelry.

"So, Sister." Wesley cut away another section of his casserole with his knife and used his thumb to hold it on the blade as he swept the food into his mouth. "I hear the Americans have declared war on us. Lord, but those people cannot tolerate an ounce of authority. Why the complaint about impressments of their merchant sailors into our own navy? Half of them are British deserters anyway. Serves 'em right to be captured and put back where they belong."

"Well, I think the Americans are incensed because they believe we're infringing on their national sovereignty. I suspect having British frigates stationed in their harbors to inspect every ship sailing in and out has made them a bit testy."

"I suppose. Clive says the Royal Navy is superior to the ragtag American fleet and that the Americans should realize their place on the waters."

"Clive is indeed patriotic," she said.

"But you agree with him, don't you, Belle? He says a wife should support her husband in all things." Wesley was eyeing her warily.

Was this some kind of pre-marital test? In her daily busyness, she'd forgotten her recent vow to talk to Clive about her intention to continue with her business. And they were only a couple of weeks from their wedding without him ever having uttered a sound about her *not* doing so, making it easy to assume that all would be well and affable between them.

Perhaps it was time she had that discussion with her betrothed. But she had to address her brother first.

"I certainly agree that our navy boasts faster ships and better sailors. Clive and I share the same opinion on that and many other matters, and I'm sure he'll have no cause to regret marrying me."

Wesley seemed satisfied enough with her answer, and signaled the innkeeper for another glass of port.

As the liquid was poured from the ewer, Wesley wiped his knife on his napkin. The innkeeper offered to bring out apple puffs and some of his wife's sweet orange wine, which Wesley accepted enthusiastically.

The distraction was enough to move him on to other news.

"So not only are the Americans rebelling to our west, but the French popinjay has invaded Russia to our east. We can but hope that Tsar Alexander squashes that brute Napoleon once and for all."

"Is that what Clive says?" Belle asked.

"Yes. He said that—" Wesley stopped in midsentence. "Are you mocking me, Sister?"

"Indeed not. I have the greatest respect for my intended's opinion, and so wished to know what he thought on the matter."

"Right. Well, Clive says that the Russians will finally give Napoleon the drubbing he deserves. And it will serve our esteemed Lord Nelson's memory, too."

Lord Nelson had been dead seven years now from his wounds suffered at the hands of the French during the Battle of Trafalgar. She and Wesley were young teenagers then, with barely an understanding of events outside Leeds, much less in the world at large.

Clive's influence over her brother was growing.

Well, it was only right that her future husband and her brother be as close as brothers themselves, wasn't it?

A small dessert platter was set before them, and the innkeeper proffered the new variety of wine. Belle waved off the drink and took one of the miniature pastries. The interior filling was piping hot and sweet. Wesley took no notice of the apple puffs, but instead took to his glass with gusto.

I hope he won't be in his cups soon.

Belle overheard a bit of conversation from a table nearby and introduced it into their own. "They say the Prince of Wales has instituted another rule in his war against his wife. While the Princess of Wales is at Windsor for the summer, she can only see their daughter once every two weeks."

The war between George and his wife, Caroline, was well-known throughout England.

Wesley shook his head. "They're like a pair of battling roosters who—"

They were interrupted by a commotion in the outer taproom. Everyone in the dining room looked up at the sounds of arguing and feet scuffling.

Henry burst into the dining room, wide-eyed and sweating, twisting his hat in his hand in his usual nervous way.

"Miss Stirling! Come quick! There's a gang planning to smash the mill tonight. They know you're out for the evening. I knew this would happen. Yes I did. It's going to be the end of us, yes it is. Oh, Mr. Stirling, good evening to you, sir. I'm sure you'll want to come, too. It's terrible bad, it is."

Belle put out a hand to calm him. "Henry, are you sure?"

"Yes, I'm quite sure. I went to check it out for myself, and they're gathering at the north end of Briggate. I found a horse and got here quick as I could. Hurry, Miss Stirling."

She rose and looked at Wesley. His face was ashen. He drew coins from his pocket and threw them on the table as he got up unsteadily from the table.

"Wesley, are you all right?" she asked. Perhaps this wasn't a good night for revelry, after all.

He nodded and followed her and Henry out of Abbey Inn to find fast transport back to the shop.

Belle saw about a dozen men, most with neckerchiefs tied around the lower halves of their faces, approaching the shop. They were still at least about a quarter mile away.

Belle leaned over to whisper to Wesley, "Except for the masks, they don't look menacing at all."

He squeezed her hand. "I'll protect you, Sister."

Would he?

"Here, here," Wesley called out as he ran to intercept the men. What did he think he was doing? If they had destruction on their minds, Wesley would fall victim to them.

"Wesley, stop!" she called.

"It's all right, Belle. Go home," he shouted back.

Not likely. Belle knew what she had to do to protect themselves and her livelihood.

She picked up her skirts and ran into the shop, heading as swiftly as she could for her work counter lining the wall, and bending over to find the pistol box among the shelves below the counter. She moved aside ledgers, material scraps, and boxes containing scissors, tapes, and leftover lengths of decorative fringes.

Ah, there it was. She pulled it out and frantically set it on the counter. Drat. She'd forgotten that the box had a lock on it. Where was the key? She lifted her key ring from a nail on the wall in front of her, and shuffled through the keys, searching for the right one.

Hurry, Belle, hurry.

She could hear the din of voices rising angrily nearby, as the men came closer.

Please, God, help me find that infernal key.

Ah, this one must be it. She fit it inside the lock and the top sprang open. The guns were old, but the brass appliqué on the handles still gleamed brightly.

Two pistols. Meaning she could, at most, hope to get off two shots, which would, she hoped, be enough to scare them off. After all, a rough-made club was no match for a gun. Even if the gun was managed by a woman.

Now to remember how to load the things. It had been too long since she'd last practiced.

She searched under the counter where the pistol box had been and retrieved the ammunition kit. The gun man in Birmingham from whom she'd purchased the guns had given her written instructions that he'd tucked inside the kit. She unfolded the page of instructions and scattered the other contents across the oak countertop.

Her hands were beginning to tremble, for fear of not being able to load the guns in time. Or load them at all.

Belle selected a piece of flint and tucked it into the hammer. Next, she tapped a measure of black powder out of its container and onto a piece of tissue paper. Half-cocking the hammer on one of the pistols, she shakily poured a measure of black powder down the barrel. With one hand still holding the gun, she wrapped a lead ball inside a wad of cloth and rammed it down the barrel on top of the gunpowder, using a metal ramrod. The cloth would prevent the ball from rolling back out of the barrel.

Almost done.

She picked up the container of black powder again and sprinkled a tiny amount in the flash pan underneath before fully cocking the piece. Ah, right. When she pulled the trigger, the flint in the hammer would crash down on the pan, creating an ignition to send the bullet hurtling off to its target.

She hoped.

More noise and arguing from outside distracted her. Was that the sound of Wesley apologizing?

Shaking her head in anger and frustration, she gently set the pistol upright against a jar on the counter and set to work on the second pistol, relieved that she loaded it far more quickly than the first one.

Before she could move to pick up the first gun, a hand came from nowhere and grabbed her wrist, shaking it and forcing it to release the second pistol. It fell to the counter, and Belle was momentarily blinded by a flash as the hammer came down on what black powder remained in the flash pan. It wasn't enough to fire the pistol.

She turned toward her attacker, struggling against him. The man wore a brown wool hood over his eyes. The jagged eyeholes of his mask had tilted and she couldn't even see his pupils. The cloth was oddly familiar.

"Leave me be!" she said. "What is your business here?"

"We mean you no trouble, Annabelle. We just need to see that mill dismantled."

So you're not a stranger to me.

"How dare you address me so familiarly. Who are you?"

"Never mind that."

He yanked her away from the counter, but she was able to grab the first pistol as he did so, hiding it in the folds of her skirt.

Careful, she thought. *You'll only get one chance.*

She tried to squirm out of his grasp, but he held her arm tightly. As the man prodded her toward the door of the shop, the other men came tumbling in, Wesley and Henry on their heels.

Most of them were carrying weapons of some sort, from clubs to knives to sacks full of something—probably stones.

Wesley was in the middle of the group, fully surrounded by the men. Catching Belle's eye, he shrugged, his eyes sending her a plea she couldn't understand. Henry looked as though he might faint dead away at any moment.

She lashed out at the man who was handling her so roughly. "I'll say it again; leave me be, you oafish dolt. You've no right to be here and I'll see every one of you hanged."

He let go in surprise at her outburst.

One of the gang laughed. "Hey, you said she was a lively thing. Truer words never spoken. But let's get to business."

Before she could react with the weapon clutched in her hand, three of the club-wielding men went to the gig mill and began beating against it. It wasn't long before the mill was cracking and splintering before her eyes, collapsing in a heap of rubble.

No, it couldn't be. She'd worked so long and hard to save the money to buy the mill. It was the future of cloth finishing and focus of her dreams. It would take years before she could replace it.

You'll never be able to replace it, a tiny voice whispered.

She felt dizzy.

Belle gripped the pistol tighter, although it was sliding in her grasp as her nerves caused her to sweat. She had one shot, and she wasn't sure where to place it. At the man holding her? The range was too close. At the men who had just hammered away at her precious new mill? What if one of them was her own employee who thought he would lose his job because of it? Besides, it was too late to stop their work.

As their exertion against the machinery caused them to breathe more heavily, the men tore their masks away to allow for more air passage. None of them were her workers. Their forearms were rippled with muscles, so they were obviously croppers from elsewhere.

Part of George Mellor's gang, perhaps? Maybe Mellor himself had escaped prison and was now underneath the wool mask?

Wesley seemed paralyzed, staring in fascination at what was going on and doing nothing to stop it, not that there was anything to be done to save the machinery.

But Belle could and would get these men out of her shop.

In one fluid motion, she brought her pistol out into plain view and pointed it at her attacker while reaching up with her free hand and yanking on her captor's wool covering. It easily came away in her hand.

Clive Pryce.

What?

She stared back and forth between the wool and his face. And realized that the cloth looked familiar because it came from her shop. It was part of an older batch of drab that Henry had hand-finished.

She shook her head in disbelief. They were affianced, due to be married in a couple of weeks. And Wesley's best friend. He was—

She looked over at Wesley again. "It can't be," she breathed.

But Clive stepped toward her again. She whirled on him with her pistol and raised it at him.

He lifted his hands in supplication. "Belle, darling, this was all only for your own good. You know deep inside that this mill is immoral. In two ways. Not only because it produces inferior cloth that will drive expert craftsmen like Henry into starvation, but because you know that managing this shop is your elder brother's job, not yours. You've stepped outside your role as his younger sister to assert yourself in a distasteful, mannish way. Assuredly, I won't tolerate it when you become my wife."

"You won't tolerate . . . I've stepped outside . . . my own good . . ."
Belle was nearly speechless in shock.

"Besides, even if I permitted you to continue with this draper
shop, it wouldn't do for the wife of a respectable Luddite to introduce an evil piece of machinery into it."

Once again, Belle was grasping for an understanding. "What are
you saying? Have you done this before?"

"Done it before? Why, I'm a King Ludd, just like George Mellor. My men are expert in smashing gig mills, stocking frames, and
the like. Notice how we didn't touch anything else, just the mill.
It's a lesson to arrogant shop owners without destroying their entire livelihood."

"Therefore I should be grateful to you for doing this?"

Clive laughed. "I suppose that's true."

Despite his shaking nervousness, Henry spoke up. "Now, Mr.
Pryce, I don't much like this new machinery, either, but I'd never
destroy it."

"Your opinion concerns me little. Belle, you hire insolent men,
and Henry will be the first to go when we're married."

Belle readily found her astonishment overtaken by pure, white-
hot fury. How dare he presume to know what was good for her?
For that matter, how dare he think to know anything about her at
all? For if he believed that for one second Belle could be happy
outside of the cloth shop, then he should be taken straight to York
Asylum for confinement. In fact, she'd escort him there personally.

"You'll not tell me—" But before she could finish her thought,
Henry stepped forward toward Clive, his hands raised. She didn't
know whether he meant to attack or supplicate, but it didn't matter. Clive took it as a threatening gesture, grabbed Henry, and
threw him bodily onto the demolished remains of the gig mill.
Henry landed violently on his back with a clatter that sounded almost as terrible as the smashing of the mill. He groaned and fell
eerily silent.

"Henry!" Belle cried, running forward to help him, but Clive
seized her and shoved her to one side.

"He's not important, Belle. You first need to apologize to me and your brother for the vain way you've been handling things in this shop. It's not befitting a woman."

"*I* need to apologize? To *you?*"

Henry moaned again. *Thank God, he's still alive.*

Wait. Did Clive say she also needed to apologize to Wesley? Her brother shared the profits from this shop with her and had every interest in the gig mill being a success. Unless—

She wheeled around on her sibling, still pointing the pistol forward in her wrath. "So, tell me, Wesley, my dearest brother. Is this little celebration of any surprise to you whatsoever?"

"Of course! I knew nothing about it!" Wesley straightened his back in indignation.

"And so how did Clive manage to obtain this piece of cloth from our shop to wear to this little gathering that you knew nothing about?"

"He must have stolen it."

"Indeed. Your closest companion made it his business to break into our shop when no one was here to steal a piece of cloth to wear in his plan—that you knew nothing about—to obliterate the item in the shop that holds our livelihood. Is this what I'm supposed to believe, *Brother?*"

Beads of sweat broke out on Wesley's forehead. "Sister, surely you wouldn't consider using that weapon on me."

"I'm really not sure what I would consider doing. Right now I'm waiting to hear what your part in this was."

"I, well, I, er, you see . . ." Wesley looked helplessly at Clive, who stepped back into the conversation.

"Sweetheart, you must realize that although I certainly supported this instructive lesson for you, it was actually Wesley who instigated it. He has long desired to gain control of the shop back from you, and this was an ideal way to scare you into handing it over to him."

Belle could scarcely believe what she was hearing. Her own brother really was the source of this destruction?

"How could you do this?" she asked him.

"I didn't! Clive is lying. It was his idea to do it. He wanted to scare you into giving up the shop so that you would be a proper wife. He told me you'd be the better for it. Besides, he's the one who has been an active leader with the Luddites."

Belle was confused. Was this Wesley's scheme, or Clive's? Either way, they were in collusion against her.

But her attention was diverted once again by Mr. Wood stumbling noisily into the shop. "What ho!" he said. "I heard there was some trouble here. Who are you men, wearing disguises like that? Show us your faces as God made them."

The remaining miscreants with kerchiefs still around their faces pulled them down. No one dared disobey a man of the cloth.

The vicar noticed Clive. "Ah, Mr. Pryce, I see you got here ahead of me. Took me some time to run over here after I got word at the rectory that there was a disturbance. I suppose you have things well in hand." He looked at the destroyed mill. "Or perhaps you got here too late."

Belle spoke up. "Actually, Mr. Wood, I'm afraid my former fiancé does not have things well in hand. In fact, I've just discovered that he, or my brother, or both of them together, are responsible for this mess."

"Surely you must be joking, my dear. Why, Clive Pryce is an upstanding citizen of this community. His father has been a city alderman for years, and Mr. Pryce is destined to follow in his footsteps. You're talking nonsense."

"I never talk nonsense. You know that. And my brother and Clive would be well served to hear what I have to say, for I am deadly serious. I despise you both. How dare you consider for one moment doing such a thing to me? If either of you loved me, it would never have crossed your pea brains to do this."

Wesley interjected, "But Sister, it was only because we loved—"

"Silence!" she thundered so loudly that everyone in the room jumped. "You're my own blood, but you betray me as easily as the turncoat on his own country. And you!" She now addressed Clive. "Mr. Pryce, our wedding is officially called off. I suppose I should thank you for showing me your colors before our marriage. I hope to never lay eyes on you again."

"Belle, dearest, you don't mean that."

"And already you've forgotten that I don't talk nonsense, ever. I'm finished with you, and Wesley, and my life here. This, however"—she held up the pistol—"I do believe I'll keep. For good luck."

She backed out of the shop, pointing the pistol out, daring anyone to molest her further. Once she was through the front door, she stormed into the night air. Mr. Wood ran out after her. She continued walking and he matched her stride. "Belle, my dear, I know that the boys were perhaps a little overbearing in their behavior, but I think you're overreacting. Come back, let's pray and come to a resolution on this. I think they both really had good intentions."

"You pray, Mr. Wood. Pray for both of their souls, because I'll see them punished."

"Belle, I'm afraid I must remind you again that Clive is an alderman's son. Alderman Pryce's influence in our town cannot be overstated, and it's best that we consider the impact any reaction against his son would—"

Belle stopped and turned to face the vicar. "Clive Pryce is a criminal. He's been sabotaging mills and stocking frames and who knows what else all over Yorkshire. He should be in prison. And you're about to suggest that we have to be considerate of him, aren't you, since Alderman Pryce might have his afternoon tea disturbed otherwise."

"Miss Stirling, no good can come of persecuting Clive for his youthful indiscretions. Remember that our good Lord said to 'bless them that curse you, and pray for those that persecute you.'"

"So, you're saying you'll defend Clive in his criminal activities?"

"I must be a peacemaker. . . ."

"A peacemaker doesn't create peace by allowing gangs to maraud about the countryside. If you won't take care of him, I will. I'll have justice for what he's done to me."

"What will you do? You're being very unwise. You have no plan."

"That's where you're wrong, Mr. Wood. I know exactly what I'll do."

Belle picked up her purposeful stride once again, leaving the vicar standing helplessly in the street.

While Mr. Wood returned to the shop to disperse the mob and presumably restore order, Belle marched to the rectory to visit Amelia, who stared wide-eyed at her friend's ferocious appearance and the pistol dangling from her fingers.

With as little explanation as possible, Belle asked to borrow some money and clothing, with a pledge to repay Amelia as soon as possible. Amelia gave her everything she asked for, and helped her to pack it into a traveling bag.

And so, she hurriedly kissed and hugged her friend, whose eyes were full of questions. Belle felt guilty leaving her old friend in this way, but Belle had business to attend to, and didn't want anyone to know about it, lest someone try to stop her.

For Belle knew precisely where she was headed.

She was headed to Parliament.

❧ 2 ❧

He that wrestles with us strengthens our nerves and sharpens our skill. Our antagonist is our helper.

—Edmund Burke, Irish statesman, 1729–1797

June 1812
London

Belle almost lost her nerve. The grandiose, imposing Gothic exterior of St. Stephen's Chapel inside the grounds of Westminster Palace was breathtaking. And a bit daunting.

Mustering her courage by reminding herself of what had happened to her shop, she climbed the long flight of outside steps to the entrance.

Inside the entry room, a uniformed man stopped her almost at once.

"How can I help you, miss?"

"I want to speak to Lord Perceval. I want to report a violation against the Frame Breaking Act, and I expect him to give me recompense against a mob of Luddites."

The man shook his head. "Miss, have you been on a long ocean voyage? Lord Perceval was assassinated last week. Right here in this very room, in fact. Lord Liverpool's the prime minister now. And he doesn't preside over the House of Commons, anyway, the Speaker of the House does."

The prime minister had been killed? How was that possible?

"Assassinated? By whom?"

"A cracked-brain named John Bellingham. Had some idea that the British government owed him compensation for a time he spent as a guest in one of the tsar's prisons. Like I said, a complete nutter. He was hanged just yesterday. Miss, how could you have not heard about it?"

Because I've been spending the last week riding and walking to London, that's why.

"I suppose I've been otherwise occupied," she said.

The man's eyes narrowed. "And you say you're here now for compensation, is that right?"

"Yes. I mean, no. What I'm trying to say is, I'm not off my head like Mr. Bellingham. I just need to speak to whoever is the— Speaker of the House, did you say?"

"It's the Right Honorable Charles Abbot. But you don't just walk in and interrupt proceedings, miss. They're having a debate in there."

"I've come a long distance, sir, and will not leave until I've had my say with Mr. Abbot."

"No."

No? He said no?

Belle hadn't eaten or slept well in more than a week while making her journey into the city. She'd finally reached her destination, and this muttonhead thought he was going to prevent her from seeing the Speaker?

"Well, sir, I say *yes.*" And with that, she moved to open one of the two arched doors leading into the chamber.

"You can't do that!" The guard pushed the door closed. "Really, miss, I'm going to have to ask you to leave."

"I won't leave without seeing Mr. Abbot."

The man sighed. "Well, aren't you just the fair lady of the joust. I'll let you go up into the gallery to watch the debate. It's highly improper to let a woman up there, but I suspect you'll worry me into the grave otherwise."

"Thank you, sir."

"But remember: You can only observe. No one interrupts the proceedings. Do you understand me?"

"I understand."

Belle followed him up a flight of stairs to a viewing gallery on one side of the chapel. The guard let her step in and shut the door behind her as he returned to duty.

Another gallery faced her. Beneath each gallery were four rows of pews facing each other, across a center aisle. Hundreds of men filled the pews. The aisle was dominated by a desk and very tall altar chair behind it, both of these at the opposite end of the chapel from where she'd entered.

Presiding over the session from the chair was a man with sharp, regal features. He projected strength and confidence. This must be Mr. Abbot.

The Speaker addressed someone on one side of the pews.

"The Honorable Member for Chichester may speak," he said.

A middle-aged man, dressed like most of the others in a finely tied, snowy white cravat and dark jacket and pants, stood. "Thank you. Mr. Speaker, today I raise the issue of the New Street and its unconscionable impact on Cavendish Square. The architect Mr. Nash has presented a very grand rerouting from Marylebone Park to the prince's Carlton House residence, and certainly there is no objection to a naming of this route after the Prince Regent, but the plan is too extreme, too extreme."

Belle heard mutterings of "Honorable Member Huskisson speaks true" on one side of the aisle and "No, no, too many men out of work from the war and we need building projects" from the other.

What in heaven's name were they talking about?

Huskisson continued. "We are in great financial straits because of our lengthy wars with the little Corsican, and this further folly will only serve to empty the treasury even more. Moreover, the plan calls for the homes on the east side of Cavendish Square to be torn down, a most unhappy prospect for the men of rank who live there."

Well, if the members of Parliament could argue over the wisdom of destroying homes, surely it would be willing to debate the ruin of her gig mill.

"And so I . . ." Unfortunately, the man spoke so tediously and unremarkably that when his speech was combined with her travel exhaustion, Belle found herself nodding off. She sternly shook herself awake. She hadn't come all this way to sleep through her opportunity.

And so the day went on. Various members were recognized from either the Tory or Whig side of the aisle to discuss a variety of bills, measures, and reforms. Some were debated wildly, some politely ignored.

A gentleman from the Whig side of the House, named Sheridan, petitioned for funds to support the Royal Navy's effort against the Americans. Mr. Abbot verbally pushed him aside, saying that since the Member for Ilchester's loyalties had not always been with Great Britain but had in earlier years been with the Americans he now proclaimed to be against, Sheridan could cool his heels a little longer on the subject.

On and on it went.

Finally, the Speaker moved to close debate for the day after allowing a moment of silence in memory of Lord Perceval. This was her chance. Belle jumped up and went to the rail of the gallery.

"Mr. Abbot! Mr. Speaker! My lord Speaker!" she called out. *Drat, what is the correct form of address?* Her voice reverberated high and clear against the chapel's high ceilings.

All eyes were on her.

Abbot's eyes narrowed. "And just who might you be, madam, disrupting the rules of this House?"

Stand firm, Belle.

"I am Annabelle Stirling, my lord, from Leeds in Yorkshire. My family have been respected drapers there for many years. We were set upon by a gang of Luddites last week, who smashed our new gig mill. It seems to me, sir, that the House of Commons is not properly addressing the violence and destruction of these marauders. I demand compensation for our destroyed mill."

"You do, do you?" he asked.

Belle stood as straight as she could, grasping the rail with both hands to keep from trembling.

"Yes, my lord, I do."

"And where is your husband to make this case for you?"

"I have no husband."

"Well then, what of your parents?"

"My parents are dead, sir."

"No husband? No parents? Who, then, owns this family shop?"

"My brother, sir, Wesley Stirling."

"And why is he not here to plead your case?"

"He was one of the Luddite attackers."

The House of Commons erupted in laughter. Belle felt her neck and cheeks turn scarlet. She clenched the rail in front of her more tightly, frustrated but determined.

"So, to be clear, Miss Stirling, your brother owns this cloth shop and decided to destroy his own gig mill in an apparent act of self-destruction, and now his sister has descended upon Parliament to demand restitution for it? Is this what we are to understand?" Abbot was barely maintaining a somber expression, while the other members were pointing up at her and screeching like a tribe of monkeys who have just discovered a new insect that might be interesting to devour.

Belle could have happily torn Abbot's unsympathetic look right from his face.

She waited for the laughter to subside.

"No, sir. What I am saying is that my foolish brother was deceived by my fi— by some Luddites into what he thought was a harmless prank against me. He didn't know what he was doing. Nevertheless, the mob destroyed the mill, which cost me dearly. I demand that Parliament make restitution, for its inability to keep these packs of wild dogs from vandalizing the countryside at will. Shops like mine are vital to England's trade and cannot be permitted to fall prey to these creatures. So I ask you, sirs, which of you will stand up for me?"

The chamber's laughter gave way to a few appreciative murmurs, in addition to several scandalized gasps. Then the monkeys began chattering among themselves again, Tory and Whig alike, their differences forgotten in light of this interesting new development.

The Speaker spoke up. "Ahem, we would do well to be quiet. Members, I ask for your attention. Gentlemen, *SILENCE!*"

The chamber stilled.

"Miss Stirling, I believe your complaint is with your brother, not us. I suggest that you return to Yorkshire to resume your family squabble, and not waste the House's valuable time. You may not realize that we've been a bit busy, between the loss of Lord Perceval, the Americans' declaration of war, and now Napoleon's rampage through Russia. We are also facing another election in September. A woman's troubles with her jackanapes brother are hardly of concern to us."

Belle was losing control of the situation, but she wouldn't give up now.

"Pardon me, sir, but I will not leave London until I've been reassured that Parliament will take care of the damages."

"You may be waiting in London an excruciatingly long time, Miss Stirling." A slow smile spread across his face. He was toying with her now.

"Possibly you are right, sir, but assuredly if you will not hear me I'll find others who will."

"Is that so? And to whom will you plead your case if I refuse to listen? Where else could you possibly go? The prime minister and I are of one mind, so you'll get no assistance there."

She swallowed. Indeed, where would she go if the Speaker were to ignore her? Who was more influential than he? But she wouldn't be cowed by this man, nor any of the others watching their exchange with amusement.

"I'll tell you where I'll go. I'll go to the Prince Regent. He'll listen to one of his subjects if you won't."

This elicited a barking laugh from Abbot. "Ah, madam, I see you don't know the prince well at all. By all means, you should seek him out for reparations. In fact, we would be glad of a return visit from you to let us know of your grand success with him."

And with that, she was summarily dismissed. Furious, she whirled around to fling herself back down the stairs, and stopped short, nearly toppling over a man who had slipped into the gallery at some point and was now blocking the door. He sat in a chair with a writing box straddling his lap, and was scratching his quill pen furiously across a piece of parchment, presumably to record the proceedings. He looked up to dip his quill in a pot of ink, and realized Belle was gaping at him. He moved his legs to one side to allow her to sweep past, making a single, curt observation: "Interesting."

Interesting, indeed. Belle returned to her temporary lodgings in the city to lick her raw wounds and plan her next steps.

Perhaps she really *would* try to obtain an audience with George Hanover.

Lord Liverpool waited patiently from an armchair while the prince's valet crammed his master into a corset and struggled to tie the laces tightly enough so that the prince's figure might be made somewhat fashionably slim. A pair of pantaloons in the style Beau Brummell had made famous lay across a chair next to him.

The Prince Regent was slavish to Brummell's style even though the two were no longer acquaintances. In Liverpool's opinion, Brummell had tried to best the Prince Regent at being a complete horse's rear. Not caring for the competition, George had discarded him. Yet George could not ever discard his desire for fashion, and so Brummell's influence lived on in starched neatness against the prince's body.

The prince rubbed rouge on his cheeks while the valet worked on his clothes. Peering closely into the mirror to examine his own facial artistry, George Hanover said into his reflection, "So you say this little chit actually interrupted the proceedings over some foolish grievance against the government?"

Liverpool swirled the claret in his glass with one hand, while holding the *London Gazette* report in the other. "Yes, apparently it was quite remarkable. I spoke to Abbot after reading the report. He says he's never seen anything like it. She practically accused the assembly of being at fault for those idiotic Luddites."

"She sounds like an utter harridan."

"That's just it, Your Highness. He says she wasn't that at all. She was more . . . impassioned than anything else. The members were quite taken with her."

George's valet fitted the prince's waistcoat over his torso. George grunted in irritation as the valet stepped between his master and the mirror to button it.

But he returned his attention to Liverpool. "Taken with her, you say? Was she comely? Was she dressed fashionably?"

Liverpool considered. "According to Abbot, yes. Very black hair, almost ebony, done up against her head with curls like women do. Comes from a line of drapers, so I imagine she knows more than most about the cut of cloth. Well proportioned. Although I suspect her tart tongue is not for a fainthearted man."

"Indeed?" With the valet now off unfolding a cravat from a nearby chest, George examined his eyebrows in the mirror before applying some cream to smooth them down. "She sounds most intriguing. I should like to meet her."

"Actually, Your Highness, she threatened Parliament to seek an audience with you herself if the Commons wouldn't do something for her."

"Did she? She sounds more and more captivating. What's her name again?"

"Annabelle Stirling. She's from Yorkshire."

"Well, I insist that you find Mistress Annabelle Stirling and have her brought to me here at Carlton House. It is my express wish to grant the young lady's desire for an audience with me."

And with that, George stepped his stockinged feet into a pair of satin-heeled shoes topped with extravagant red bows, while his valet tied his cravat. The prince was ready for whatever social engagement he had planned, therefore Liverpool's meeting with him was over.

After spending a couple of days nursing her fury inside her temporary lodgings, Belle borrowed writing implements from her landlord so she could pen a letter to Wesley, instructing him to send her all of the inventory from the shop, as well as a bank draft for what she felt was her fair share of the shop's value. As for the rest, Wesley and Clive could rot together for all she cared.

She would start over in London, far from the madmen of Yorkshire.

But before she could follow through on her threat to the House Speaker, she was startled by a courier carrying a summons for her to attend to the Prince Regent at Carlton House, two days hence.

Bewildered, she wondered who was responsible for this. And how had the prince discovered where she was staying? The Crown certainly had resources beyond her understanding.

She spent the interim time scouring London for a shop location, finally deciding on a reasonably priced lease on an abandoned draper's shop, fortuitously located in between a wallpaper printer owned by two brothers, and the C. Laurent Fashion Dolls shop, run by a woman of French descent, at the lower end of Oxford Street, which she quickly learned was a more fashionable shopping district than Cheapside. She could do no more with it until Wesley sent her goods to London, which could take weeks, so she decided to focus on finding a proper gown to wear to meet the Prince Regent.

And just what did a tradeswoman wear to be presented to a prince?

And for that matter, how was a curtsy to a prince actually executed?

Lady Isabella, Marchioness of Hertford, glowed with pleasure over the note she'd just received. Breaking open the prince's personal seal, she scanned his scrawled handwriting, which promised that a very special, no, an exquisite, gift would be arriving at Manchester House before his own appearance later that evening. Could she ensure Lord Hertford was otherwise engaged?

Her husband, Francis, would certainly oblige the prince. Her relationship with George Hanover was in its fifth year, and her husband had been very obliging for four of those years, ever since the prince's private secretary had revealed the affair to Francis and Isabella had to explain the great benefit her special closeness to the prince would mean to the family name.

Francis had been much more understanding after that.

Isabella put the note down to finish her toilette. Waving her maid away from the dressing table, Isabella pulled her ring box toward her.

Now what kind of bauble might the prince be sending over? She'd recently hinted that the sapphire necklace she'd seen in Rundell and Bridge's window would set off her coloring well. If he was obliging her in that, then she must be ready with a bare neck and perfectly bejeweled wrists and fingers.

Isabella pulled out a ring containing a plump pearl surrounded by diamonds and placed it on her right forefinger. Except that it wouldn't slide on. Must be the heat swelling her fingers. She pulled out a different ring, this one a large square of jade flanked by a single round diamond. It, too, refused to be worn.

Had she really gained so much weight lately? She put a hand to her cheek. Certainly it was fleshier than it had been ten years ago, but wasn't the prince just as rotund? After all, she might be nearing fifty-three, but he was just five years her junior and required many more stays and ties than she did.

And he seemed to enjoy her stoutness. She smiled in satisfaction as she closed the ring box. She'd leave her wrists and fingers bare, the better to display her new necklace, with its fine loops and swirls of tiny, glittering diamonds punctuated by large oval sapphires across her ample bosom.

No sizing required.

When two of George's liveried servants arrived an hour later, she stood serenely by the window in her bedchamber, a practiced air of nonchalance about her.

This air was swept away when the men entered, not with a small casket to hold her anticipated jeweled delight, but struggling with an immense, cloth-wrapped monstrosity. They propped it against the fireplace mantel.

"What is this?" she demanded. "Surely this is a mistake."

"No, madam," said the shorter of the two men. "His Highness said specifically to be sure we brought this today." The two men bowed their way out of the room.

Servant humility was always a good assurance of her continued favor with the prince.

She examined the package. Obviously a painting. And life-sized, too. She and Lord Hertford were great art collectors, but had enough fortune to buy whatever pleased them. Didn't the prince know by now that jewels and titles established a mistress's special position with her royal lover, not some dust-collecting, fifteenth-century painting of the Madonna?

Yet . . . what if this was not the Blessed Virgin? What if it was the prince himself? Perhaps he'd personally done a sitting just for her. Ah, now that would be of particular value. A painting to hang at one end of their dining room so that all of their guests could feast on it.

She removed a pair of snips from her dressing table and carefully clipped away the ties holding the cotton wrapped around the painting. She took several steps back to admire the portrait of the prince.

Except it wasn't the prince.

No, not at all. In fact, who in Hades *was* this?

For it was a full-length portrait of a young woman seated in a pastoral setting, a faithful dog at her side. The girl's eyes were languid, her nose straight, and her lips full. The sitter held a miniature in her hand, but Isabella couldn't make out whose portrait it was. She bent down to look at the signature. Thomas Gainsborough.

Well, George certainly paid a princely sum for it.

But who was she?

Lady Hertford didn't have long to wait, for her royal lover appeared promptly at his appointed time. She had to admit, even after five years as his mistress, she was still impressed by his ability to make an entrance. Although his figure resembled nothing less than six feet of sausage stuffed inside six inches of casing, he strutted into her drawing room like a bantam rooster.

Lady Hertford touched her own waistline self-consciously. *Well,* she thought, *those of us who live well may expand an inch or two. Or three. It just demonstrates my own beauty is such that the prince finds me delectable anyway.*

"Ah, my sweet Prin," she called, rushing to him eagerly to accept his wet kiss. "I insist you come to my bedchamber right away."

"Not even wine first, eh, Lady Isabella?" George's eyes disappeared into the fleshy folds created by his lascivious grin. Was it her imagination, or was he a tad larger than last week? She took his arm and led him up the stairs.

"No, my amorous Prinny. We must discuss the gift you sent. It intrigues me greatly."

"Did you like it? I thought you would. It's of great value, you know."

A servant closed the door behind them as they entered her bedroom, leaving Lady Hertford alone with the prince. She went to the painting and tapped the subject's face. "She's quite lovely. Who is the sitter?"

George smiled broadly. "You don't know? Why, it's Maria Robinson. A remarkable likeness to her. Although the portrait must be thirty years old now."

Maria Robinson?

Lady Hertford blinked rapidly. Surely this was some kind of jest.

"Did you say this is a portrait of Maria Robinson?"

"Yes. She was quite a beauty at her peak."

Lady Hertford tried to maintain a calm composure in front of the man for whom she'd sacrificed the last five years of her domestic tranquility.

"My dear, are you saying that you are presenting me with a gift of one of your previous mistresses?"

Maria had been George's mistress long ago, an actress whom he met in 1779 and nicknamed Perdita after a role she performed onstage. Her liaison with the prince had not ended well. She left the stage on his promises of financial support—what an idiot the girl was—and within two years was abandoned by him through a curt and unfeeling letter. Maria died in 1800, after nearly two decades of paralysis following a horrific miscarriage while under the protection of her new lover, Colonel Tarleton.

Heavens, Lady Hertford thought. *As though I would ever be as a big a fool as that chit.*

"Of course, my love," he said. "Isn't it a remarkable likeness?" George spread his hands wide, as though waiting for her to come to him.

One of the buttons on his waistcoat popped off under the strain and tinkled gently as it hit the marble floor.

They both pretended not to notice.

"What is remarkable is your audacity." She hoped her voice was even, but feared it had poisonous overtones. She had to watch herself.

"Whatever do you mean?" He let his hands drop, as it was apparent that Lady Hertford would not be bounding into them. A useless loss of a pearl button, she supposed.

"Sir, do you seriously think I intend to hang a portrait of your previous *mistress* in my home?"

He looked puzzled. "It's a Gainsborough," he said.

"I don't care if Gainsborough and Reynolds woke Rembrandt from the dead and all three congressed together on it. The mistress of your youth will not reside in my home."

She made a mental note to have her great-grandfather's portrait rehung in the dining room.

George pulled a lace-edged handkerchief out of a sleeve and mopped his perfectly dry brow.

"How you wound me, Isabella. Already that dreadful Lord Liverpool maltreats me by withholding the financial support necessary for a man of my station. Can't a man give his most adored lady, the woman of his heart, his truest of loves, a gift without undeserved persecution?"

"Not when it is a gift reminding his true love of his previous inamorata!"

"Dear lady, you misunderstand me. My heart is racing to the point of leaping from my breast, so deeply have you wounded me. I do believe I need a glass of refreshment."

He headed to the sideboard that she'd placed in her room years ago to hold the prince's favorite libations. He ran a pudgy, beringed finger across the front of the decanters and selected a brandy. He expertly poured himself a full measure into one of the Baccarat crystal glasses Lady Hertford had imported from France especially for him. Only when he was within her private rooms did he pour for himself.

He turned back to her, raising the glass to his lips. But as he caught Isabella's eye, all of a sudden his hand began shaking violently, sloshing a little of the brown liquid on his snowy white cravat.

Lady Hertford narrowed her eyes. *A neat trick my wounded suitor performs. But I am a fine actress, too.*

"Oh, my love!" She rushed to daub at the finely tied cloth hiding the prince's many jowls. "Have I caused you to drop a spot of brandy?"

He set the glass back down and allowed her to minister to him.

"Do you see the pain you cause me, my dear heart, my perfect match? I can hardly conduct myself as a man when my sweetheart beyond compare accuses me of a devious act when none is intended. Perhaps my affections are wasted here."

Isabella removed the diamond-head pin holding his cravat in place. She wiped off the gold stick and reinserted it back into the fabric. "Wasted? This many years I've spent in complete and total adoration of your person, and now my own tender feelings are called into question?"

She bit her lip. That was a mistake. Never compete with the prince over injury. Now she would need to compensate for her transgression. Isabella brought his hand to her lips for a kiss, then put her cheek to it in submission. As well as to hide her impatience with this ongoing charade.

Such deferent moves were typically sufficient to restore his good humor, but the prince was more prickly than usual. She couldn't imagine why. Bonaparte was mired in downpours in Russia, his wagons sunk to their hubs and his horses dropping from exhaustion. Not to mention the dysentery and disease raging through his ranks. There was probably little hope for the French madman there. Of course, Tsar Alexander of Russia now needed watching, but the final defeat of his greatest enemy should have George feeling very expansive.

But he wasn't.

"Ah, ah!" George stumbled away from her, clutching his heart. "I am overtaken!"

His pain didn't affect his ability to find her bed, climb the two steps up to her overstuffed mattress, and collapse heavily backward against her pillows, his hand still planted on his chest.

"The pain you cause me, cruel woman, is exquisite. I'm quite certain I'm about to expire." The prince tossed back and forth, no simple task given his girth. It amounted to a barely imperceptible rocking, but with his hands now flailing and grasping at unseen objects.

Oh, honestly.

Isabella went to his side and knelt on the bedside steps. "Prin, my dear, you mustn't die! My world will collapse without you. I'll ring immediately for a servant to fetch you a doctor." She reached for a bell rope dangling next to the bed hangings.

"No, no, sweetest angel, fairest of the fair, I believe the attack is subsiding now. It must be all of the anxiety you place me under." The prince heaved himself up on Isabella's arm. "Ah, much better. Really, you must watch your gross mistreatment of me. And this mattress—when did it become so uncomfortable? I believe your stoutness has practically flattened it into a custard. Have it replaced."

Isabella blinked.

The prince placed his thick hand on her shoulder. "Never fear, my cherub. I forgive your unintended damage to my soul, which exists only to worship you to the exclusion of all other divinities. It's relieving to know the depth of your sorrow for offending me over my sincere and well-meaning gift. For a prince cannot tolerate those who would intentionally harm his delicate feelings."

Indeed.

"And since we are good friends once again, my lovely Isabella, and since I'm already perched here in our favorite place, why don't you join me for an affectionate visit?" he asked, helping her into the bed.

Although the prince thought he'd won the day, it was Isabella who was ultimately victorious. For during their secret caresses, she extracted a promise for the sapphire and diamond necklace she wanted, and she intended to see the Lord Steward first thing in the morning about the purchase. In fact, she'd tell the Lord Steward that George had promised a matching bracelet, as well.

And that should compensate for having to look at George's youthful doxy at the dining table every night.

* * *

Belle was shown into Carlton House by a uniformed servant, who led her through the magnificent home into a drawing room. Her heels echoed against marble floors, reverberating against vaulted ceilings and exquisitely carved columns.

She wondered if her gown was adequate for a residence such as this one, much less for presentation to the Prince Regent. There was no time to have a dress made from one of her own fabrics, so she visited a local dressmaker, who assured her that this dress, a reject from Lady something-or-another who decided at the last minute that she wanted a violet-trimmed gown, not this pink one better worn by a younger woman, was quite appropriate for such an occasion. Belle wondered now if the woman just wanted to get rid of it. The complementary embroidered spencer jacket was well made, and the flounces bordering the hem of the dress did add flair to the plain skirt. In any case, it required only a simple alteration to suit Belle's thinner frame so it could be ready in such a short time.

Even with her fashionable white satin bonnet trimmed with ostrich feathers, accompanied by matching gloves and a simple cross necklace—the only jewelry she could presently afford—she wondered now if she wasn't appallingly underdressed.

This prince had a reputation for exquisite taste and high fashion standards. Surely he would take one look at her and be instantly repulsed.

Courage, Belle.

Another soul was already waiting in the round drawing room where she was escorted. An elderly tradesman by the look of him, dressed neatly but simply, and not troubling to cover or disguise his balding head. She nodded politely to the man, and sat on a red velvet gilded chair on the opposite side of the room.

As the minutes ticked by and still no summons came for either of them to see Prince George, she became bored and walked to the center of the room to get a better look at the décor. She realized the room was actually an oval. Fantastic crystal chandeliers were impossibly suspended from the center of the ceiling and from various points around the perimeter of the room. The light fixtures reminded her of lightning hurtling down from the sky in explosive bolts.

They were really quite hideous.

As were the fringed seat covers on many of the big, stout benches around the room.

"Is something wrong?"

Belle whirled around on the voice coming from over her left shoulder. It was the tradesman.

"Oh, no sir. I was just admiring the room."

The man smiled kindly. "I would hardly call it admiration. Perhaps you see a problem in here?"

"Not really a problem, no." How horrifying that he may have read the distaste on her face. But it couldn't hurt to pass the time talking to this man, though, could it? "I'm just not sure that these particular benches belong here."

He nodded. "I see. What about them is an affront to you?"

"They're too . . . bulky. They aren't right for the airiness of the space." She frowned. "And this shade of blue fabric on them just isn't right inside a room with so much gilding in it. Not that I would have overdone the gold leafing in this way, either."

"You have very clear opinions on matters of design. Is your husband perhaps an architect?"

His words mocked, but the twinkle of his eyes suggested he meant no offense.

"My family owns a cloth shop in Yorkshire, so I've always been interested in fabric use in décor. I had some red and cream brocade that would be dazzling on these seat frames."

"Hmm, I see. So, in your opinion as a draper, are there other fabrics in here that require changing?"

She looked at the massive windows swathed with layered, fringed draperies. The marine blue draperies extended out to cover half the walls.

"The windows are covered in a way that is certainly grand, but look at the ceiling. It is painted in soft pastels to give the illusion of clouds gently floating past the room. It suggests light and cool breezes. The draperies are better suited for protecting the occupants against a gloomy thunderstorm, don't you think? Whoever designed the room should have used a botanical print, to represent the green earth beneath the English sky, and in a much lighter fabric. This silk is too heavy. I would pull them off the ground more, perhaps tying them up more with tassels, to give a look of grandeur without depressing visitors to death."

"I believe the intent was to imitate a Roman tent."

"Truly?" *Belle, don't show your disbelief so obviously.*

The man was too lost in contemplation to notice her bad manners.

"I presume you have other fabrics in your shop more suitable to the room?" he asked.

"Actually, the shop is why I'm here today to see the prince. Our new gig mill was destroyed by some Luddites, and I want the prince to help me."

"Help you? How? Do you expect the prince to pay for your broken machinery?"

"Yes. And to force Parliament to take action against these gangs of wild men."

He looked at her thoughtfully, much like a loving uncle would at a wayward niece. "You've never actually met the prince, have you? Don't know anything about him?"

"Well, no, but—" Her words were interrupted when a cream and gilded door opened, and in entered a man whose cologne descended upon her before he had fully crossed the threshold. His girth explained the size of the benches.

Next to her, the tradesman made a shallow bow. This must be the prince! She dropped into a curtsy, keeping her head down and hoping she was accomplishing it properly.

"Ah, Nash, welcome to the Circular Room. Think you that Mr. Holland does work as fine as yours?" the prince said.

Nash? Where had she heard that name before? Belle rose when she sensed the man next to her doing so.

The prince's gaze turned to her. He must have been handsome in his youth, but folds of flesh obscured his past good looks, and instead revealed only blue eyes that squinted as he broke into hearty laughter.

She dropped back into a curtsy.

"This must be the bewitching Miss Stirling. Please rise, my dear, so I can look at you. Why, you're as exquisite as Lord Liverpool described you. I see you've met my esteemed architect, Mr. Nash. He's responsible for my favorite projects, although Carlton House is Mr. Holland's work."

Now she remembered. Nash was the one responsible for the street renovations that had engendered discussion in Parliament. And here she was, insulting his competitor's work inside the prince's house. No wonder Nash was so bemused by her assessment.

"I, I think it's quite, um, lovely," Belle faltered.

"Actually, this young lady was offering me her candid opinion of the room, and I'm pleased to say that she was simply overwhelmed by it all."

"Ah, so the lady shares my excellent good taste, is that so, Nash?" The prince winked at Belle. At least, that's what the twitch on his face appeared to be. "This room is my inner sanctum, if you will. I bring only my closest friends here to visit."

The prince invited them to be seated, and he lowered himself down heavily on one of the enormous benches Belle had just criticized.

"Ahh. So, Miss Stirling, I understand you have a grievance you wish me to hear."

"Yes, Your Highness." She looked uncertainly at Nash. Would she be forced to petition the prince in front of him?

Apparently so, for the Prince Regent merely nodded at her to continue. Once again, she explained what had happened in Leeds, leaving out the details about her fiancé and her brother. So caught up was she in her story that she found herself pacing and gesticulating as she relayed her tale of woe. She sat down again, once again discomfited at her own poor etiquette.

"And so I come to you, sir, for your great influence on Parliament, to have restitution made to me and to bring action against the Luddite mobs roaming the countryside. These brutes are not good for the loyal millers and drapers of England, and they're not good for the Crown's reputation."

The prince again nodded at her. Did that mean he would take action on her behalf? He turned to Nash. "I say, doesn't Miss Stirling give the most impassioned speech you've ever heard? Sweet as a kitten about it, but I sense ten deadly claws behind her delightful demeanor. What should I do?"

"I think you wish to help her, Your Highness."

"Indeed, a pleasure it would be to help such a winsome lady in distress. Yes, it would. So, Nash, what have you heard about moving forward on the new street? Or Regent Street, I'm proud to say it will be called."

And from there, the prince and Nash absorbed themselves in talk about the demolition and rerouting of London streets that would provide for a direct promenade route from Carlton House to Marylebone Park. The prince's excitement for the project was palpable. The two men talked as if Belle didn't exist anymore. Being ignored was almost as bad as the members of Parliament mocking her.

When George finally looked up again and noticed she was still sitting there, he dismissed her casually, as though she were a servant. Her cheeks flamed as she retreated backward out of the Circular Room, and into the presence of another servant who stood waiting outside to escort her out of Carlton House.

Had she been completely disregarded by both Parliament and the prince in just a few short days?

It didn't matter. She still retained enough anger and fervor to return and fight another day.

As the door clicked behind Belle, Nash looked knowingly at his patron. "She is an interesting girl, isn't she?"

"Quite. Positively enchanting. Lots of pluck." The prince laced his fingers across his belly, contemplating.

"She would be an entertaining guest to have about at the Pavilion."

"Yes, but she's no one. No connections. Just a tradeswoman. Different from you, of course."

"Of course. And quite different from my wife, Mary Ann, yes?"

"Ahem, yes, different there, too. But Mrs. Nash holds reign in our hearts well. As do her children."

"Of that, she and I have no doubt. Miss Stirling did have very insightful ideas about décor, though. It's too bad she isn't working with me on the Pavilion project, for then she'd be passing through the halls regularly."

"Yes, it would be a divine happiness to listen to her righteous passion as she claps those delicate little hands together to make her points. Most unlike the braying and carping of my supposed wife." The prince shuddered. "I've restricted that harpy Caroline's movements and her access to our daughter in order to curb her foul disposition and to show her that I am her master, but still she plagues me. You've heard the rumors of her paramours, I presume? Disgusting for a princess of England to behave so immorally."

"Most distressing for you, I'm sure, to have your wife acting in a most unbecoming manner." Nash and everyone else in London had listened to the prince's complaints about Caroline of Brunswick for years. The couple had spent only the first twenty-four hours of their 1795 marriage together. George hated Caroline on sight for her poor hygiene, and spent their brief time together drunk. She returned the sentiment because of his obesity and unchivalrous manners, and was stoic through two nights of rough fumbling in the dark in an attempt to get an heir. They parted mutually almost immediately afterwards.

The miraculous result of their brief, loveless union was a daughter, Charlotte, whom George kept sequestered away from her mother, in order to teach Caroline vague and incomprehensible lessons.

But the prince was becoming diverted from the point. Nash must bring him round.

"True enough, the princess cannot compare to the charming Miss Stirling. If only Miss Stirling had some sort of role at the Pavilion, so that I could bring her there on working visits."

George sat up straight. "D'you know, I have an idea. Have Mr. Crace use her as the Pavilion's exclusive draper. Let her pick out fabrics and trims and other decorative gewgaws. I should definitely like to spend more time in Miss Stirling's company."

"An excellent idea, Your Highness. I'll take care of it straight-away."

And so John Nash knew he had secured himself even further in the prince's affections. Presumably he could convince Frederick Crace of the great wisdom in bringing Miss Stirling into their merry band of players.

His only problem would be holding the prince at an acceptable length away from Miss Stirling. Even their brief encounter was making the prince's favorite architect fond of the young woman. If he wasn't careful, he might consider her his own daughter. He hoped he wasn't making a mistake in giving the girl too much royal exposure.

― 3 ―

It was a pleasing gay Retreat,
Beauty, and fashion's ever favorite seat:
Where splendor lays its cumbrous pomps aside,
Content in softer, simpler paths to glide.

—Mary Lloyd, "Brighton: A Poem," 1809

July 1812
London

Belle resigned herself to the idea that she'd accomplished nothing for all her efforts thus far, other than to acquire a shop location. And if Wesley didn't send her any inventory, her new plans might be terminated quite soon. She'd had no word at all from home, and didn't know if her brother had burned her letter, shared it in laughter with Clive and his friends, or in his own anger burned the letter along with the shop while standing around fanning the flames with his friends. But she was ecstatic when a long wagon piled high with her belongings rolled up in front of her lodgings.

Surprisingly, he'd sent her goods.

Even more unexpectedly, Wesley himself accompanied the wagon.

His sheepish appearance nearly melted her hardened heart on the spot. Perhaps he really had been influenced by Clive and had come to his senses. After all, they were family. The only family they had was each other with both parents gone and neither one of them married.

Belle now had no intention of ever encumbering herself with a husband if it meant he would be another Clive: an enemy clothed in a friend's warming cloak.

Wesley begged her forgiveness to the point that it embarrassed her. "Sister, I was a complete idiot. Just extend me some grace, and I swear to you I will never, ever again be misled by men like Clive Pryce. I can't imagine what I was thinking to agree to do something that would destroy our livelihood and dishonor the memory of our parents."

But as much as she was glad to be reunited with her brother, she'd learned a hard lesson.

"I do forgive you, Wesley, as though it had never happened, and we will never speak of it again. However, this is a fresh start for me in London, and the shop I'm forming will be mine alone. You are welcome to work here with me, but you will not own it. Am I clear?"

"Yes, yes, anything. Just so we can be affectionate siblings again. Oh, and I brought this for you." He pulled a folded letter from his pocket and handed it to her.

Her first name was written across the front in a scrawl she recognized.

It was from Clive.

The letter was undated, and contained no greeting.

> *Although you have turned your back on everyone who loves you, I still consider you affianced to me. I may have made a simple error of judgment, but this in no way excuses your appalling abandonment. Banns are being said in church each week, so you can return right away to resume your promised place as my wife. I will forgive you all if you will only return to me. But you must do so quickly to secure my forgiveness.*

Belle looked up at Wesley, who shifted uncomfortably.

"Do you know what this says?" she asked.

"I think so."

She crumpled it up and tossed it back to her brother. "If you ever see my former fiancé again, you may assure him that my greatest hope is for his perpetual roasting in hell."

Which concluded any further discussion about Clive.

"How is Henry?" she asked.

"Mostly recovered, although I suspect his back will always give him trouble. He found work in a heckling shop, where the work is easier than cropping."

"What of everyone else?"

"Gone to other cropper shops. A couple of them left town altogether."

They arranged additional lodgings for Wesley with Belle's landlady, then took the goods to Belle's new shop location, working all through the night to set everything up. Wesley had brought nearly everything, even managing to dismantle and stow the counter on the bottom of the wagon. All that remained back in Yorkshire were about a dozen bolts of fabrics, which he promised would arrive soon.

Despite the lack of sleep, Belle was happy. She made mental lists of what still remained to be done. First and foremost, she needed to have a sign made to hang outside, one painted to show the ram with the golden fleece, the motif of the Drapers' Company, underneath the name "Stirling Drapers."

She also needed to create a tableau in the shop window to show off her fabrics. Except she would not do what the average draper did, which was to dangle fabric in long, softly folding cascades in the window from the ceiling. Such arrangement was designed to show women what fabric would look like when constructed in a dress, which she found tiresome and boring. Instead, Belle planned to create frequently changing vignettes in different color schemes, to show off the fabrics as potential chair coverings, draperies, and other interior décor.

She'd done this to a small extent back in Leeds, except there weren't many of her neighbors seeking to redecorate their homes. Most of the women just wanted to see the latest fabrics being used for the current season's fashion. Humdrum.

As for the rest of the shop behind the windows, she made use of the existing shelving lining the walls. Rows of deep, round openings lined the back wall, in which they stored the cloth bolts, letting about three feet of fabric dangle down from each bolt so that customers could browse the cloth, rubbing it between their fingers. Along one of the long sides of the shop, shelves stored and displayed laces, ribbons, threads, and buttons. The other wall presented tassels, buttons, and upholstery padding.

She stowed her pistols, now reunited with one another, back under the counter, which Wesley had rebuilt at the front of the shop, hiding them behind her usual collection of cutting and measuring supplies. Unfortunately, the shop was entirely too small for her to consider bringing in another gig mill to finish fabric, so from now on she would only sell ready cloth to the public.

So on a bright, sunny morning, she and Wesley threw open the front doors, inviting in their very first patrons. Belle prayed for success and Wesley's continued dedication to the new shop.

She had no notion of how remarkable the success might be. Just days after opening the shop, she received a request to call on Mr. Nash at his home on Dover Street, to discuss an important commission he might have for her.

She was shocked by what she found there. In front of his spacious home were several wagons being loaded up with household goods. A dozen workers were carrying out tables, mirrors, paintings, chairs, and other furnishings for loading onto the wagons, under the severe supervision of a beautiful, if exasperated, woman standing in front of the four-story home. Wearing a gown of radiant yellow, she was issuing orders from beneath the shade of a columned portico shading the front entrance.

Belle approached the woman. "Excuse me, madam? I am looking for Mr. Nash. Is he here?"

The woman passed an irritated glance over her. "We've no more charity to give today, and we're very busy. Try elsewhere."

Belle's cheeks flamed. Couldn't the woman see that her clothing might be simple, but she wore a fine cut of cloth? Was her wardrobe really that awful? "No, madam, I don't seek charity. I have an appointment with Mr. Nash."

"Regarding?"

"I don't actually know. A possible commission for my shop. I'm a draper over on Oxford Street."

The woman shrugged, unimpressed, but opened the door behind her, calling for a servant. When a sweaty and out-of-breath maid in uniform appeared, the woman gave her instructions.

"Margaret, take this young lady—what is your name again?"

"Annabelle Stirling, madam."

"Take Miss Stirling to the drawing room, go find Mr. Nash, and tell him he has a visitor."

The maid nodded in obedience. "Yes, madam, but the drawing room has been nearly emptied of furniture."

The woman sighed. "Yes, Margaret, half the rooms of the house are nearly empty, but this girl insists she has a meeting with him."

The maid bobbed toward the woman and turned back into the house, leaving Belle to follow. Belle wondered if the woman was Mr. Nash's wife, but the maid gave her no opportunity to ask a question, instead hurrying through the circular, domed staircase hall into a dining room filled with sketches of homes, and to the drawing room beyond that.

Belle nearly ran to keep up, but it didn't prevent her from noticing that Mr. Nash lived almost as regally as the prince himself.

They entered a room that was, indeed, nearly empty. "Wait here, please," the maid said as she closed the door behind her.

A few minutes later, the door opened again, and Mr. Nash entered. Like everyone else Belle had seen so far, he looked overexerted, and beads of perspiration covered his forehead. But his smile upon seeing her was genuine.

"Ah, Miss Stirling! What a delight to see you again."

She held out her hand to his. "And you as well, sir. I would like to apologize for my unforgivable behavior at—"

Nash waved away her concern. "Think no more on it. Actually, as I told the prince later, it was all quite amusing. You are an unusually outspoken young woman. Perhaps it is no wonder you aren't married yet."

Belle drew herself up to retort, then realized he was gently teasing her. "Well, my brother has more than once accused me of lacking an appropriate amount of humility."

"And yet somehow you do not lack for charm. No, the apologies due are my own. I regret our rather sparse circumstances here. My household is headed down to Brighton for a time, and there's quite a bit of confusion as we decide what will go with us and what will stay here."

"Brighton?"

"Yes, it's in Sussex, directly on the Channel. A marvelous place for the health, really. People have been bathing in the seawater there for more than sixty years. The prince's interest in that town is making property values rise there. He has a residence there, called the Marine Pavilion, and I am making grand modifications to it. Would you like to see my drawings?" He searched through an open crate of long scrolls standing on their ends until he found what he wanted, and unrolled it on top of a stack of crates marked "Books—Architectural."

It was a sketch of the front exterior of an immense home, the centerpiece of which was a round, domed entry surrounded by columns, and this center section flanked by two wings echoing the curves of that center focal point. It expanded out farther on either side in a jumbled, uncoordinated way. It was impressive from a size standpoint, but utterly lacking in ornamentation and style.

"So what do you think of it, Miss Stirling?" Nash asked.

"I believe that I have no opinion whatsoever, sir."

He chuckled, his eyes crinkling in their amusement. "Fear not, Miss Stirling, your opinion is clearly expressed on your face, and I am of the same view. It looks like an undecorated cake, does it not? It is missing the rosettes and edging that would make it a confection suitable for a prince."

"I must agree with you."

"This is how Henry Holland redesigned the farmhouse that sat there. I cannot blame him, for it was conceived as a seaside retreat, never as a royal palace. But the prince is now enamored of the Oriental style, and I intend to use his preference to create the most audacious and improbable home ever designed for a sovereign, which he will in due course become. So now I will show you my own plans to improve the home, which I am determined to call the Royal Pavilion."

He went back to the crate and selected another rolled-up drawing, unrolling it on top of the first.

Belle drew in a breath. The architect was right. It was bold and extraordinary. The classically styled columns in the center of the house were to be replaced with tall Indian pillars, and a mild, rounded top was built up further by an onion-shaped dome. The flanking wings remained the same except for some minor architectural detailing, but the expanding pieces of the house to either side were brought to heel through a restructuring of their fronts, which incorporated even more onion domes. At corners on each side of the plan's domes were tall columns topped with what looked to be miniature onion domes.

"What are these?" she asked, pointing to the rooftop columns.

"My interpretation of minarets. They go well with the domes, don't they?"

She had no idea what he was talking about. But the effect was otherworldly.

Belle knew she looked like a wide-eyed calf, but there was no help for it. "Mr. Nash, I know that I am no jaded London sophisticate, but this is the most astonishing thing I've ever seen."

"And what do you suppose the interior of such a residence should look like?"

"Why, I don't know. Something Hindu? Moorish? Chinese?"

"In fact, it will be all of these. Don't you think it would be quite a feat to make the interior complement the exterior?"

Belle's mind raced over her cloth inventory. She had nothing suitable on hand. She would probably seek out some of the new copper-roller printed fabrics. She imagined something in Turkey red, or perhaps chrome yellow, colors dramatic enough to do justice to such a palace.

The wallpaper finisher next door to her could probably create an appropriate design, given the right instruction. How she envied Mr. Nash's good fortune to not only work for the man who would eventually be king but work on such a project!

"That is an understatement, sir. You are fortunate indeed to have such an opportunity."

"But it is an opportunity I am willing to share." Nash rolled this second drawing back up and inserted it back into the crate. "How would you like to work under the Pavilion's artist-designer, Mr.

Crace, as an assistant, if you will, to provide all of the drapery and upholstery fabrics for the project?"

Had she just heard aright? Was she, an unrefined girl from Yorkshire, being offered a prospect that the most respected members of the Company of Drapers could only dream of? Why was Nash presenting it to her on a silver salver?

"I don't understand, sir. I'm just a draper recently arrived from the north. You hardly know me. And surely the prince wouldn't risk money and time on someone as untried and inexperienced as I am?"

"Ah, but you're not just a draper. You're a woman of mettle and spirit. You've got innate talent that could be easily developed. More importantly, the prince is impressed with you."

Impressed with her? How could this be? He'd stopped short of mocking her out loud, and then dismissed her without any assurance that he would give her petition any consideration.

But so what? Would the opportunity of working at the Pavilion not only be a great coup for her, would it also give her a chance to urge the prince once again to take action against the wild Luddites?

She had to admit, though, that the idea of working on a royal residence was the most tantalizing consideration. Her mind turned to more practical considerations.

"How often would you—or Mr. Crace—expect me at the Pavilion? I have a new shop and I'm trying to build up business there. What will I do with it?"

"Surely you have a trusted servant. Did you close your shop to come here today? Can he not manage your shop when you need to be in Brighton?"

Hmm. Could he? She'd forgiven Wesley, but did she trust him yet?

If I want to take advantage of this project, there's no help for it. I have to leave the shop in his hands.

"Yes, I suppose he can. How long do you estimate the project to last, Mr. Nash?"

He spread his hands and shrugged. "The prince is a man of many, er, changing opinions. My design could expand, contract, and change many times before the project is complete. Assume a few years, although your visits would be infrequent. Mr. Crace handles much of the design, but he'll confer with you over complementary fabrics to his designs. You'll still have a firm hand in your shop."

The project could last for years. What a reputation she could establish if she didn't fail at the work. Although failure was a distinct possibility, if the prince was as finicky as Nash implied him to be.

"Sir, you yourself say I only have an unrefined talent. I'm not sure I'm ready to be an advisor to the prince's artist-designer."

"I think that will be easily enough done, Miss Stirling. I'll engage you as sort of an associate, giving you a wage for working with me on the project, although in many ways you'll be more of an apprentice to Mr. Crace. I'll give you colored plates to study, texts to read, and will tour you past some of my own completed projects, so that you can understand things beyond the perspective of a mere draper. I'm sure Mr. Crace will also want to tutor you, much as I did with my current associate, James Morgan, who is staying behind to manage the Regent Street project, but whom I expect you will meet in due course. And so, what say you to my offer?"

She was light-headed by what the man was suggesting. And was there really any doubt she'd do it?

"Mr. Nash, I would be honored to be your draper."

"Splendid. I'll give you some materials to examine and expect you to join Mrs. Nash and me in Brighton in a month."

Belle left Dover Street with her arms piled high with leather-bound books and sheaves of watercolor plates tied together with twine.

She could hardly believe her own good fortune.

Business in the shop picked up almost instantly, once she had Wesley letting out word that the proprietress was to be providing fabrics for the redesign of the Royal Pavilion. They adjusted their hours to stay open longer, and were even visited by the master of the Drapers' Company, who was curious to meet the city's newcomer who had already garnered royal recognition.

More interesting to Belle than honorific visits, though, was the increased contact with society women. She and Wesley quickly adapted their manners and speech to that of their clients. In Leeds, much of her custom was done through letters and via agents. Her personal contact with customers was generally limited to the ordinary residents of Leeds. Now, she never knew when a lady of rank might wish to see her goods. It was a heady experience.

And these more important customers required far better service, which frequently meant visiting them at their homes with samples. Belle was glad that Wesley was throwing himself into their new circumstances with enthusiasm, always happy to stay behind, tending to walk-in patrons while Belle was out meeting customers of distinction.

When Belle wasn't working with customers, her nose was buried inside the materials Nash had provided her. She'd no idea there was so much to learn. Most interesting to her was the extent to which the reigning monarch impacted home fashions. What a king found fashionable, so did everyone in the country, from fabric color to the primary woods used for every stick of furniture in the house.

Her initial reading was of the classical architectural orders: Doric, Ionic, and Corinthian. The differences among the styles bored her, and she knew that Nash wasn't one to slavishly adhere to any particular architectural style, anyway, hence his popularity with an extravagant, unrestrained patron.

She learned that interiors of the Tudor period reflected the heavy ornate dress of its courtiers: heavy fringes and braids against green, red, and yellow fabrics. The wood of choice was oak, plentiful in England's forests. Fabrics were frequently shot through with gold or silver thread, a sewing effort Belle could not fathom.

Green was the most popular interior color during the Stuart reign of the seventeenth century, and it was accompanied by the heaviest furniture designs she'd ever laid eyes on, carved mostly in walnut, a dark wood. The Stuarts also popularized single color schemes in each room. The great tester beds and Jacobean sideboards were downright colossal.

Furniture design lightened up considerably in the early eighteenth century with the ascent of Queen Anne and the King Georges I, II, and III, although the penchant for single-color rooms remained. The beauty of mahogany was appreciated, and furniture in this sturdy wood began filling the best homes. Belle recognized some of the famous, more modern names associated with the period: Adam, Hepplewhite, Sheraton, and even Thomas Chippendale, who practiced his trade in the then-colonies, were all well-known even to a neophyte such as her.

Even more interesting were the names of artist-designers, such as Frederick Crace and Robert Jones. Mr. Crace she would soon meet. Would she maybe one day meet Mr. Jones, as well?

According to Nash's notes, the wealthier families were discarding the Georgian décor of the last hundred years, creating great opportunities for architects and artist-designers. Aristocratic and affluent merchant families were today remaking their homes to reflect the emerging style dictated by the man who would become George IV but was now merely titled the Prince Regent.

Nash offered his opinion of the impact the Prince Regent would have on interior style. The prince had eclectic tastes, and loved nothing more than mixing them together in a chaotic blend of color and style. Straight, neo-classical lines could be happily combined with chinoiserie wallpaper and French over-gilding, making the prince giddy with joy.

No wonder Belle thought the Circular Room at Carlton House looked ridiculous.

And now she understood Nash's outrageous ideas for the Pavilion.

For further study, Belle even paraded about London, seeking out the designs of architects Nash had listed as noteworthy. The Drury Theatre façade improvements by Robert Adam; Henry Holland's East India House, home to the British East India Company; and Nash's multitude of terraced homes, as well as the beginnings of his planned Regent's Canal, opened Belle's eyes to the magnificent world of London architecture.

She also spent time near Carlton House, walking the length of the street improvements Nash planned between the residence and Marylebone Park. She grasped now why there was such animated discussion in Parliament, given the extraordinary scope of it, and the number of existing homes and buildings to be torn down in the process of creating this straightened thoroughfare. An impressive and ambitious project, she decided.

Inside Marylebone Park was a sign describing a canal that had just been approved by Parliament as part of the redevelopment of the area. The canal would begin from the River Thames at Limehouse, running under bridges, through locks, and past basins on its way to the Paddington Basin. The sign boasted that upon the project's completion, London's shipping efficiency would be unparalleled. The project was being financed by the Regents' Canal Company. She ran a finger across the list of company leaders. John Nash was a director.

Was there anything in London he wasn't involved in?

Belle hardly slept during these few weeks, instead transforming herself into a sea sponge, absorbing information then lying down to dry out before absorbing even more. Between studying and visiting customers in their homes to opine on their décor based on her newfound knowledge, she was exhausted.

A Lady Derby sent a note summoning Belle to her residence at 23 Grosvenor Square. Belle arrived there with a bundle of samples, unsure whether Lady Derby was shopping for dress material or draperies. She soon realized that the countess really just wanted to see who Belle was.

"Surely you've heard of me, Miss Stirling."

No, she hadn't. It seemed a peculiar habit of the aristocrats she was meeting to assume that everyone knew of them and their great accomplishments.

"I'm afraid I am at a loss. . . ," Belle said helplessly.

Lady Derby, a tall, slender woman of probably fifty years, who was nevertheless still quite beautiful, played the coquette with an increasingly uncomfortable Belle. "As notorious as I am, and you've never heard mention of me?"

"I'm afraid I'm quite new to London. I've been many years in Yorkshire, madam."

"I started my own life from humble beginnings, too, in Liverpool. But I came to London and became the darling of Drury

Lane. Are you sure you've never heard of me? I was Berinthia in Sheridan's *Trip to Scarborough*, and Miss Tittup in Garrick's *Bon Ton*. No? I married Lord Derby after leaving the stage, oh, fifteen years ago."

Something the woman said struck a memory in Belle's mind. "Sheridan? Do you perchance mean the member of Parliament?"

"Yes, he's held posts in the government for years. It's all he has since his theatre burned down three years ago. He and the prince are famous carousing partners. Have you met him?"

"Not exactly. I saw him speak in Parliament when I went there to complain about the Luddites."

"You went to Parliament? And spoke during session?" Lady Derby looked at her thoughtfully. "How very remarkable."

Belle was uncomfortable under the scrutiny. "Yes, madam. About the fabric you wished to inspect?"

Lady Derby cast a bored eye over her samples. "Yes, these all look adequate. I understand you were quite frank with the prince's architect when you visited Carlton House. They say the prince was quite taken with you and has talked of little else. I had to meet you for myself. Tell me, Miss Stirling, what do you think of our townhome? What changes would you make to this drawing room, for instance?" She swept a hand around her parlor.

Was this a test? Was she expecting an honest assessment or was she intending to mock Belle? Best to be politic.

"Well, if I may, Lady Derby, I'm guessing by the curved niches and the curves in the vaulted ceiling, as well as the rounded mantelpieces, that this home was designed by Robert Adam. And if this is so, then I would not change a single thing."

"Ah, well done, Miss Stirling, well done!" Lady Derby laughed, revealing teeth that were still white and perfect, despite her advancing age. "You would do well at court intrigue. As for me, I am more comfortable with rehearsed lines than with spontaneous witticisms. I wish Lord Derby were home. He would enjoy a look at you."

"Madam, I am not a zoo creature." Belle had done it again. *Learn to control your tongue,* she swore inwardly.

But the countess took no offense. "No, I suppose you are not. Being onstage does make one a zoo creature, albeit a cosseted and adored one. I don't mind it myself. So we've established that you are neither a monkey nor a Bengal tiger. But you are certainly quite interesting. You've been requested to work on the prince's Pavilion, have you not? I hear Mr. Nash has some rather devastatingly exceptional plans for it."

"Yes, madam, they are quite unique. I don't believe there will be anything like it east of India. No baker has ever made a cake so layered with decoration and outrageous ornamentation," Belle said, remembering Nash's own description.

"Really?" she breathed. "Lord Derby and I simply must get invited to his new palace when it's finished. Derby says he wants to look for a property to buy in Brighton. He says I will marvel at how the resort town is growing."

"I hope to visit the town soon myself."

But Lady Derby was too absorbed in her own musings to care about Belle's impending visit to Brighton.

"I wonder if the princess will be permitted to see the Pavilion? Or will he make it the paradise of Lady Hertford, much as it was once Mrs. Fitzherbert's heavenly realm? Maybe he even plans to sequester someone else there. There's much to contemplate, isn't there?"

"Madam, I know of the prince's troubles with his wife, but who are Lady Hertford and Mrs. Fitzherbert?" Belle couldn't keep pace with what the countess was talking about.

"Is there no newspaper in Yorkshire? Dear girl, if you are going to successfully serve the prince, you'd best know what he is about. Mrs. Fitzherbert was his wife. Or *is* his wife, depending upon your viewpoint. And those who surround the prince make sure not to have a viewpoint. He married her illegally nearly, what, three decades ago. She's Catholic, you know. But when the king offered to absolve the prince's debts if he married his cousin, Caroline of Brunswick, well, he discarded Mrs. Fitzherbert like a tattered old glove. It was quite the scandal.

"Now that I think about it, Mrs. Fitzherbert still lives in Brighton. I wonder if . . . no, he couldn't be thinking to do that.

Anyway, he married the princess, and hated her on sight. Could hardly make his parts work in order to ensure an heir."

Belle winced at Lady Derby's crude phrasing.

The countess continued. "They've a daughter, Charlotte, but he never lets the princess see her. He screeches like a banshee to all who will listen about how distressed and maligned he is about his marriage, but he slanders himself by carrying on with married heifers like Lady Hertford. Of course there have been others. Let's see. . . ." Lady Derby held up a hand to count off on her fingers. "Mrs. Robinson, Mrs. Eliot, Lady Melbourne, Lady Jersey, Mrs. Armistead, and I'm sure there will be more after Lady Hertford."

She stopped as if only just realizing Belle was still there. "Goodness, whatever possessed me to talk like this to you?"

Belle hardly knew how to respond. "The prince must be a rather extraordinary person."

"Extra-corpulent, yes. Extra-repulsive, maybe. But extra-ordinary—you might think so only if you are his mistress or his architect."

"Yes, madam. I suppose I shall have to be extra-cautious and extra-vigilant while I'm around the prince. Lest I raise Lady Hertford's ire." Belle gathered up her samples, realizing there was no actual business to be conducted here.

"Ha! You do know how to fire a verbal broadside, don't you? You're not afraid of me at all as your superior."

"My only fear is that I've wasted time here without making a sale, and that I've made enough of a fool of myself that you'll warn your friends not to hire me, either. My apologies for my frankness, Lady Derby; I'm afraid my tongue is usually three steps ahead of my good judgment."

"I take no offense, Miss Stirling. I was on the stage for years, you know—"

Yes, so you've mentioned.

"—and there's very little anyone can say to surprise me. And when someone speaks so cleverly, well, it's simply a grand divertissement, isn't it? Never fear, everyone here on the square will hear how talented you are and will be calling on you in no time."

Belle rather doubted it, but bid proper good-byes nonetheless.

* * *

The Prince Regent examined his cheek in the mirror, picking at a blemish while his visitor continued talking behind him. He unscrewed a small pot of concealer and daubed it at the reddened remains of the pimple. Was it covered? He wanted his skin to be flawless for his assignation with Lady Hertford tonight, since she so admired his complexion.

He turned back to the center of the room, which was dominated by a large, round table awash in architectural drawings.

"Tell me, Mr. Nash," he interrupted his visitor. "How does my skin seem to you?" The prince jutted his cheek forward.

"Sir?" Nash said.

"Do you see any flaw on my face?"

"No, none at all. Did you wish for one?" Nash smiled broadly at him.

Damned pert, the architect was. And lowborn. But he did have outstanding ideas, unmatched by any others except the prince's own.

He mentally forgave Nash the slight and returned to the subject. "So, before you depart for Brighton, what's the progress of Regent Street?"

"Sir, as you know, there were many objections and criticisms to my plan, including the new sewer down the center of the street and the considerable compensations required for owners of property not already belonging to the Crown. I am confident, though, that a bill approving the necessary expenditures will pass next year."

"Excellent. And what of your canal company?"

"I've passed responsibility for the project on to my associate, James Morgan, so that I can more fully concentrate on the Royal Pavilion. I expect construction to begin in October."

"Then everything proceeds on course. Let's talk of more important things. What do you have to show me about my dearly beloved Pavilion?"

Nash's perpetual smile widened into a grin. The two men were much of one mind on the reconstruction of what had once been a small seaside villa. And the architect's vision for it was nothing less

than an Oriental confection of spires, turrets, and minarets. It would
be simply fantastic beyond compare when it was complete. And if
his father would stop holding on so ferociously to his own miser-
ably crazy life, why then, George would be king and could exert
far more control over his own purse strings.

Parliament was to blame, too. He couldn't remember a time that
they weren't colluding with his father to prevent him from accomplishing his dreams. If they'd only granted him a reasonable allowance to start with, he'd never have run up a pesky debt, forcing
him to marry that disgusting creature from Brunswick. And the
Pavilion would be much further along now than it was.

Did no one care about his ruined life?

Well, Lady Hertford did. As did Mr. Nash. Ah, that reminded
him. He should mention something about a lack of funds to get
caught up on the architect's fees. But as Mr. Nash continued talking animatedly about his plans for the Pavilion's kitchen, George
thought it best to drop the matter for now.

"You say you'll be installing steam heating? I can just see the
looks on foreign ambassadors' faces when they see it."

Nash nodded. "And, of course, the kitchen will adjoin your new
Banqueting Room. Your guests will not only be dumbfounded by
the proximity of the kitchen to that room, but will go apoplectic
with jealousy over the innovations and modernizations. It will be
your greatest triumph."

"Superb, Nash, quite divine. My palace will be the envy of the
Continent. Next time we meet, I want to discuss more Hindu in-
fluences to the interior. And finally, were you able to secure the
Stirling girl?"

"Of course. She is quite flattered to be hired to work on the
Pavilion, and is also honored to have an opportunity to be in your
presence again."

"Quite so. Then we'll meet again on the coast."

Nash gathered his papers and gave a bow before leaving. It wasn't
deep enough to be called respectable, though. Come to think of it,
Nash hadn't called him "Your Highness" at all during their meeting. In fact, Nash rarely addressed him properly. No, the architect
was entirely too brash.

Brash, but extraordinarily talented. The prince supposed he'd have to beg for more money from the government in order not to lose Nash.

But the prince forgot all about Nash's fees as his valet finished preparing him for his evening with Lady Hertford. After all, a man of his prowess needed to satisfy his own personal needs before he could possibly worry about something as mundane as financial details, didn't he?

Belle was enthralled by the resort town of Brighton. Unlike the expanding industrial vista of Yorkshire, or the ancient mien of London society, Brighton was vibrant and alive, practically pulsing with energy now that the Prince Regent had decided to remake his residence there.

London's elite visited periodically to bathe in the waters of Brighton as a cure of any number of diseases. Some had even taken to sipping glasses of seawater, hoping to cure lingering or persistent diseases. Belle purchased a cup of it, which had been mixed with milk and heated, but nearly gagged in her valiant attempt to finish it.

Visitors to Brighton, situated as it was on the Channel, had unfettered views of the great river's activities. Standing on the brown, pebbly-sanded beach, Belle watched fishermen plying their trade near the shore, while pleasure yachts and merchant sailing ships occupied the waters farther out.

Entertainment abounded, from the delightful to the crude. Tea parties, fireworks, theatre, bull roasts, horse races, shopping bazaars, coffeehouses, and cockfighting all had their devoted patrons. Members of society also went to dances and played cards at one of two Assembly Rooms, one at the Old Ship Inn and the other at Castle Tavern.

The prince's influence lay everywhere. Belle attended her first play with John and Mary Ann Nash at the Royal Theatre, so named because the prince gave his assent to have a theatre built on the site in 1806. They watched an actor by the name of Charles Kemble, playing Macduff in Shakespeare's *Hamlet*, his performance drawing fervent applause. Mr. Nash, though, spent a great deal of time grumbling about who the architect of the theatre may have been, speculating that it was a Mr. Hides, whose work he didn't appreciate.

But it was a rare occurrence to see Mr. Nash in a petulant mood. Almost nothing seemed to permeate his personality, which was as cheery and sparkling as the sunshine warming Brighton's copper-colored beaches.

The Nashes had luxurious lodgings only a few blocks from the Pavilion. The lodgings consisted of two townhomes connected by doors on the ground floor and the floors above it. One entire home and the upper floors were for the family's private use, and the ground floor of the second house, with its separate entrance, was dedicated to Mr. Nash's architecture practice.

The family lived almost royally, with so many servants Belle could hardly keep track of them, and a houseful of valuable art and furniture.

Contrary to Belle's first impression of Mrs. Nash upon meeting her on the front stoop of their London home, she soon learned that Nash's wife was kind, if a bit flighty. Mrs. Nash seemed to enjoy having another woman around her. She never mentioned her first meeting with Belle outside the Nashes' Dover Street residence, having seemingly forgotten it.

Most of the woman's attention was centered on her five children, who ranged in age from four to fourteen, and who she said were the product of an earlier marriage. They ran through the house in a joyous but completely undisciplined way whenever their father was not there, but skittered off to the spacious nursery on the top floor when he arrived home. As for Nash, he seemed to take very little notice of them whatsoever.

Nash and his wife, the former Mary Ann Bradley, made an unlikely pair. Unfailingly polite to each other both in public and in private, they seemed neither to be particularly enamored, nor to bear animosity, toward each other. Their marriage struck Belle as amiable but distant.

In fact, both husband and wife were warmer toward Belle than to each other. Peculiar, but no business of hers.

As with the books and drawings he had given her to study, Belle threw herself into absorbing everything the architect had to say about his past.

"I apprenticed in London under the great architect Sir Robert Taylor—did I not recommend you look at his work on the Bank of England?—but separated from him in 1778 after many years together, upon inheriting a substantial fortune from an uncle. I proceeded to invest the legacy in a property in the fashionable neighborhood of Bloomsbury, transforming a block of connected houses into one flamboyant, stuccoed mansion. London had never seen anything like it, and I was absolutely certain of its success.

"Yet it was not to be. That highly regarded architect and idiot Sir John Soane famously criticized it. The building was a financial disaster, and I am sad to say I declared bankruptcy in 1783.

"Some say it's unwise to both plan for structures as well as to be the project's financier," he told Belle. "But I still think there is great profit to be had from such a scheme. I intend to try again one day."

Nash went on to say that he returned to his birthplace of Wales and resumed work as an architect, focusing primarily on the design of country houses and expanding his work to include romantic landscape plans.

He eventually returned to London in 1796, his reputation restored and on parallel with that of other noted architects, such as Holland, Cockerell, Wyatt, and even Nash's biggest detractor, Soane. Nash thrust himself boldly into the London architectural scene, seeking high-profile work and traveling all over England and Ireland to pursue his projects. He picked up and dropped a variety of partners and assistants along the way. In 1798, he diverted his attention enough to marry Mary Ann Bradley.

"My bride was still a comely woman of twenty-five, even after bearing five children, and I was a mere lad of forty-six, Belle. And look at me! All squat bottomed, snub nosed, and squint eyed. One might call it a miracle that she married me. But then one wouldn't know how it was between us."

Belle couldn't deny that even though Mrs. Nash was becoming plumper daily, she was still very striking, made more so by the various shades of yellow she preferred in her clothing. And Mr. Nash's kind and jovial nature went far toward obscuring his rather harrowing appearance.

During the early days of his marriage, Nash caught the attention of the Prince Regent, who admired the architect's grand, sweeping visions for home and streets alike.

"I am also a director of the Regent's Canal Company. We're going to provide a canal link from west London to the River Thames in the east. My plan is to run the canal around the northern edge of Regent's Park," he said. "My man Morgan is handling the details now, although I'll be inspecting it when I return to check on other aspects of the Regent Street project."

"I saw where the canal will start, sir," Belle said excitedly. "I visited the park while studying everything you gave me."

"Indeed, indeed. If all goes well, the first section should open in a couple of years. Perhaps you should accompany Mrs. Nash and me to see my work. Would you like that?"

"Yes, sir, I would."

Nash shook his head, a broad smile on his face. "A young lady in my offices on the path to learning architecture. Oh, the order of the universe will be in upheaval, won't it? Greatly distressing. Greatly distressing, indeed."

But Belle sensed that, quite to the contrary, her new employer was enormously satisfied.

Nash told Belle that she would not be permitted access to the Pavilion until presented to the prince there once again and the prince had not yet arrived for a visit. Some point of etiquette that must be obeyed, Nash said. So, each day while waiting, Belle helped in the office by straightening papers, sweeping, and greeting the occasional visitor.

In the evenings, Mrs. Nash sequestered her children away in their nursery and joined her husband and Belle in the library. Nash stretched out in front of the fire with a glass of port in his hand, and spent time quizzing Belle on what she'd learned about interior design thus far, but talking more about his opinions on the direction of design under the prince's influence. When Nash was done with lessons, he shifted conversation to more gossipy topics. Belle sat in rapt attention, listening to his stories of dealings with unscrupulous suppliers, sloppy craftsmen, and jealous competitors. But she was most drawn in by his stories of the Prince Regent.

According to Nash, George Hanover, the Prince Regent who would one day become George IV, had had a poor relationship with his father from the time he was just a young lad. The Hanoverian court was dull and moralizing, and provided no outlet for a high-spirited boy like the prince. In turn, the king viewed his son as self-indulgent and irresponsible.

The prince nursed his resentment of his father until it bloomed into a permanent rebellion and he set out to distance himself as far as he could from the family patriarch.

Because the king was a Tory and despised Whig politicians like Charles James Fox and Richard Sheridan—there was that name again!—both of whom sided with the American colonials against their king, his son immediately surrounded himself with both of these men.

The two men led Prince George down a merry path of debauchery. The king complained publicly that Fox was the one principally responsible for the prince's many failings, including wasteful spending and his propensity to vomit in public.

And because the king maintained an unusually chaste domestic life, the son made sure to be dissolute and wanton. The Act of Settlement of 1701 forbade marriage to any other than a Protestant, yet the prince had secretly married his beautiful Catholic widow, Maria Fitzherbert, in 1785.

Belle already knew the rest of this sordid story, but didn't want her new mentor to know that she had actually been gossiping with Lady Derby. What he revealed that Belle didn't know was that, even after his marriage to Caroline, the prince had continued his liaison with Maria Fitzherbert, not finishing with her permanently until last year.

He was currently taken with the Lady Hertford, who was turning his loyalties back to the Tories. A small comfort to his father. George III had been living in a blind, rheumatic, and nearly permanent insane state since 1810, obliging Parliament to install his son as regent two years ago.

Today, because the prince was a spendthrift in response to his father's lifetime of frugality, John Nash found himself the recipient of many lucrative contracts for improving the prince's various properties.

"The prince has an enormous appetite, both for food and love," Nash told Belle. "Sometimes he is too ravenous for both, and diverts his own attention through these little building projects that greatly benefit my practice. And so, while you are working here, you will always speak highly of the prince no matter what you hear. Or what you may experience with him. Do you understand, Miss Stirling?"

She did, but why was such a warning needed?

Finally, the Prince Regent would be in Brighton in another two days. But first, Nash asked Belle to sign on at the circulating library.

"Here, take this," he said, handing Belle some coins. "You'll need to give the master at the library this, and in turn you'll be able to sign the Master of Ceremonies book. Sign in as 'Annabelle Stirling, ward of John Nash, the Prince Regent's architect.' "

Belle was puzzled. "Why am I to do this?"

"The master ensures that balls held in the Castle Tavern don't conflict with those being held at Old Ship Inn. Therefore, he's the nucleus of society in Brighton. Once your name is in his book, everyone in town will know you're here and under some notice of the prince's. And that will lead to some social invitations for you, Miss Stirling. You're young and shouldn't be quite so serious."

"I hardly think that while I'm here I'll have time for—"

"Maybe you will, maybe you won't. But it does no harm, does it?" His eyes crinkled in response to his smile, and Belle was helpless to refuse her new mentor.

That evening, she wrote to Wesley, telling him of her adventures to date, and of her planned visit to finally see the existing pavilion the next day. And to remind him to lay a yard or two of that new tambour-worked muslin in the window.

* * *

Belle and Nash set out the next day around noon, with Nash assuring her that the prince would most certainly not be awake and receiving guests before then. They approached the residence from what the architect referred to as the Steine front. A decorative fence partially enclosed an expansive, triangular-shaped green containing a stream ambling placidly through it. Homes surrounded the street that enclosed the green, including the Pavilion, which Belle thought had been accurately portrayed in Nash's drawings, except for the scaffolding that now climbed the exterior like an orderly creeping wood vine.

When the scaffolding was eventually removed, she knew the exterior would be rejuvenated in stucco and Bath stone.

Belle was anxious to see the interior of the prince's residence, but Nash held her back.

"I want you to understand this vista from the prince's perspective. The green here is where fishermen used to lay out their fishing nets for drying after bringing in their daily haul from the Channel. But the town began erecting the railing about forty years ago to contain the fishermen's activity, because fashionable visitors were offended by it while promenading near the prince's house. It angered the fishermen but pleased the prince, so . . ." Nash shrugged. "The redbrick house you see to the right of the Pavilion? That will be demolished to make way for my additions."

Nash then pointed to a row of houses on the west side of the Steine. "See those homes? All built in the last few years by London's elite who know that the prince now favors this coastal town. That one in the middle? It belongs to Maria Fitzherbert."

"You mean . . . ?"

"Yes, the prince's old mistress. She had this residence built in 1804, a half-dozen years before the two of them split permanently. She always maintained a separate residence from the prince, I suppose for appearance's sake. Yet she's decided to stay on. The lady is quiet and gracious, and hasn't a spiteful bone in her. But it's best not to mention her to the prince. He still harbors a passion for her, among others."

Nash turned and swept a hand in the direction of the lawn leading toward the Pavilion. "That section of the prince's lawn was once part of the Steine, but has of course been acquired for his use. I predict Brighton will one day surpass places like Bath as a retreat for the beau monde, provided the prince maintains his passion for the place. And we, Belle, shall be the ones to help them establish their fine residences and keep up with changing décor tastes, will we not?"

"It's too exhilarating a thought to really grasp."

He smiled at her as though she were his favorite niece. "Let's go see the Pavilion now, shall we? Oh, by the way, Mr. Crace will be meeting us here, as well."

So she would finally get to meet one of the prince's artist-designers.

They strolled the lawn up to the home that until now she'd only seen from a distance, and more intimately in Nash's drawings. The interior was a beehive of activity, with workers having torn out so many walls and floors that Belle couldn't begin to assess where she actually was in relationship to the drawings.

Nash led her down a long corridor, through another space that was either another hallway or perhaps a large pantry, and into a cavernous space under construction. Along one side was a gigantic cooking-sized fireplace being swarmed over by masons.

"The kitchen?" she asked.

"Yes. There will be rooms far grander and more magnificent, but this one is a source of great pride for me. And it will be the first room to complete." He pointed to the fireplace. "The fireplace will contain a smoke jack. The upward draft from the fire will turn a metal turbine in the chimney, and a series of gears, pulleys, and chains will transfer the motion to a set of five spits. The prince's chef will be able to present multiple roasted dishes for any given menu. There's nothing of its design anywhere else in England."

"Impressive."

"Furthermore, I intend to use the support columns around the center of the room to bring in the styling of the Banqueting Room."

"I don't understand. How will you make them decorative?"

"Ah, Miss Stirling, you will see in due time. Speaking of time, I think we should see where the prince is."

They found him, or rather, he found them, in a room untouched by construction. After their requisite deferential greeting, Nash evaporated from the room.

The prince wore a gray-striped waistcoat with a neck so high it almost completely obscured his voluminous chin. A gold watch fob dangled perilously from the top of his dangerously stretched black leggings, which disappeared into high-topped boots. He looked like a melon perched on two spindly twigs.

"You admire my suit, Miss Stirling?" the prince asked.

"Your Highness, I've never seen anything quite so unforgettable in my life."

The prince brushed off an imaginary speck from the sleeve of his dark overcoat, a poorly disguised attempt at modesty.

"Our happenstance meeting here today is quite fortuitous, Miss Stirling."

"Happenstance, sir? Mr. Nash said—"

"I've given you much thought since our first meeting. And of how compatible we could be."

Compatible? What was he talking about? She didn't like the direction of this. Where had Nash gotten himself off to?

"I have much to offer the right woman. The right woman is, of course, one who pleases me. And I believe you would please me well." The prince folded his hands across his belly. "Are you ready to try to please me?"

Belle's mind raced. Mr. Nash had arranged this meeting so she would be permitted to work in the palace, hadn't he? Surely Nash wasn't trying to broker an arrangement between her and the Prince Regent.

Or was this the prince's way of being coy and clever?

Oh, honestly.

"Your Highness, as tantalizing as your offer is, it is completely impossible for me to become your mistress." She hoped she looked sufficiently disappointed.

"Dear girl, what impediment could there possibly be?" The

prince reached over and rubbed a sausage finger along her cheekbone. Belle kept her smile stitched in place.

"Why, sir, everyone knows that you prefer married ladies as your companions. And since I am clearly still just a maiden, I am therefore totally unsuitable as a mistress." She dropped her voice to just above a whisper. "But, sir, the moment I take a husband, I'll surely let you know."

The prince dropped his hand from her face, blinking in disbelief.

She held her breath. Would he now banish her from the royal property?

A small quiver of his lip was only a precursor to his subsequent hearty laugh.

"Miss Stirling, you do tickle me. What a breath of sweet, fragrant air you are. Right then, I take your challenge. A lovely bottle of perfume like you won't sit on the shelf long before an enamored buyer comes along, so we'll be discussing a liaison in no time, won't we?"

"But sir, I am a fragrance that smells sweet in the bottle but bitter on the wrist. So I shall probably linger on the shelf until I turn to vinegar. And then a man of your delicate sensibilities would never be interested in putting such a foul container among his other fragile, crystal-stoppered flagons."

The prince's eyes nearly disappeared in the folds of his face as he grinned at her. "If only my harpy of a wife had your qualities, I wouldn't be forced to seek love and companionship elsewhere. I am *most* unfortunate in my marriage, you know. She is my worst enemy. If only I were the king, I'd rid myself of her. She's done nothing but cause me heartache—"

The prince continued on his tirade for several more minutes, until he exhausted himself and dismissed an equally worn Belle to return to Nash. She did her best to avoid skittering out like a gazelle being tracked by a lion, and immediately sought Nash out.

She cornered him in a vestibule for answers as to where the prince had gotten the idea that she would be amenable to being his mistress. When no answer was forthcoming, she nearly quit on Nash, but the desire to actually work on the Pavilion was too great.

Chastened but still in good humor, Nash led Belle farther throughout the property. A man's voice called out to Nash as they entered a room whose décor looked old and shabby. He followed them in and Nash shook hands with him. The man was flat faced and wore a measuring tape about his neck.

"Ah, Crace, there you are. May I introduce Miss Stirling to you? This is the young woman the prince wishes to provide fabrics for the Pavilion's new interiors."

Crace was half of Nash's age, and possessed half his humor. He tilted his head back in order to look imperiously down his nose at her. "So you're the little orphan I must feed and succor," he said. "How very unpleasant."

What was this? First the prince was overtly flirtatious, now Mr. Crace was utterly disdainful of her.

"Sir, have I caused you some injury?" she asked, dropping the hand that he refused to take in greeting.

"Not yet, but undoubtedly you will. Nash, I'd like an opportunity to discuss the windows in the Music Room when you've time. Alone," he added, with another derisive glance at Belle.

But Nash was never one to lose his happy demeanor. "Of course," he replied, his smile wide. "It's unfortunate that Miss Stirling will be returning to London soon, so she'll have to extend her regrets at not being able to join us."

"Quite." Crace turned on his heel and left.

Belle looked at Nash questioningly, but he merely patted her shoulder. "Never mind him. His brain is fogged by wallpaper paste. He'll soon come to appreciate you as much as the prince and I do."

So, she'd definitely offended Mr. Crace, and probably offended the prince. Her main concern, though, was whether the prince would still welcome her back to the Pavilion. However, she soon got a report from Nash that she still remained in the prince's favor. Far from being insulted by her refusal of his advances, he was charmed.

She sighed in relief. Mr. Crace, however, would require more work to earn his cordiality. If he was capable of it.

Belle spent a week further at Brighton, walking through the Pavilion with Nash, drawings in hand, and further understanding his and the prince's vision for it. Mr. Crace never reappeared.

She returned to London, her head stuffed with her own ideas for fabrics to complement the planned exotic Hindu exteriors. She promised to return soon with cloth samples for Mr. Crace's inspection.

❧ 4 ❧

Are we aware of our obligations to a mob? It is the mob that labor in your fields and serve in your houses—that man your navy, and recruit your army—that have enabled you to defy the world, and can also defy you when neglect and calamity have driven them to despair. You may call the people a mob; but do not forget that a mob too often speaks the sentiments of the people.

—George Gordon Noel Byron, maiden speech
to the House of Lords, February 27, 1812

February 1813
London

The memories of Clive's betrayal, Wesley's treachery, her humiliation in Parliament, and the king's immodest proposal all flew from Belle's mind as she immersed herself into the world of room design. She remained up late each night in her rooms, surrounded by samples clipped from her bolts and her growing collection of books, floor plan drawings, and colored plates representing Mr. Crace's designs.

She matched and rematched samples together against the artist-designer's plans, finally wondering how it was she thought she was capable of any of it. *You're just a draper. You sell cloth. You're not a designer. You have thoughts of grandeur way beyond your station.*

Yet she loved the challenge and wasn't about to relinquish her task.

And, besides, Mr. Nash told her before she left Brighton not to obsess to perfection over her suggestions, for he and the prince were sure to make numerous changes.

Wesley was of great comfort to her, for he'd taken to his role of her assistant with great aplomb. He was charming and affable to the women who visited the shop, and although Belle suspected he succumbed to the attentions of the more persistent female patrons, she closed her eyes to it. Her brother was discreet, business was thriving, and how could she stop him even if she so desired?

She had to shut her eyes even tighter against his periodic disappearances for hours, so reminiscent of his behavior in Leeds, but she trusted that all would work out.

In January, her Luddite wound was reopened briefly when she heard that George Mellor and his mob of men were convicted in the uprisings in Yorkshire. Thirty-six hours after their conviction—with no time for appeal—he and two of his compatriots were summarily executed before a silent crowd. Dozens more Luddites were transported to the Colonies, and another round of executions resulted in the deaths of fourteen more of Mellor's followers.

Belle hoped this was the end of worker fanaticism in England.

"So a bunch of rabble were executed, and the court may have been corrupted," George said to Lady Isabella, who had just shared the news with him. "What of it? They were criminals terrorizing the countryside. Besides, their anger is at Parliament, not *me*. I've done nothing. Therefore, there's nothing to worry over. When will supper arrive?"

On cue, a servant entered with an overloaded tray of steaming dishes, which he set on the table between the prince and his mistress. Lady Isabella had suggested that they dine here in her rooms, but now questioned the wisdom of that idea, given that the table might collapse under the weight of their food.

The prince signaled for another glass of wine, and endeavored to acquaint himself with selections from every plate.

Lady Isabella sighed. Her royal lover didn't understand that the people could bring great ruin to the country if their ire was sufficiently roused and they might find the differences between Parliament and the Crown to be mere nuances.

He held up his knife, which had a slice of crispy-skinned duck on it. "Besides, there are so many other problems plaguing me that

I can't be worried about what goes on in the north. Jane Austen has a new novel out, and I've yet to secure an inscribed copy for Carlton House. She's very evasive. Must have my librarian Clarke see to it.

"And of course Caroline continues to try my patience. I've isolated her as best I can, and now all of the *ton* patronize my parties, not hers. But she's in league with that cursed Whig, Henry Brougham, and together they're stirring up propaganda against me. But I can wage my own campaign, can't I? And one that might get Parliament's attention enough to help rid me of that millstone."

Apparently the ongoing war with the Americans and Napoleon's unrelenting agitation on the Continent were of little concern to him in light of his personal domestic matters. Lady Isabella felt her patience being tried. If only his fixation were limited to obsessing over his wife, she wouldn't be concerned. But now he was consumed with his building projects. It didn't bode well for the future if his attentions were to be diverted so far from her.

"My dearest heart," she began, reaching over for a piece of gingerbread cake. "How often will you be leaving me to go to Brighton to visit your new residence? You know how much I miss you when you're away."

"Not too often. Just when Mr. Nash needs me to make approvals. And for periodic checks on progress."

"You haven't invited me to accompany you yet. I should like to see the progress, too. Or don't you plan to have me preside there as your hostess? Have you someone else in mind?"

"No need for you to worry, my love. I am as constant as the North Star. You know that, don't you?"

And that's what was so worrisome. George's constancy was well-known to everyone. And now he was focusing his attentions in Brighton, where Maria Fitzherbert still resided, and where the prince had now employed some young chit to paper his walls and unroll rugs.

Lady Isabella's own constancy these days was a peculiar feeling of dread.

* * *

Belle stared at the letter in her hand. Was she angry? Sad? Over a year had passed since her life had so dramatically changed. Ambivalence was the most passion she could muster. She read it again.

14 June 1813

Dearest Belle,
I have momentous news to share with you. Clive and I have married, and are leaving for Wales to be near some distant relatives of his that have promised him work.
I pray you are not too terribly shocked or angered. You know Papa always liked Clive. He thought what went on at the shop was a complete misunderstanding, and that you would soon return to your rightful place here in Leeds. When you didn't, and we never heard from you except to return that bit of borrowed money, well, Clive gave up hope and sought my father for comfort.
It led to us developing a close friendship, which Papa encouraged. And, truthfully, I saw no other prospects for myself and welcomed Clive's attentions. Please, dearest friend, may I have your blessing on our union?
Your faithful friend,
Amelia

Belle shared it with Wesley. He read it impassively. "So your best friend is marrying your fiancé."

"He was no longer my fiancé. Not once he connived you into ruining my life."

"Sister, I've apologized for—"

She held up a hand. "I'm sorry, I wasn't trying to unearth the dead. Consider the topic reburied."

Wesley held up a length of Osnaburg linen. It had a grease stain on it. He threw the cloth on a pile of other fabric scraps to be discarded.

"It does bring up an interesting question, Belle. When do you plan to get married, and stop your obsession with decorating people's homes?"

"Why, Brother, the minute you decide to get married and stop carousing the streets at night like a wharf rat."

"Peace, Sister, peace. Although, in my defense, if I bring a bit of joy to a lonely woman's life, what harm have I done? But I believe we should agree to leave each other alone on this topic, eh? Besides, there are more important concerns for us. For instance, I've served this shop well and faithfully for a year. Isn't it time you let me share in its management?"

Except that you haven't been faithful, Wesley. You slip out for hours at a time with no explanation. If I run an errand, I never know if you'll be here on my return.

His overt affection for some of the shop's patrons reminded her of his fancy for the girls who frequented the Pack Horse Inn. A little too indiscriminate.

And there were some of his strange comings and goings late at night. Occasionally, Belle could hear him banging into their lodgings in the wee morning hours and stumbling off to his room to sleep for an hour or two. That day, there would be no odor of rancid alcohol on him, but he would behave like a man in the aftermath of a drunken stupor, tired and slow. By supper he was fine again. It never affected his sales, for women were too enamored of his cocoa-colored eyes framed by long lashes to notice that he was a little off.

Belle noticed. She'd not said anything because it had only happened a handful of times. But the tiny kernel of doubt that had sprouted inside her was beginning to flourish. She loved Wesley, but, regrettably, she didn't trust him.

"I don't know if the time is right for that yet," she said, turning away so he wouldn't see the unease on her face.

But she didn't move fast enough to avoid seeing the resentment in those narrowing brown eyes.

Wesley had the dream again. Not a dream, really, more like a tortured limp through a maze of pain and confusion.

It began as so many of them did.

He was walking through a park late at night, alone. The moon hung low and bright, its dark surface shadows stark against the glow. It was warm and utterly still, without even a stray bat flying overhead for company.

Wesley strolled through the park with a cane, whistling aimlessly. He was always happy in the beginning of the dream, his whistling carefree and joyous and his body that of a hale and hearty young man. He had the sense of being wealthy, and being respected by all he encountered. That feeling of importance was calming and satisfying.

But as he neared a copse of trees in the center of the park, clouds drifted across the face of the moon, sending the park into gloomy grayness as the moon struggled futilely against the jagged-edged mist beginning to obscure it.

His instincts now prickling him with the urge to flee, Wesley kept walking toward the trees, his mind issuing an alarm but his legs unheeding of the warning.

He now reached the canopy of overhanging branches from the oaks and elms on the outer edge of the copse. The leafy spreads served to conceal the filtered moonlight even more.

Still he continued. Now he knew that someone was calling him from inside the grove. A woman's voice, pleading and begging. For her life? For Wesley to do something? The sounds were indecipherable. Where was she? He could hear her, but couldn't find her.

In the darkness of the trees, the temperature dropped low enough that Wesley knew he should be shivering, but instead he was sweating profusely. His disobedient legs continued their pace forward, and he was incapable of ordering them to do otherwise.

The woman's voice was rising, becoming more hysterical. And now he was closer, so he could make out words. "It's you, Wesley Stirling. You did this to me." The "me" ended in an anguished choke. "I'll be with you forever. I'll never let you go."

Wesley stopped to mop his brow with a kerchief. But his legs only permitted a moment's rest, so determined were they on their course.

"Why?" The woman's voice was rising to a screech. "How could you leave me behind? To be devoured?"

Wesley put his hands against a tree, in an effort to stop his legs from carrying him to what was surely hell. "I didn't mean it, Alice," he whispered. "Truly. I couldn't help it."

"You're a liar, Wesley Stirling."

Wesley jumped. He could feel the warm breath against his ear as the words flowed in like poison.

"No, you must listen to me. I was forced to leave you there." He wasn't even sure where to address his words. Up in the treetops? Next to him? Toward the center of the woods? But surely he was near the center now.

"You're a liar, and will burn on a pyre." In his ear, the voice cackled happily at her own rhyme. "Liars burn on pyres, pyres are for liars, liars roast in fire on the pyre, heeeeeee!"

The voice seemed to swoop quickly up away from him into the tree branches, shaking and rattling them. Small acorns struck him in the face. And then the voice, or woman, or whatever it was, plunged back down, settling at his ear again.

"I thought you loved me, Wesley, my dearest."

"I did, Alice, I did." Sweat was trickling in rivulets down inside his collar.

"But not now?" Her—*its*—breath was now burning hot on his ear. The stench of something acrid assailed him. Had Death finally come for him? Was it the final divine joke to face your guiltiest moment before descending into Hades?

"No. I mean, yes. Of course yes. I don't know what you want, Alice." Wesley could feel his hands being pushed off the tree trunk. Was he falling? He clawed out in front of him, grasping for anything solid. He regained his footing as he made contact with something unrecognizable. It was soft and pliable, like the sweetest of women, yet thick and gummy. His hands were lodged securely in it. He pulled back gently, but could not extricate his hands.

What the hell was it?

It was at this moment that Wesley realized there was no light at all in the woods. Or had he been blinded? He tried again to extract his hands from the gelatinous substance in front of him.

"Pl-please, Alice. It wasn't my fault. What can I even do now about what happened to you?" If he wasn't careful, he'd start weeping.

"You can do nothing, my love. But I can do many things. Over and over. Forever and ever and ever. You'll never leave me behind again, sweetheart." Her giggle was barely perceptible over the echo of the word "sweetheart."

And with that, his arms disappeared into the viscous substance up to his elbows and he tipped forward, his face against the slimy, jellied *thing* in front of him.

And then it was gone.

He was standing alone again in the dense grove of trees. He was no longer sweating, but instead was overtaken by a distinct chill. The chill rapidly plummeted into frigidity. He flexed his hands to work warmth into them, and tried to turn around to once again quit the landscape.

But again his legs were uncooperative. So he stood rooted to his place, shivering and blowing our great plumes of frost. For how long would he be made to stand here, taking this punishment?

And then she was back.

He preferred her in her gelatinous form.

For her voice was back against his ear, hot and heavy with a malicious desire. "No, sweetheart, you'll never leave me behind. Not while I have you in my arms."

And those arms, strong as the tree limbs above him, wound their way around his chest, gripping him in a deathly vise. Alice had been fleshy and strong, but he didn't remember her as being quite so powerful. And with such a long reach.

For her arms were now endless, wrapping around him again and again, a spider entangling an unwary insect in her secret web. And he was the fool who had wandered—no, dashed—into it.

She was squeezing him now. He couldn't breathe. Wesley could feel a small tingle in the back of his throat, as though she had inserted a thin, hairy leg in his mouth and was probing him.

Not just probing him, choking him. Seizing his breath by both her embrace and her evil scraping from within. He closed his eyes, willing her away, but knowing that she would eventually claim him as her own. He fell to the ground, staring sightlessly through the tree canopy at the moon's reappearance from the cloud cover, unable to do more than emit a faint gurgle.

And then he awoke.

Wesley sat straight up in bed. The moon was indeed bright. It couldn't be past midnight. He frantically checked himself in his fading panic. There were no deadly tentacles around him and his hands were not covered in anything gummy. He swallowed. Nothing there, either.

But he was sweating profusely, the only reminder of his nightmare. He picked up the package on the table next to his bed and examined it.

I'll eat no more opium. Ever.

But he knew there would be more. There would always be more. More and more and more until Alice completely devoured him from beyond the grave.

August 1814
London

While Belle's business grew, and Nash's projects expanded, war raged relentlessly across the Continent for the next year. Following Napoleon's disastrous retreat from Russia in October 1812, Prussia, Sweden, Austria, and a number of German states reentered the war, seeing opportunity in the emperor's defeat. Even the indefatigable Napoleon Bonaparte could not long survive the coalition built against him. In June 1813, the Duke of Wellington broke the will of the French Army at the Battle of Vitoria in Spain. Napoleon was subsequently defeated again at Leipzig in October 1813, and by March 1814 his forces were stretched too thin to effectively protect Paris, which succumbed to his enemies on March 30, 1814.

The hopelessness of his situation forced Napoleon to abdicate at Fontainebleau on April 4, in favor of his son, Napoleon II. However, the allies refused to recognize his successor, and instead reinstalled the House of Bourbon, placing Louis XVIII on the French throne.

Napoleon himself was exiled to the island of Elba, off the coast of Tuscany. Chillingly, Napoleon promised his troops that it was not the end but that he would return to France "when the violets will bloom." His troops rested assured that their god-like leader would come back for more victories.

Despite Napoleon's confidence of his eventual retaking of the French throne, England's happiness over the peace resulting from his abdication lasted for months, and now a splendid exposition, called the Jubilee Fair, replete with fireworks and entertainments celebrating peace, was to take place at Hyde Park on August 1.

Wesley, who hadn't had a nightmare episode in weeks, asked Belle if she would like to accompany him to the event. "I've been reading about the planned festivities in the paper. Let's close up for the day and attend. I think most of the shops on Oxford Street will be shut down, anyway."

"What? Miss Smythe or Miss Davidson didn't want to accompany a handsome gentleman such as yourself?" she asked, smiling.

"Many of the ladies who patronize the shop would think that only drunkards, escapees from Newgate, and fallen women will be there. I prefer your company, anyway. And I flatter myself that you prefer mine. Of course, our appearance together might ruin my chances for obtaining a proper wife." Wesley's eyes rolled upward as he laughed at his own joke.

Wesley's initial resentment of her refusal a few months ago to make him her equal in the shop had vanished quickly, and he was much as she remembered him in Leeds: fun and lighthearted.

Her brother was in good spirits as they approached the crowded grounds of Hyde Park. The rectangular park, with its serpentine lake slicing it vertically down the middle, was teeming with people, tents with gaily flapping flags, and temporary booths set up to sell pies, drink, and souvenirs. Jubilee nuts and Regent cakes were popular offerings, with anxious buyers crowding the stands to purchase what were surely just bags of sugared almonds and plain biscuits.

Tapped barrels of ale, porter, and stout were flowing regularly into tankards, and men were carrying their refreshments with them to enjoy any of the myriad of impromptu entertainments spread all over the grounds. A fiddler sawed his instrument merrily with several drunken bystanders sloppily dancing nearby.

Stages had been erected, each offering different performances representing Napoleon's defeat against their fancy, painted backdrops. Actors shouted to be heard against competing theatrical troupes, vendors hawking, and the booming of a band from the other side of the lake. Belle and Wesley strolled from stage to stage, trying to catch all of the shows.

Children ran everywhere, shouting happily and enacting their own versions of the emperor's downfall.

Belle had never seen anything like it. Her mouth must have been hanging open, for Wesley looked at her and laughed.

"London is madness, isn't it? But I think the best is yet to come. Look there." Wesley pointed to the lake. She'd not noticed the fleet of ships on its surface.

A fleet of ships in the middle of a park? How could that be?

Belle frowned, and Wesley laughed again at her confusion.

"Fascinating, isn't it? The papers referred to it as a Naumachia, which I believe is scheduled to start shortly." He pulled out a pocket watch to confirm his statement. "Yes, any time."

"But what is a . . . what is it called?" Belle asked.

"A Naumachia. A mock sea battle. I'd say this one is Trafalgar. They're just reduced wooden replicas of great sailing ships. The ships will chase each other around and the sailors aboard each one will fire blank shot at the enemy."

As if in response to Wesley's words, several distant pops rang out and plumes of white smoke rose from one of the smaller ships. Men on board the French-flagged ship screamed in imaginary distress, but were soon laughing uncontrollably. Onlookers at the water's edge joined in the merriment, shouting encouragement to the "French" sailors to jump into the water and drown themselves.

Soon all of the ships were firing at one another in a melee of good humor, as those watching kept up their taunts and jeering that the French should surrender and strike their colors. At the conclusion of the "battle," in which the French ships did indeed lower their flags in defeat, the crowd's cheering was raucous and deafening.

It was also completely thrilling.

A great whoosh emanated from one of the French ships and Belle could see a tower of flames rising from it. The crowd was now delirious, and she found herself clapping and cheering. A small rowboat appeared on the lake, carrying one portly passenger and an oarsman. It came to the center of the lake while the play ships scattered to either side. The passenger stood, revealing the finery that couldn't conceal his puffy figure. Spectators gasped in recognition and rushed to the water's edge on both sides of the lake to hear what he had to say.

Wesley gripped Belle's shoulder. "It's the Prince Regent!" he said as he pulled her along to get a better view.

Prince George was unsteady on his feet in the rowboat, and put his hand on the rower's shoulder for balance. With his other hand, he brushed something from his waistcoat, an affectation she'd seen before. His garments were the most elegant she had ever seen on him so far, but then, she knew little about royal attire. His clothing was dark, and he wore a high collar with a white neck cloth artfully arranged inside it. The medallion attached to a wide sash across his shoulder winked brilliantly even at a distance in the waning hours of daylight. He also wore what looked to be an admiral's hat. In the distance behind him, the fired ship continued to spark flames upward.

Belle held her breath. What would he say?

"Dear people, fellow countrymen, what happy news brings us to this day." The prince's voice carried clearly across the water. "First, we celebrate the Glorious Peace that comes from our victory over that tyrant and oppressor, Bonaparte."

Huzzahs filled the air.

"Our fearless military commander, the Duke of Wellington, showed that despot that even a hundred thousand of the best-trained French troops are no match for a handful of our brave and intrepid lads."

"Long live the Duke of Wellington!" shouted someone from the crowd. The people responded with cheers.

"Quite right." The prince raised his free hand to quiet everyone as he nodded toward the sound of the voice.

"May this Glorious Peace reign over our country as long as the House of Hanover has reigned in gentleness and compassion over its people. For today we also celebrate the centennial anniversary of Hanoverian rule in England!"

The applause and shouts of approval were more scattered this time. But George held up a hand again as though quieting a roaring crowd.

"Yes, for one hundred years my family has presided over Great Britain, with no thought for our own comfort but only for the solace, cheer, and well-being of the citizenry."

He paused for the crowd's approval, which was even sparser this time. Undaunted, he continued. "And so, my good friends, let us eat to contentment, have drink in good cheer, and place our faith in God's providence that He will maintain the peace and Hanoverian rule for a hundred years more! I hereby decree that the tapped barrels throughout the park be made to provide one free tankard to all who gather here!"

And this did stimulate widespread applause and shouts, as people stampeded to be the first to secure a cup of beer. Hardly anyone noticed as the prince sat down heavily again in his boat and was rowed back to shore, where he was helped into a waiting coach by no fewer than three liveried footmen.

Belle and Wesley continued their promenade around the park, finding a secluded path away from much of the chaos produced from the free-flowing liquor. Wesley plucked a rose of deep coral from a bush and handed it to Belle, who tucked it over her ear inside her bonnet.

Belle was strangely pleased by her brother's tender action. Maybe she was wrong not to make him her equal partner. He was her only blood relative, after all. And he really had been very dedicated to the shop's success. She would have to think more on it.

They stopped at the sound of distant booming. Across the lake, behind the cluster of now-inactive ships, fireworks were exploding into the air in an animated display of reds, blues, whites, and yellows. The drawn-out screeching, followed by the rapid-fire pops of each fireworks spectacle, sent the blood coursing through Belle's veins. She was alive, and happy, and proud to be a Briton in her country's hour of glory. She was especially proud to be here with her brother, Wesley, who was—

Where was he?

She looked all around her. She was alone. She stood on tiptoe to see over the shoulders of people in the distance. Why would Wesley have abandoned her?

And then she saw him, slipping rather furtively in between the flaps of an unmarked tent. A man stood in front of the flap, facing out, with his arms crossed on his chest, after Wesley went in. Belle started to go after Wesley, but realized that perhaps she wouldn't be welcome there.

He had invited her to accompany him to the fair. Why was he disappearing so mysteriously, without a word about where he was going?

She shook her head. Sometimes her brother was impossible to decipher.

She left the path to visit a long row of booths offering commemorative souvenirs near her brother's tent. Vendors barked and hawked their wares at her, nearly driving her senseless. She fled to the end of the selling area, to a tented booth where the seller wasn't booming about the quality of his wares. Instead, he sat quietly in an ornately carved chair before a spread of equally figured smoking pipes and walking canes on a table.

Gentlemen's accoutrements.

Even though he was seated, Belle could see the man was tall and lean, yet he had the sinewy muscles of a hardworking craftsman running through his arms. He rose as she approached his booth, revealing that he wore a carpenter's leather apron.

"Madam," he said. His voice was warm and good-humored. "May I interest you in something for your father? Or perhaps your husband?"

"I have neither. But I'm here with my brother. He's somewhere nearby. I thought I'd do some shopping."

"He left you alone?"

"No, no, he went to . . . visit with friends. He'll be by shortly."

The man nodded slowly. "I see. Perhaps he would like a walking stick. This one"—he held up a cane of ebony, topped with a bust of Napoleon wearing his famed military hat, carved in a pale, yellow wood—"allows the user to keep the former emperor under his thumb at all times. Actually, all of the wood here was taken from one of Napoleon's supply carriages."

"Truly? How did you take possession of one?" Belle ran her hand over the cane's carving. It was exquisitely detailed.

"There is a waxworker, Madame Tussaud, who has a traveling exhibition in Great Britain. She purchased a selection of Bonaparte's artifacts to create a tableau of his capture. I sometimes create furniture pieces for her tableaux. She did not need the carriage, and I had good use for its wood."

A waxworker? How interesting. The man's face was interesting, as well. Or, rather, arresting. Particularly his eyes. The right one was a more intense shade of green than the other. The green of a dense forest where one could become frighteningly lost without a map to retrace one's steps. And almost as if that eye knew it had an advantage over the left one, he used it to appraise her more fully, turning his head just slightly so that his right eye was dominant in her line of sight.

She cleared her throat and broke from his gaze. "Yes, well, what of these objects?"

He smiled lovingly at the smoking pipes, as though they were his own children. "I particularly enjoyed carving these. As you can see, each one has a face carved into the bowl. Here is the Prince Regent, this one is the Duke of Wellington, and this is one I did from a painting of Lord Nelson. I use imported woods, like olive-wood and mesquite, to ensure hardness. These pipes will last forever."

Belle picked one up. They were just as detailed as the walking sticks. This man took great pride in his work. She wondered if Wesley was interested in picking up smoking.

"I'm no expert, sir, but it seems to me that you are a fine craftsman."

The man blushed. "You honor me."

"It is no honor to hear the truth. My only dilemma will be which one to purchase."

The man gently took the pipe from her hand. His calloused

thumb brushed her palm. Belle was surprised at the tenderness of his touch.

"My apologies, miss. I didn't mean to offend. Let me show you something else I have." He lifted the lid of a plain oak trunk that sat on the ground next to him. Belle gasped.

The exterior of the trunk was completely unfinished, raw, and ordinary, but as he pushed the lid back on its brass hinges she was taken aback by the interior. It was decorated with a bouquet of roses, pansies, and daffodils, done entirely in different-colored woods, each petal somehow cut and glued together perfectly, with no gaps between them. The flowers sat in a Greek urn, the pattern of which was also delicately cut from multiple types of wood.

In fact, every inch of the interior was covered with designs: Fleur-de-lys, vines, and geometric patterns lined the sides, bottom, and trays of the trunk. Ironically, the trays contained mostly dusty tools.

As usual, Belle spoke before thinking. "Such a beautiful home for such unattractive guests." She put a hand to her mouth as though she could somehow stopper her words back up.

The man reached into the depths of the trunk and pulled out another pipe, bringing it to her. He smiled as she took it. "My tool chest is my calling card. Every cabinetmaker owns one and takes great pride in it. But we never finish the outside, since it sits in the shop and is subject to wood shavings, splinters, and falling tools. I open it to show potential customers the inlay and marquetry I'm capable of making. I'm hoping to find some new customers while selling these tributes to the Great Peace."

She barely glanced at the pipe, so entranced was she by the chest. "I've been reading lately on those very subjects." She pointed at the chest. "The patterns and designs that don't actually create a picture, such as the scroll along that one tray, that's inlay. Whereas your spectacular floral bouquet is marquetry."

"And just how did you come to read about wood designs?"

"I'm a draper, but I've been called on to do work on the prince's Pavilion in Brighton. I've been studying everything I can about interior design. To include furniture."

"Is that right, Miss . . . ?"

"Stirling. Annabelle Stirling." Drat him, he didn't believe her. She held out her hand. "And you, sir, are . . . ?"

He took her hand and bowed over it across the table of pipes. "Putnam Boyce. My friends call me Put. Rhymes with 'shut.' "

He said it like a poem he'd repeated thousands of times. He probably had.

"We Boyces have been cabinetmakers for four generations, and before that, my great-great-grandfather was a sailmaker who did odd carpentry jobs on a ship. Myself, I've been cabinetmaking for about ten years now, since I was fourteen."

"Do you work with your father?"

His smile faded. "My parents are both gone. I keep the shop by myself except for a couple of apprentices and a journeyman. I saw no need to turn it over to anyone else just because my neighbors thought I was too young to manage on my own."

Why, he's just like me.

She gave him her own tentative smile to try to restore his good humor. "Well, I'm pleased to meet you, Mr. Put-rhymes-with-shut Boyce."

Oh dear, but his face did gleam when he was amused. He held her gaze an uncomfortably long time.

She cleared her throat again. "And so, you wanted to show me another pipe?"

"Yes. I wasn't planning to sell this one. Thought I might keep it. But I'll sell it to you."

She held it up for closer inspection. The dark bowl was shaped like a stallion's head, its mane carved to look as though the horse was galloping. It had a long stem that tapered up into a fine point for a mouthpiece.

"Mr. Boyce, I couldn't buy this. First, it must be very expensive, but also, it's a grand piece that you should probably hand down to your son."

"I suppose that one day when I'm married and have a son, I can carve another one."

She was oddly pleased to learn he wasn't married.

Belle, get hold of yourself. What difference does it make what this man's status is? You've no interest in men. Remember, you'll lose control of your shop if you permit a man to share your life.

A good reminder to keep Wesley at bay a little longer.

"So how much do you want for it?" she asked.

He named a price far lower than what he was asking for the other pipes on display. She started to demur, but he was already reaching over again and folding her hands around the pipe. His hands were rough and thick with years of shaping wood, yet held hers as though she were a delicate teacup. They belied his relatively young age.

"Your brother should be able to enjoy many years of smoking with this. My salutations to him."

She handed over a few coins to him, which he dropped inside his apron. "Ah, while I'm thinking of it, you should also have this." He reached once again into his trunk, and pulled out a wooden hair comb. The teeth were perfectly spaced on the dark brown wood, and the spine of the comb contained a small rose inlay in a pale wood.

"It's beautiful, Mr. Boyce. Are you sure?" She didn't even attempt to say no. The comb was a spectacular piece of art. And he was making a gift of it to her.

"It is my pleasure. And if you ever have any furniture needs, I hope you will come to my shop on Curtain Road in Shoreditch. I also make musical instruments, wall and ceiling moldings, and sconces."

Oh. He was just using the comb as his calling card. Very well.

"Thank you, Mr. Boyce. I will remember you. I'm sure I'll have need of a cabinetmaker in the future. For the prince's residence."

He smiled. "Yes, Miss Stirling."

She turned to leave, but he stopped her. "I believe the wine and ale are free-flowing now, and it will be dark soon. Please be careful with your person, Miss Stirling. I wouldn't like to see you come to any harm."

She tucked both the pipe and the comb inside her reticule. "I'll be careful."

Not seeing Wesley anywhere yet, Belle decided to return to the path she was on, to see what other fragrant blooms she might find. She quickly lost interest in the flowers and shrubbery as the sun sank lower in the sky. The darker the sky became, the blacker her mood grew, despite her interesting conversation with that cabinet-maker.

Why hasn't Wesley returned?

Mr. Boyce was right. The drunkards, thieves, and who knew what other rabid creatures would be marauding about soon, wreaking havoc with their addled pates and foolish courage brewed in mugs. Wesley had left her alone and defenseless.

How dare my brother simply abandon me?

Enough. Belle raised her chin and marched with determination to the tent where Wesley had disappeared. Not only would she retrieve her brother so they could go home, but she was feeling just spirited enough to give him a stern lecture about leaving her alone to be preyed upon by wandering criminals.

To poor Wesley's shock, she did just that, loudly demanding his presence from outside the tent, fixing him with a glare reminiscent of the one she'd given him during his feigned Luddite attack, and sermonizing the entire way back home about his poor treatment of her. And after his activities in the tent, he had little presence of mind to respond to her verbal lashing, which angered her even further. She concluded her lecture by hurling the pipe at his chest, demanding that he learn to smoke tobacco.

As he nursed his emotional wounds later that evening over a nibble of opium, Wesley wondered: Why couldn't a man ever have some peace?

He flipped the pipe over in his other hand. Excellent work. And he'd heard that some fellows were beginning to smoke opium blended with tobacco, not just eat from the sun-dried bricks. Smoking supposedly made the sensations more intense. Interesting.

December 1814

Arthur Thistlewood and his comrades had been forever changed. Their beloved leader, Thomas Spence, died in September, and more than three dozen of his followers, including Thistlewood, buried him quietly but with resolve.

Calling themselves Spence's "forty disciples," they vowed that his struggle would not end here. On the contrary, they would move forward with enthusiasm and at great risk to their own lives. They renamed the movement the Spencean Philanthropists, and endeavored to start branches of the group all over London, encouraging them to convene clandestinely in public houses all over London to formulate the best ways of achieving an equal society.

Thistlewood became the de facto leader of the Spenceans, and was elevated to a level of esteem he could have only imagined when one of the followers reported to him that the government had become concerned about him and the newspapers were reporting him to be a "dangerous character."

Thistlewood preened under the new respect and deference shown him by his fellow Spenceans. Not that he ever showed his pleasure in public, for it wouldn't have been in keeping with their philosophy of all-men-are-equal. Nevertheless, at night, when lying in the darkness of his room with Susan snoring and wheezing beside him, he realized that he was finally achieving a dream. He just wasn't sure what that dream would morph into eventually, but it was building steam.

He looked over at his wife. Although he wasn't particularly sure what the end of his dream would be, he was fairly certain she didn't belong there.

7 January 1815, Saturday

Had another dream of Alice last night. How can she be plaguing me from the dead like this? What will I have to do to rid myself of her?

Ordered four bolts of bird-and-thistle chintz. B—— says it is an excellent drapery fabric, but I wish she would remember that customers also desire to have clothing made.

Weather dreary today. Endless rain the past three days.

B—— plans to return to Brighton again for a visit.

Asked her again to make me her partner. Again she

*refused. What will I have to do to prove myself? It is not
seemly for a man to be under the thumb of his younger
sister.*

*Must remember to find seamstresses for hire for drapery
work. B—— keeps reminding me.*

April 1815

Belle's work in the shop overtook her as she prepared her own
sketches and ideas for the Great Corridor at Brighton.

It was to be the spine of the Pavilion, linking all of the important state rooms together, and was also the most Chinese part of
the palace. Nash had shown her a sample chair—a Chinese export
of intricately designed satinwood and bamboo—as well as a panel
of Mr. Crace's intended wallpaper, consisting of repeating murals
of waving bamboo plants on linen. Her task was to choose fabric
for seat covers in the palm green and salmon–colored gallery.

Only the comb, which occupied the center of her dresser top,
provided an easily forgotten reminder that she planned to thank
Put personally for having provided her with a gift Wesley loved so
well.

Finally remembering that Put had told her his shop was in
Shoreditch, she settled for dashing off a quick note the day before
leaving in a privately hired coach.

Aghast at the expense of the private hire, Belle reluctantly
handed over the fee to take her back to Brighton. Mr. Nash assured her by letter that he would submit it to the Pavilion's Lord
Chamberlain for payment as part of the Pavilion's cost. Nash
wanted all of the material samples and drawings Belle was bringing to be as clean and undamaged as possible. Hauling bags on and
off public transport would never do.

She relished being back in Brighton, although it was bitterly
cold and wet on the coast this time of year. The chill made her
hands feel like glass that might crack upon any impact.

Mrs. Nash still spent most of her time with her children, but
joined her husband and Belle in the evenings to chat trivialities.

Mary Ann Nash was partial to sweet almond liqueur, whereas Nash preferred cognac. Belle kept her own imbibing to a minimum, only because she'd witnessed how foolish it had made Wesley in the past.

Belle treasured these quiet, comfortable evenings with the Nashes. Both husband and wife were affable in their own ways, and John Nash's knowledge, which he happily shared, was vast and comprehensive.

Outside of Amelia, from whom she hadn't heard since her move to Wales with Clive, the Nashes were the closest things Belle had to real friends.

Belle and Nash decided on an impromptu visit one morning so Nash could finish showing Belle the kitchen. Since her last visit, the fireplace and its smoke jack were completely installed, the surround painted green, and the entire thing topped with an elaborate copper awning.

In fact, copper was the order of the day, with a similar awning on the opposite wall to cover a lengthy cooktop. Open crates full of copper stockpots and saucepans were stored in a corner.

Large paned windows high up on the wall flooded the space with light, accented by a multitude of chandeliers strung from the ceiling.

And the support columns, why, they'd been made over to look like tall bamboo sticks. Her awe must have shown on her face, for Nash said, "And they aren't done yet, Belle. Wait until you see what else I do with them."

Belle avoided more than a polite visit with the prince this time, enough to get his approval on her suggestions for the Great Corridor, which she knew was presumptuous of her, since Mr. Crace had not yet heard her ideas.

She returned to London quickly, anxious to implement everything according to Nash's patient explanation. She was once again amazed and humbled to be working on a royal residence.

Napoleon escaped Elba on February 26, 1815, and returned to France. With sixteen hundred troops at his back, he invaded Paris on March 1, successfully taking control of the government once again.

Bonaparte was on the loose again, determined to have Europe for himself.

The residents of Brighton were alarmed. The seaside resort lay open on the English Channel, and Bonaparte had threatened invasion before. Knowing that Bonaparte was capable of massing great strength, would Parliament send troops to protect them?

Nash talked to the Prince Regent to express his concerns for the people and the safety of the Pavilion project, but the prince's airy reply focused merely on moving progress forward on the Pavilion as quickly as possible.

"Either the prince is confident British troops can repel the French, or, well, he doesn't understand. . . ." Nash let his words drop inside his library one evening.

Mrs. Nash's brow was furrowed. "I'm sure it's the former. In the meantime, I guess we should carry on as though nothing is wrong."

As though nothing is wrong? Belle thought as she stared distractedly into the fireplace. She'd lived through her parents' deaths and Clive's betrayal, which still sometimes gave her nightmares. But the idea of French troops landing on Brighton's shores to invade England, and pillaging their way north to London, made her tremble uncontrollably.

Perhaps Mrs. Nash was made of sterner stuff than she was.

She bent down to pick up a copy of Mr. Chippendale's *The Gentleman & Cabinetmaker's Director* from the floor. It was a book Nash had not loaned her as part of her training. Nash must have carelessly tossed it down after using it. She flipped through the book. The oversized leather volume was finely tooled, and not only contained an explanation of the classical architectural orders but included Chippendale's drawings of bookcases, chests, commodes, mirrors, frames, chairs, bed frames, and all manner of tables.

A page titled "China Case" was dog-eared. It contained a drawing of a closed, three-section cabinet atop eight thin, squared legs. Fretwork decorated the front of the cabinet, and the top of the center section of the cabinet had a decoration on it made to resemble a pagoda. A note in Nash's hand on this page read: *Styling for Aqualate Hall, Staffordshire—Entrance Hall—Lord Boughey—approval 25 March 1808.*

Belle ran a hand across the furniture sketch. How very exotic. It finally brought back to mind Putnam Boyce. Did he have enough talent to build such a piece? She was sure he did.

Enough woolgathering, Belle. She shut the book and slid it in between companion cabinetmaker directories from Mr. Sheraton and Mr. Hepplewhite.

"Miss Stirling, I've decided to give you an important assignment," Nash said, as he stretched out his legs before the fire during their evening talk. The April evenings were still quite chilly.

"Shall I get my sketchbook?" she asked.

"No, this is a different sort of assignment. More of an errand, really. The Prince Regent greatly admires a certain author, whose books he keeps in all of his residences. He realized that he does not have a set for the library at Brighton, and is quite insistent that he must have them immediately. He's written to his librarian, a Mr. James Stanier Clarke, instructing him to have the author deliver copies to Carlton House. I want you to go to London and retrieve the books personally."

"But, sir, can't the books be sent by mail to Brighton?"

"I'm afraid not. The prince is quite adamant that they be handled carefully and that they are brought down right away. I'd like you to leave tomorrow morning for London."

5

I do not want people to be very agreeable, as it saves me the trouble of liking them a great deal.

—Jane Austen, letter to her sister, Cassandra, December 24, 1798

May 1815
London

Even when the prince was not in residence at Carlton House, it was still staffed by a full complement of servants. She was shown into a drawing room, only to realize that the librarian was already there meeting with the author.

Mr. Clarke was short, wiry, balding, and full of a nervous energy that couldn't be contained even behind his thick, wire-rimmed spectacles. He was rather the opposite of his royal employer.

Even more startling to Belle was the fact that the author was actually a woman. One with whom Belle felt an instant connection, for she was also slender, and possessed eyes that bespoke of a life lived well beyond her years.

Mr. Clarke introduced Belle to Miss Jane Austen, whose latest book, *Emma*, would be published soon.

"Miss Stirling, I was just telling Miss Austen what a great admirer the Prince Regent is of her works. He's read everything she's written, and maintains her books quite prominently in the libraries of all his residences. Which is, of course, why you're here."

"Yes, sir, to pick up a set for the Pavilion."

From a nearby table, Miss Austen picked up a bundle of nine books tied together with a strap. She handed the bundle to Belle, who turned them to their sides to read the titles. *Sense and Sensibility. Pride and Prejudice. Mansfield Park.* Each in three volumes. She'd never heard of any of these titles, but then, she wasn't exactly a member of London's great literary circles.

And, judging by Miss Austen's wan appearance, a literary career might not be the healthiest of choices.

"Miss Austen's next book will be out imminently, and then we'll have another book to add to the shelves of each of the prince's houses." Mr. Clarke was practically rocking back and forth on his heels, so excited was he by the very idea of it.

And although the eminent librarian didn't notice it from his vantage point, Belle saw Miss Austen make an exaggerated pained expression and shake her head.

Before she could help herself, Belle giggled, and was rewarded with a smile from the author.

Mr. Clarke blinked gravely from behind his spectacles. "Is something amusing, Miss Stirling?"

Belle bit her lip. "No, sir, I'm sorry."

"Humph, well then. As I was saying to Miss Austen, the prince is very much looking forward to her next book, *Emma*. He talks of nothing else."

Certainly Belle didn't know the prince very well, but she would hardly say that Miss Austen's books were his foremost thought.

"Truly?" Miss Austen put her head to one side. "What does he say regarding Mr. Darcy's abominable treatment of the innocent Jane Bennet in *Pride and Prejudice*?"

"Er, I don't quite recall him mentioning that chapter of the book."

"That *chapter?* Why, it forms Elizabeth Bennet's entire opinion of Mr. Darcy. It is central to the novel."

"Yes, well, the prince and I have many important books to discuss and don't have the opportunity to discuss them all in as much detail as I'd like." Mr. Clarke pushed his spectacles against his face. A nervous gesture, since they hadn't slid down his nose.

"It seems to me the prince would be particularly interested in reading about a man who has utter disregard for the state of a woman's marital happiness."

"Miss Austen, why would a man of the prince's stature be consumed with that?"

"So that he can use it as an example of how his own subjects must not behave toward long-suffering women."

Mr. Clarke removed his spectacles and tapped them in one hand, his eyes blinking rapidly to focus. "Are you making a particular point?"

"None at all, sir, none at all."

And with that, Jane turned slightly out of Mr. Clarke's view to wink at Belle.

"Humph. Regardless. Where was I? Oh yes, the prince simply cannot say enough about his admiration for your novels, and speaks of nothing else."

"Nothing else," Jane repeated solemnly.

"He doesn't extend this sort of—dare I call it patronage—to just any author, particularly novelists, you understand."

"No, it would be quite insensible of him to do so."

"Quite. Imagine how gratifying it would be for you as a writer to have all of Great Britain know the great esteem in which the prince holds you."

"Highly gratifying indeed, Mr. Clarke. Particularly with his expansive knowledge of my books' lessons in goodness and decency."

Mr. Clarke put his spectacles back on, this time leaving them on the end of his nose and looking at Miss Austen over the top of them. "And so, because of the prince's very generous support of your works, don't you think there is something you might do in return for him?"

The author put a hand to her breast. "Does the prince suggest that I become the fourth member of his marriage?"

"Miss Austen, you greatly try my patience. No, I refer to your upcoming novel. Isn't there a way to express your gratitude to the prince for his continued championing of your efforts?"

"With *Emma*? Express gratitude? Oh, I see. You want me to dedicate the novel to His Highness."

"My dear Miss Austen, what a capital idea you've just had! The prince will be simply delighted that you've made this offer. Undoubtedly you will be the toast of London when he spreads word of it."

"Undoubtedly."

"I have more ideas for you, as well, Miss Austen. For example, when you next appear in print, you might want to dedicate your volume to Prince Leopold of Saxe-Coburg-Saalfield. In fact, why not write a romantic novel illustrative of the history of the august House of Coburg? It would be most interesting. Perhaps we can continue to correspond and I can provide you with further suggestions."

"You are very kind in your hints as to the sort of composition which might recommend me. But I could no more write a romance than an epic poem. No, I must keep to my own style and go my own way; although I may never succeed again in my writings, I am convinced I should totally fail in any other way."

Mr. Clarke accepted her declaration without seeming to understand the sarcasm dripping from it like ink from a bent pen nib.

After more discussion as to when Miss Austen would deliver copies of *Emma* to the librarian for distribution to each of the prince's residences, they engaged in more verbal swordplay as Mr. Clarke coerced the author into donating even more copies for the prince to distribute to his friends. Finally, the visit was mercifully concluded.

Jane and Belle left together, and the older woman invited Belle to sup with her nearby, before they would each need to find coaches to take them to their destinations, Jane to Chawton in Hampshire, and Belle back south to Brighton.

Over veal pasties covered in white wine sauce, the author chatted happily about her writing and her quiet life in the cottage she shared with her mother and sister, Cassandra. She was already working on her next novel, *The Elliots*, and a second edition of *Mansfield Park* was being prepared for publication after *Emma*.

Belle's mind whirled at what must be required to write hundreds and hundreds of pages of interesting stories. Before she realized what she was doing, she blurted out, "I think interior design work is far simpler than what you do, Miss Austen."

Belle's comment was met by bright, intelligent hazel eyes. "I can't imagine that being so. Tell me about these designs. Do you actually work as an artist-designer?"

"Well, not exactly . . ." Belle proceeded to tell Jane about losing her parents, managing the cloth shop with her brother, her subsequent run-in with Luddites, her flight to London, and her resulting work for John Nash. She omitted any mention of Wesley's wrongdoing, her devotion to him overriding any desire to be too garrulous with a newfound friend.

"So you stormed Parliament! How I should have loved to have seen that."

Belle shook her head. "It wasn't quite that dramatic. It mostly resulted in my looking rather foolish."

"I somehow doubt that. It must be fascinating to work for such a well-known architect, Miss Stirling, although his association with the prince does not garner him praise in every corner. Be careful that your own reputation does not always stay hitched to his."

Belle was silent. John Nash was her only hope for success. What did it matter to her what his eventual reputation might be?

"Do you have to be in the prince's company often?" Jane asked.

Jane made it sound as though to know the man, who was effectively the ruling monarch, was a dishonor. The man was a bit forward, but, then again, he was the Prince of Wales.

"I've met him more than once."

"And what is your impression?"

"He is, well, determined in his nature."

Jane laughed aloud. "Yes, he is that. But I confess that I despise his shabby treatment of his wife, the poor woman."

"Is this what you were referring to in your mention of your characters Mr. Darcy and Jane Bennet?"

Jane clapped her hands together. "Did you catch that?"

"I knew that you intended something rather mocking, but I've not read your book and so I'm not sure what you meant."

"I will rectify that immediately. I'll send a set of books to you."

"Would you? I'd be glad of it, although I've nothing to give you in return." Belle's mind flashed to the inlaid comb on her dresser, but she just as quickly decided she wouldn't give that up.

"No, wait, I do have something. I'll send you a few yards of a nice gauze. You can wrap your books in them to protect them from sunlight and insect droppings."

The two women exchanged addresses before departing from each other with a warm handshake and promises to write letters straightaway.

Belle was elated. She'd made her first real friend since leaving Yorkshire. It made her trip back to Brighton to deliver the books and finish her current work there a much lighter burden. She even considered going out of her way to Hampshire to visit Jane on her next return to London, but knew she'd already been away from her shop too long.

She would save the visit for another time.

Most everything in England was interrupted when the glorious news arrived that Wellington had once and for all smashed Napoleon in June 1815 at the Battle of Waterloo, in Belgium. The little Corsican abdicated again, surrendered to the British, and was exiled to the remote island of St. Helena. Belle looked at it on a map. It was a tiny speck in the South Atlantic Ocean, far off the coast of Africa. Remote indeed.

This time, the newspapers assured the Britons, there was no escape for Napoleon. He would die on this rocky, forbidding landmass.

For the condemned, exile was always better than an execution, wasn't it?

The long-lasting good news of Napoleon's exile was replaced by the immense news of Mount Tambora, which reached Belle's ears in September 1815. The volcano in the Dutch East Indies blew its top during a series of eruptions in April, killing nearly eighty thousand people. Sailors returning to port spread talk about the devastation that had taken place more than seven thousand miles away across two continents, sending a colossal propulsion of gases high into the atmosphere. Belle could hardly imagine the destruction being wreaked in that part of the world.

She shivered. At least England didn't have volcanoes, and an eruption that far away could have little to do with the subjects of

Great Britain, who were already suffering under the new Corn Law, which placed an import tariff on foreign crops to protect the profits of British farmers following the dramatic drop in prices at the end of the Napoleonic Wars. The law prevented any foreign grains from being imported until the domestic price reached a certain level. The effect was disastrous, resulting in grain shortages and, consequently, rioting and strikes in many places, even in London.

The rioting was, thankfully, in other parts of the city and they hadn't experienced it on Oxford Street.

Yet.

22 February 1816
Chawton House Estate
Hampshire

Dear Miss Stirling,
Enclosed please find a copy of Emma, *which I promised you when we first met. I hope you have found an opportunity to read the other books I sent you. My new publisher, Mr. Murray, will be releasing* Mansfield Park *again this month, and I hope that sales from it will help to improve our situation here. Mother, Cassandra, and I have lived simply but comfortably at the beneficence of my older brother, Henry. Did I tell you he serves as my agent? He is also a banker, although I think his talents are better suited to agenting. Of course, we are hopeful for the best of outcomes with regard to his bank.*
I do thank you for the package of gauze you sent, the finest I've ever touched. I've encased a set of my own books with it, and have more left over for the next edition of Mansfield Park. *You have my greatest thanks.*
Please do let me know how you're getting on in Brighton.
Yours affectionately,
J. Austen

Belle carefully traced Mr. Nash's rendering of the proposed Music Room in the Pavilion, and snipped small samples of fabric and trims she hoped to use in it, and sent it all to Jane along with a letter wishing her well.

As she became overwhelmed with customers, Belle put aside her efforts to nurture this burgeoning friendship. Then, by late summer, Napoleon was long forgotten as England experienced an unexpected misfortune. Heavy rains had cascaded from the sky in bleak, unending sheets throughout the growing season, which was far colder than normal. In fact, Belle couldn't remember the last time she'd been without a heavy wool cloak. The resulting failed harvests drove food prices up even higher than before, and the poor all over Great Britain were suffering from starvation and sickness. Many of them were streaming into London as refugees.

The Worshipful Company of Drapers responded by asking its members to donate whatever spare cloth they could afford to the city's hospitals, to be used for makeshift blankets, cots, and shawls.

Belle contributed as much as she could, making trips to St. Bartholomew's poorhouse in Smithfield once each week to deliver bundles of cloth. She began to think there wasn't enough wool in all of England to comfort the suffering. She was more fortunate than most, though. Food might be more expensive and difficult to procure, but the aristocracy hardly knew the difference, and as long as the *ton* craved new fashions for their clothing and their interiors, Belle would be able to continue feeding herself and Wesley.

In the midst of misery was a moment of national happiness. On May 2, 1816, the Prince Regent's daughter, Charlotte, was wed to Prince Leopold of Saxe-Coburg-Saalfield in a complete love match.

Belle immediately ordered a vast quantity of a cotton print commemorating the marriage. In vivid colors of red and green on a white background, and the Prince of Wales's insignia set prominently within, the fabric sold out in mere days.

She welcomed the excitement and flutter generated by the royal marriage, and was almost disappointed when Londoners returned to their daily routines.

Belle finally set aside time to write to Jane, who she hoped had not experienced difficulties from the failed harvests.

> *I'm sure you know that Bonaparte has been exiled, presumably for the final time. I know that your animosity resides mostly in the prince, but I think you will agree that the emperor was of far greater threat to our country's happiness and well-being. I myself am relieved to go to Brighton now unworried about a French invasion.*
>
> *I trust you have not been in dire straits as a result of the food shortages. The London newspapers are now reporting that it was the eruption of Mount Tambora, so very far away, that is responsible for all of this misery. That it is volcanic ash drifting around the planet that has caused everything from the prolonged cold to the endless rains. I can hardly believe it. My visits to a local hospital, though, convince my eyes of what my mind refuses to comprehend. They say that even the Americans are experiencing crop destruction because of frost and snows long into their growing season, which might have helped Britain defeat them had Lord Liverpool not signed the Treaty of Ghent with them already.*
>
> *Please let me know soonest how you and your family are faring.*

Belle tried not to wait too anxiously for a return post from Jane.

The ongoing cold and rain temporarily stopped work at the Pavilion, giving Belle some free time in between checking on the shop and visiting her growing client list. Her constant scanning of the newspaper for information about the increasing refugee problem led her to an advertisement for Madame Tussaud's traveling wax exhibition, which had arrived in London for a limited time.

That was the woman Mr. Boyce had mentioned, who had sold him Napoleon's supply carriage. Thinking that a visit to see famous people sculpted in wax might be an interesting diversion, Belle decided to go. She invited Wesley to accompany her, but he declined, claiming he wanted to go to the tobacconist's for some new Cavendish tobacco that had just arrived from Virginia.

She smiled, pleased. He did really seem to like the pipe she'd given him. He stayed locked up in his room with it for hours at a time.

The wax exhibition was crowded with patrons gawking at wax figures artfully arranged in vignettes suggesting that person's notoriety or fame. She instantly recognized the interior of a House of Commons meeting, with figures both standing and seated, made to look as if in debate. She paused at one middle-aged figure that dominated the scene, and read the plaque next to him. *Sir Francis Burdett, born 1770, the member from Westminster. House of Commons. Figure made in 1803.*

Belle couldn't recall him at all from the parliamentary meeting she'd attended. But then, she hardly remembered anyone from that day.

She stopped at another tableau of Louis XIV of France, surrounded by courtiers. The king held a walking stick in his hand. Interest piqued, she knelt and examined the cane's knob, which was carved into a large sunburst. The plaque next to him indicated that King Louis carried ornate, jeweled walking sticks but restricted their use to the aristocracy, the king not wanting the peasantry to carry sticks in his presence. Fascinating. Yet, just a few months ago, she could have purchased one of many that Mr. Boyce offered in his booth.

She'd nearly finished her tour when she realized there was a curtained-off area she'd not yet visited. A young man stood guard there, collecting an additional admission fee for it.

"It's our Separate Room, miss. An extra twopence. Be cautious, it's not for the faint of heart nor those with delicate sensibilities."

She smiled. "I'll be careful."

Behind the curtain, the area was darker with only a few sconces illuminating it. Accustoming her eyes to the dark, she realized she was the only patron back here. The display was a macabre blend of wax heads on pikes, criminals meeting their ends at the hands of the hangman, and examples of execution instruments, including a guillotine blade that looked rusted from blood.

She shivered. What a clever spectacle it all was. She wondered if the blade was an actual artifact.

An exhibition worker was on his knees, his back to her, adjusting the legs of an ironically exotic writing table inside a mock prison cell, in which the prisoner was the Earl of Essex, courtier and onetime favorite of Queen Elizabeth, who met his end with an axman after being convicted of treason.

Belle approached the man. "Excuse me, can you tell me if the guillotine blade—oh!"

The man turning toward her was Mr. Boyce, wearing the same leather apron as at the Hyde Park celebration.

A slow smile settled across his face, reaching up to those unusually mismatched eyes. "Why, Miss Stirling, isn't it?" He rose from his work, dusting off his knees. "How did your brother like his pipe?"

She was surprised he remembered her so well. "He likes it greatly. He didn't even want to join me here today because he wanted to visit the tobacconist's. Why are you here?"

"Madame Tussaud wanted me to make her a writing desk for the earl here. I guess he would have been permitted more luxuries than most Tower prisoners. I even put a secret drawer in it. Would you like to see it?"

Without waiting for her response, he opened a drawer, then gently pressed down on the bottom of it. It slid away to reveal a narrow space where a document could be stored flat.

"I like to think Essex would have had something like that, much as he enjoyed intrigue and deception," Put said.

It gave Belle an idea. "Mr. Boyce, can you make Oriental-style cabinetry?"

"You mean using ebony wood, lots of fretwork? Of course."

"Then perhaps I could commission you to make a desk for Lady Derby. She wants to remodel her home in the style of the Royal Pavilion before everyone else in London begins copying it."

Realization dawned in his eyes. "So you really are doing work for the Prince Regent?"

"Of course I am!" If she were an aristocratic lady and held a fan, she would have swiped him across the shoulder with it.

"Interesting. I'd be happy to do this for you, I mean, the Lady Derby. What if I were to escort you to see my workshop tomorrow, and you can see examples of what I'm capable of."

She gave him her shop's location and left the wax exhibition, oddly pleased with her visit.

Put arrived as scheduled, only this time not wearing an apron. In fact, it seemed he'd dressed for the occasion, although his nearly fashionable pants and waistcoat were clearly paining him.

Belle hid a smile. The poor man needed a tailor, and quickly.

She introduced him to Wesley, who took great interest in Belle's male visitor but just as quickly lost his curiosity when he discovered Put was only there to construct a desk for one of Belle's clients.

Belle kept her rolled-up room drawings in her lap as they rode in awkward silence in a hired hack, with Put constantly fiddling with his buttons and the cravat badly tied around his neck.

His cabinetmaking shop was at one end of Curtain Road, and was actually in the basement of a building. He escorted her down a flight of steps to his shop.

His cabinet shop was long and narrow, consisting of an outer room containing random pieces of completed chests, chairs, and picture frames, separated by a doorway from another room, presumably a workshop, beyond it.

Even from a distance, the open doorway revealed rows of pegs and nails all over the walls, from which hung saws, chisels, and planes. Waist-high tables were covered with wood shavings and partially finished pieces: Table legs, chair splats, and clock cases all had their assigned spots in the room. A scraping noise let Belle know that someone was back there working.

She thought it might be rude to ask to see the workshop, so instead Belle asked about the finished pieces. Put referred to them as speculation pieces, intended both to demonstrate the cabinetmaker's skill and also for quick sale to any patron who didn't have time to wait for custom pieces.

"Your aristocratic clients, of course, will be satisfied only with highly customized pieces."

Belle nodded her head in agreement as she ran her hand across the top of a spinet that sat proudly against one wall. She knew nothing about cabinetry, but instinctively knew the piece was beautiful. The musical instrument's wood had a pattern that swirled and danced, as though it could hear the music the spinet would produce. The words "Boyce Fine Furniture—London—1815" were inset in brass across the band of casing above the keys.

Put stepped up behind her, his voice close to her ear. "What do you think, Miss Stirling?"

"It's beautiful. I didn't know that a cabinetmaker could create wooden musical instruments."

"Actually, we're virtually the only ones who can create them. This one is particularly fine, isn't it? Do you know how to play?"

"No, my fingers were intended for cloth, not ivory."

"And well made they were for it, Miss Stirling."

He reached around her and tapped on the keys, which made a melodious, if disjointed, tune.

His nearness was creating disjointed thoughts in her mind, too. She stepped away from the spinet.

Put noticed her discomfort and moved away himself. When he turned back, his manner was grave.

"May I see your sketches, please?"

As she proffered the drawings she'd brought with her, Put lifted the lid to a tall desk at one end of the room. The lid folded on a hinge to create an easel, on which he placed her drawings, placing a book on either end of the drawings to keep them flat.

She recognized the books as the Chippendale and Sheraton directories, although they were far poorer quality copies than what Mr. Nash had in his offices.

Belle described her idea for a desk for Lady Derby's private chamber. Put nodded with understanding, and made notes about dimensions and proportions. He pulled out a second piece of paper, making some calculations, and presented her with a price and a delivery date of a month hence.

"I'll confirm with Lady Derby, but I believe she'll pay that. Please pick me up on your way to deliver it, so that we may present it together."

"As you wish." He tugged at the material surrounding his neck again.

And with no more business to conduct, Put escorted her home. Belle's stomach fluttered as he bent over her hand in farewell.

Stop that. He's a craftsman, nothing more. Nor need he be more.

Still, she looked forward to seeing him again in a month.

But she was to be disappointed, for he sent one of his apprentices to her shop with the piece and she was trapped riding to Lady Derby's with a young man, a boy really, who nattered on incessantly about the new Bilbo Catcher toy his employer had taught him to carve and the number of times he'd managed to swing the wooden ball into the cup thus far.

It made for a long and dissatisfying expedition. And yet, it was a comfort, for now she knew that the cabinetmaker was not interested in her, else he would have come himself, and she would no longer be even the tiniest bit diverted from her resolve to stay in the unmarried state.

Although a draper's shop would be quite complementary to a cabinetmaker's, wouldn't it?

There will be no more thoughts like that, Belle Stirling.

But think about it she did, until Nash summoned her back to Brighton again.

❧ 6 ❧

Name or title what has he?
Is he Regent of the sea?
By his bulk and by his size,
By his oily qualities,
This (or else my eyesight fails),
This should be the Prince of Whales.

—Charles Lamb, 1812

August 1816
London

"Your Highness, the food riots occurring across the country are of grave danger to your regency. Tens of thousands of people are dying. Your subjects need to know that you are concerned for them. Combine their suffering with the clamor for parliamentary reform that isn't forthcoming and I believe we may have a dark confrontation with your subjects." Lord Liverpool watched as George poured three different liqueurs into crystal glasses. The prince was experimenting with some new flavors imported from Italy.

"But I do have sympathy for the plight of the downtrodden. Haven't I told you so many times?" George sniffed appreciatively at one of the glasses, which held a thick, lime green liquid.

The Prince Regent claimed to champion the Whigs and their desire for parliamentary reform, but Liverpool suspected his support was only due to his great hatred for his father, who was a staunch supporter of the Tories.

Liverpool tried again.

"Yes, but telling your ministers is not quite the same as the people seeing your face. Please, Your Highness, your subjects need comfort and assurance."

George drained the glass. "How often must I remind you that the people always love their monarch as long as Parliament defends him. If you were doing your work properly, the people wouldn't need constant assuaging."

"But this is not a matter of simple unity between Parliament and monarch, sir. There are not only riots occurring, but typhoid fever in Ireland. If we do nothing, we may experience dangerous uprisings."

"Then perhaps I should repair myself to Windsor while you manage things."

Liverpool resisted the treasonous urge to strangle the Prince Regent. He hoped the monarchy could survive this man after he became king.

Mr. Nash was waiting impatiently for her at the coaching inn in Brighton this time.

"Heavens, my girl, what happened?"

"A storm passed through Blindley Heath, and with the ground already so soft this year, trees were uprooted in the roads. We were rerouted twice."

"I see. Well, Mr. Crace is impatient to see you. Did you bring your samples?"

Belle held up one of her two traveling cases. "In here."

"Then let's not delay."

So without a moment to change or freshen up, Belle was whisked to the Royal Pavilion. Nash parted from her at the entrance so that he could find the prince, leaving her to face the Pavilion's artist-designer on her own.

Mr. Crace was standing in the middle of what was to become the Music Room, and which the artist-designer declared would be his finest achievement inside the palace. Crace had dictated colors of bright crimson, peacock blue, and burnished gold for this room that would eventually accommodate hundreds of guests to be entertained with selections from the prince's favorite operas. For now, though, the room was barely more than an open space full of scaffolding. Belle's draper shop could fit in here four times over.

Mr. Crace looked up from where he was discussing some measurements with a carpenter. Visibly scowling, he gestured the workman away and crooked a finger to Belle to join him.

"So I suppose you have the samples?"

Belle opened the case and laid out several groupings of fabrics. Each group also had a coordinating wallpaper strip with it.

"My shop is next to a wallpaperer. I had him make some samples, as well. I thought this grouping of cream and gold might—"

Mr. Crace's voice sliced through her. "So am I to understand that I am not only required to buy my fabrics exclusively from you, but my wallpaper, as well?"

Belle was startled by the venom in his voice. "No, I just thought you might like to see—"

"You think entirely too much, Miss Stirling. Keep your presentation to simply fabrics. Lest I soon have you telling me what musical instruments and dance chairs to put in here."

Belle blinked. What had she done to offend this man? Somehow, she was certain it was the prince's doing, but there was no help for it at the moment.

Clamping down on the oath forming in her mind, she instead replied, "As you wish," and tossed the wallpaper sheets back into her bag.

Having scored this victory over Belle, Crace was much more civil for the rest of the discussion, eventually deciding on many of Belle's recommendations, including a long, knotted gold fringe for the festooned draperies planned for the room.

He haughtily informed her of the deadline for the fabrics, a date that was nearly impossible to meet.

"Mr. Crace, the mills will never be able to produce so much of this blue silk-satin so quickly. Even the mills that have machinery couldn't do it. I'll need a month more, at least."

"Naturally, I shouldn't have expected that you could fulfill such a simple request."

Such a *simple* request?

And then she realized that Frederick Crace had no interest whatsoever in tutoring her, or buying a single scrap of cloth from her. Somehow the prince's fondness for her had resulted in Crace being forced to take her on. The question was, what was Mr. Nash's participation in it?

And was she in any position to question it?

But for certain she wouldn't be questioned and harangued by this dour, ill-tempered brute.

Her next words tumbled out with abandon. "Mr. Crace, I've no doubt that you are a brilliant designer, and justifiably command the prince's respect. However, you are quite despicable in your practices with your equals. And make no mistake, Mr. Crace, I *am* your equal. We both serve the prince, and we both enjoy the patronage of aristocrats. I provide high-quality goods and am fair in my pricing. I've spent many hours matching the best fabrics and passementerie possible according to your own instructions. I will *not* be misused like some French doxy just arrived in port." Belle emphasized her words by thrusting all of her samples back into her bag and latching the straps closed.

Crace stared at her, eyes bulging, though whether from shock or anger she wasn't about to wait to find out. Belle escaped with her yardage orders as quickly as she could.

Quickly realizing that Mr. Nash had already left the property as well, she set out back to his lodgings on her own, calming her temper as best she could and not thinking about the repercussions to come from her outburst.

As she walked along the Steine, she noticed an elegantly dressed woman carrying a parasol stepping out of one of the large homes facing the green. Belle paused. Wasn't that the home Nash had pointed out as belonging to Maria Fitzherbert, the prince's earlier wife?

Belle paused by the gate, waiting for the resident to exit onto the street. She dropped her bags and curtseyed before the woman, which seemed to please her.

"Mrs. Fitzherbert?" Belle asked.

"Yes. And who might you be, miss?" the woman said, a smile on her aging but kindly face.

"Annabelle Stirling, madam. I'm the draper to the prince's refurbishment of the Pavilion. Pleased to make your acquaintance." Belle dropped another quick curtsy.

"Draper? Hasn't Mr. Nash employed Mr. Crace?"

Belle felt her cheeks redden. "Yes, madam, but my shop has been selected to provide the fabrics."

"Is your shop in Brighton? I've never seen you before."

"No, back in London. My brother runs it with me."

"How lovely for you, dear. The prince has always been a generous man, as you have now experienced. I hope to visit the Pavilion once it's finished, but"—Mrs. Fitzherbert held up her free palm—"I doubt I shall be invited." She giggled, a move that would be unseemly for most women her age but on Mrs. Fitzherbert was just charming.

"So," she asked, "I presume you've been all through the Pavilion?"

"Yes, madam, several times."

"Wait, I remember your name. Weren't you registered at the circulating library?"

"Yes, as a ward of Mr. Nash's."

"Yes, of course. Would you like to come to supper here soon? I don't hold as elegant a court as I used to, but I still have a very talented chef. I should like to ask you about the work going on at the prince's residence."

Belle was intrigued with the idea of dining with Mrs. Fitzherbert. After Belle told her that she was scheduled to leave Brighton imminently but that she would be back in a few weeks, they agreed upon Belle visiting Mrs. Fitzherbert when she returned.

Belle arrived back in London, exhausted. With barely the strength to push open the door to the shop, she untied her bonnet and tossed it on a hook behind the door while smoothing her hair and readjusting pins. Wesley looked up from the counter where he was busy scribbling something.

Belle greeted him and apologized for arriving so late. "The trip to Brighton was delayed by rains, and on the return there was difficulty getting a new team of horses at the Dorset Arms in East Grinstead, which postponed us by hours. I'm so glad to be back. I thought I'd stop to see how things were here before returning home to bathe. What are you working on?" Belle put up a hand to stifle a yawn.

Wesley slid the pages under the counter. "Nothing, just some notes."

"All right. Well, if you don't need me for anything . . ."

"No, Sister. I'll be along shortly myself. Here, a letter came for you."

She opened the letter. It was from Jane, assuring her that all was well with her family. What a relief to know that she was healthy and sound during these difficult times.

Belle retied her bonnet and left. Wesley pulled the journal back out and finished his current entry.

> *Mrs. Naughton purchased five yards of embroidered Tree of Life fabric. Refused my recommendation for less expensive, printed variety.*
> *Doorbell broken. Will repair tomorrow.*
> *Have experimented with pipe. Provides a much more satisfying outcome, although dreams are even more vivid.*
> *Still raining. Still cold. Still people coming in from the countryside. Have not yet recognized anyone from Yorkshire.*
> *B—— returned from Brighton. She was tired so I didn't press her. Must talk to her again soon.*

He tied twine around the journal and took it home to his lodgings to store under his mattress.

Belle entered St. Bart's with a pile of blankets and a basket full of bread, which had cost her dearly. The attendant on duty at the door asked if she would mind distributing the food herself, since they were overwhelmed and short-staffed because of the ongoing influx of refugees from all over Great Britain.

Families were huddled together in pathetic clusters, shivering. Many adults were coughing, and children stared at her with dull, lifeless eyes.

She pulled her cloak closer around her, resisting the urge to shiver herself. Ignoring her own trepidation, she pulled out loaves, breaking them in half and distributing them where she could.

Most of the refugees were too weak to do much more than clutch the bread in dirty hands. What a stark contrast this was to the opulence of the prince's Pavilion.

Belle entered another room where an emaciated couple shared a narrow cot together. The husband's painfully thin arm was wrapped around his wife, as if to protect her from starvation and the never-ending damp air.

"Hello?" Belle said as softly as she could. "I have a blanket and some bread for you if you want it." She pulled out a loaf.

The woman lifted her head weakly and opened her eyes, confused. She wore broken glasses repaired in the center with filthy twine.

"Belle?" she asked. "What are you doing here?" The woman struggled to sit up on the edge of the cot, while the man remained lying down.

Belle realized they were Clive and Amelia. She rushed to the bed, dropping the basket at the foot of it, and sat next to her old friend.

"Amelia! How did you come to London? What happened?" She grabbed her icy hands and rubbed them between her own.

"Oh, Belle, life has been so difficult this past year. Nearly everyone is starving in Wales. We lost our poor daughter, Lizzy, two months ago. I was dried up and had nothing to offer the poor mite. Nothing at all." Tears welled up in Amelia's eyes. "She just sort of took a deep breath and gave up. What sort of mother has no milk to offer her baby? I miss her so, but Clive says I have to quit talking about her."

Amelia's lips trembled in the grief that she had to bear on her own.

"We were told that anyone with any strength left should head to London, that the Prince Regent wouldn't let anyone in his city starve, right, Clive?"

Clive, once a tall, proud man, was not interested in talking. He gave Belle a baleful glare and rolled over, away from them both.

Amelia shrugged. "So far, though, this has been the only place where we've gotten help, and it's not been much. Is that for us?" She was eyeing the loaf of bread still in Belle's hands, and devoured it greedily when Belle gave it to her.

"But why didn't you come to me? I would have given you lodging."

Amelia pointed at Clive's prone body, still except for his shallow breathing. "I suggested it. He said no. Said it wasn't proper." Bits of bread flecked out from her mouth onto her chin. "I didn't dare find you on my own. So we've been here about a week now. But we're weak as kittens and can't even venture out to find employment. If there were any jobs to be had. Oh, Belle, what's to become of us?"

Belle hardly knew what to say, and so instead gathered her friend in her arms. Amelia's entire body heaved as she sobbed against Belle's shoulder. Belle sang softly to her friend and stroked her hair, until finally Amelia calmed down.

Belle held Amelia out by the shoulders. "Now listen to me. The first thing we're going to do is make you strong again. I'll return tomorrow with some clothes and hot food and enough money to keep you in your own place for a while. After all, you loaned me money once, remember?"

Amelia's tearstained face was broken by a smile. "Yes."

But her happiness was short-lived.

"Don't want charity from the likes of you," Clive said without even turning to face them. "Take your basket and go. We'll be fine."

"But Clive," Amelia said. "Belle wants to help—"

"Doesn't matter what she wants to do. I'm your husband and I say we don't need her charity. I'll not say it again, woman." Clive coughed violently, rattling the cheap bed frame.

Amelia was crying silently again.

Belle got up and lifted the basket, which still contained a few blankets and loaves of bread, from the floor, setting it next to Amelia. She mouthed, *I'll be back tomorrow,* but said aloud, "Well, it was good to see you both. I pray for your good health."

"Belle, wait." Amelia reached out her claw-like hands and spoke softly. "Please, I want you to know how sorry I am for . . . for . . . what happened. Can you find it in your heart to forgive me?"

Belle glanced down at Clive, who grunted his irritation.

"There's nothing to forgive, sweetest. Nothing at all."

True to her word, Belle returned the next day with a packet of coins, more food, and one of her own dresses to give Amelia. Wesley had protested loudly over her taking so much money out of the lockbox, even though it was for his own friend. After a great argument, though, he'd acquiesced and even accompanied Belle back to St. Bart's, thinking he could convince Clive to accept their charity.

It was a wasted trip for Wesley, though, for when they arrived there the cot was empty. Belle inquired with an orderly who was sweeping the hallway outside the room, and learned that their stiff bodies had been discovered early in the morning and taken away to a potter's field.

"Strange it was, too, because he was lying atop her, with a pillow between his face and hers. Fellow was so sick he probably didn't realize what he was doing. More'n likely suffocated his poor wife to death."

The package of gifts tumbled out of Belle's arms as she grabbed at the wall for support against the swirling images of Clive and Amelia that reverberated in her mind. This wasn't possible. There was still so much to say to Amelia, about Belle's love for her friend, and her understanding about Amelia's marriage with Clive, and her own sorrow over the loss of Amelia's baby. Yet Belle had chosen to wait until the next day, when Clive's mood might be improved.

Now she would never be able to say anything to Amelia ever again.

A peculiar loneliness descended over Belle after Clive's and Amelia's deaths. Amelia had always been a shy follower. Always satisfied to live in Belle's shadow, and even content to marry a man Belle rejected.

I never took Amelia seriously enough. I was too consumed with Fafa, and the shop, and becoming a respected draper. Did I ever ask her what her own dreams were?

Never.

Belle couldn't muster any regret for Clive's passing, but it was just as well since her remorse over Amelia consumed her for several weeks, nearly rendering her immobile.

Compounding her grief was the realization that she'd made no real friends since arriving in London, other than Miss Austen, who lived in faraway Hampshire. The London elite's interest in her was tepid fascination, sure to disappear when her work at the Pavilion was over. The Prince Regent's attentions lacked propriety. Mr. Crace despised her presence. And Mr. Nash she wasn't quite sure about.

Except for Wesley, she'd lost everyone who'd ever meant anything to her. And Wesley was disturbingly unmoved by their deaths. Within a couple of days, he was no longer mentioning his friend and was once again pre-occupied with campaigning for Belle to make him an owner of the shop.

She evaded his arguments and pleadings, finally fleeing the shop to find peace and solace elsewhere.

She was surprised by where she headed for it.

Belle pushed open the door to Putnam Boyce's shop. There was no one in the outer display room, but she could hear a raucous combination of laughing, sawing, and hammering coming from the workshop. She stepped tentatively toward the back, still unsure as to why she was actually here.

Inside the workshop, Put stood in the middle of the activity in his apron, his right thigh steadying a long plank of wood as he held it with his left arm and sawed it with his right. The work was demanding, evidenced by his straining arm muscles and the beads of sweat on his forehead.

Around him, three other workers were in the process of finishing various pieces. The boy who had escorted Belle to Lady Derby's was pulling a scraper across a table to smooth it out. Another man was partially curtained off from the others. He used a rag to apply a noxious oil to a frame that looked as though it might eventually hold a mirror. The third man was organizing planks of wood by size and color inside a large, shelved cupboard.

Belle stood in the doorway, taking in the noise, the smells, and the obvious camaraderie of the men. She was about to interrupt when Put looked up and saw her standing there. He put down his saw and casually passed a hand through his hair. Wood shavings sprinkled down from his forearms, littering his shoulders and the floor around him.

Everyone else stopped what they were doing, as well.

He smiled. "Miss Stirling, welcome. I didn't hear you in the outer room or I would have come to greet you. How can I help you? Was Lady Derby pleased with her desk?"

Belle suddenly felt very foolish coming here. She was sure to make a spectacle in front of these men.

"Ah, yes, the desk was fine. Just fine. I only wanted to, er, come here, to, um . . ."

Belle, you idiot, how could you possibly be faltering in such an innocuous setting?

She had to give it to Mr. Boyce, though. He had instinct. "I need to get something else from the woodpile. Perhaps you can accompany me outside and tell me about the order you need to place? The rest of you, no need to gawp." He crossed the maze of worktables, tool chests, and half-finished projects in just a few steps, and guided Belle through the back door into his lumberyard.

Here she saw immense stacks of wood planks, one end facing her, piled up between trees used as bookends to contain them. Canvas tarps were hung from tree to tree, presumably to protect the woodpiles from rain and snow. Each treed-off section held planks of varying thickness, but all looked to be at least eight feet long.

Belle pointed to one of the stacks' ends. "That looks like an entire tree trunk was sliced up and layered back in its original formation. How did you manage that?"

"That's Caribbean mahogany. I pay extra for it from the sawyer. He has it cut just as you say, in planks as even as possible, then reassembled with spacers in between the planks so air can circulate around them while they season."

"Why would you pay extra for that? What difference does it make?"

"It makes it easier to book-match the pieces. In other words, if I want the wood grain on one cabinet door to match that of a door next to it, it's much easier if I'm working with wood that has literally grown up together."

"I see." She ran her fingers across the ends of the planks, recalling what she'd read about various woods in her studies with Mr.

Nash. She became distracted by her own thoughts again. Was Mr. Nash to be her only friend in the world now? If so, what did that say about her ability to manage relationships? What if she'd never decided to purchase that bedeviled gig mill in the first place? Maybe Clive would have never lost his reason. Her marriage to him wouldn't have been perfect, but then he wouldn't have dragged Amelia to Wales, and then . . .

Put cleared his throat. "Miss Stirling, your face is troubled and you're as jumpy as a cat tied to a mule's leg. What worries you?"

And without warning, tears spilled down her cheeks. She turned to wipe them away, completely irritated by her own weakness. She never cried, not even in front of Wesley. Now she was a blathering little ninny. What in the world had possessed her to come here?

"Come now, Miss Stirling, what's on your mind? My shoulder is strong." He patted his right shoulder for effect.

Although she knew he didn't seriously mean for her to cry on his shoulder, the temptation was too great, and to her own mortification, she flung herself at him, crying as heartily as Amelia had just days ago.

Put allowed it, wrapping his right arm around her waist and stroking her hair with his left hand. "Hush now, what could be the matter that a little spitfire like you becomes so distressed?"

How she hoped no one could see them, standing together amid the trees in what looked like an embrace. This was all terribly inappropriate. Yet she liked his comfort. His leather apron, blended with the odor of wood, was soft and reassuring.

Finally, she sighed and broke free of his embrace, still unsure why she was here with this man she hardly knew. He led her to a half-sawn log on the ground and sat down on it with her.

He put a calloused finger under her chin to make her look at him. One green eye looked at her, looking for unspoken answers. "If you stay here much longer without stating your purpose, I'll have to assume you are seeking employment, and I'll set you to hauling planks into the workshop." He tried to look very stern, but his exaggerated frown made her laugh despite her misery.

Swallowing, she told him everything that had happened to her over the past few years, from the deaths of her parents to Clive's and Amelia's miserable endings. She left out nothing, uttering for the first time her disappointment in Wesley's betrayal. Put listened patiently without interruption.

She sniffed and wiped the back of her hand across her face when she was finished, embarrassed by her most unladylike act. He pulled a cloth from the front pocket of his apron, shook the wood chips from it, and gave it to her.

It reminded her of a wood fire burning on a chilly autumn evening.

Comforting. Calming.

"Well, Miss Stirling, you've certainly done well for yourself, given your circumstances. But, may I ask, did you actually say you handled a pistol?"

"I had to. They were threatening my livelihood."

Put laughed and cupped a hand around her cheek. "Delightful. Miss Stirling, I know my question is rather untimely, but may I have permission to pay you court? Or should I ask your brother? Perhaps we can stroll through Vauxhall Gardens, and take some refreshment there together."

She hadn't expected this. Or had she? What was she thinking, prostrating herself before a fellow merchant whom she hardly knew?

Mr. Boyce probably thinks I came here with a tale of woe just to ensnare him.

Although the idea of being courted by him was not entirely unwelcome.

Yes, it is. Remember what happened before.

She gently removed his hand from her face. "I cannot, Mr. Boyce. I told you about Clive Pryce. He pretended to love me for who I am, and in reality planned to take away everything in my life that was significant to me. I won't let that happen again. My shop is my own and I won't share it with a man—a husband—who will take it from me."

Put frowned. "And you would toss me into the same stockpot of chicken as the inestimable Mr. Pryce?"

"Well, no, not exactly. But I must protect myself."

"From what, *exactly?* Miss Stirling, I would merely like to escort you to a pleasure garden, not see you off to the gallows that you call 'marriage.' I'm a cabinetmaker, what do I know about fancy cloths? I only see the yardage my clients give me to cover their chair cushions and I take little note of it. In fact, it seems to me that our work is complementary to one another. There's no need to fear me."

"You're right," she said before she could swallow the words.

"Then you'll accompany me out one evening soon?"

"No, our relationship must remain platonic. One tradesman to another."

Put grunted in exasperation. "Miss Stirling, I've never once in my life begged for anything, and I'll not start now. But I will ask one final time, why not?"

"Well." She laughed weakly. "I promised the Prince Regent I'll become his mistress once I get married, so I have to do all I can to avoid that fate."

She provided no explanation to his confused countenance, instead jumping up and fleeing the cabinetmaker's lumberyard as quickly as she'd once fled Mr. Crace's presence.

So is this your new solution for all of life's problems, Belle Stirling? Run like a frightened rabbit into your safe little warren whenever you feel the slightest threat to your livelihood?

Well, it certainly worked for most rabbits. Except for the ones who didn't see the fox coming.

Her reaction of fear to Put's proposal was justified, though. For she and Wesley attended Guy Fawkes Night celebrations on November 5, their first London experience with the event's bonfires, fireworks, and the spectacular practice of setting blazing tar barrels in the streets. While there, she saw Put in the distance with another young woman on his arm. He was laughing and gesticulating with the happy, open expression of a man in love.

I guess Mr. Boyce forgot me quickly enough, didn't he?

Or else he'd played her false and this was a woman he'd been squiring for some time. He was behaving quite familiarly with her. And looked content.

Even worse, perhaps he'd made overtures to Belle because he sought work at the Pavilion.

She suddenly felt nauseated, and handed Wesley her kidney pie without explanation, asking that they go home immediately. She realized that her rabbit instincts were serving her well.

In all of Belle's self-pity, she'd forgotten her friendship with Miss Austen. But a letter from the authoress changed that.

> *Dear Miss Stirling,*
> *My heart is too heavy over what I will share with you now in our private correspondence. My family is greatly affected, and the pall over the cottage almost forbids discussing it. But my pen and paper are quiet confidants, and I'm grateful for this medium in which to reveal my unhappy news.*
> *I believe I told you that my brother Henry is a banker, in addition to having brokered agreements to have my books published. He has always taken great care to protect my works. Several months ago, he even repurchased the copyright for an earlier work,* Susan, *so that we could republish it ourselves.*
> *Alas, publication of that novel has been postponed, possibly forever. For Henry's bank failed in March, leaving us all in dire financial straits, since all of my brothers were invested in the bank and they were supporting Mother, Cassandra, and me from its profits.*
> *I have felt poorly as of late, undoubtedly due to this alarming turn of events. But I am determined to finish* The Elliots *quickly, so that Mr. Murray can publish it and perhaps I can make some small contribution to my family's welfare. Did I tell you that the second edition of* Mansfield Park *was published last month? It has not done as well as hoped, although* Emma *has thus far proven successful.*
> *I longingly await your news, dearest Belle, which must surely be happier than my own. Although I cannot abide*

*the prince, I do admire his highly capable draper and
eagerly long to know how she fares at Brighton.
Yours affectionately,
J. Austen*

Belle wrote back immediately, grateful for the companionship, albeit long-distance, of another female. She consciously avoided discussion of her troubles, instead sharing news about her latest work on the Pavilion and that she'd met the famed Maria Fitzherbert.

Belle was delighted to receive a quick reply, accompanied by a small, wrapped package containing a book.

*Dear Miss Stirling,
Your fortunes grow. I am in wonder that you met Mrs.
Fitzherbert, and confess myself to be nearly agog that
she will have you to supper. You must write me soonest
afterwards and tell me of your visit. I am most
particularly interested in her attitudes and feelings about
the prince, although you seem loath to discuss him outside
of the details of your project.
And now, you may recall that certain gentleman, the
prince, who, through his man, Mr. Clarke, contrived to
assist me in a complete conversion of my writing practices.
I, of course, view it as a change to my entire realm of
existence, into one that the highly esteem'd prince, whom
you know I hold in the highest regard, might view with
approval.
It would prove to be my proudest moment as an
authoress to find that not only the prince himself, but his
insightful and gifted librarian, should find the enclosed
guidance for prospective writers to be of any small value.
Perhaps he will maintain copies at all of the royal
residences. In my pursuit of having it published as quickly
as possible, I erred in forgetting to make a dedication to
His Grace, to credit him with the idea of writing it in the
first place.*

I trust you will enjoy it.
Yours affectionately,
J. Austen

Jane made no mention of her family's financial situation. Belle wondered if sales of *Emma* had resolved things. She unwrapped the book. It was a thin volume, titled *Plan of a Novel, according to Hints from Various Quarters.* Leafing through it, she saw that it was a satire on how to outline a book, employing the full force of Jane's scathing wit. Although Mr. Clarke was unnamed in it, Belle recognized how Jane was poking fun at his suggestions during their visit to Carlton House. Belle stayed up far into the night with her friend's book, enjoying it immensely and nearly forgetting all of her worries at Brighton.

December 1816
London

Arthur Thistlewood was pleased with the turnout at Spa Fields. Although he'd doubted the success of his plan, especially after his fellow radical Mr. Hunt had refused to hear him out, things had turned out well.

Or, dare he say, almost with divine intervention?

Perish *that* thought. Man was in control of his own destiny. A man's reason was what made a difference in his fate, not reliance on some old-fashioned, foolish religion. His time in France during the Revolution had taught him that truth.

Yes, Mr. Hunt had ignored Thistlewood, but had answered the call from someone else to address a meeting in November at Spa Fields, in north London, to whip up support for a petition to the Prince Regent from the people of London, asking for relief from all of the distress they were suffering. Sweeping reform of Parliament was a centerpiece of the petition, to include universal suffrage for men, annual general elections, and a secret ballot.

Mr. Henry Hunt was the perfect man to give the speech asking for support. After all, he not only agreed with Thistlewood and the other reformers, but he was such an impassioned speaker that he was nicknamed "Orator."

Exceeding even Thistlewood's expectations, the meeting at Spa Fields had over ten thousand people in attendance, a sure sign that the time was right for these reforms. With the enthusiastic support of the peaceful crowd, it was decided that Hunt and Sir Francis Burdett, a member of Parliament sympathetic to the movement, would deliver the petition to the Prince Regent. Burdett, however, declined the honor. Good riddance to a false friend.

But the petition fell on deaf ears anyway. Hunt made two futile attempts to secure an audience with the prince, both of which were refused.

And it was what happened after that for which Thistlewood was so greatly contented.

Hunt returned to Spa Fields to tell the crowd that he'd been unsuccessful, but arrived to find Thistlewood there, standing on a platform decorated with banners, already declaiming against the prince and exhorting them as the patriots of Paris prior to their storming of the Bastille.

And eerily reminiscent of the attack on that famous prison, the Londoners reacted in nearly the same way. They marched on a gunsmith's shop and robbed it of its weapons, killing a pedestrian or two in the process.

Thistlewood, Hunt, and the rest of the mob made their way to the Royal Exchange, where they were greeted by a group of constables.

The resulting melee was predictable, and Thistlewood along with Hunt and several others were arrested and charged with high treason, and they now languished in jail awaiting trial.

Thistlewood's spirits were high, though. He had great confidence that he would be freed. His reason and faith in himself dictated it.

Change was coming to England. And no jail cell would prevent Arthur Thistlewood from being at the center of it.

❧ 7 ❧

Human nature is so well disposed towards those who are in interesting situations, that a young person, who either marries or dies, is sure of being kindly spoken of.

—Jane Austen, *Emma*, 1815

April 1817
Brighton

Belle's next trip to Brighton involved more interaction with Mr. Crace, although he seemed to have gained a modicum of respect for Belle and didn't treat her quite so harshly. She showed him the embroidered seat covers she'd ordered for the Music Room, and they went over more measurements and Crace's further plans for that room until Belle felt she had enough information to do more ordering.

Once her business was completed, she was free to do what she had really looked forward to: have supper with Maria Fitzherbert. It was a much more pleasant affair than Belle could have imagined.

They discussed trivialities during a meal centered on some poached cod caught that morning in the waters along Brighton's coastline, during which Belle could easily observe Mrs. Fitzherbert. Although the woman had to be in her sixties, she still retained a beautiful mass of golden hair, complemented by hazel brown eyes set in a creamy complexion. Her few wrinkles indicated that they had only developed in response to a life of laughter.

The prince's ex-wife also wore an interesting ruby cross around her neck that glittered in the candlelight.

Mrs. Fitzherbert was kind, solicitous of her guest, and carried no airs about her at all. It was remarkable, given the lady's previous status as practically the Princess of Wales.

It made Belle understand perfectly why the prince might have risked his father's wrath to have secretly married her.

Afterwards, Belle followed Mrs. Fitzherbert into her parlor and they took seats at a square gaming table. Maria took a deck of cards out of a wooden box.

"A game of Speculation?" she asked.

"Madam, I've never played cards before."

Mrs. Fitzherbert blinked her sympathetic round eyes several times. "Truly? Well, no matter, I'll show you." She poured out a quantity of different-colored round disks, made of mother-of-pearl, from the bottom of the card box. "Since you're new at this, I believe we should play without real money."

And soon Belle was immersed in the fast-paced card game, selling and buying visible trump cards as well as risking bets on face-down cards. Once the game was well under way and required less concentration on Belle's part, Maria opened up conversation.

"So, Miss Stirling, tell me how things fare at the Pavilion. Are any rooms complete yet?"

"The Music Room is started, as is the Great Corridor, which will link the Banqueting Room, the Saloon, and the Music Room. The Corridor is more than a hundred feet long. Also, the kitchen is finished, and it is a wonder to behold."

Maria sat forward. "Tell me everything about it."

So Belle described as best she could the mechanical marvels of the Pavilion's kitchen: the lead ice-bins, enormous bread furnace-ovens, and expensive water-pipe system.

"There is even a steam table that allows dozens of covered dishes to be kept warm before being carried into the Banqueting Room. The prince wants to be able to serve at least a hundred dishes at his state dinners."

Maria smiled sadly. "I once presided at the Pavilion, you know. What marvelous parties His Highness and I used to host. Everyone flocked to Brighton to attend. They still come to Brighton in droves, of course, but rarely to see me. But"—she brightened considerably—"I can imagine that now the Pavilion's kitchen will light everyone's imagination afire. Oh! I believe I just made a pun!" Maria's laugh tinkled in the room, and Belle could not help but join her.

Mrs. Fitzherbert had more questions. "Are there rooms in use during the renovations?"

"Most of them are. Mr. Nash tries to ensure that there are elegant spaces available for the Prince Regent to do any entertaining. He has imported a French chef, Antonin Carême, and wants to make use of his talents frequently."

Mrs. Fitzherbert sighed. "Yes, the prince has the finest taste. Has he hosted any grand meals recently?"

"I was not present for it, of course, but Mr. Nash told me of a grand affair in January with four soups, four fish dishes, and no less than thirty-six entrées, an assortment of soufflés, and eight majestic dessert molds designed to look like palaces and mosques."

"A delight to his guests, I'm sure. And how is the prince himself? Is he well? Happy? I do hope so." Maria dealt more cards.

"I don't know the prince very well, madam, but he doesn't strike me as *un*happy."

"People misunderstand him, you know. He's led a very difficult life. What we had together was . . . transcendent of mortal descriptions such as 'love' or 'marriage.' And I know some have thought it tawdry, and have called it a mere liaison, just because the prince was forced to end it. But I know that I will always be the wife of his heart, and we are married in God's eyes." Maria absently fingered the cross at her neck.

The conversation had taken a decidedly maudlin turn, but Belle decided to press an advantage here. Keeping her eyes studied on her cards, she said, "I understand that the prince has formed other relationships beyond that with the Princess Caroline, madam."

"You mean Lady Hertford? Yes, he dallies with her. I imagine his hands are quite full with her, too. Oh! There I am again! I don't suppose you've seen Lady Hertford before."

"No, madam."

"Ah, never mind, my little joke is lost on you. I'm certain she and her husband are colluding to bankrupt my naïve prince."

Mrs. Fitzherbert was proving to be the prince's staunchest defender, a bullmastiff in a ruby collar.

"You're right, I'm sure. Do you know if he has cast his affections toward any other women?"

Maria hesitated. "Another mistress? Do you suspect someone in particular as his inamorata?"

How have I managed to ask such a brainless question?

"No, madam, I just think His Highness is a man of many appetites, that he might desire . . . rather, that I, I think . . . what I mean to say is . . ." Belle faltered.

Maria turned up another card before holding Belle in her stare. "Miss Stirling, are you trying to entice the Prince Regent yourself?"

"Heavens, no! I mean, of course not. How could I possibly? He's so corpu— Er, I realize that you once were his mist—I mean, his wife—oh, fiddlesticks, madam, I must apologize for being the most harebrained person who has ever crossed your threshold."

A deadly silence filled the room, nearly swallowing Belle whole.

And then Maria Fitzherbert laughed, her attractive voice replacing the terrible quiet. "You mean you're attempting to divine the prince's proclivities without calling attention to my own previous attachment to him? Please, don't look so troubled. I know the prince doesn't seek out younger women for company. After all, he can hardly tolerate his own daughter's presence, much less the vigor that a youthful companion would bring."

"I understand. Please forgive my boorish questioning."

"No matter. I caution you, though, Miss Stirling, to remember that no matter how unpopular the prince might be to the public, it is always wise for those around him to keep quiet counsel."

First Mr. Nash, now Mrs. Fitzherbert, were warning her from being too inquisitive where the prince was concerned.

Knowing Mrs. Fitzherbert must now think she had windmills in her head, Belle turned the conversation to the paintings that filled the room. Maria enthusiastically provided details about the artist of each one. Many had been gifts from the prince.

By the end of the game, Belle had the highest trump and claimed the winning pot, although she was certain Mrs. Fitzherbert had let her win.

September 1817
London

Belle received a letter, but this time the handwriting was unfamiliar. She gasped at its contents.

> *Dear Miss Stirling,*
> *It is my unfortunate duty to inform you that my dear sister, Jane, passed away on 18 July, of a wasting disease. She had been unwell for more than a year, although such awareness has not lessened the blow for our family in the least. My brother Henry moved us temporarily from Chawton House to Winchester in May, as he'd heard of a doctor there who might be able to cure her, but it was to no avail.*
> *I found some of the correspondence between you among her papers, and, remembering her fond recollections of you, took it as my personal responsibility to advise you of her passing.*
> *My sister is buried at Winchester Cathedral, should you find the means to visit and pay your respects.*
> *With kindest regards,*
> *Cassandra Austen*

She laid the letter down in utter shock. Jane, gone? First her parents, then Clive and Amelia, and now this. It seemed God was determined that she be alone in the world. At least there was still Wesley.

She spent the day locked in her room, reading and rereading Jane's letters and fingering her books. The following morning, finally spent of tears, Belle rejoined her brother to resume her duties. He didn't seem to notice a difference in her, although his distance from her was growing marked. He wasn't exactly surly; it was more like he was somewhere else and grumpy about being there. She needed to talk to him about it, but her own grief overrode her concern for her brother.

And then she was distracted by a visitor.

One morning while she was on a ladder, rearranging bins of silk and cotton gimp, Put Boyce entered, carrying a folded slip of paper. He was wearing the same ill-fitting dress clothes as he'd worn when he escorted her to see his shop for the first time.

Climbing down to greet him, Belle shook her head. Put-rhymes-with-shut Boyce was a man meant for leather and homespun, not silks and buckskin.

An image of Put enjoying his time with the young woman at the fair appeared unbidden in Belle's mind. She wondered what the woman thought of her beau's lack of style and quickly dismissed the thought. Mr. Boyce must be here on business, else why be here at all?

"How may I be of assistance?" she asked.

He glanced around. "Is Mr. Stirling not here?"

Actually, she had no idea where he'd disappeared to this morning. "Wesley's on an errand for me."

"Ah. Yes." Put cleared his throat. "I found this and wished to offer my condolences." He unfolded the paper and handed it to her. It was a copy of Jane's obituary, torn from a periodical magazine.

> 18 July. At Winchester, Miss Jane Austen,
> youngest daughter of Rev. George Austen,
> Rector of Steventon, Hants, authoress of
> "Emma," "Mansfield Park," "Pride and
> Prejudice," and "Sense and Sensibility."

The print blurred before Belle's eyes. *I never even realized she was ill.*

"Yes, Mr. Boyce? I am aware of Miss Austen's passing," she said, handing the notice back to him.

He frowned. "My apologies, I did not intend to cause you further distress. But I remembered your mention of the lady as a friend you'd acquired since arriving in London, and wanted to pay my respects."

"I told you about Jane?"

"Miss Stirling, there was little you *didn't* tell me that day."

And despite herself, Belle laughed. "I suppose I was a chattering magpie that day."

"Without the thieving habits. Actually, you were quite charming."

Belle was saved from responding to his comment by the arrival of a passerby, who stopped in to ask when the wallpaper merchant next door would be opening for the day.

After the shopper left, an uncomfortable silence ensued. Put obviously had more on his mind, but Belle didn't want to think about what that might be.

He cleared his throat again. "I've been working on some interesting pieces lately. Right now I'm finishing up an ebonized mantel clock for a Mr. Ashby. He said your brother referred him to me."

Mr. Ashby? She'd never heard Wesley mention the name.

"Young Merrick, my apprentice, is advancing in his skills. I believe he'll make journeyman before his seventeenth birthday. You remember Merrick?"

Of course. The boy who escorted her to Lady Derby's when it should have been Put himself. "Yes, I remember. I'm glad for him. And you."

"How does your own business fare?"

"Very nicely. Because of my work at the Pavilion, some of London's aristocrats are using me as their exclusive draper, and, as with Lady Derby, some are even consulting me over interior design. I've had some valuable commissions."

"So one day you'll be noticed by one of their eligible second sons, who will whisk you off to marital bliss before heading off to his naval commission."

"Hardly, Mr. Boyce. And you know my feelings on the subject."

"Isn't it time you called me Put? After all, I know such personal details about you as your propensity to wield pistols at intruders. Surely we are on familiar terms."

Yes, you are on familiar terms with someone else, too.

Why did it feel so comforting to be near this man, as full of dust and shavings and peculiar smells as he was? There was something very reassuring about his collection of saws, his jars of stains and varnishes, his stacks of planks, and his display of finely crafted furniture. But it wasn't the shop that was the comfort, was it? The comfort was in the owner.

Belle shook her head to dissolve the tears once again threatening to spill forth. Where was her pert attitude hiding? Really, she had to stop this infernal blubbering whenever she was around him. Except now she wasn't sure if she was crying for Jane or crying for something indefinable that was missing from her life. She loved her independent life, but it all seemed ethereal. Just the result of chance and of no permanence. Ultimately, her success lay in whatever Mr. Nash wanted it to be. Or what the prince wanted it to be. Or Mr. Crace.

She wanted warmth. And comfort. And stability.

And how in the world did an odorous, sloppy place like a cabinet-maker's shop make her feel any of these?

"I'm not sure we're as familiar as you think, Mr. Boyce. You seem to know everything about me, whereas I know little about you."

"Easily rectified, if you'll join me for a walk through Vauxhall Gardens."

No, she would not be his secondary bit of baggage.

"I'm very busy lately, and have little time for frivolities. Here, I'll show you the latest drawings for the prince's Pavilion. You'll easily see how much ordering has to be done for such an immense residence."

She retreated to the counter, going to its other side and pulling her set of rolled-up sketches from behind it. At least she now had a barrier between her and Mr. Boyce.

Belle cleared a space on the counter and smoothed the drawings out on the wood top, and for the next half hour she pointed out details of the interior design for the palace. She distracted Put well, for soon he was caught up in suggestions for table heights, mirror frame patterns, and chair leg motifs.

Their examination of the drawings concluded, Belle moved to roll the drawings back up, but Put laid his hand down in the center of them to stop her.

"One moment, Miss Stirling. There's one thing we've not discussed. And that's the real reason why you came into my shop all those months ago resembling a warped walnut board: beautiful, but completely unmanageable. I left you alone, hoping you might return on your own once you'd overcome your feelings, but you're stubborn."

Not stubborn, Mr. Boyce, just wary.

"My apologies, sir. I had a temporary lapse of judgment in coming to you. A weak moment. I'm sorry I troubled you, and assure you I won't allow it to happen again."

"Hmm." Put kept his hand in the center of the papers so that she couldn't move them. His gaze was intense, and she knew she would soon falter under it. She responded to him lightly.

"Must I remove your hand with one of those terribly dangerous blades I saw hanging on your walls?" she asked.

Something in his eyes shifted. He realized she wasn't going to lower her guard. "I'm terribly sorry about your friend. I remember when my brother died, many years ago. He was kicked in the head by a horse. Terrible how he suffered before he finally died. That's why today I won't ride one of the beasts if I can help it. I walk almost everywhere."

"You walk? Everywhere?"

"I'm used to it." Put shrugged and removed his hand from her papers.

"But we took a hack to your shop."

"Wouldn't have been right to ask you to walk that far. You deserve better than the calloused hands and feet I have, Miss Stirling."

But do I deserve better than your other young lady?

Belle picked up the sheaf and began straightening the pages.

"I, too, am sorry for the loss of your brother, for I don't know what I would do if something happened to Wesley. And now, Mr. Boyce, I have one final question before I must return to work, as my day will soon be busy with customers."

She finished tying the twine on the drawings and laid the rolled tube of drawings back under the counter before leaning over it as far as she could to stare at him, hoping that her eyes were half as penetrating as his.

He laughed uncomfortably but didn't step back. "This does sound serious."

"It is. I know I'm being a bit impertinent, but I must ask. Why are your eyes so . . . different . . . from each other?"

And now Put did take a step backward, scowling.

Oh dear. I've erred in asking this question.

"What do you mean, different?"

I've waded this far in, I may as well soak my head.

"I don't know. Different in a way that is intriguing, I suppose. Both look at me, but you only focus one on me. It's almost . . . unnerving. Do you do this on purpose? Is it a trick you are playing on me? Are you teasing me?" Belle had finally voiced the questions that had been bothering her.

"Teasing you? You think this amounts to an attempt to mock you?" Put pointed at his left eye. "If I didn't know you for a serious woman, I'd think *you* were teasing *me*."

"Why in heaven's name would I tease you? I'm asking a civil question." At least, it seemed like a reasonable question when she'd asked it.

But now Put was nearly belligerent.

"Questions are apparently civil only when *you* ask them, Miss Stirling. My questions are to be evaded at all costs."

"Mr. Boyce, I—"

"Damnation, woman, I have great regard for you and I told you to call me Put!" His fist came down, sending everything atop the counter into tremors. Startled, Belle backed up against the shelves on the wall behind the counter.

How had he not broken his hand against the hard oak?

Belle could read many things at once in his face. Regret for having behaved boorishly. Embarrassment for admitting affection. Hope that his plea had not fallen on deaf ears.

But she was too stunned to formulate a response. She remained against the shelving, one hand on her waist and the other clutching an empty shelf behind her.

He shook his head sadly. "Very well, Miss Stirling, I'll answer your question. My left eye seems, well, weaker, then my right eye because it is. In fact, it isn't really an eye at all. I lost my real eye from a large splinter that kicked up while I was splitting a particularly knotty piece of wood. It felt like I'd taken an entire log into my eye socket. I'll spare you the details of what the surgeon had to do to me, but in the end I was left with a patch to cover the void."

"Oh," Belle said. It sounded like a squeak in her own ear.

"You recall that I do some work for Madame Tussaud, the waxworker?"

Belle nodded.

"I was helping her son set up a tableau of Lord Nelson one day, and she commented that the admiral and I had something in common, except that she could help me, whereas the good admiral was long in his grave. And so she did help me. She procured a glass eye for me; I have no idea where she gets them. She makes them herself for all I know. She matched the color as closely as she could, but said my shade of green was difficult.

"The surgeon helped to set it, and now I'm as good as new, except that I don't see as well as I used to, which is why you notice me focusing with my right eye."

"Mr. Boyce, I mean, Put, I didn't mean to—" Belle stepped forward to the counter and tried to put her hand out to his, but he jerked away angrily.

"I don't want charity from you."

Belle shuddered. Weren't those Clive's last words to her? What else of Clive might be hidden beneath the surface?

"And now, Miss Stirling, I believe we are fairly matched in confessions. You are a stubborn draper who will be very successful one day if you can manage to control your tongue, and I am a dented, scratched man of wood who has never learned to control his sentiments. A sorry pair we make. Good day, Miss Stirling."

"Put, please, I—" But there was no use in it. He turned on his heel and left, tugging at his collar as he roughly pulled the door shut behind him.

More death and disharmony followed on the heels of Jane's passing and Belle's explosive call from Put. This time, however, all of England suffered the effects.

On November 6, Princess Charlotte, daughter to the Prince Regent and Princess Caroline, was taken back to bed with severe stomach pains after fifty hours of labor, in which she was finally delivered of a dead baby boy. The princess then began to vomit uncontrollably, and soon lapsed into convulsions, dying herself before the day was out. She and her husband had been married just over a year, and by all accounts were very devoted to each other.

Belle remembered Mrs. Fitzherbert saying that the Prince Regent could hardly stand his daughter. It seemed incongruous to the newspaper reports of his hysterical outbursts and dramatic calls to be sealed away in his room forever. Apparently, Princess Charlotte's husband, Prince Leopold, had the unenviable and utterly ridiculous task of soothing and comforting his wife's father during his frenzied and frequent outbreaks of dramatic lamentation.

Charlotte was buried at St. George's Chapel in Windsor, and the entire country joined her husband and the Prince Regent in mourning, for the princess had been immensely popular with the public. George's own sense of empathy and suffering was not so great, though, that he even bothered to send a letter to Princess Caroline, now residing in Italy with a lover, to inform her of her own daughter's passing.

The public was shocked to hear that Caroline learned of her daughter's death only because George's letter to the pope informing him of such was intercepted from the courier passing through her town.

For George, the good news was that with his daughter now departed, Caroline had little hope of regaining her standing in the royal house by virtue of her daughter's succession to the throne.

The rest of the country also realized this, and wept silently.

Belle imagined, however, that the Prince Regent was enormously heartened by Caroline's weakened position.

"My suffering is great, too great for someone as gentle and sensitive as I am." The Prince Regent, seated before a writing table, waved away the servant carrying the carafe. It wouldn't do to have wine poured while he was working himself up into a righteous state of self-indignation. Others might misconstrue his sincerity. He settled for a quick bite of one of the pastries on a platter at his elbow.

And perhaps he should have chosen a different location than the Circular Room inside Carlton House. It was too vast a meeting place for the men before him to adequately appreciate his distress.

He'd summoned Lord Liverpool, Speaker of the House Charles Abbot, and Sir Francis Burdett to once again drum up support for a divorce from that screeching, grubby trollop he'd been forced into an unholy alliance with. She was now cavorting about in Pesaro, Italy, and rumored to have publicly taken a mere servant into her bed.

Good Lord, how did the man climb in bed with her each night without retching?

And how could the men seated before him not understand how ghastly the past year had been for him? Must he reiterate it again?

"Gentlemen, as you know, this year has been particularly difficult for us. First was that distasteful delegation trying to submit their nitwit petition to me for parliamentary reforms. As though that was of any concern to me. In fact, it was apparently more the concern of one particular person here." He purposely avoided looking at Burdett.

"Then there was the shooting incident that occurred while I was driving out to Westminster to open the new session of Parliament. I've said it before: We were perilously close to a crisis. Had whatever deranged person who took the shot at me had any sort of good aim, I might not be here to address you this day, and England would be adrift without my steady hand.

"Parliament's messages to me of loyalty after the incident were, of course, greatly appreciated, but then I had so much more to endure after the passage of the Gag Acts, since the public, having no comprehension of the danger to the nation's stability, reacted so violently to the suspension of Habeas Corpus and the suppression of reforming societies and clubs."

Lord Liverpool sat before him like a statue.

"Then my own dearest, darling daughter was taken away from me by the angels, lifted up to heaven where she now sings lullabies to her son." George made the motion of cradling an infant in his arms.

Would nothing generate a reaction in these idiots?

"Yes, I have endured many calamities this year, and this latest indecency by my so-called wife is beyond the pale. I am collecting evidence against her, sirs, for I know that she is committing treason in her sordid liaison with that Pergamo, her servant. I think he's her stable boy, or some such thing. It's really too much for me to contemplate on top of all of my other concerns; however, as a loving prince, I must. It is my intent to begin proceedings against the Princess of Wales for treason once my case is solidified. But I can't be successful in this on my own."

Liverpool muttered something to Abbot, seated nearby, but they were too far away for George to catch the comment.

Indeed, this room was entirely too large for the performance, er, discussion he had intended. But he wasn't finished yet.

"And so, my lords, I throw my weakened and frail self upon your mercy. *Will no one rid me of this turbulent woman?*"

He resisted the urge to grin. He'd been thinking up that last bit for days now, as his pièce de résistance. It was a reference to Henry II's grousing about his Archbishop of Canterbury, Thomas Becket. Henry's plea to be rid of his turbulent priest had unwittingly set several of his men out to literally rid the king of the archbishop, hacking him down inside Canterbury Cathedral.

Although such a fate was entirely too kind for Caroline.

Liverpool finally spoke. "Your Highness, thus far, there is no real evidence of the princess's infidelities, just rumors. If the people believe that you are persecuting her, they will turn against Your Highness's government. It is a great risk for very little reward."

"Little reward! Shedding that albatross would be no little thing. Sending her to prison—or at least into permanent exile—would bring sunshine back to England."

"Sunshine has already returned, sir, with the dissipation of volcanic ash from Mount Tambora."

Gads, what an iron pole the prime minister was. George contemplated throwing himself on the floor in a fit, but settled for mopping his forehead with a lace-edged handkerchief taken from his waistcoat pocket. Who had given this to him? Was it old enough to be from Maria, or was it from Lady Hertford, or perhaps . . . ?

He realized Lord Liverpool was waiting for an answer.

"Indeed, Lord Liverpool, the literal sun has returned. But my wife has blocked the figurative light from the land. She is Caligula, Beelzebub, and Jezebel tied together in one hideous package. It is your *duty* to help me. For England."

George sensed that the men were not with him. They were sitting there, disengaged, despite his best speechmaking.

Well, no matter. The prince was determined to be rid of his wife.

Whatever it might take.

Wesley was glad Belle had gone off to St. Bart's again with her basket of charity. The flood of refugees into London had stopped, but Belle continued with her weekly visits there. Must be her attempt to feel better over the death of her author friend, Jane whatever. His sister hadn't been herself since that girl's death. As far as Wesley was concerned, it was taking Belle entirely too long to get over it.

Or maybe Belle's trips to St. Bart's were to assuage her guilt over Clive, although it was misplaced guilt in Wesley's opinion. Clive had duped them both, hadn't he? Nearly ruined Wesley's relationship with his sister.

In fact, because of Clive, Wesley had been forced to come groveling to Belle in London, the complete opposite outcome of what had been planned with the shop back in Leeds. It was all Clive's idea. And Clive's fault.

Of course, there was the matter of Belle's friend Amelia. Mousy girl, as Wesley recalled. Scared of all shadows except Belle's, whose shadow she resided under. It was difficult to remember what Amelia even looked like, so unremarkable was she.

Nevertheless, Wesley enjoyed his Sunday afternoons away from the shop, with Belle also gone. The free time gave him an opportunity to write in his journal, prowl about town, indulge in his favorite pastimes, and dwell on how unfair life had been to him thus far.

How was it that Belle was achieving success, and a certain amount of fame, too, whether she realized it or not, while he was languishing in the background? He'd cozied up to the wealthiest of women and their daughters, and although they'd been pleasant diversions, none had resulted in any sort of progress for him. At most he'd gotten gifts: a fine suit of clothes, a pocket watch, a chess set. Nice, but of little value in establishing his own name.

Belle gave hardly anyone the time of day, other than that cabinetmaker who hadn't been around in a while, yet she was profiting handsomely. What the deuce did Belle have that he didn't?

She was too outspoken, enjoyed verbal thrusts and parries, and didn't understand her place at all. Whereas Wesley was charming, well liked, and understood exactly what his place in the world should be.

If only Wesley knew how to harness Belle's power and make it his own. His attempts at sarcasm and rebellion since Belle's ascension had only led to his own humiliation, heartbreak, and an increasingly untidy fascination with opium. How much better life would be if he could surge and flow the way his sister did.

Would it always be like this? He, a daring, fearless man, always under the dominance of his younger sister? There must be a way to achieve supremacy over her.

The thought made the hair on his neck prickle in a satisfying, secret sort of way.

And he just as quickly banished it. *Fool. Your sister loves you and forgave you when you didn't deserve it. You're fortunate to still have a place with her, and you're incapable of managing a shop on your own, anyway.*

God, how he hated this ongoing argument with himself.

He scraped a little opium from his brick, dropped it into the pipe Belle had given him accompanied by one of her sharp tongue-lashings, and packed some tobacco on top of it. This diversion was perilously close to becoming a habit, but Mr. Ashby provided it so conveniently, sometimes even stopping by his lodgings to check that he had enough supply.

He waited for the comfortable, floating feeling to overtake him, hoping that it wouldn't lead to one of those periodic walking nightmares. They were almost always about Alice, who had become his own personal Medusa, turning him to stone every time he dreamt of her.

Wesley had been seriously interested in marrying a woman only once before, and it hadn't been Alice. It was a disaster, and mostly his parents' fault. He'd harbored a secret crush on a boyhood friend's wife, Lucy, and when that friend accidentally drowned in one of Yorkshire's many canals he considered it divine approval for him to pursue Lucy.

His parents had been horrified by his desire for his dead friend's wife, and kept the story away from Belle. So as not to "damage" her, they said. His father had left no stone unturned in attempting to dissuade him on his quest for Lucy's hand, even threatening to disinherit him from the shop. It had scared him enough to abandon his suit of the widowed woman.

Fat lot of good it was, given that Belle was running everything anyway.

Nursing his own hurt and fury, he'd ended up in India with Alice Treadle, one of the Pack Horse Inn's more pliable and agreeable maids, after seeking employment with the East India Company. They were happy to take on someone who had earlier been importing cheap Indian cottons from them. He'd thought life with her would be easy and companionable. And his new position as an agent smuggling opium into China, where it was forbidden, had no end of financial reward. He'd found a boon companion in Mr.

Nathaniel Ashby, who had also fled England with an accommodating young woman to pursue interests in the opium trade.

Table delicacies, luxurious surroundings, and servants were all Wesley's. He'd learned to skim a bit from the shipments for his own personal use, but it never hurt anyone.

Except that Alice wanted more. Of everything. More opium. More of his affection. More dresses, jewelry, and entertainment. She was exhausting to a man whose intent in bringing her along on his assignment was so that *she* could serve *him*, not the other way around.

And so they drifted apart, although Wesley would never have turned her out, not so far from home. But without his knowledge, Alice fell in with a bad lot of Indian natives, and soon he suspected that she was prostituting herself to earn more money for her lifestyle. It was hard to believe that she was even more extravagant than he was.

Alice's appearance disintegrated. She went from pleasing plumpness to cadaverously gaunt. Her hair became greasy and unkempt, and she lost a tooth or two. She turned into a bony little shrew, disgorging vileness and heaping daily insults on him.

Then the real trouble started.

The demands for her services as an exotic Englishwoman grew more persistent, despite her crumbling looks. Wesley turned the other way when men appeared at the doorstep of his bungalow to call on Alice, and he swallowed his bile when she laughingly took them up to one of the guest rooms.

One afternoon, a man arrived with his two servants. The man's dress identified him as Vaisia caste, so probably some businessman wanting to entertain himself with a rare treat: an Anglo doxy in India. He and Alice went upstairs together while the servants waited on the landing, Alice's mocking laughter in Wesley's ears once again.

But within a short time, the mirth had turned malevolent. Shouts and curses drifted over the transom of the bedchamber, reaching Wesley in his study. He heard what sounded like slaps, then Alice's voice rising in anger above the man's. Or was it in fear? Wesley returned to his newspaper, but couldn't concentrate.

Should he go up there and see what was the matter? No, Alice would just mock him. And how humiliating would it be for a cuckolded man to ask if his mistress was comfortable in bed with another man in his own house?

He threw the paper aside and reached for his comforting brown brick. Ah, now the noise upstairs didn't seem as loud or unpleasant.

But even his pleasant haze couldn't block out the clamor as the two of them came tumbling down the stairs to the intermediate landing in a deafening rush. He decided to confront the group. Best to see if Alice planned to be out all night.

What greeted him was appalling, even if it felt remote. Now all four of them were on the landing, and as Wesley stepped out of his study he was in time to witness the businessman punch Alice in the face while the servants held her still. Blood spurted from her nose and soaked the front of her dress.

"You promised!" he shouted. "I paid good money for you and you'll do as I tell you." He kicked Alice and she fell from the landing down the stairs to the floor.

Wesley knew it was his responsibility to save Alice, but something—fear? revulsion? his altered condition?—caused him to shrink back inside the doorway of the study, where he could observe but not be seen himself.

Alice was bleeding more profusely now, but the fall had not broken her spirit. She gamely stood up and shook a fist at them as they came down the stairs after her.

"I'll not be ordered around by a filthy bludger. I'm the lady of this house and I say what jaunts will be had inside the bedroom. Not you pack of—"

She couldn't finish her words because the businessman grabbed her by the throat.

"Watch your next words, English doxy." He nodded at his servants. The two picked Alice up and carried her struggling body to the front door. The businessman opened it in an almost gentlemanly fashion, bowing as the servants carried Alice onto the verandah, and quietly closing it behind him as if letting out the cat.

Wesley crept to a window at the front of the house to see what was happening. Alice was on her feet now between the two men, but still struggling. Wesley struggled, too.

Go, man, go help her. You don't love her, but she's your responsibility for God's sake.

But he stayed rooted to the spot.

You don't know where they're taking her. Or if they'll bring her back. Save her. Rescue her from them.

And still he didn't move. Only when they were out of sight did he turn back to the study and pick up his opium again.

But they did bring her back. The next morning he found her crumpled, lifeless body dumped outside his study window. As if they knew he'd been watching from there and were mocking him.

He'd quit his post and jumped aboard the next packet ship headed for England after that, never explaining to anyone his sudden return. His parents had been only too happy to forgive and forget.

He was back in Yorkshire with his old haunts and new friends, including Clive Pryce, in charge of his own destiny, and he didn't have to divulge to anyone what had happened to him in India. Other than the occasional waking dream about Alice, it was as if that chapter of his life had never occurred.

Except that he wasn't really in charge of his destiny, was he?

And he needed to be. It was the only way to erase Alice's lingering stain on his dreams. Well, there was no help for it. He had to talk to his sister again.

As if on cue, he heard Belle entering the lodging house. Rebelling against the inner whisper telling him to wait, not to approach his sister when he wasn't in full control of his faculties, he jumped up from his bed and went out to confront her.

He clamored up the stairs behind her to her room.

"Wesley, what's got you so excited?" Belle asked. "What's wrong? Your face looks so pinched."

No, he wouldn't allow her to control the conversation by pointing out some imagined flaw.

"Sister, it's time we talked again." Did he sound firm?

"All right." She removed her bonnet and sat down in a chair, while Wesley walked back and forth in her room.

"Tell me, Sister," he said. "How do you enjoy working in Brighton, at the prince's Pavilion?"

She stiffened visibly. "I'm faring well enough, I suppose. Why do you ask?"

Wesley ignored her question and posed another of his own. "And my work at the shop, do you find it to be agreeable?"

"Agreeable? You're my brother. We've always worked well together."

An evasive answer. Belle had a wily mind, he must admit.

"Yet, you don't think we work that well together, for you still don't entirely trust me, do you?"

Belle was wary of a trap now. He could see her mentally pacing back and forth, anticipating his next move.

"I trust you."

"If you trust me, then surely you would like me to be independent of your considerable restrictions."

"What restrictions do you mean, Wesley?"

"I mean nothing untoward. Just that I'm capable of helping you far more than I'm now doing, and we both know I've proven my worth. You never would have been able to start the shop without my arrival with everything from Leeds."

"Oh, you mean your arrival with *my* goods that *you* nearly destroyed?"

He winced. That was probably not his best point. Better to press on.

"And I've managed the shop well during your frequent absences. I've also attracted many new customers into the shop. More than you have, since you require your patron's assistance to build your customer base."

"*My* frequent absences? Wesley Stirling, have you lost your senses? You bring in customers with your winking, flirting, and who knows what else. That is, when you haven't run off without warning for days at a time to seek some unknown amusement. Our customers don't complain, so I don't ask questions. In return, I expect you to let me be, to run the shop as I see fit."

"But that's just it, Sister. Your days of running it may be very close to an end. Do you really think that an esteemed architect like

Mr. Nash was so impressed by your ability to select fabrics that he championed you to the Prince Regent of England? Honestly? Has it not ever occurred to you that he has other motives in mind?"

"My acquaintance with John Nash was purely coincidental, and we are just colleagues now."

Wesley gave her a look of pity. "Has it ever occurred to you that Mr. Nash wants to take possession of your shop? I'm sure he knows our family's reputation for good cloth. He's put you in a position to attract many wealthy clients. You can be sure Mr. Nash will figure out how to profit handsomely from it. He's a man of business, after all."

"Mr. Nash doesn't own me, Wesley. He has no power to do it."

"No, but he has the prince's ear. And, ultimately, the prince *does* own you. Maybe John Nash plans to ruin you through scurrilous gossip, rumors of cheating customers, that sort of thing. Simple enough for someone in Nash's position. He'll buy you out for pence on the pound and reap for himself a good secondary business.

"Then you'll be left with no customers and be forced to sell. Not only that, your only prospect will be to find some old lecher to marry you. After you lose the shop, you'll be spending your time managing your elderly husband's household accounts on his far-off Cornwall estate."

He could see Belle's mind working behind her eyes. Excellent. Let her worry a bit first. Not that Wesley thought for a moment that Mr. Nash had any intentions on something as far beneath him as a draper shop.

"You know," he said, raising a finger in the air as though struck with a brilliant idea. "I have a thought. I believe I know how we could solve both our problems."

"Is that so?" Belle narrowed her eyes. Why did the woman have to be so suspicious of him?

"It occurs to me that, since you will have no taste whatsoever for a decrepit old lecher, and I am anxious to be my own shop owner, it's really just a matter of legitimately removing you from Mr. Nash's control."

"Thus far, you're making no sense."

"What I'm saying is that if you were to turn the shop over to me, a mere piece of paperwork that wouldn't really mean anything between brother and sister, then no poacher could ever take it away from you. It would always be here for you, just in my safekeeping. And of course I wouldn't make any decisions without you."

Belle stood utterly still, her mouth open. Poor dear thing, she was overcome by the offer. It was hard not to laugh in delight at her complete shock.

"Don't you see how perfect it is, Belle? What a force we will be together. Under my guiding hand, the shop will flourish, and you can rest assured of your legacy in the cloth industry. In fact, with my elevated position, I might be able to help you make a grand marriage one day."

"So you would . . . we would be . . ." Belle was incapable of speech, her eyes wide open and unblinking. He'd best finish before she fainted dead away from astonishment.

He dropped to his right knee, and took Belle's right hand in both of his own. "Annabelle, dear sister, please, let's improve both our lots in life together by reversing our roles in the shop."

Belle was quiet. That was a good sign, for she didn't immediately singe him with a dismissive, caustic comment. Wesley started to imagine himself as the proprietor of the shop. His first order of business before the ink had been blotted and dried on their legal agreement would be to have a new sign made for the outside, replacing Belle's name with his own as proprietor of Stirling Drapers. And no more extravagant donations to St. Bart's. Enough had been done there already.

What's more, she had nicer rooms here at the lodging house. He should ask her to switch. Besides, her upper-story location was far more private for late-night, er, meetings, and Belle certainly had no need for the convenience.

". . . not be possible."

Wesley was jarred out of his pleasant daydream.

"What did you say?"

Belle withdrew her hand from his. "I'm sorry, Brother, but no matter how John Nash or the prince or *you* might try to control my life for me, I'm still confident that I can take care of myself."

What? Had Belle just refused him?

"I don't understand. I'm offering you a grand opportunity, Belle. A girl of your station couldn't hope for better."

Belle stood, her arms crossed in front of her. "And that's just it, Wesley. Just as Mr. Nash doesn't recognize 'stations' in life, nor shall I. I'll make my own way. I am my own mistress. No man will own my business, and that includes my brother. But I do thank you for this most amusing performance. For the briefest of moments, I actually thought you had a valid point. But you're just being foolish. Now, if you have nothing further to say . . . ?"

"Belle, please, I only want what's best for us. Why do you always work against me?" How the hell was he all of a sudden pleading with his sister again?

He suddenly very much wished for a smoke of opium. He patted his trouser pockets. Nothing. His earlier smoke hadn't lasted nearly long enough. He needed more and more of it these days.

He caught a movement out of the corner of one eye. What was it? Belle continued explaining to him her nonsensical ideas about maintaining independence and not turning her life over to another Clive. Chatter, chatter, chatter. Endless chattering. Wesley put his hands over his ears and his sister's voice faded away.

The room started swaying, so he stood up and backed up against the window for balance.

She had returned.

He felt Alice whispering in his ear again. *Did you think you could find happiness without me? That you could do anything in your life to forget me? That I wouldn't find out what you're doing? Foolish, foolish boy.* The way she said "foolish boy" reminded Wesley of Belle, but he was too overcome to consider why.

"I'm not foolish. This is my only hope of shedding the past and finding peace."

He knew Belle was responding to those words, but she'd receded into the wallpaper and he couldn't hear a word of it. Not with Alice clinging to him, burning him with her stinging, sour breath.

How many times must I tell you, sweet one? Your destiny is with mine. There is no happiness for you without me. We will be together. Always. You owe it to me. Remember how you allowed those men to take me. Remember? Alice raised her voice to a snarl.

"Yes, yes." He hoped he wasn't weeping in front of Belle.

And now I see that you're trying to abandon me. To replace me with your family's business. Do you truly think that would enable you to be rid of me? Alice punctuated her comments by sticking her forked tongue in his ear, pointing and searching wetly for what? His inner thoughts? His entire brain?

Wesley jerked away from her, but she was already doing what she always did, wrapping her endless arms around his body, laughing and singing all at once. Why must he always be her helpless fly?

No, he wouldn't do it this time. He would cast her off. He struggled against her suffocating grasp, thrusting his head and trying to run in any direction he could. He was no longer sure where he was in his room. If he was even still in the room at all.

There. He could feel her loosening her grip on his legs. He must run faster, harder. If he could only get some distance from Alice, he'd be free of her. Free of her mocking demands for his attention. He was certain Alice would disappear entirely from his life once he was settled in the shop with Belle in her proper place.

Wesley heard hollow laughter in the distance. He thought it was Alice, but realized it was coming from his own throat. Why was Belle above him, calling his name?

"Wesley? Wesley? What happened? Are you ill? Why did you fall?" His sister's face was blurry above his.

No, he wasn't ill, just trapped by the women in his life. Belle in his waking hours and Alice in his nightmares. How ironic, the charming and roguish Wesley Stirling held hostage by two women.

And now his laughter was hysterical.

❧ 8 ❧

Under the pressure of the cares and sorrows of our mortal condition, men have at all times, and in all countries, called in some physical aid to their moral consolations—wine, beer, opium, brandy, or tobacco.

—Edmund Burke, Irish statesman, 1729–1797

May 1818
London

Belle had now been in London for six years. It was hard to imagine that work still continued at Brighton, seemingly without end.

Wesley spent more and more time away from the shop, although he managed to be on hand when Belle needed to be away at Brighton. Their relationship had reached a polite impasse, with neither one of them willing to bend any further to the other.

Their strained bond made it impossible for Belle to make comment on Wesley's activities. In particular, she didn't like that Mr. Ashby, whom Wesley claimed as a tavern friend, and who came skulking about the lodging house at all hours. She also suspected Wesley was lifting coins from their money box, but had no heart for accusing him.

Things were only slightly better with Put Boyce. Belle had sent out a peace dove by making a request for his shop to build her a new counter for the shop. She wanted one with more shelves and drawers on the proprietor's side, including a secret cabinet in which to hide her pistols.

Put crafted the counter in several pieces, and came personally to first dry-fit the pieces together, then do a final assembly. Ironically, he replaced her old oak counter with one made of walnut.

Yet she was certain he was only charging her an oak price.

After that, they continued to send each other small commissions. He purchased fabric from her for his occasional chair seats, and she gave him orders for various custom pieces for her London customers who sought her design assistance.

But Mr. Boyce was keeping himself a yardstick's length from her.

Belle sighed. How had she managed to distance herself from both Wesley and Putnam Boyce?

But things were at least cordial with Mr. Crace. He might not be particularly enthused with the prince's draper, but Belle had at least earned a bit of respect for her taste in color and texture.

Mr. Nash and the prince continued to champion her. In fact, the prince had just imported a carpet from Turkey for Carlton House's entrance, and he wanted all of the chairs in the space to be recovered in complementary shades of green and yellow. Nash was currently in London monitoring his canal project, and suggested that Belle handle it on her own.

The carpet was rolled up alongside one wall of the home's spacious entry. Belle first pushed all of the chairs and occasional tables up against the wall. She then cut the muslin ties securing the cotton casing around the folded rug, and struggled to remove the casing and unfurl the carpet so she could see the entire pattern and get a feel for what fabrics would be right to blend with it. Once she made notes about colors, she planned to measure out how much fabric would be needed for the furniture in the room.

She was sweating and had nearly tumbled over in her skirts several times before finally getting the carpet unrolled. She should have brought Wesley with her to help, but he was just so moody these days that she wasn't sure how helpful he would have been.

As she stood gazing down at the carpet, tapping a pencil against her cheek, lost in thought, she heard an "Ahem!" behind her.

She turned to see the Prince Regent there, dressed in an Oriental kimono emblazoned with large, colorfully embroidered dragons worn over his pantaloons. The prince's love for Oriental design was permeating every aspect of his life.

It required several dragons to fully enclose the prince's girth.

"Ah, Miss Stirling, so you're here to improve my pitiful little hovel?"

Belle curtseyed. "Your Highness's home is beautiful as it is, but I am happy to help you complement your new carpet."

"I selected the colors specifically to enhance the artwork in here." He pointed to one wall. On it was a half-length portrait of a stunning woman wearing a mass of dark curls, sitting at a table and leaning on an open book.

"It's a Gainsborough," he said.

"It's beautiful."

The prince perked up. "You appreciate the fine work of Gainsborough? Not everyone does."

"I'm not sure I'm qualified to judge art, sir, but the woman in the portrait is breathtaking. Is she a princess from some royal house?"

The Prince Regent laughed. "Far from it. I bought this painting because of how the subject's story touched my heart. Her name was Giovanna Baccelli, and she died, let's see . . . has it been nearly twenty years ago? She was an Italian ballerina whose heart was broken into brittle little pieces by her lover, the Duke of Dorset. After ten years with her as his sun, as the dancing center of his universe, he was forced by his family to cast her off in order to marry an heiress. The Baccelli moved from the duke's country estate into a small townhome in London, and died there a few years later. Of a broken heart, I am certain."

Belle looked again at the woman, whose soft gaze only reflected a deep, inner serenity. *Smooth runs the water where the brook is deep.* What would Giovanna Baccelli have to say about marriage and the wisdom of relying on a man for happiness?

She realized that the prince was looking back and forth between her and the portrait, his expression amused.

"My apologies, sir, I forgot myself."

"Your beauty requires no apology. Standing here, I am reminded of how much you are like the talented Baccelli."

"Sir? I've taken no duke as my protector. Nor would I."

"No, but the Baccelli relied on something unreliable—the duke—to satisfy her life. She refused to marry elsewhere when her youth and beauty might have made her a better marriage match. Instead, she waited until she was nearly an old woman, and wed herself to some droopy man of insignificance. I wonder, Miss Stirling, if you rely too heavily on your independence, and will end up sacrificing great happiness."

"As long as I have my shop, sir, I'll always be happy."

"Indeed. But of course I speak selfishly, for I'm in great need of you to take wedding vows, so that we two can become lovers, eh? I've not forgotten your promise to me, Miss Stirling." He playfully wagged a finger at her.

She teased him in return. "Well, Your Highness, it does seem as though for me to live up to the considerable charms of Miss Baccelli, I will have to start right now to find myself a duke. Although I have no skills in the art of dance to woo my potential husband, so perhaps I'll have to settle for an earl, or a lowly baron. Someone willing to marry a cloth merchant."

The prince's demeanor turned grave. "I could secure someone for you."

"I'm sorry?"

"I can find a titled man, someone older and more experienced—a widower, maybe?—who would be more than happy to marry you. Would you like me to help you? Think how much sooner we could achieve our goal of being together. Ha!" The prince snapped the pudgy fingers on his right hand for emphasis.

Belle blanched. Their banter had turned serious, and was eerily reminiscent of what Wesley had intimated.

"Your Highness, sir, I was just jesting. I'm too busy and happy working on the Pavilion to even consider a husband. But I'll remember your generous offer."

At that moment, a servant entered to notify the prince that his bath had been drawn, to ready him for his planned outing to the theatre with Lady Hertford that evening. With the prince's attention diverted to his own toilette, Belle made her escape back to the safety of her shop.

The Horse and Groom had become Wesley's favorite retreat. The ale was plentiful, the fare was served hot, and someone was always willing to throw dice. He could forget everything that irritated him when he was here.

Especially when there was the delightful Darcey White to entertain him. She'd finally made eye contact with Wesley after several weeks of just winking at him but otherwise ignoring him. In fact, Darcey White simply fascinated him. The daughter of a member of the House of Commons, she didn't behave at all like a young lady from an important family. What would Mr. White think if he knew his eldest daughter was frequenting taverns when she was supposed to be visiting an ailing friend?

Darcey lounged about the taproom in the Horse and Groom like any common trollop, but her dress and manners spoke the truth of her refined upbringing. This was a woman who should be attending dances in the Assembly Rooms, not lounging about in a taproom with disreputable persons, on hard benches with her elbows on rickety tables.

Wesley's interest in her had started as it always did. Once he'd finally captured her attention, getting her to nibble at the hook, he'd pull on the line with imperceptible gentleness, so that she didn't realize she was being drawn to his boat until he was lifting her over the side.

Or was Darcey the one actually tugging on the line, determined to bring him over the side into the water with her?

Darcey drank dark ale from mugs, wiped her mouth with the back of her hand, and swore like the lowest jack-tar in His Majesty's navy. All while wearing the prettiest, filmiest dresses with her hair done up in the fashionable face-framing curls the ladies liked these days.

It was over one of these mugs that Wesley suspected he might be falling in love.

"So, tell me, Wesley Stirling, what do you do to earn money?" She hid a belch behind her hand. "You're here at the Horse and Groom as often as I am, you cur."

"I'm a draper. I have a shop on Oxford Street."

"That right? Do you think you've got anything that would make my bosom look smaller?" She sat straighter and turned to give him her full profile.

Wesley knew exactly what Belle would think of such a woman; moreover, he knew what he should think, too, but to have a member's daughter thrusting herself teasingly at him was too much.

"I believe that in your case, Miss White, 'less' would be the watchword. I don't think such delicacies should be kept too well hidden."

She laughed, her even, white teeth another reminder of her gentle breeding.

"My father would disagree with you. Course, he is a most disagreeable sort. Never allows me any freedom."

"Yet you're here."

"That's because I make my own freedom. What the father doesn't know about, he can't punish." She licked her lips. "You won't be telling on me now, will you, Wesley Stirling?"

And risk losing her company? Never.

Darcey tapped her empty mug on the table. "Speaking of disagreeable sorts of people, I'm all out, and may turn into one myself soon."

Wesley happily got her a refill.

"So, Miss White, how does your father restrict your freedom?"

"He's obsessed with his position in Parliament. Nothing can interfere with his reputation or his dignity. He parades my younger sister and me in front of his important guests, and we curtsy, and say, 'Good evening, my lord,' and, 'Would you like to see my embroidery sampler, my lady,' and other nonsense, then we're sent to our rooms like little children."

Darcey tipped her mug back for a large swallow of drink.

"I'm not permitted to attend any parties or dances because Father is concerned that I'll get myself in trouble and ruin his plans to make a brilliant marriage for me. Which is just his way of saying he's hoping to make a brilliant alliance for himself. He's my papa, so I love him, but I also hate him. I want to be free to have fun, not skulk about in secret."

And that was when Wesley knew the hook was lodged firmly in his own cheek. For here was a woman who could understand exactly how he felt about Belle.

"So time spent here at the Horse and Groom eases the pain, doesn't it?" he asked.

BY THE KING'S DESIGN   171

She looked at him in surprise. "Hardly. I'm here to get a breath
of air away from my stuffy house, while I plot my revenge on him."
She laughed, throwing into question her seriousness.

Revenge. Now that was something Wesley hadn't considered
before.

He decided that Darcey White was a worthy companion for
sharing his opium.

"Where did he put it?" Belle muttered to herself several days
later. She'd closed the shop for the day, no thanks to Wesley, who
had disappeared once again that afternoon.

She knew she'd seen Wesley perusing the price list from one of
their preferred mills. She needed the list so she could place an
order of toile that they'd just run out of today when she sold their
remaining length to a woman who planned to make matching bed-
covers, canopy, and draperies for her bedchamber.

Where had he hidden it? Would he have taken it back to his
rooms for some reason?

After searching everywhere she could think of, she locked up
and returned to their lodgings. She tapped on his door, and, hearing no response, jiggled the latch. It was unlocked.

She entered, tentative about trespassing on her brother's domain. His bedclothes were jumbled on his bed, and clothes were
equally cluttered about in piles, both on the bed and on the floor.
Belle shook her head. How did he ever find anything?

She poked as gently as she could through his belongings in his
room. Not finding the list anywhere obvious, she moved aside
his bedclothes. How did he sleep with so much debris littering his
bed? She touched a piece of fabric that did not belong to his bed-
coverings and lifted it up. What was this?

A folded length of cotton batiste. Nearly three yards' worth.
Why had he snipped it and brought it here? She had just reviewed
the shop ledger this morning, and knew that he hadn't recorded
the cut, either.

She sighed. Wesley was becoming more and more difficult these
days.

Belle noticed a shallow wood box poking out from underneath

his bed. It looked like something that might hold documents. Might he have accidentally stored the price list in there?

She knelt down, pulled it out, and placed it on her lap, sliding the lid out from its grooved tracks on either side of the box. Ah, Wesley's smoking supplies. She smiled as she pulled out the pipe she'd given him, which he seemed to love so much. She also tried not to let it remind her of Put.

Wesley had several pouches of aromatic tobacco in the box, too, and the fragrance was heady. And what was this?

She pushed aside the tobacco and picked up a murky brown brick. What was this? His latest tobacco find? She pulled it closer and sniffed at it. It was cloyingly sweet. A fragranced tobacco? There was no maker's stamp on it.

"What the hell are you doing?" Wesley banged open the door, causing Belle to jump up, dropping the box and scattering its contents. She still held the brick out to him.

"Looking for the Harrington Mill price list. I need it and I know you last had it, yet it's completely missing from our catalog box. But now I'm looking at this. What is it?"

He came around the bed to where she was and snatched it from her. "None of your business. And I'll thank you not to intrude on my personal belongings. I threw the damned thing away, if you must know, because I did a comparison with their last price list and they'd escalated prices ridiculously."

"But the food riots and—"

"Have nothing to do with cotton and wool prices. And I'm sure you didn't think I could be conscientious enough to even compare prices, did you?"

"Don't sneer at me, Wesley Stirling. I thought no such thing. It would have been helpful if you'd at least *told* me you discarded the price list. Which I will ask you not to do again. Despite whatever price increases they may have had, they are one of the best manufacturers of cambric and toile in England, and I intend to continue purchasing from them for as long as I can."

Wesley bowed mockingly, holding the brick out in his right hand. "Of course, dear sister. You are, after all, lord and mistress of both our lives." He bent over and threw the spilled smoking supplies back to their storage box, slid the lid back on, and shoved it back under his bed.

When he rose, Belle saw that he was not only unshaven, but his eyes were bloodshot, and had a distinctly unfocused glaze to them. "Wesley, what's wrong? Are you ill? Is that why you're so tetchy?" And when had he gotten so thin?

His laugh sounded like a gunshot report in the room. "Ha! So you invade my room, snooping about where you don't belong, and then accuse me of ill humor."

Belle straightened. "You're obviously not yourself, Brother. I'll go to my room now. Perhaps you'd like to join me in the morning for breakfast, and we can talk then."

She strode out of the room before he could snap at her again.

What was happening to her brother? What if he abandoned her? He was all she had left in the world. And what was that strange substance he'd snatched away from her without explanation? For certain it wasn't tobacco.

But by morning, Wesley was a different man. His eyes were clear, his face was smooth, and he offered Belle an apology for his behavior and promised to be a better brother and a more conscientious employee as he daubed butter on a bite of raisin scone.

Belle, desperate to find the sibling she'd loved so well when she was younger, accepted his apology without questioning him further about the curious substance she'd found under his bed, nor asking about the fabric that he'd taken from the shop without explanation.

"Never mind, Wesley. For me, it's as though yesterday never happened. Let's not speak of it again."

Wesley grinned sheepishly, and told her he'd be along to the shop as soon as he cleaned up his room.

But Wesley really just wanted a few minutes of peace in his room after the exertion required to apologize to Belle.

10 July 1819, Saturday

Apologized to B——. D—— won't be happy, but I will explain.

Moved box to a more secure location.

Must remember to see Mr. Ashby. D——— is depleting what I have. May need to nick a few shillings from the lockbox again.

She says her father is considering several marriage options for her, mostly with the second sons of fellow parliamentarians. She thinks I have the ability to break any ensuing engagement, but I don't see how. A Yorkshire draper transplanted to London hardly has any influence anywhere, much less in Parliament. But I can't lose D———. I already can't imagine an existence without her.

D——— says my sister should be able to help, given her relationship with the Prince Regent. As if I would ever ask such a great favor from B———. No, if I'm to break D——— free of her father, I have to do it on my own.

During breakfast one morning, Belle's interest was piqued by the sound of someone shouting, "Peterloo Massacre!" outside their lodgings. She got up from the dining table where she and Wesley were sharing a quick breakfast before heading to the shop, and peered out a window. A boy was traversing the street outside their lodgings with a cartload of newspapers, calling out, "Peterloo Massacre!" repeatedly, and people were rushing up to buy copies. She excused herself, went outside, and was intrigued enough by the sign propped up in the boy's cart to spend twopence for her own copy.

PETERLOO MASSACRE!!!

JUST PUBLISHED NO. 1 PRICE TWOPENCE OF PETERLOO MASSACRE. CONTAINING A FULL, TRUE, AND FAITHFUL ACCOUNT OF THE INHUMAN MURDERS, WOUNDINGS AND OTHER MONSTROUS CRUELTIES EXERCISED BY A SET OF INFERNALS (MISCALLED SOLDIERS) UPON UNARMED AND DISTRESSED PEOPLE.

She carried the broadsheet back into her lodgings and read aloud to Wesley.

The Manchester Observer
21 August, 1819

The morning of the 16th was hailed with ex-ultation by the many thousands, whose feelings were powerfully excited on the occasion. At an early period, numbers came pressing in from various and distant parts of the country, to wit-ness the greatest and most gratifying assem-blage of Britons that was ever recorded in the annuals of our history. From Bolton, Oldham, Stockport, Middleton, and all the circumjacent country; from the more distant towns of Leeds, Sheffield, etc. came thousands of willing votaries to the shrine of sacred liberty; and at the period when the Patriotic Mr. Hunt and his friends had taken their station on the hustings, it is sup-posed that no less than 150,000 people were congregated in the area near St. Peter's Church.

Mr. Hunt ascended the hustings about half-past one o'clock, and after a few preliminary arrangements, proceeded to address the im-mense multitude, recommending peace and order for their government. Whilst thus en-gaged, and without the shadow of disorder oc-curring or likely to occur, we were surprised, though not alarmed, at perceiving a column of infantry take possession of an opening in the as-sembly.

Our fears were raised to horror, by the ap-pearance of the Manchester and Salford Yeo-manry Cavalry, who came galloping into the area, and proceeded to form in line ready for ac-tion; nor were they long delayed from their hellish purpose - the special constables were called in from their previous stations - the bugle sounded the charge - and a scene of murder and carnage ensued which posterity will hesitate to believe, and which will hand down the authors and abettors of this foul and bloody tragedy to the astonished world. Men, women, and children, without distinction of age or sex became the victims of these monsters.

The people in the crowd were so compact and stood so firm that they could not reach the hustings without halting. Few, if any of the meeting, even yet, supposed that this martial display was intended for anything more than securing Hunt, Johnson, Knight and Moorhouse, for whom they had warrants. Mr. Hunt was called upon to deliver himself up, which he offered to do to a Magistrate, but not to the Manchester Yeomanry Cavalry. A gentleman in the commission presented himself, and Mr. Hunt acknowledged his authority, and departed for the rendezvous of the Magistrates; where Mr. Johnson and Mr. Saxton were taken, and from thence conducted, along with Mr. Hunt to the New Bayley prison; Mr. Knight escaped, but was afterwards arrested at his own house and Mr. Moorhouse was soon after taken into custody at the Flying Horse Inn.

It is impossible for us to ascertain the extent of loss in lives and limbs which has been thus wantonly and inhumanly occasioned - people flew in every direction to avoid these hairbrained assassins, who were supported by detachments from the 15th Hussars. The latter, however, did not deal out death and wounds with the same liberal hand as our townsmen.

A secondary article indicated that an estimated eighteen people had been killed and around five hundred were wounded, many of them women.

"How terrible," was all Belle could choke out in response. "Those poor families, losing wives, mothers, and children like that."

Wesley was, as usual, detached. He shrugged his shoulders. "It's the price to be paid for reform. Besides, what does the government expect after four years of the Corn Law?"

The Corn Law? What was he talking about? They'd already seen that the disaster of the Corn Laws had been further worsened by the dreadful harvest in 1816, a consequence of the eruption of Mount Tambora. The country had suffered inestimable loss, in people like Clive and Amelia, literally starving to death all across the country. Why would the people's suffering result in the government exacting even harsher retribution on them?

"How can you say that? These were innocent women and children standing alongside their menfolk. It says here that one woman was thrown into a cellar and sabred to death. And here's another, a Mary Heys, who was ridden over by cavalry. She was pregnant, with six young ones at home. She gave premature birth and followed her infant into the grave. I can't imagine."

"Ha! That's because you can't even imagine being married, much less having a child in apron strings."

"What's that to do with anything, Wesley? You also have never partaken in the matrimonial state. And remember we promised not to bring that up with each other again. The point here is whether this tragedy could have been avoided."

Wesley shook his head. "It couldn't. Soon this country will undergo a revolution like France did."

"That's not possible. We have a duly elected Parliament and a crowned king. Revolutionaries are only effective in uncivilized countries."

"That's not what Mr. Thistlewood says."

"And who is Mr. Thistlewood?"

Wesley narrowed his eyes. "Just a friend. He knows much about such things. More than you or I ever could."

And with that, Wesley departed the dining table for the shop, without offering to walk there with Belle.

Wesley jammed his hat on his head as he left their lodgings. Who was Mr. Thistlewood, indeed? Just the brilliant leader of the Spencean Philanthropists was all. In fact, if it were so early in the day he might consider skipping the shop today and instead heading over to the Horse and Groom. He stopped to check his pocket watch. No, it was entirely too early, even for a man of strength and purpose like Arthur Thistlewood.

But surely this afternoon he'd find him there. And Darcey, too. Darcey thought Mr. Thistlewood would prove to be very influential in the country's future, and that Wesley should join the Spenceans.

They'd discussed it at length in a private room in the inn over a new brick of opium he'd purchased from Nathaniel Ashby. Afterwards, Darcey heightened his senses and pleasure in the way that only she knew how to do. Now Wesley was a little foggy as to exactly why she thought he should join the Spenceans.

But as long as Darcey was willing to wrap herself around him long into the night and help him forget Alice, he was willing to follow her ideas just about anywhere.

That afternoon, he slipped out of the shop while Belle was in the storage room. She'd be furious, but he would make sure to come home long after she was asleep, which would take the edge off her anger the next day.

The walk to the Horse and Groom was a pleasant one, a few blocks north up Edgware Road to Cato Street. Entering the tavern's taproom, he immediately saw Darcey at a game table, attempting to play a game of chess with an opponent Wesley didn't recognize. She was concentrating intently, licking her lips as she decided her next move.

So attuned to her was he that he nearly came undone at her subconsciously alluring move. He pulled her away from the game, leaving her opponent grumbling.

He put his lips close to her ear. "Were you waiting for me?"

She stopped. "Now why would I be waiting on the likes of you, Wesley Stirling? Have I not better things to do?"

Her eyes were challenging, but her smile was seductive. His gaze traveled downward to the cut of her bodice, which was low but respectable, and which he planned to divest her of soon.

She shook her arm free from his hand. "Besides, it's about time you showed your mangy cur face in here. I saw Mr. Thistlewood earlier, and he's planning a meeting of the Spenceans tonight. You should attend and ask if you can join his group."

"Tonight? What time? I've a powerful thirst that needs slaking first."

"Is that right, now?" She ran a fingernail lightly down his arm. "And just how do you propose to take care of it?"

"Quickly and firmly and to the great satisfaction of all concerned. Come, woman." He took Darcey by the arm once again and led her to their favorite private room upstairs.

Afterwards, feeling sated and drowsy, he allowed her to drag him to the tavern's ballroom, which had been set up with chairs in rows facing one end of the room. A gathering of men were already seated and waiting for their speaker. Wesley sat down with Darcey near the front. Her face was flushed and her hair untidy, but a bonnet covered most of the damage. She stared straight ahead, looking neither at him nor anyone else in the room.

He refrained from looking down at her bodice again, fearful that he might drag her out of the meeting and back to their room again.

But his attention was soon diverted for real, as Arthur Thistlewood entered, a mug of ale in his hand, which he downed and handed off to a serving boy before stepping onto the six-inch platform at the head of the room.

"Ah, friends," Thistlewood began. "Are we not well served by the proprietor of the Horse and Groom? He's an honest man doing an honest day's work, is he not, and deserves our praise."

Wesley couldn't see the proprietor anywhere in the room, but it didn't stop the group from breaking out into huzzahs for the provider of libations in the tavern.

Thistlewood motioned for quiet. He was a man of intense, fiery passion. A man Wesley would not want to have Darcey become too well acquainted with. Thistlewood's thick, expressive eyebrows were upstaged only by a shock of curly hair on top of his head that smoothed out and grew straight below his ears. He opened his mouth again, and Wesley noticed the man's graying teeth, which in no way detracted from his magnetism.

"Many of you here tonight already know me. But I see new friends, and I hope you are thinking men, rational men, men who care for the safety and welfare of your fellow tradesmen. For those of you who have never joined us before, let me introduce myself. I am Arthur Thistlewood, the son of a farmer and the husband of a butcher's daughter. I am one of you.

"Yet, would you believe, the authorities have declared me a dangerous character? Someone who advocates revolution and sedition?"

He bent over to address the audience in hushed tones. "I fear they may be right."

People leaned forward to hear more.

"For the government has imposed unprecedented suffering upon us of a magnitude not seen since our civil war. And I have personally been the victim of their inhumane and brutal aggression. You know about the riots of Spa Fields from three years ago, do you not?"

Heads nodded.

"You know that the Prince Regent refused a hearing of our grievances—our reasonable request for parliamentary reforms. And you know that a group of evil-minded constables attacked us, determined to run us to ground.

"But what you may not know is that, I, Arthur Thistlewood, was humiliated by arrest right before the eyes of my wife and infant child, followed by a prison stay. Of course, they had no case against me, and I was quickly released.

"Then, two years ago, I was greatly insulted by Lord Sidmouth, the Home Secretary, who also refused to hear my complaints against him. When Lord Sidmouth wouldn't grant me an audience, I did the only thing that any man of honor and courage could do: I challenged him to a duel. Coward that he is, he wouldn't face me, but instead had me arrested with threatening a breach of the peace."

Thistlewood shook his head dolefully. "For shame, Lord Sidmouth. You bring disgrace upon the country."

Murmurs of "for shame" and "coward" floated through the room. All eyes were riveted on Thistlewood.

"And so I was proclaimed guilty and sentenced to twelve months' imprisonment in Horsham Jail. Further indignity found me there, for I was forced to share one bed with three men, in a cell measuring a mere seven by nine feet! A dog should not be subjected to such conditions.

"But my constitution is such that I endured with as much poise as I could muster, and I earned the admiration of the men in my cell for my composure and self-confidence. But by this point I was a man of experience in oppression, wasn't I?"

More nods.

"And we all here have heard about the recent tragedy, now known as Peterloo in comparison to Waterloo, where the military was sent in to overwhelming victory against its enemy. Only in this instance, the cavalry galloped in to trample upon and murder more than five hundred innocent men, women, and children peaceably assembled at St. Peter's Field to demonstrate for suffrage and reform."

The audience was visibly agitated at this. News was just flowing into London about Peterloo, and it looked as though not everyone knew the details about the altercation. Wesley sensed that Mr. Thistlewood was not overly concerned about the slaughter of innocents in St. Peter's Field, for it advanced his important movement.

And on that point Wesley could agree, although recalling Belle's horrified expression about it did give him a moment's pause.

But what was Belle's opinion as compared to Darcey's rapturous expression and Thistlewood's inflamed oratory? She was a mere draper.

"And so, my friends, I ask you: What is the only way such indiscriminate violence against us can be addressed? Is it by hiding behind our womenfolk's skirts? No! For they will hack our women to bits. Is it by pleading and begging for redress of our grievances? Again, I say, no! For they will ignore us and throw us into prison."

Once again, Thistlewood dropped his voice for effect. And effective it was. Even Wesley was holding his breath.

"Friends, we will only accomplish our aims of freedom and equality for all men by the shedding of blood." He raised his fist and his voice together. "The blood of our oppressors, our tyrannical leaders, yes, even of our neighbors who stand in the way of our noble goals."

Flecks of foam appeared at the corner of Thistlewood's mouth. The orator seemed overcome by his own speechmaking, mopping his forehead with a kerchief. "I submit to all of you that we are all coming to a momentous decision. That decision is whether we will stand or fall, be brave or cowards, preserve or lose our very lives. And so the question is: Will you join us? Will you join those of us who will conquer the unbearable, inhumane forces that persecute us?"

The room exploded in elation.

"We'll join you!"

"Eliminate the oppressors!"

"Death to Parliament!"

Thistlewood extended his arms as though to embrace everyone in the room. "It pleases me to have so many generous supporters who understand my vision. You are joining a great movement by uniting with the Spenceans. I will lead you to victory. My genius is so great just now, I don't think there is any man alive who has so great a genius as mine at the moment."

He paused dramatically, looking upward as though in deep cogitation with the divine. "If it is the will of the Author of the World, should He exist, that I should perish in the cause of freedom, His will, and not mine, be done! It would be quite a triumph to me!"

Thistlewood threw his arms up in the air, and the audience cheered. Wesley glanced at Darcey. Her eyes were shining and her cheeks were wet with tears as she clapped wildly in support.

And so Wesley knew that he would happily join the Spencean Philanthropists to please the very enthralling Darcey White.

Awake! Arise! Arm yourselves with truth, justice, reason.
Lay siege to corruption. Claim as your inalienable right,
universal suffrage and annual Parliaments. And whenever
you have the gratification to choose a representative, let him
be from among the lower orders of men, and he will know
how to sympathize with you.

—Thomas Spence, founder of
the Spencean Philanthropists, 1793

August 1819
London

*W*hy did I have to choose this moment to go out? Belle asked herself
as she retreated back inside her shop.

Having left an unusually happy Wesley to manage alone one
afternoon, she went shopping. She planned to buy a packet of
paper while she was out, but also wanted to browse windows. She
started with the C. Laurent Fashion Dolls shop next door, which
she'd only visited once since arriving in London.

The proprietress, Lady Greycliffe, was an older French beauty,
tall and willowy. Her blond hair was shot through with silver
bands, revealing her to be at least in her fifties, even though she
looked younger. She possessed beautiful manners and a delightful
accent, although she told Belle she'd been in England for more
than thirty years. Born Claudette Laurent in Paris, she'd been or-
phaned at a young age and fled to England, scratching her way up
to finally opening this fashionable shop on Oxford Street, even
having met and married a minor lord along the way. Although she
now had a fine estate in Kent and a London townhome, Lady

Greycliffe could never give up her passion for dollmaking, and still spent considerable time in her Oxford Street location.

Belle lauded the dollmaker's tenacity and courage.

The shop had dolls of extraordinary proportions, from the tiniest creatures to fit little baby houses up to life-sized creations set on iron frames with translucent wax heads and hands.

The shop's specialty was fashion dolls made to resemble real people. Belle was so intrigued by them that she gave the proprietress a list of Amelia's features, to have a keepsake made of her friend. Lady Greycliffe promised to have it in three weeks' time.

From there, Belle browsed nearly every shop window on her side of Oxford Street. She hadn't realized the number of various businesses in this shopping district. Confectioners, jewelers, dressmakers, bootmakers, milliners, penmakers, and stationers all displayed wares in their windows. She wandered in and out of the shops, splurging only to buy herself a steel-nibbed pen and some India ink, in addition to a small sheaf of paper for writing up the shop's sales.

She came out of the stationer's shop, intending to return back to her own, when she looked across the busy road, full of pedestrians, carriages, horses, and their droppings, and saw something that made her heart sink.

Put Boyce sat at a table outside a coffee shop with that attractive woman she'd seen him with before. This was certainly far afield from his cabinetmaker shop for him to be.

He said he liked walking everywhere, didn't he? And this is *the most fashionable shopping district in London. Why shouldn't he be here with his lady love?*

Put was dressed again in his uncomfortable dark tailcoat over a striped waistcoat with buckskin breeches. Except he didn't look ill at ease at all. No, in fact, he appeared quite jovial. He and the lady, with her fashionable bonnet tied with a dark green sash—silk if Belle wasn't mistaken—were laughing at some terribly funny joke.

Put leaned in to speak to her, and the woman leaned toward him as well, offering him the side of her face.

He was close enough to kiss her cheek.

Surely he wouldn't commit such an act in public, would he?

At that moment there was a long gap in horse traffic in the street. Put looked across Oxford Street and saw Belle standing there. She knew she must look a complete idiot, but she was rooted to the spot.

She half hoped he would look embarrassed, but he didn't. He held up a hand in greeting, then stood and directed a bow her way. The lady with him saw that Put was looking at Belle, and raised a gloved hand to her, as well.

And that was too much. To have the woman waving to her energized Belle into motion and she fled back to her own shop, once again the rabbit acting on instinct.

The shop was empty except for Wesley, thank goodness. She hung the "Closed" sign in the window and locked the door.

"I think we're done for the day," she said.

Wesley looked up from where he was writing in a journal. "What's wrong, Sister?"

"Nothing. Nothing at all. How were things in my absence?"

"Mostly lookers, only one sale of some palm-and-bird-of-paradise damask to Mrs. Jennings. Oh, and Lady Logan sent along a note that she wants to meet with you. Something about seat cushions and her new Italian greyhound."

Oh dear.

"Anything else?"

"No. Except that I've been having an interesting time lately."

"Have you?" She looked around, and noticed that the floor was littered with threads, broken buttons, and scraps. She retrieved a broom and began sweeping the floor.

"Yes. I've been to some meetings led by my friend, Arthur Thistlewood. He makes some valid points about the Peterloo Massacre."

"Thistlewood? Isn't he the one you said knows more about anything than we could possibly hope to?"

"Well, er, I may have spoken harshly, but he really is very clever. He heads an organization called the Spencean Philanthropists, dedicated to destroying the oppressive power of the government. I've joined them and have already impressed Mr. Thistlewood with my quick grasp of politics."

Belle shook her head. There was a pile of scraps at one end of the cutting table. It must be days' worth. Why did Wesley have time to scribble in a book but no time to clean up scraps?

"Did you hear me, Belle?"

She snapped back to attention. "I'm sorry, what?"

"I asked what you thought about my joining the Spenceans."

"If they're radicals, I don't approve."

Wesley slammed his journal shut. "No, of course not. You'd never stand firm for principle or ideals."

"What do you mean? I merely said I don't support extreme movements."

"What you really mean to say is that you don't support anything in which I might involve myself."

"I said no such thing, nor did I intend it." Belle scooped all of the litter into a dustbin. "Must you constantly go off your head with me, Wesley?"

Especially when I'm this tired and disheartened.

"Must you constantly insult me and oppress me?" he retorted.

"Oppress you? Honestly, I don't know where you get such ridiculous ideas."

She put away the broom and attended to other tasks to avoid further conflict, not noticing the burning glare in Wesley's eyes.

September 1819
London

Wesley was attending regular meetings of the Spenceans. At Darcey's urging, he volunteered for various small tasks and errands for Mr. Thistlewood, resulting in the leader pulling Wesley into his inner circle of cronies.

Darcey was pleased by his advancement.

"You're at the forefront of this movement, love," she said, drawing languidly on his pipe while stretched out on the bed in their room at the tavern. He always found it devilishly amusing not only that she was smoking a pipe but that it was the very one Belle gave him.

Smoke swirled around Darcey in a wispy, exotic dance. She wore only a gauzy shift, made from a length of cotton batiste he'd cut without Belle's knowledge, and which was now wrinkled from the stays Darcey had removed earlier. Darcey had teased him about it when he gave it to her, saying she was surprised he'd had the nerve to steal something from his sister.

It was the only moment of irritation he'd ever had with Darcey.

Wesley joined her on the bed, propping himself up on one elbow as he took the pipe from her to draw from it himself. Now they were both enveloped in the sweet, fragrant smoke.

"So, are you ready for more?" Darcey asked, slowly blinking her almond-shaped eyes. Wesley felt that familiar stirring.

"Already?" He grinned at her and handed the pipe back.

She pushed it away as she sat up. "No, addlepate, I don't mean that. I mean are you ready for more involvement with Mr. Thistlewood?"

"More? You don't think I'm close to him?"

"You are, but I want further glory for you." She snuggled back down next to him, inserting one foot between his legs and sliding it up and down from his ankles to his kneecaps. "You should be Mr. Thistlewood's closest confidant, my love. He implies that a close, inner circle is meeting outside of the Horse and Groom. I'm certain he plans to do something dramatic against the government, and it should be my Wesley at his right hand, don't you think?" She gently nipped his chin.

"Yes, you know best. Just tell me what to do." Between the opium and Darcey's teasing, he was quite beyond even paying attention to what she was saying.

"Don't worry, love, I will. We'll start with you getting into that inner circle and finding out where they meet." She giggled as she tugged at his clothes. "Now, let's entertain ourselves."

Wesley could hardly remember the next hour after that.

5 October 1819, Tuesday

D—— is pleased with my progress with the Spenceans.
Mr. Thistlewood has been giving me more responsibilities,

*and last week assigned John Harrison and me to find a
secret meeting place for the Spencean inner circle. We
happened upon a clean hayloft over an unused stable on
Cato Street, almost directly across the street from the Horse
and Groom! The owner was more than glad to rent the
abandoned space, which I told him was for meetings of a
new chapter of the British and Foreign Bible Society. Very
clever of me, I thought.*

*Mr. Thistlewood praised our find, and today called me
his "boon companion." He says I will be integral to the
inner circle's future plans.*

*D—— was a bit put out, now that she realizes she
can't be present for the same meetings I will be attending.*

Promised I will repeat to her every word that's uttered.

*She said she'll have to be satisfied with it. She wants me
to influence Thistlewood to act against the House of
Commons. Wants her father to be punished somehow.*

I don't see how it can be done, but I will do my best.

*Found a mouse nesting under the cutting table.
Drowned it in a bucket, but forgot to empty it before
B—— found it. Ha! I keep reliving her horror in my
mind. Very gratifying.*

*Have not had a visit from Mr. Ashby lately. May have
to seek him out.*

*November 1819
Brighton*

Progress on the Pavilion was moving along rapidly. However, no
matter what stage construction was in, there always had to be sections of palace in good working order so that the Prince Regent
could entertain at a moment's notice. So, if on a whim the prince
desired a twenty-course meal with fifty of his closest friends, it was
expected that his new French chef would have the cooking facili-
ties to do so and that a dining room would be elegantly serviced
and ready.

If the prince wished to stroll about a perfumed and pastoral-set garden, it must be available.

If he wished to bring Lady Conyngham for a visit, why, flawlessly appointed rooms must be prepared.

As Belle witnessed the extraordinary lengths to which workers and servants went to satisfy these requirements, she realized that part of a monarch's privilege was to have his world set perfectly around him.

How did a king or prince contend with a world that, as she well knew, could change in an instant?

❧ 10 ❧

Lady Conyngham has completely gained the summit of her ambition, and has all the honors paid her of the Royal Mistress . . . to be anyone's mistress is a miserable lot. To be a royal man's mistress worse still, for how seldom is a Prince constant!

—From the diary of novelist Lady Charlotte Bury, 1775–1861

January 30, 1820
Carlton House, London

"I insist that the Lady Conyngham have a place of precedence, of course. And I must have new robes, as well. I'll provide you with an entire list of my requirements in due course, but I expect events to progress quickly. Most quickly." George waved his hands in emphasis.

Lord Liverpool cleared his throat. "Your Highness, er, Your Majesty, the late king just passed on yesterday. It might be wise to see his funeral to completion before initiating your own coronation."

"Lord Liverpool, need I remind you, of all people, of the people's great desire to have a smooth and happy transition between monarchs? The people will be very anxious to see me crowned, and I don't intend to disappoint them."

Liverpool gritted his teeth. Lord, the man was insufferable as regent. Now he was king and had already added another foot to his stature in his own mind. What came after insufferable?

"Yes, Your Majesty."

"Now, where was I? Oh yes, I've always admired Queen Elizabeth's coronation activities. A weak woman, but she knew how to impress the masses. Have poets, musicians, and actors posted along my coronation route, each delivering odes and prayers to my forthcoming glorious reign. I'll keep a purse of coins on me and distribute them to each of the performers."

Liverpool resisted the urge to roll his eyes. He tried again. "Majesty, I just caution you that it may be impossible to pull together a coronation so quickly."

"Nonsense. Elizabeth's men did it in two months. You can do the same. Oh, and another thing: I do not want that harpy in Italy at my coronation under any circumstances. I do not intend to allow her to be crowned."

"But sir, she is your wife, and therefore legitimately the queen."

"She has no legitimacy! And she wouldn't still be my wife if Parliament was of any use or assistance to me whatsoever."

"Yes, Your Majesty."

"Now that I am king, perhaps you can see your way to ridding me of my treacherous, boorish, ill-behaved wife. Bless me, such talk makes me ill." The new king patted his face with a handkerchief, his favorite accoutrement. "Please send Lady Conyngham in on your way out."

Liverpool bowed and exited, signaling to a servant outside the door to send in the king's new mistress.

Lady Elizabeth, the Marchioness of Conyngham, bounced up at her summons to meet with the new king. She was as voluptuous and greedy as Lady Hertford, but twice as beautiful and not nearly as cantankerous.

It had taken the forty-eight-year-old Lady Elizabeth more than a dozen years to supplant Lady Hertford. At least her husband, the Marquess of Conyngham, was willfully blind to her ambitions; else it would have taken her longer.

She supposed that she had an accommodating husband in common with Lady Hertford, too. But she would never make that lady's mistakes. Poor Lady Hertford, she simply wasn't experienced enough in managing men to maintain the Prince Regent in her thrall long enough to see him become king.

But Lady Elizabeth intended to hold on to the new king until one of them was laid in a coffin.

"Your Majesty!" she exclaimed as she was permitted entrance to the Circular Room. She swept into a low curtsy at his feet. She had a flash of inspiration, and dropped to the ground nearly prostrate at his feet, kissing the tops of his beribboned shoes.

"My dear one, please, you know you are my dearest friend and do not need to resort to such displays of reverence."

"But sir, you are my king now. Whatever adoration I had for you before, and you know how considerable it was, has been swept away, to be replaced with indescribable esteem for your new and magnificent person. I can hardly be held accountable for my actions."

"Quite so, my sweetest heart, quite so. You do bring me great comfort during these trying times. I suppose you saw Liverpool on his way out? He still won't do anything to rid me of Caroline. Was ever a prince, nay, a king, more harassed than I?"

"Never, Your Majesty," she replied in her most soothing voice.

He smiled. "You bring me great comfort, Lady Elizabeth. How I wish it were in my power to give you what I know would be your greatest wish, the holy union of matrimony with me. I can tell you nothing would give me more pleasure. But as long as Parliament stalls and refuses to charge Caroline with anything . . ."

Now the king was just toying with her. Not only was her own marriage an impediment, but if the king were actually able to obtain a divorce and remarry, it would most certainly be to a princess.

For Lady Conyngham, mistress was the highest title she could hope for, and she was pleased enough with it.

The king was ready to move on to other subjects. "I believe I am tired of Carlton House. Besides, it's an inadequate palace for my new, glorious monarchy, don't you think? Perhaps St. James's Place would be more fitting? What do you think, Lady Elizabeth?"

Actually, neither would do. She had a better idea, but she pretended to consider. "Your Majesty is too grand for merely St. James's. Why not Buckingham House?"

"Never! That was my father's favorite residence. Besides, it's entirely too small."

"Does it have to be?"

"What do you mean?"

"Isn't it only fitting that Your Majesty renovate Buckingham House, first to make it a residence fit for your splendor, but also to eradicate the—shall we say—odor of its previous residents?"

"Ah!" Light dawned in his eyes. "Lady Elizabeth, this is one of your more brilliant ideas, and you do tend to radiate them with regularity. You are a lovely adornment and always know how to bring me to a jolly mood."

"And does this lovely adornment deserve a reward for her imagination and intelligence?"

"Sweetheart, you've read my mind." He pulled her to him for a sweaty kiss.

Not exactly the reward she had in mind, but Lady Elizabeth was nothing if not patient. After all, she'd enjoyed liaisons with Lord Ponsonby, the handsomest man in England two decades ago, as well as with Nicholas, heir to the Russian throne, when he passed through London a few years ago.

In both cases, she merely had to bide her time. As she had done while waiting to catch George's eye. And when Buckingham House was transformed into a palatial residence, she intended to have her own suite of rooms there. Fully furnished at the king's expense, of course.

Hmm, perhaps she was becoming more and more like a spider who sits patiently, waiting for an unsuspecting fly to bumble its way into her web. A distasteful thought, wasn't it?

She shrugged and returned her focus to the king's pleasure, wondering if the job of king's mistress would be a more difficult one than that of the prince's mistress.

The poor old king was not even buried yet, and aristocrats from all over London were sending servants to Belle, summoning her to their townhomes for redecoration advice in anticipation of their own personal balls to be held in anticipation of the coronation.

Belle just hoped the ceremony would be held off long enough for her to complete all of her new projects. Her aristocratic clients were always demanding, but with an impending coronation they were shrill and peevish.

Wesley continued to be irritable, as well, but he was making more effort around the shop. He'd recently found a new supplier of Indian calico. The dyeing work was exquisitely vivid, and for an instant Belle imagined it covering one of Put's chairs. She dismissed the thought and instead complimented her brother for his find. He shrugged off her praise, but she caught a satisfied smile on his face as he turned away from her.

His expression reminded her of the old Wesley, the Yorkshire boy who came home at the end of a summer's day, whistling and jangling his winnings inside his pocket. But that boy was long since gone, wasn't he?

Tuesday, February 1, 1820

Arthur Thistlewood was in rare form this evening.

The hayloft across from the Horse and Groom had been furnished with some spare pieces from the tavern, mostly rickety benches and a couple of tables, hastily brought up via its ladder entry from the stable below.

Thistlewood addressed his inner circle, which consisted of Wesley and ten other men: his fellow hideout seeker, John Harrison; George Edwards; John Brunt; James Ings; Richard Tidd; William Davidson; Charles Cooper; Richard Bradburn; James Wilson; and John Strange.

They were tightly packed inside the unheated, twelve-by-sixteen-foot room. Two grimy windows tried vainly to filter in light, but Mr. Thistlewood insisted that they not be cleaned, so as to maintain the hayloft's illusion of abandonment. The beamed ceiling was low, and the unplastered walls emitted an odor reminiscent of the horses and hay bales that would have once shared this space. Two rectangular holes in the floor along one wall, originally meant for tossing hay down to the stable, occupied more floor space and made the room seem even smaller.

No one cared, though, for every man leaned forward to capture and digest Thistlewood's impassioned speech. The only break in the tension was from William Davidson, a Jamaican mulatto with an interesting, lilting accent, whose passion for cigars could not be quelled even during a meeting such as this. Smoke enveloped Davidson and Richard Tidd, sitting next to him.

Wesley's own throat ached to share his pipe with Darcey. He hoped she wasn't using up the last of his opium across the street while he was in this meeting. 'Twould be dreadfully unfair of her, since his presence here was mostly at her urging.

Mostly.

There was a sense of self-importance he felt to be sitting among these men who might one day be very significant in His Majesty's government. Maybe Wesley could one day have a prominent position. Then Belle would finally understand that he was worth more than being just her fetch-and-carry boy.

Wesley didn't know any of the other men particularly well, since he spent most of his spare time with Darcey, but he was acquainted enough with them to know that they passionately believed in Mr. Thistlewood's vision of a radically changed government.

And tonight, Thistlewood was roused to a feverish pitch, even as plumes of cold vapor swirled from his mouth as he spoke.

"And so, friends, fellow patriots, we've been presented with a glorious opportunity. One that might almost be construed as a sign from the Almighty Himself. Fortunately for those of us assembled here, we do not need to wait for firm signs of divine approval, for you have me to interpret recent events as the smiling of the heavens upon our righteous efforts."

The man knew how to grab attention. Even Davidson threw his cigar to the floor and stamped on it, so as not to be distracted from a single word Thistlewood uttered.

"You know the old king held on an unconscionably long time, living in his addled state locked up in Windsor. We've had the so-called rule of a regent, but the Punch and Judy man in St. James's Park has more concern for Britain's subjects than the new king does. And he doesn't eat nearly as much.

"I am now convinced that the old King George lived so long to provide me with the time necessary to gather you, my closest associates, into my confidence, so that when the time was right, we could strike against the government. His death three days ago was the sign I needed. For now we have the moment. A moment of upheaval, a moment of chaos, a moment created for revolutionary change!" Thistlewood pounded his fist against his breast, then stopped to close his eyes and breathe deeply.

Wesley knew Darcey would be on the verge of a swoon if she were here. He was glad she wasn't.

"But the Regency is gone. Instead, that bloated ignoramus now claims himself to be our king. As though men of our disposition and good sense will tolerate the rule of such a totty-headed squab, who cannot even manage to find a mistress who is an actual improvement upon his wife!"

The men clapped their approval.

"The old king was a staunch Tory, the new king a Whig. The old king a devoted family man, the new one an adulterer. The old king was abstemious, the new king a drunken glutton. The people will be nervous now, you mark my words. It is one thing for Prinny to be the regent; it's another thing entirely for him to wear the crown.

"We are now at the precipice, fellows. Will we leap forward, or will we cower backward like ninnies? Others may say we are trying to milk the pigeon, but I say our goal *is* possible, and that we will be the catalyst for a brighter, better England!"

Now the men roared in agreement.

And as he always did to control his audiences, Thistlewood dropped his voice to nearly a whisper. "So we are in agreement that the uncertainty created by this change in the monarchy provides the right timing for rebellion. All that remains is to decide exactly what to do, eh?"

James Ings spoke in enthusiasm. "I was once a butcher, until everything dried up during the year without a summer. I'll slaughter all of them in Parliament right proper and put their heads on exhibition at Westminster Bridge!"

Cheers went up all around.

Thistlewood laughed. "So we have one suggestion to send Mr.

Ings in with his butcher's knife to make steaks of the members. But may I present you with another plan?" Thistlewood motioned to George Edwards to join him at the front of the room.

Edwards, a man of average height and looks, unfolded a newspaper and read from it.

ANNOUNCEMENT

On 23rd February
Seven o'clock in the evening
Cabinet dinner to be held at the home of
Lord Harrowby, Lord President of the Council.
Lord Liverpool to speak on issues of great importance.
All members from both houses invited to attend.
39 Grosvenor Square, London
Members will enjoy fine libations
and cigars following dinner.

Edwards looked back to Thistlewood, who clapped him on the shoulder as he took the newspaper from him. "My thanks to Mr. Edwards, my boon companion, who uncovered this advertisement in the *New Times.*"

Wesley frowned. How many boon companions did Mr. Thistlewood claim?

"I suggest that this dinner provides the perfect opportunity to overthrow the entire government at once, because the fools will all be sitting together, stuffing themselves into fatted calves, and we will simply go in, and, as Mr. Ings suggests, slaughter them."

"And put their heads on pikes on Westminster Bridge," Ings reminded him.

"As you wish, sir. Shall we make you Chief Dispenser of Justice, then?"

"I'd wear the title proudly, I would." Ings sat back, smug.

Wesley spoke up. "What then, Mr. Thistlewood? After Parliament has been destroyed."

Their leader smiled warmly. "Ah, excellent question, Mr. Stirling. From there we will set up a Committee of Public Safety to oversee the revolution that we initiate. From my experience, I believe we may have bloodshed in the streets for about six months. After that, we will form a provisional government. Mr. Edwards has suggested that Mansion House is a likely candidate for housing our government, since the Lord Mayor will no longer have use for it. We'll hold the king prisoner until we decide if he can be of any use."

So Mr. Thistlewood had already worked out this entire plan with George Edwards, and was just presenting this to them to gather support for it. Part of Wesley was irritated. This was how Belle made decisions, completely without him.

Yet, on the other hand, if all went well and his own goals were achieved, what cause for complaint did he have? For now Wesley understood that, through revolution, more could be accomplished than the mere overthrow of the government and the establishment of an important position for him. For surely in a revolutionary melee the loss of any member of the House of Commons would be blamed on the revolution.

Wesley looked across the room. Or, more likely, the melee would be blamed on someone like an ex-butcher placing heads on pikes. He brought his focus back to Thistlewood.

"So all we lack are details about the cabinet meeting itself. We would be well armed to know if they are planning more tyranny for England's subjects. We also need a way to get past Harrowby's servants in advance, so we can figure out the exact lay of his home. Any suggestions?"

Wesley wondered if Thistlewood really sought ideas or if he already had that worked out, as well.

Ings piped up again. "I say we storm his home like it's a castle defended by lily-livered Frenchmen!"

"Ha! An excellent idea if they were indeed Frogs. But what we need here is the element of stealth, not brute force."

"I suggest even more," Edwards said. "While some of us gain entry to Lord Harrowby's home, it would be fitting for others to set fire to nearby houses, and throw hand-grenades into passing carriages to divert attention."

"My friend," Thistlewood said. "You think like a true revolutionary. But I fear such activities are better left for the critical day of overthrow."

William Davidson, the Jamaican whose burnished skin reminded Wesley of cacao beans, stood and snapped his fingers to draw attention to himself.

"Mr. Thistlewood," he said in his singsong voice. "May I propose myself as your instrument of stealth? I worked at Lord Harrowby's former residence some years ago, and am quite sure he still has staff of my acquaintance. I can find out what you need to know."

All focus was now on Davidson, including that of Thistlewood, who motioned for Edwards to sit down so that Davidson could step forward. Davidson received the same shoulder-slapping, boon companion treatment.

"Mr. Davidson, 'tis another sign of heavenly favor that you have joined our group. For how else could we have been blessed by a former servant of the Harrowby household? Indeed, I charge you with getting the exact details of the cabinet meeting—what they will be discussing, how many meal courses, even what kind of port they'll be serving. We'll also need to know what hours Harrowby keeps at Grosvenor Square. Most important, we need a layout of the home, and you should find out if his dining hall is large enough for the event or if he will move it elsewhere. Can you do all of this?"

"Indeed, sir, I can."

"And you will report to us again on the morrow?"

"Yes, sir."

Thistlewood brandished the paper above his head. "And so you see, my fellow compatriots, the English government is too stupid by far for the likes of the Spenceans!"

Everyone in the room was murmuring with excitement. Revolution was coming to England.

It was nearly midnight before Wesley slid down the ladder and back to the Horse and Groom. Bottles of vinegary wine were produced to celebrate their upcoming victory, with Thistlewood promising to open the well-stocked cellars of every palace in

Britain once the goals of the revolution were accomplished. Wesley drank his fill, then decided he'd been gone long enough that Darcey might now be in a fit of pique.

If she hadn't already left the tavern.

But she was waiting for him in their room, eyes blazing both in anger over his long absence and in fervor over what had happened. He took great pleasure in drawing out the story as long as he could, until she was finally begging him for details.

When Wesley concluded the details of the plan, Darcey got up and sat on the bed, lost in thought.

"A Committee of Public Safety, you say? Exquisite. My father is so bound up in etiquette and protocol that he'll have no idea how to function inside a revolutionary form of government. It will send him completely off his beetlehead. Although"—she tilted her head at Wesley—"I suppose by that point he may no longer be in existence to have a nervous attack. My sister and I will be completely free of him."

"And you won't have to marry any of Mr. White's selections."

Darcey brought her knees up and hugged them, still facing Wesley. "No, I won't. I'll be as free as a falcon, soaring through the clouds and snatching whatever I want on the ground."

"And what do you want on the ground?"

"I'm sure there will still be a tasty morsel or two for me to capture in my talons." She reached out and cupped Wesley's neck. "But first we have to be sure this will work. When did you say the dinner is?"

"The twenty-third of this month. Three weeks away."

She nodded. "I'm going to go home and pack a traveling case, steal some money from my father's desk, then come back to the Horse and Groom. It doesn't matter now if he knows I've run off, for he'll have more serious matters to consider in a short time. Will you live here with me? Until everything is in motion and we can move into rooms at Mansion House together?"

"I'll need to make excuses to Belle. It may take me a week to sort things out, but I'll join you here."

Wesley ignored the tiny nugget of warning deep inside himself. That inner voice sounded too much like Belle.

Wednesday, February 2, 1820

Belle put down the newspaper to greet her first customer of the day, a familiar face who frequented the shop regularly. Belle addressed the lady's chattering with absentminded nods as she continued to think over what she'd read.

The Prince Regent had just become King George IV two days ago, but was already issuing orders that British ambassadors on the Continent use their diplomatic skills to ensure that monarchs in foreign courts follow his lead in recognizing Caroline only as a queen consort. Not queen. He was also demanding that the church omit her name from the liturgy.

The article went on to say that the new king was gathering incriminating evidence against his wife, evidence of gross misconduct and adultery while living abroad. The king intended to produce this evidence for Parliament soon. But Lord Liverpool was already hinting that he was disinclined to bring any action against the queen, no matter what evidence the king brought.

Belle cut a length of striped silk taffeta and handed it to her smiling customer, who asked for the purchase to be placed on her husband's account. The doorbell tinkled behind the woman as she left, and Belle returned to the newspaper and her thoughts.

How could the king, such a philanderer and cruel husband, be obsessed with punishing Caroline? True, the new queen's manners were reputed to be ghastly, and her personal hygiene only marginally better than that of a corpse. But she'd been sincere in her desire to be a good wife, and had provided the king with a daughter. Didn't that count for something?

And if, after years of abuse heaped upon Caroline by her self-centered husband, she'd fled to Italy to find happiness, why was the king so consumed with this notion of bringing her to justice? Wasn't marriage to him penalty enough?

And how would the prime minister's refusal to examine the evidence affect the relationship between him and the king? And affect the ruling of the country?

Mr. Nash said she was not to ever gossip about the king, but a private thought was acceptable, wasn't it? She sighed. Ah, well, she wasn't in a position of influence over the king, was she?

Mind your business, she admonished herself. *The king pays handsomely for your cloth.*

She shook her head to clear it of her tangled views. After a review of what bolts had fewer than ten yards on them so she could prepare her next order, Belle stepped outside to check the weather. It looked like it might rain soon. Or snow. She shivered and stepped back into the warmth of the shop. For the thousandth time, she wondered where Wesley was today. She never heard him come home to their lodgings last night.

She glanced at the watch pinned to her dress. Eleven o'clock. Where was he off to all the time these days?

Every time she thought Wesley was finally coming round, he began his disappearing tricks. Belle needed to make a trip to Brighton to see what rooms were to be finished in time for the coronation and what fabrics and trims she would need to buy for those rooms. Wesley's unreliability was making it impossible for her to leave the shop.

Honestly, maybe she should just shut the shop down and move to Brighton. She could serve the new king much more easily there, and so many of London's aristocrats were buying seaside homes in Brighton that she could have business there for decades.

She wouldn't have to run into Putnam Boyce anymore, either. Belle knew she needed to place an order with him for an ebonized writing box to go in Lady Logan's bedchamber. Lady Logan had placed her old one atop her bed one day, and her Italian greyhound had wet on it as well as her bed pillows. The dog was given a biscuit afterwards, while Belle received a summons for a tongue-lashing, with Lady Logan castigating her for not having the pillows made in a fabric unattractive to canines.

But Belle hadn't had the heart to face Put since gawking at him in the middle of the street. Soon, though, Lady Logan would be tapping a foot in impatience. Well, perhaps if Wesley finally showed up this afternoon she'd make a trip over to Shoreditch.

The door's bell tinkled as another customer entered the shop. A young woman, probably younger than Belle, with the most beautiful, almond-shaped eyes she'd ever seen. The woman entered the shop as if she owned it, examining the shop's layout as if determining whether to insist it be changed.

Belle went to the woman and folded her hands in front of her. "Good afternoon, madam. May I help you?"

"Perhaps, perhaps. You are, I assume, the proprietress here?"

"I am. I'm Annabelle Stirling, madam. Are you looking for material for a gown or for interior décor?"

"Hmm, I'm not quite sure yet." The woman walked along the wall opposite the shop's counter, fingering the hanging cloth from almost every single bolt in the store, and running her hand through baskets of buttons, thimbles, and threads.

"Madam, are you sure I cannot assist you in finding something?"

Those eyes blinked unhurriedly at her. She was as graceful as a leopard watching its prey from high atop a branch, deciding whether the prey was worth the effort of climbing down to capture it.

Belle reflexively stepped away from her customer, who had returned to examining another bolt of cloth. "That's a lovely dotted muslin we just got in. It would make a fine day dress."

"Yes, it probably would. Tell me, are you the sole owner of this shop?"

What? What difference did that make to a fabric purchase?

"Yes. I come from a long line of drapers, madam, originally from Yorkshire, which is, as I'm sure you know, the center of the cloth industry."

"Actually, I didn't know. Interesting. I come from a long line of important officeholders. So you say you run this shop entirely alone?"

Belle didn't much care for this woman, who seemed determined to taunt her for some unknown reason.

"This shop belongs to me alone. Now, if you've a specific need, I'm happy to help you, Miss—?"

"White . . . Whitecastle. I'm Miss Whitecastle."

"Very well, Miss Whitecastle, if you've no actual business here . . ."

"Oh, but we do have business together, Miss Stirling. Perhaps

we'll resume it another day. For now, I just wanted to meet you."
And on that, Miss Whitecastle strode out of the shop. Belle wouldn't
have been surprised to learn that the woman had a tail swishing
underneath her dress.

What in heaven's name was that all about?

Sometimes the oddest people came through the door.

Belle brushed all thoughts of Miss Whitecastle from her mind as
she steeled herself for a visit to Put. Drat Wesley and his long absences.

Put was conferring with a couple in his outer room when she arrived with the old and rank-smelling writing box. She placed it on
a chair seat and tried to look as interested as she could in a grand-
father clock near the door while he finished with them. Other than
their conversation, the shop was quiet, so his workers must be out
somewhere.

After an interminable length of time spent avoiding Put's eyes,
she was relieved when the couple left.

When she turned to face him, she saw that he was at his most
comfortable, in his worn, leather apron over a white shirt and
threadbare trousers. His hose needed darning, his shoes were
scuffed, and, as usual, there was a sprinkling of wood shavings on
his forearms. The man was noticeably happier in his trade garments.

It was baffling, though. How could she, a *draper*, actually find
appeal in someone so raggedly dressed?

"Miss Stirling," Put said with a bow. "It has been long since I've
had the pleasure of your acquaintance, since that day in Oxford
Street—"

"Yes, I remember the day well."

"I wanted to introduce you to my—"

Fiancée? Lover? Sweetheart? Whatever she was, Belle needed
no introductions.

"Not to worry, Mr. Boyce. Your relationships don't concern me
anymore."

"Anymore? What does that mean? Did they once concern you?
And anyway, Frances is—"

"As I said, I can't be concerned. I need to place an urgent order for a writing box to replace this one." She picked it up from the chair and showed it to him.

He took it and sniffed at it. "What the hell happened to it?"

"An impudent, mannerless dog got the box, as well as some pillows I had made, into his sights, and the result was, well, this."

Put shook his head. "The wood has been left to sit too long in urine. I might have been able to save it if your customer brought it to you sooner."

"Yes. Well. Anyway, I recommended to her that we do something ebonized instead of in oak, since the new king has made ebony all the rage. She agreed that that was the thing to do."

"Same dimensions?"

"Yes."

"Any inlay? Marquetry? Secret compartments?"

"No, just what she had before."

"As you wish, Miss Stirling." He folded down the hinge of his work desk so that the surface area was flat, then put the writing box down on the center of it.

"How does your own business fare?" he asked.

"Well, thank you."

"Can I interest you in some other pieces? Another gift for your brother, perhaps? A mirror for your dresser top? I just received some Brazilian cherrywood I can show you—"

"No, nothing else." She didn't dare step into his lumberyard with him. Too dangerous.

"Very well. I guess you're too busy to spend time with a friend." Put took her arm and slowly walked her to the door. "I can deliver the new writing box myself in two weeks' time—"

"That won't be necessary."

"You'll pick it up personally?"

"No, have Merrick bring it round. That would be most convenient."

They had reached the door of the shop. Belle put her hand out to the knob, but Put reached over and threw the latch, trapping her between him and the door.

She wasn't sure she liked being this close to him.

"Miss Stirling, what is bedeviling you? If I recall correctly, I am the injured party between the two of us. So if I'm willing to make amends, on what grounds will you not?"

She laughed weakly. "I'd no idea we were scheduled to make apologies today. I assumed this to be a business transaction."

"Stop it," he growled. "No more foolishness."

He was pressed up against her, his head slightly turned so that his good eye plumbed the depths of both her own eyes.

"I don't know who you think that woman was, but let me assure you, she's not who you think she is. If you'd just let me explain—"

"That's just it! You can't explain. Because the explanation doesn't matter. She could be your wife or your sister or a complete figment of my imagination, but it's immaterial because I can't allow myself to destroy one more relationship, nor to let anyone take control of my life. I've already made such a wreck of things with my brother, and I don't even know how. He's so distant and cross and incensed over I know not what, and I'm—"

Put bent down, his lips almost touching her ear. "I'm not your brother, Belle." He brought both hands up to cradle her face, and gently bumped his forehead against hers.

She held her breath. What would he say next?

He said nothing.

Instead, he brought his mouth down to hers, startling her with its warmth and deep affection. Put didn't force her to accept him, he merely enveloped her in his heady and intoxicating essence.

Good Lord, was this what it felt like to fall in love with someone? To have this tingling sensation of both floating away yet melding to the man who held you?

She responded eagerly to him, both lost in the feelings he was generating in her and irritated that she was losing control over her emotions.

She tried to ignore the knot of annoyance. But when Put finally broke the kiss and whispered her name, the irritation won out. She wrenched away from him, fumbling for the lock behind her. She knew her eyes were wet, but she couldn't help it, and cursed herself for her weakness.

"I cannot," she whispered, finally yanking open the door and fleeing back into the chilly streets toward the safety of her shop.

How had she so quickly succumbed to Put that *he* had been the one to end their kiss? How wanton would she have become had she stayed there?

He didn't follow her, and she never heard him say, almost to himself, "How can a man be rejected for spending time with his cousin?"

She was also unaware of the opportunity Put would soon receive to place himself in her path again.

Wesley waited expectantly in the hayloft for Mr. Thistlewood to arrive. Gads, but it was cold up here, although the others didn't seem to notice as they joked and conversed with each other in the dark room. A lone candle burned on the table at the front of the room, giving the gathering a mysterious atmosphere.

Wesley sat alone, quietly, to think. He'd just left Darcey in their room, where she'd relayed her visit to Belle to him.

So Belle hadn't even mentioned that he was even a worker in her shop, much less an integral component to its success.

Darcey was more excitable than Wesley had ever seen her before. Her eyes were unnaturally bright, with beads of sweat gathered above her lip and eyebrows, making him wonder if she'd been rummaging in his box without him. In this agitated state, she told Wesley that this was the proof he needed that Belle would never, ever share control of the draper shop with him, and that Belle, like her father, needed to be taught a lesson about oppressing those closest to them.

"Tonight, my love, you have to make your grandest gesture yet. Mr. Thistlewood already has the outline of a plan. Make yourself as useful as you can in it so you will not only be sure that my father is taken care of, but so that you can obtain a high place for yourself."

Wesley had argued weakly his concern about the plan being discovered and what might happen if he and the others were caught, but Darcey dismissed him airily.

"Once the Revolution started in France, there was no going back. The king and his ministers were powerless to stop it."

"Yes, but Robespierre ended up under the same blade as the king."

"Oh, Mr. Thistlewood is much smarter than Robespierre. He has learned from whatever mistakes the French made, so that the revolution here will be much more successful. And you, my love, will rise to the top of the milk pitcher."

And so, armed with Darcey's confidence and kisses, as well as the promise of a new intoxicant she wanted them to try together when he returned later, Wesley waited for Thistlewood to start the meeting so he could find a point in which to assert himself.

Ah, finally Mr. Thistlewood's head appeared in the ladder shaft. He emerged into the hayloft, drawing himself up with grace despite his imposing size. He headed to one end of the room and lifted his hands in a gesture for everyone to pay attention to him.

The room was instantly quiet.

"Friends, thank you for returning again tonight. We have so little time that I'll get right to the heart of things. Mr. Davidson, what have you to report to us?"

William Davidson stood, his dark skin nearly invisible in the murky shadows of the room. Thistlewood lit two more candles, increasing the visibility in the room.

"I was able to speak to one of Lord Harrowby's coachmen. He said the earl isn't even in London at the moment, but is off to the country visiting friends. There is no cabinet dinner planned."

Murmurs of disbelief filled the air.

George Edwards jumped up. "What do you mean? The newspaper advertisement was very plain that Lord Harrowby was planning a cabinet dinner on the twenty-third. The coachman must be mistaken." He looked to Thistlewood for affirmation.

Thistlewood pursed his lips and nodded thoughtfully. "I tend to think you're right, Edwards. Such an advertisement couldn't have been placed by mistake, after all. Either the servant is lying, or is confused about his master's whereabouts."

Davidson shook his head. "I don't think he is lying, nor is he confused, sir. Benks and I were close friends while I was at Grosvenor Square. There's no reason for him to lie to me. And surely the earl's coachman knows where his master—"

Edwards interrupted again. "If Lord Harrowby is in the country, why isn't his coachman with him? How does the earl plan to return to London?"

Davidson turned to Edwards as though addressing a child. "I'm sure the earl has more than one carriage, and certainly more than one attendant for each carriage."

"Why, you insulting little—"

"Friends, please, let's maintain our temperate constitutions," Mr. Thistlewood said. "Save your heated passions for the moment you hold knives and pistols in your hands, eh? Now, I think the only way to resolve this is to decide who holds more credence, one of the earl's servants, or the earl himself, who placed announcement of the dinner in the newspaper. I suggest it is the latter. Therefore, Mr. Davidson, we will proceed with our assassinations as planned. However, you are to be commended for your excellent work thus far."

"But now we don't know where the dinner will be held inside his home," Davidson said. "How will we figure that out, if no one on the earl's staff knows about the dinner?"

Thistlewood smiled. "Let's not assume too much. I think what we need is an excuse to get into Lord Harrowby's home ourselves and examine it. Suggestions?"

James Ings piped up. "We'll break in through the servants' quarters in the middle of the night and club any of them over the head that gets in our way."

"Fool!" Davidson hissed. "The servant quarters are in the attic. Are you going to make your approach by balloon?"

"I must agree," Thistlewood said. "A late-night entry attempt is not only risky, but completely unworthy of men who call themselves Spencean Philanthropists. We need to be clever, yet bold."

John Harrison spoke, probably for the first time in one of these meetings. "I know what to do. Let's send the good earl a gift, one of great value that he'd be happy to receive. A couple of us will serve as the deliverymen, and can inspect the place freely if we manage it during a time that most of the servants are out. Davidson can't go, for obvious reasons."

Thistlewood clapped slowly and bent his head in acknowledgment to Harrison. "Excellent idea and good reasoning, Mr. Harrison."

"Hear, hear," the other men called out.

Blast it all, why hadn't Wesley thought of such a good idea? *I should volunteer to deliver the gift.*

"And so, what remains to decide is exactly what this gift should be."

William Davidson stood again. "If memory serves me, the earl and his countess are celebrating their twenty-fifth wedding anniversary soon. Perhaps an anniversary gift from his old servant who still esteems him?"

They shouted suggestions as though whoever was loudest would win. "A diamond bracelet for his wife!" "A fancy dog!" "A rare book!"

Thistlewood shook his head at all of these suggestions. He raised his hands again for more quiet. "Friends, all of these gifts are small tokens, and would be taken into the house by whatever servant answered the door, and we would promptly see that door closed in our faces. It must be heavy, or bulky, or both, to allow us access to the home."

"How about a piece of furniture? Bet the earl would like an elegant desk that he can sit behind so he looks important."

Wesley turned at the voice coming from behind him. It was Richard Tidd, a balding man with heavy jowls and thin lips, giving him a simian appearance.

Now Thistlewood granted Tidd a beaming smile. Being shown favor by Thistlewood felt as though you were one of Christ's apostles and had just figured out the meaning of a parable while sitting at His feet.

Wesley wanted that smile. He cast about in his mind for something to contribute. The conspirators would gain access to Lord Harrowby's, offering the gift of a desk as a way to access the inner reaches of the home. And once they did—oh, of course!

Here was Wesley's opportunity to be as useful as Davidson, Edwards, and Tidd.

"I know a master cabinetmaker, Mr. Thistlewood."

Thistlewood's eye was upon him. "Do you now? And is he discreet?"

Was Putnam Boyce discreet? Wesley hardly knew the man.

"He is, sir. And he makes aristocratic-quality pieces. He'll make one for us without asking questions, long as we apply enough guineas to his palm."

Thistlewood nodded. "Well done, Mr. Stirling. Go see your cabinetmaker, and offer him whatever it takes to have the desk done in the next two weeks."

Wesley breathed deeply in self-satisfaction. He'd pleased his savior.

The meeting broke up soon thereafter, and Wesley hurried back to the Horse and Groom, where Darcey waited for his news. He told her everything in great detail, except the part where Thistlewood cornered him at the end, to ask if he could meet with him privately elsewhere to discuss further details. It made Wesley realize that he wasn't quite ready to give up his room at the lodging house to move in with Darcey.

In celebration of his accomplishment, Darcey brought out a bottle full of a dark liquid. She jiggled it back and forth. "Laudanum. Have you tried it before? It's an opium tincture; this one is blended with brandy."

He hadn't. But he was more than willing to rejoice over his success in whatever way Darcey wanted. And as his mind mellowed from the potent substance, he realized it was quite easy to ignore Darcey's increasing power over him, and to believe that it was his own decision to embroil himself in a massive conspiracy.

Thursday, February 3, 1820

Put was pleased with his new commission, especially since it came from Belle's brother. The boy was a bit cagey and probably a ne'er-do-well in Put's opinion, but Belle was blind to Wesley's faults, and so for her sake he would also be blind to them.

Besides, the boy seemed earnest in his desire to make a surprise gift for Belle, in the form of a secretary. Although Put understood the secrecy that had to be involved, he didn't understand the immediacy of the project. Two weeks was hardly enough time to create the piece.

But Wesley was eager for the desk and offered entirely too much money for it. Put suggested about half the price for it. They discussed specifications, shook hands on it, and Wesley left the shop, whistling.

Which left Put to figure out how to produce the finest desk he could possibly imagine in a mere two weeks. He had to finalize the design, select wood from his seasoned stock, then cut, shape, glue, nail, and possibly veneer pieces together.

It was an impossible task. The only way he could complete it in time would be to dig out some old desk carcasses from the storeroom and see which one might serve as a good foundation for what he had in mind.

He would get it accomplished for Belle. Maybe she would actually listen to him for five minutes when he delivered it.

Belle returned to her lodgings, exhausted from a busy day followed by a trip to St. Bart's to drop off some lengths of Welsh wool flannel. Once again, Wesley had disappeared from the shop early, and she'd had to manage completely on her own the entire afternoon.

It was time to talk to her brother again. How could he expect to have a greater role in the shop if he was going to randomly evaporate without warning?

She heard his voice from behind his door and went to it, raising her hand to knock on it. She stopped when she realized that there was a second masculine voice in the room. Their voices were low, and Belle could hardly distinguish one from the other. Snatches of their conversation floated through the door.

". . . is almost ready for delivery . . ."

"His wife will be none the wiser. . . ."

"Need to keep these lodgings . . . may need to hide here."

"Pains . . . penalties . . . for the king."

"Timing is right . . . prime minister . . ."

". . . be rid of the tyrannical wretch . . ."

". . . great reward for you, Mr. Stirling . . ."

Belle felt a knot forming in her stomach. Dear God, what were they talking about? What was Wesley involved in? She heard shuffling in the room, and scurried up the stairs to her own room, lest they open the door and find her eavesdropping on them.

She ran to her window overlooking the street to see who would emerge from their lodging house. It was a tall, hulking man whose long, dark sideburns hung low underneath the rim of his beaver hat.

As if he realized he was being watched, he paused and turned to look up at Belle's window. She stepped back, but not before seeing the hateful intensity of the man's gaze underneath his frown.

She shivered. What manner of men was Wesley associating with? And what were they plotting?

Furthermore, what did it mean about someone's wife being "none the wiser" and that the timing was now right? And exactly what sort of reward was Wesley being promised?

She sat back down and pressed her fingers to her forehead, rubbing her brow as though it would somehow inspire answers.

It sounded as though they were talking about the king's ongoing battle with the queen, and that Wesley was somehow engaged in it. Was he being paid to help gather evidence? Was that what was almost ready for delivery? But that was impossible. Surely she was just imagining things based on the scurrilous articles she was reading in the newspapers. Besides, how could Wesley have any connection with the House of Hanover, except through her?

She dropped her thumb to her lap as her heart thudded to a halt. *Am I responsible? Have I unwittingly given Wesley access to the king?*

It couldn't be. Wesley couldn't be *that* foolish.

But he'd been mysterious for months, and the king's vitriol against his wife had been going on even longer. Who knew what men of the gutter the king might be seeking out to gather evidence? And what men of the gutter Wesley was secretly associating with?

And if word reached the king that Wesley was her brother, then the king might think Wesley was a trusty conspirator.

She rubbed her eyes. She was being ridiculous.

Belle had a sudden urge to run to Put's shop, another outlandish impulse. As though the man would want to see her again after her last jumpy performance in front of him. If only she didn't have an overwhelming desire to flee to him when she was troubled.

Well, there was no help for it. She'd have to confront Wesley, lest he get himself in over his head. There might still be time to prevent him harming others. Or himself.

She went back downstairs and knocked on his door. He opened, and seemed confused to find Belle there.

"Oh, I thought you were—never mind. What do you need, Sister?" Wesley leaned inside the door frame, his arms crossed in front of him.

"Let me speak plainly to you," she began.

"Ha! Yes, please do. It's so rare that you speak your mind to me."

"May I come in?"

Wesley shrugged. "Depends what you want to say."

"Who was the man that just left here?"

"You mean Mr. This—why do you ask?"

"So that was your bosom friend, Mr. Thistlewood? He has the look of the devil about him. I heard you, Wesley. Talking. Or should I say conspiring?"

Her brother went rigid. "What did you hear?"

"Enough to know you're up to something dangerous and stupid. Something that you think will earn you great favor but will probably result in catastrophe."

Wesley grabbed her arm and roughly pulled her into his room, slamming the door shut behind her.

He held on to her arm and put his face close to hers. Through gritted teeth he said, "What did you hear?"

She pushed against him with her free arm and he released her. Enough was enough. She'd been patient with Wesley for years, but rough handling her like this was beyond the pale.

And before she could quite stop herself, Belle unleashed several years of anger on her brother.

"How dare you! You are the most arrogant, self-centered man, no, boy, I have ever encountered. One would think you were the spoiled, pampered pet of a rich mistress, as much as you strut about thinking that you're owed some special place and favor in society for no effort. Even with me you do it. You think you deserve ownership in the shop because you wink at the female customers and make daring suggestions with them. And when I don't consider that proof of maturity and responsibility, what do you do? Why, you take revenge on me by disappearing from the shop for hours at a time, to meet who knows what tramp or trollop.

"Is that supposed to impress me? Do you think as I stand here that I'm overcome with remorse at not making you an owner of the shop? Truly? Especially since I just overheard you discussing something that probably amounts to treachery at best, treason at worst.

"Tell me, Brother, what ingenious plan do you have for achieving the recognition that has so long eluded you? Are you helping to manufacture evidence for the king to use against the queen? Will you aid in seeing that poor woman dethroned?"

Wesley grew still. "What did you say?"

"I'm asking you if Mr. Thistlewood is an agent of the king's. Are you two conspiring to bring false evidence against Queen Caroline so that the king can divorce her?"

Wesley blinked as if he couldn't believe what he was hearing.

"Yes. Yes, that is what's happening. You've rooted us out, Belle."

Such imprudent people were always shocked when they were discovered in their foolhardy plans, Belle thought.

But Belle didn't like his tone. It was too . . . smug. And confident. Quite unlike his attitude just moments ago.

Hmmm.

"So what will you do now?" she asked.

"What do you mean, what will I do? Do you think your sniffing presence changes anything? We'll proceed as planned. After all, the king wants it, and what the king wants he shall have. Making it none of your concern whatsoever. In fact, I suspect His Majesty would be quite angry if he learned that you knew anything about this."

Yes, that was probably true. Belle felt as though she'd been pricked by a sharp pin, and all of the righteous, principled air was released from her body.

"And what shiny gift has he offered you, Wesley?"

Wesley slowly smiled. "You wouldn't believe me if I told you. Enough, now. Run off and tend to your own affairs, and don't worry about mine. Things will be concluded soon enough and you'll find that all's well."

He pushed her out of his room like an errant child, and once again she was facing his locked door.

Once again she couldn't begin to fathom her brother's behavior.

And once again she fought the desire to run to Put. What could he do about it, anyway?

❧ 11 ❧

To feel much for others and little for ourselves; to restrain our selfishness and exercise our benevolent affections, constitute the perfection of human nature.

—Adam Smith, Scottish moral philosophizer, 1723–1790

Friday, February 18, 1820
London

Put brushed long strokes of mordant—a combination of alum and water—to the drawers of the secretary-style desk he was building for Belle. The mordant saturated the wood and prepared it for accepting color. Sitting nearby was his own stain concoction of freshly cut brazilwood boiled in water with some more alum and a bit of potash. The ingredients were heated together for just the right amount of time to create a magnificent shade of red-brown.

Long after he shut up the shop for the day and his workers went home to their wives or to a tavern for a pint, he remained behind to work long into the night in the light of gas lamps. He'd even set up a pallet in the shop's attic so that he didn't need to waste time walking home each day while completing the piece. After all, a single intricately carved chair could take up to two weeks to create, making his time frame for the desk very short indeed.

He was content with the progress, though. Remembering Belle's delight with the Earl of Essex's desk at Madame Tussaud's, he came up with an idea for a double secret compartment for Belle's.

He looked out the window at the night sky. The light purple tinges of dawn were appearing above the buildings across from his, and soon the street vendors would be rolling their carts into place and hawking their wares.

It was probably time to climb the ladder into the attic to catch a few hours of sleep on his lumpy mattress before his employees returned to start a fresh day. But he needed to supervise the drying of the mordant, then the stain needed to be applied in up to a dozen coats, so, once again, he would work twenty-four hours straight without sleep.

He added more wood scraps into the fireplace and stoked the dying fire to warm his fingers for the work that lay ahead of him, work he knew was a labor of love.

Mr. and Mrs. Nash were in London, and paid a visit to Belle's shop for the first time. Frigid February air blew into the shop behind the couple, but Belle was delighted to see them, and apologized for the scraps littering the floor.

"Never mind, Miss Stirling," Nash said. "We can see you've built yourself quite a profitable business here, eh, Mrs. Nash?"

"Indeed so. In fact, I think I need a length of this tamboured muslin. My fichus have become quite tattered and I need to have new ones made."

Belle cut the requested fabric, adding extra yardage to the cut, and presented it to Mrs. Nash as a gift. "You are too kind to give this to me, Miss Stirling. I'll not forget it. You must join us for lunch, I insist."

For once, Wesley was in the shop, working at something behind the counter. He was congenial to the Nashes, and nodded agreement to look after the shop before Belle could even finish the request. She joined the Nashes for luncheon at the same café where she'd seen Put and that woman dining together. She understood why he picked the place. The food was delicious. Midway through their Madeira-soaked pound cake, Belle and John Nash were absorbed in discussion about the Pavilion's progress.

Belle hadn't realized the extent to which they'd excluded Mary Ann Nash until she interrupted them. "You know, I do believe I'd like to go shopping for some hats and hairpins. After all, what good is a spruced-up bodice if one's coiffure isn't covered fashionably?

Besides, I've never really walked through this area. Mr. Nash, I know you want to take a turn to look at Regent's Park. Why don't you and Miss Stirling do so, and I'll meet you later at the hotel?"

Mary Ann Nash gathered up her cloak and gloves and left for her shopping jaunt along Oxford Street.

Nash watched his wife's retreating back. "I suspect my wife wants to be seen strolling about this fashionable area, no matter that she may snap like an icicle out there, eh?"

And so Nash and Belle went to view the progress of not only the park but all of the new street between Carlton House and Regent's Park. Nash offered her a fur-lined blanket to wrap around herself as they started out. Mrs. Nash's initials were embroidered on one corner and it smelled faintly of her perfume.

The park and the construction surrounding the area were less than a mile away from Belle's location on Oxford Street, yet her duties and constant travel to Brighton had prevented her from visiting the area herself.

Progress on the street and park itself was slowed during the bitterly cold month of February, but work continued on buildings surrounding the area. They rode past the demolition of the Little Theatre in nearby Haymarket, a century-old, decrepit building that would now be replaced on the same site by the new Theatre Royal, designed by Mr. Nash.

"The new theatre will be shifted just south, to line up with St. James's Square, you see. I understand the new manager intends to stage Sheridan's *The Rivals* as its first production." Nash smiled as though pleased with that decision.

As their carriage rumbled along past other partially completed buildings, Belle used the opportunity to broach what she had learned from Wesley.

"Mr. Nash, if you knew that the king was plotting something dreadful, what would you do?"

"Have you somehow come into such knowledge?"

"Yes. I've learned that the king is gathering evidence against Queen Caroline in an effort to discredit her."

"Miss Stirling, who *isn't* in possession of that information? The king has been trying to rid himself of his wife since five minutes after he took his vows. And the newspapers are full of his outbursts and tirades against her."

"Yes, but he's employing others to manufacture evidence against her. She could end up at the tip of every satirist's pen, if not locked up in the Tower."

"I don't think a queen has seen the inside of a Tower cell since Elizabeth. Besides, the visitors who now tour the Tower would find it immensely entertaining, hardly the king's goal. The royal couple has already been lambasted by the likes of Rowlandson. One more piece of gossip won't affect his scribbling one way or the other."

Nash gazed thoughtfully at her.

"Miss Stirling, from where did you get this piece of scurrilous information?"

"I . . . I can't say. I overheard a conversation somewhere."

Nash smiled. "Ah, perhaps your eye was to a keyhole when it should have been on a measuring tape, eh? Overheard conversations are generally misconstrued."

Belle reddened. "I assure you, Mr. Nash, I overheard this conversation correctly. In fact, I confronted one of the parties involved, and he confessed as much."

"So the exchange involved a man with whom you are well acquainted enough that you could confront him. You've mentioned no other men in your life, so who could that possibly be, besides your own brother?"

Belle didn't reply, merely turning her head to look out the window.

"I see that I am prescient. And what could your brother, a mild-mannered lad if I ever saw one, have to do with any schemes of the king? Listen to me well, Miss Stirling. I don't know your brother, but I can hardly countenance that he would be scheming at the uppermost heights of the kingdom. You, after all, are closer to the king than he could ever hope to be."

"Yes, but—"

"And regardless of the sheer absurdity of your brother plotting such a thing with King George, who has an army of connivers and schemers surrounding him from which to draw, remember what I told you long ago: Mind your tongue where the king is concerned. He pays us well and we benefit even further from our society clientele. No good could come to you as a result of your groundless suspicions."

"They aren't groundless."

"Moreover, what of your brother? If such a story got out, do you seriously think the king would suffer for it? No, he would let others, such as your brother, assume all blame. Your wisest course, Miss Stirling, is to stay as far away from this as possible. Believe me, there are many things you don't necessarily understand about the king."

"Such as?"

But Nash refused to say anything more, and a couple of days later he and Mrs. Nash returned to Brighton.

Belle, however, made up her mind. She would stop Wesley.

Saturday, February 19, 1820

Put's first thought when Wesley entered the shop was that the boy was gaunt. Was Belle aware that her brother looked ill?

"I've come to check on the desk, Mr. Boyce," Wesley said. "Have you made something worthy of my sister?"

"I believe so. Let me show you." Put removed the burlap loosely draped over the secretary to protect it from the ever-present wood dust in the shop.

"Handsome," was Wesley's entire assessment.

Put considered throttling him. The desk was a masterpiece of marquetry and function. He showed Wesley its construction.

"As you can see, I've made the bookcase part separate from the drop-front bottom piece for easy transport, but it slides back on easily atop this raised rail." Put slid the top part of the secretary forward so Wesley could see how it attached.

Damn the boy, he didn't seem all that interested, given his great excitement over having the piece built right away.

"And here's the truly unique aspect of the desk." Put pulled down the slanted front of the desk, which served as a working space when open and resting on support rails that automatically popped out from below as the top was opened.

Inside the working space were a myriad of drawers and slots for holding papers, writing instruments, and whatever else Belle desired. Each drawer had a gleaming brass knob in its center. Put had furiously rubbed and polished each knob until his arms were sore.

He pulled out a drawer from inside the compartment and removed a thick pin that rattled around inside it. He set the drawer to one side, and inserted the pin into an unnoticeable hole in the wooden divider between the drawer and a vertical decorative column next to it.

The column popped forward, revealing it to be the front end of a thin compartment. Not wide enough for a book, but certainly large enough to hold some folded parchment or other narrow items.

Wesley waved his hand in the air in dismissal. "Yes, a common trick. Anyone knows about such secret compartments and could find it in an instant."

"Is that so?" Put asked. "Perhaps you should watch further."

He pulled the compartment out completely. He'd paid attention to detail everywhere in the desk, and had even carved a design in the sides of this compartment that no one but Belle would ever see. Put handed the entire box to Wesley.

Wesley peered down into the slot and turned it all around, examining not only the carving but Put's signature along the bottom of it. He shook his head. "I don't understand. What am I looking for?"

Put took it back from him. At the back of the narrow compartment, opposite the column, he slid a thin shaft of wood, meant to look like an immovable support piece. It revealed a narrow space running along the entire bottom of the compartment.

Wesley reached for it again to inspect the opening. He looked up again in admiration. "No one would ever find this twice-secret space," he said. "And it's large enough to hide money or jewelry in it, provided you put some wadding in here to prevent it from jangling around. In fact, it's an ideal place to lodge one's personal documents, or a diary. Must say I'm impressed, Mr. Boyce."

Put nodded in acknowledgment of the younger man's praise, then took the compartment back from him, slid the wood shaft back down, tucked the secret box back into the desk, pressing until he heard the click that let him know it was securely in place, and replaced the original drawer he'd removed.

"I believe Miss Stirling will be both pleased and amused by it. May I deliver it to her for you?"

Wesley handed him a slip of paper containing an address in Cato Street, not too far from the draper shop. "No. These are my new rooms. Please deliver it here."

"Not directly to Miss Stirling?"

"No, no. I, er, I've just found these new lodgings and want to surprise Belle. She doesn't know about them yet. A gift like this will make her more likely to forgive me for securing us a new place without telling her. You know how women can be, fickle and hysterical."

There was something strange in what Wesley was planning, beyond the obvious idiocy of trying to assuage his sister's wrath over a secret move by giving her a gift, but Put couldn't quite put his finger on it.

He thought back to Belle's visit. Hadn't she said she herself had mucked up her relationship with Wesley? That he was angry with her? If so, why was Wesley now seeking amends? This pair of siblings was disconnected from one another.

But Put accepted the rest of Wesley's payment for the desk, and agreed to bring it by personally in two days.

Monday, February 21, 1820

Put maintained his own delivery wagon, but borrowed a horse from a neighboring smithy whenever he needed to make a delivery. In return, Put had built several beds for the smithy's growing family. Today, Put brought one of his journeymen, Gill, with him to help with moving Wesley's secretary. He pulled his wagon up to the address in Cato Street.

Gill voiced Put's own thoughts. "Are you sure this is right? Looks like stables to me."

Gill scratched his head underneath his hat. Like Put, he despised uncomfortable street clothing. What they wore today for hauling the secretary might look unfashionable and lower-class to any member of society, but for a cabinetmaker it was like restraints.

Put looked down at his paper and back up at the wide set of doors that stretched the span of the brick building. The numbers matched.

"This is the place," he told his employee.

"Let's deliver it and get back to the shop so we can get out of these fetters, then."

Together they put muscle into lifting the two sections of the secretary out of the wagon and placed them in front of the doors. Put knocked, but got no response. He and Gill banged in unison on the door, and were rewarded with a "You'll wake last year's dead!" from inside.

One of the doors swung inwards and Wesley stepped out. "Welcome, Mr. Boyce. Let me show you where to bring the desk."

Gill stayed outside with the secretary while Put followed Wesley inside. Gill was right, this *was* a stable. And, from the smell of it, had not long ago been divested of its residents.

What the devil was the boy up to?

"The desk needs to go up there." Wesley pointed up a ladder into what was surely a hayloft.

"You must be joking. You don't actually live here, do you? And surely you don't expect Miss Stirling to join you here?"

"Oh yes, once she puts her feminine gewgaws about the place I'm sure it will be to her liking."

Either Belle's brother was an unfortunate who belonged in Bedlam or he was up to something. But he'd squared his payment for the desk, so Put was in no position to argue about where it was to go.

The three men struggled to get the two pieces up the ladder, which rose almost vertically into the space above, but managed to do so without either section getting damaged.

As Put surveyed the loft, he realized not only that Belle was not intended to reside here but that it was highly unlikely that Wesley himself lived in this primitive place. Scattered benches, tables, and a few candlesticks did not make for a habitable location.

Put and Gill assembled the top to the bottom. The completed secretary stood impossibly proud in its odd surroundings, like a chestnut tree growing in the desert.

A few minutes later, as Put jiggled the reins to put the horse in motion, Gill asked him, "Why would someone want one of our pieces for that stinkhole? It was no better than a cell at Newgate."

"I don't know."

"And it's for his sister? Wasn't that the gal you were sweet on?"

Put frowned at Gill. "Mind yourself. I'm not sweet on anyone, much less Annabelle Stirling."

There, that should keep his employee from gossiping with the others in the shop.

But he missed Gill's slowly curving smile as he wondered if Wesley really planned to give it to someone else and was extracting the best price possible from him by declaring it a gift for Belle.

Tuesday, February 22, 1820

A light morning snow was drifting down as Wesley slipped out of his lodgings with some rope he'd bought after seeing how difficult it was to maneuver the secretary up the hayloft ladder.

He stopped by the Horse and Groom to receive Darcey's embrace, as well as her complaint that he had not yet moved his belongings there. He was faintly irritated that she was more concerned that he was not there to warm her bed than with his imminent plunge into a dangerous task. He shared a pipe with her, then headed across the street.

Everyone else was already in the hayloft, admiring the desk. Even Mr. Thistlewood congratulated him for managing to commission such a fine piece. Wesley forgot his annoyance with Darcey as he basked in the older man's praise. It stirred a childhood memory in him of feeling proud when his father praised him for making accurate guesses as to the yardages on various bolts of fabrics that lay about the shop. Mr. Stirling would brag to everyone who would listen how smart his young Wesley was, and that one day he'd double the size of their business because of his sharp mind.

You were meant for more than to be Belle's fetching boy. This today proves it.

But neither the opium nor his self-assurances could quell the gnawing in his innards that had started after commissioning the desk from Mr. Boyce. His involvement with the Cato Street lads was honorable and just, he knew it. After all, Mr. Thistlewood was a man of great bearing and character and he was convinced that their plan would change England for the better. So there was no cause for concern.

And yet. He looked around at his co-conspirators, half of them intensely serious about their work, the other half still drunk from the previous evening.

What would Father think if he saw you now?

He banished that niggling thought as Mr. Thistlewood went to the front of the room, the understood signal that he was about to speak and that they should pay attention.

Thistlewood rubbed his gloved hands together and blew on them in between snatches of speech intended to rouse the conspirators.

"Friends, our time is nigh. We are on the cusp of the greatest glad tidings our country—no, all of Europe, dare I say the world?—has ever seen. For we have our example in the French events of a quarter century ago, but we have English ingenuity and cunning on our side, and their foolish mistakes will not be repeated here."

He dropped his voice.

"Imagine what a different world it will be just three days from now. Our grand uprising will be spoken of by schoolchildren for centuries. Lovers of freedom everywhere will imitate us in overthrowing their shackles of servitude. Our oppressors will accuse us of having the blood of innocents on our hands. But from where we will sit inside Mansion House, we will say to them, 'No, we *saved* the blood of innocents.' Does anyone here doubt our noble endeavor? Let him speak now."

Silence.

"And if you are with me, let me know."

Of course, the men roared their enthusiastic support. Wesley cringed inwardly. They were too noisy during this daylight meeting where passersby might notice them. But Mr. Thistlewood didn't seem concerned. He dropped his speechmaking posture, and turned to the practicalities of what would happen following delivery of the secretary later that day.

He told the men that once they established where in Lord Harrowby's house the dinner was to be held, Mr. Thistlewood would draw up exact posting locations for everyone. Only certain men would have the privilege of bursting in on the members and killing them. Everyone was to meet one final time in the hayloft the evening of the twenty-third, and at that time Thistlewood would be issuing guns and swords to his hand-selected assassins. Who those men were was his closely guarded secret.

Wesley held his breath. Would he be asked to partake in the bloodletting?

"I ask Messrs. Brunt, Edwards, and Stirling to return this afternoon and take the secretary to Lord Harrowby's home. Pretend you are from the Company of Joiners and that you are presenting this fine desk to Lord and Lady Harrowby on the occasion of their anniversary. I will wait at the corner of Duke Street for your report.

"And now, friends, return to your businesses and your wives, pretend nothing is amiss, but be here promptly at six o'clock tomorrow."

As everyone filed out, Thistlewood signaled for Wesley to stay behind. Thistlewood picked up a small leather satchel that was resting on the floor behind him and handed it to Wesley. "Do you have a secure hiding place for this inside your lodgings?"

At Thistlewood's nod, Wesley opened the satchel. Inside was a stack of letters, written plans, timetables, and maps. Mr. Thistlewood was entrusting him with such a great responsibility? Not even Edwards or Davidson had received such a task. "I do."

"See that these are well hidden. My own lodgings are above an overly educated and nosy bookseller."

Thistlewood shook his hand and the two men departed together. Or, rather, Wesley pretended to leave, heading over to the Horse and Groom, but went back as soon as he saw that Thistlewood was gone.

Still clutching Thistlewood's documents, he climbed the ladder into the hayloft, relit a recently extinguished candle, and dug around in an opening he'd discovered in the wall last week. His fingers touched the wrapped package containing his journal and writing supplies, and he pulled them out. He'd resorted to hiding his journal here ever since Belle's false—but ultimately convenient—accusations.

He sat down at the table, facing the new secretary. It really was an exquisite work of art. It almost seemed a shame that Mr. Boyce wasn't able to give it as a gift to his sister. For the man was obviously in love with Belle. Any goosecap could see that.

He pondered his entry. Wesley determined that it should be clever and glorious, like Mr. Thistlewood's speeches. Something to read to his own children one day about his grandiose exploits. He tapped the end of the quill against his nose. Nothing was coming to him.

He leafed through the papers Mr. Thistlewood had given him. Some of them were innocuous—bills of fare from the Horse and Groom, receipts from the barber, that sort of thing—but other documents were incriminating indeed: a map showing several routes from their Cato Street location to 39 Grosvenor Square; a list of all the servants who currently worked for Lord Harrowby; another list of all the members of both houses of Parliament; a receipt for a dozen flintlock pistols. It would be disastrous if they should fall into the wrong hands.

The prime minister's, for instance. Or even Belle's. Actually, he wondered what Darcey might do with such items. She might hate her father, but was she really as loyal to Wesley's interests as she proclaimed? Would she turn on him if she thought she could earn some other chance at independence and notoriety?

He shook off the thought.

But his nervousness at being in possession of the papers remained.

If Mr. Thistlewood was too afraid to keep them, why shouldn't
Wesley be equally nervous? His room was probably as safe as anywhere, but then, hadn't he caught Belle rummaging around once
already?

Even the opium haze wasn't enough to quell the barrage of
thoughts passing through him. Did Mr. Thistlewood care only for
protecting himself, and not his co-conspirators? What would happen to Wesley if—God forbid—something went wrong in their attack, and all of these documents were found in his possession?

I'll burn them.

But what if Mr. Thistlewood asked for them again? How would
he explain their disappearance?

Even more troubling was the other potential outcome of tomorrow night. If they were thwarted and Wesley was injured or killed,
how long would it take for the authorities to link him to Darcey?
What might happen to her?

They wouldn't imprison an innocent woman, would they?

And what about Belle? He supposed she couldn't possibly be
implicated.

He passed a hand over his eyes, all of a sudden feeling much
older than he was. Finally, he spent an hour making what he considered to be his most important journal entry ever. He detailed
everything about his involvement with Thistlewood, from his
meetings with Darcey to his commissioning of the secretary desk.
He put down his pen, and felt a wave of relief roll through him, as
though he'd just cleansed and pardoned himself in advance for his
sins of the future.

He tore out those pages, as well as all the others mentioning
Darcey or Thistlewood, rolled them up into a tight scroll, and went
to the secretary. Opening the slant front, he popped open the secret compartment as Put had shown him, then slid up the additional wood slat that revealed a secondary compartment hidden
below the first one. He tucked his scroll inside and brought the
slat back down to cover it.

There. In what more ironic, yet safe, place could his journal pages reside than in the home of Lord Harrowby? If Wednesday's activities were successful, why, he'd have the secretary moved into his own rooms at Mansion House. If anything went wrong, well, no one would ever be the wiser.

On second thought . . .

Wesley scooped all of Thistlewood's papers out of the satchel and stuffed them into the primary secret compartment above the hollow where his journal entry was hidden. It was far better that Thistlewood's papers not be found in the lodgings he shared with Belle.

Satisfied, he tucked the remaining pages of his journal back into the wall, blew out the candle, and headed down the ladder. He'd need some sleep in his own bed before the afternoon's activities.

Wesley didn't notice Put sitting at a window in the Horse and Groom, watching him leave.

He was also too tired to detect another, unfamiliar face staring down at him from the upper floor of the tavern.

The snow stopped long before Belle closed the shop and trudged home, weary from an unusual day of customer complaints about fabric shortages and late deliveries. She knew she needed to talk to the ever-absent Wesley about it, but what was the point?

No light shone from under his door and all was quiet. He must be out carousing again. She went upstairs, tossed her bonnet on her bed, and settled down in a chair next to the window to read in the quickly waning winter daylight. With less than three pages read of *Ivanhoe*, the latest novel by Mr. Scott, she lit a lamp on the table next to her. The reflection from the window created a comforting circle of light.

She sensed a motion outside the building, but it was too dark now to see anything. The front door opened; was that Wesley? She put her book down and took the lamp out to the landing to check.

It was indeed Wesley, who looked haggard and filthy. He carried a long length of rope slung over one shoulder.

"Brother?" she asked. "What's wrong?"

He looked up at the landing and gave her a rare, lopsided grin.

"Nothing for you to worry about. Had to help a friend move some furniture and it was heavier than I thought it would be."

"This took all day?" Drat, she'd just decided not to bother confronting him. Couldn't she ever hold her tongue?

He sighed wearily. "Yes, Belle, it took all day. I'm off to bed now. The rest of my week is very busy."

But he remained still, staring at her as though just seeing her for the first time. To her surprise, he tossed the rope down, leaped up the steps two at a time, and pulled her close into an embrace, kissing both her cheeks and tugging on one of her curls.

"Sister, sometimes I don't like you very much, but I do love you. Remember that, if in the future I don't see you anymore."

Belle gripped both his arms. "Wesley, sometimes you frighten me, but right now you terrify me. Why are you talking to me like you're about to plunge yourself into the Thames?"

"Not to worry. I just wouldn't want anything to remain . . . unsaid . . . if circumstances come between us."

"What do you mean? Wesley, please, whatever you're planning to do for the king, stop it. It's dangerous and foolhardy, and you'll only end up sorry. I beg you, Brother. Please. I . . . I'll . . . I'll do as you wish. I'll share the shop with you. Just stop what you're doing."

His smile this time had no joy in it at all. "I don't think there will be time for a draper shop in my future, Belle. I'll be too busy." He kissed her one last time and went downstairs to retrieve his rope and return to his room.

Belle put her fingers to her cheek, still moist from his lips. *Too busy? Doing what?*

She had little time to consider it. After falling into a troubled sleep, Belle rose the next morning to find that Wesley was already gone for the day. She opened the shop, and had hardly made her list of activities she wanted to complete for the day when the door banged open, sending in a bitter blast of cold air.

She looked up from the counter to find Putnam Boyce in her shop. He turned and locked the door behind him, and set the "Closed" sign in the window.

Belle came around from behind the counter. "What, exactly, are you doing, sir? This is a place of business."

"I have to talk to you, and it's serious."

Although Put was wearing a better-tailored coat than last time, he looked starched and uncomfortable, as usual.

"Mr. Boyce, I have many concerns on my mind right now, so if you'll kindly unlock the door so that I can welcome customers—"

"You can worry about your customers later. Where can we talk privately?"

"I hardly think it's proper for us to—"

"Lord, woman, but you try my patience. Is that a room back there?" He nodded toward a door at the back of the shop.

"Well, it's more of a storage closet."

"Come." Put unceremoniously swung her around and marched her to the back room.

"How dare you!" she sputtered.

"There are far more daring things going on than you could ever imagine. Where's a lamp? Ah, here we go." Put lifted the oil lamp she kept on a hook by the door next to a shelf holding a tinderbox. Opening the box, he struck a piece of flint against the firesteel, letting the sparks fall onto the char cloth and lighting the lamp with the burning cloth. He replaced the lamp on its hook. "Stop tapping your foot, Miss Stirling, and pay attention to what I have to say."

She did so grudgingly. "Mr. Boyce, you'd better have good reason for disrupting my day."

"I believe your brother is involved in something dangerous."

Put knew?

Impossible.

"What do you mean, 'something dangerous,' Mr. Boyce?"

"I mean that he is associating with a group of men that are up to no good, and I have a good suspicion he intends to do something treasonous."

"It might not be treasonous if it's for the—" She stopped.

He looked at her intently, waiting for her to finish, but when she clamped her mouth shut and refused he continued.

"Did you know your brother commissioned a very expensive secretary from me? It's one of the finest pieces I've ever made. He told me it was to be a gift for you. But he had me deliver it to a very strange address on Cato Street. Wesley claimed it was the location of new lodgings for you both, that he had rented the place without telling you, and that the secretary was to be a peace offering when he finally brought you round to see the new location. Have you seen it? Honestly, it's nothing more than an abandoned stable."

Belle's mind was whirling. New lodgings? A secretary? What was Wesley up to?

"I see you are completely unaware of what has transpired. His so-called lodgings amounted to some scattered benches and tables in a loft over the stable. The meanest felon would not be at home there; I hardly think he intended to introduce his sister to it."

"But, I don't understand. Why did he ask you to make a piece of furniture like that? I have nowhere to put it. My room is quite small at our lodging house."

"I don't know. I certainly didn't question it at the time. I was quite happy to, er, well, I was happy enough for the commission. Anyway, the whole situation bothered me enough that I returned to keep an eye out on Wesley. I've been watching him from a tavern across from the stable. He's been meeting daily with about a dozen men, and they're definitely conspiring to do something. The leader is a tall, swarthy character."

That must be Wesley's friend, Mr. Thistlewood. Oh dear, her brother really was trying to help the king build up evidence against his wife. She had no idea what to tell Put. She couldn't tell him what she knew, for he would seek the authorities. But she also couldn't have him following Wesley around like a bloodhound on the scent of a deer.

"Mr. Boyce, I appreciate your concern. But you've probably misinterpreted what you've seen. Perhaps my brother has merely joined a club of some sort, and the secretary is for storing papers."

That sounded ridiculous even in her own ears.

"If that were true, why the subterfuge about the desk being for you? Why couldn't he tell me it was for his club? And do you seriously think some men starting a social club would meet in a stable? Or that they would make the purchase of a secretary their first expenditure?"

"No, I suppose not."

"Miss Stirling, you don't seem overly surprised by any of this, other than the desk. Why do I have the impression that you might know something about your brother's activities? Is he involved in something illegal?"

"No. I don't know. Wesley hardly tells me anything anymore. I told you before that I mucked up my relationship with him somehow, and the end result is that I have no idea what my brother does, who he sees, and where he goes. He could be dining with slavers every evening for all I know about his whereabouts."

Curse Put and his penetrating gaze. She felt like he was absorbing every thought she'd ever had and keeping them for his own.

As if understanding how uncomfortable he was making her, Put relaxed his tone. "I'm sorry, Miss Stirling, I'm not accusing you of anything. I'm just worried for your brother, and by extension you, if he's up to something that's, shall we say, less than suitable for a draper. But you say you have no idea what it could be?"

Put knows I'm not telling the entire truth.

You could tell him. Maybe he could help you track Wesley down and talk some sense into him. And it would be comforting to share this.

But you don't know him well enough. If he found out how serious Wesley's connivances were, he'd run to the authorities. Then I'd be personally responsible for seeing Wesley into a cell in the Fleet.

She slowly shook her head and met that deep forest of a gaze. "No, I don't know what he might be doing."

He shook his head, and Belle sensed it was in frustration with her. Well, it certainly wouldn't be the first time she'd exasperated him, would it?

Time to change the subject. With a sharpened tongue she said, "Tell me, Mr. Boyce, how fares your lady friend?"

"Ah, finally you're willing to let me speak on the subject. My 'lady friend' whom you saw is my cousin, Frances. She's mostly deaf, and she spends a part of each year with different relatives. I try to see her whenever she's in London. And if you weren't so mulish, you might have given me an opportunity to tell you about her. In fact, you could have joined us at our meal."

Belle paused. "Oh. I see."

"I think your problem, Miss Stirling, is that you don't know who to trust. As a result, you place faith in the wrong people, and cast aside those of us you can depend upon."

"I always thought my problem was that I'm entirely too quick to speak my mind."

He laughed. "No, that's what's most interesting about you. So tell me, can I be forgiven enough to have you accompany me on a walk through Vauxhall Gardens?"

"My brother . . ."

"I hardly think your brother has voice to this anymore, given his apparent dealings."

Oh, how true. If only she could float out the door with Put this very instant, padlocking the shop forever, forgetting Wesley's despicable dealings, the king's peccadilloes, and Mr. Nash's loveless marriage, and . . . well, just everything. Just retreat somewhere idyllic where none of these men and none of her problems existed.

But she was a realist. And a proprietress. And a sister.

"That's not what I mean. How can we consider such distractions when Wesley might be on the verge of such troub—rather, while he is under a cloud of your suspicion? No, my brother must be free of distrust before I can even consider it."

"I see. And what if I'm not mistaken, and Wesley is indeed in grave circumstances?"

"Well, then, my concerns will be far greater than that of promenading through paths of boxwood, won't they, Mr. Boyce?"

❧12❧

There are few, very few, that will own themselves in a mistake.

—Jonathan Swift, Irish writer, 1667–1745

Wednesday, February 23, 1820
London

Belle closed the shop as early as she could, then practically ran back to her lodgings to see if Wesley was there. She hadn't seen him all day. In her hurry, she splashed repeatedly through icy puddles of water and was numb by the time she got home.

Wesley's room was dark and silent.

She took the opportunity to stretch before a fire their landlady had started in the tiny parlor. She closed the door to contain the heat, untied her pattens, and removed her shoes, putting them on the floor so they could dry as well as her stockinged feet. She needed this time to think. Instead, her eyes grew heavy and her mind softened.

She was in a drowsy state of half sleep when the front door opened, rousing her. She reached down and touched her shoes. Dry. As were her legs. She slipped back into her shoes as she heard the door to Wesley's room open and close.

And now for the question she should have been wrestling with instead of napping. Should she confront him? Or wait to see if he went out again, and follow him to see where he went and who he was meeting with such regularity?

Neither choice was appetizing. She straightened her skirts nervously while mentally seeking the right course of action.

But before she could decide, Wesley came back out of his room and left their lodgings again. Her decision was made for her.

Belle would follow him.

She peered out a window and watched as he headed down Oxford Street in the direction of Edgware Road. Was he headed to the Cato Street address Put mentioned? Leaving behind her noisy, clinking pattens, she slipped out of their lodgings when Wesley was far enough ahead of her that he couldn't possibly notice her.

Striding with great purpose, Wesley turned north on Edgware Road, then east on John Street. Belle was nearly running again to keep up, but this time avoided the slushy pools of water that filled every rut and dent of the street.

And now he headed south onto Cato Street. Her heart beat wildly. Where would he go next? She halted in surprise. He ducked his head as he entered what looked to be a public house, from the sign jutting out from the building, as well as the light and laughter spilling outside.

So much for Mr. Boyce's abandoned stable. But Belle still wasn't sure what to do. Enter a tavern unaccompanied? Would she even dare confront her brother in such a public place? She crept closer to the building, staying in the ever-increasing shadows along the street.

Once again, though, she didn't have long to wait. Wesley reemerged, stumbling as he came over the threshold. A pair of feminine hands reached through the doorway, pulling him back in again.

He was out again a moment later. "Wicked tart," he said to the invisible woman, whose screech of good humor followed him. Belle prepared to follow him farther up Cato Street, but instead, he simply walked across the street and knocked in a rhythmic pattern against a wide set of black doors. One of the doors opened a sliver and Wesley slipped inside.

Belle stood still, shivering even inside her warmly lined wool cloak. This must be the stable. Through the smudged and icy upper-story windows, she saw the faint but discernible glow of candlelight.

Was this where Wesley met with Mr. Thistlewood?

Shadows moved and slithered behind the windows. She could make no sense of what might be happening up there, only that it couldn't be good, else why would it be in such a strange place?

Oh, Wesley, how did this happen to you?

She stood clutching the corner of what she now saw was the Horse and Groom tavern. The overhang helped keep her secreted while she waited.

You were a fool to follow him, Belle. What do you propose to do now? March into the hayloft, stamp your feet, and drag Wesley out by the ear?

She wished she had an additional scarf to wear. It was bitterly cold enough while traipsing along behind Wesley. Standing motionless reminded her that they were in the middle of a notably frigid winter, snow having fallen intermittently since mid-October.

Come out, Wesley. Let's talk about this. We'll go back to Yorkshire and start over there. Just please don't do something you'll regret.

If she expected him to hear her silent plea, she was to be disappointed. She determined that she'd stand there all night waiting for him, and that she'd agree to anything he wanted if he promised to abandon this conspiracy of the king's.

Her internal reflection was interrupted when a stream of men burst through the same entryway of the Horse and Groom. Several spread themselves out in the street in front of the tavern, while at least a half dozen stormed inside the stable.

"Hallo!" someone shouted from inside the tavern. "They must be runners!"

Oh dear Lord, no, not the Bow Street Runners.

London's force of constables. This couldn't possibly end well.

Belle listened, paralyzed, to a cacophony of shouting, chairs scraping on wood, and the overturning of tables inside the stable. The runners waiting in the street between the tavern and the stable paced anxiously. One picked up a rock. "This'll scare 'em down," he declared, and hefted it at one of the front windows, shattering it.

The noise inside the stable was stilled for only a moment, then the struggle resumed, except now the din was more voluble as it took flight out the broken window into the cold night air.

The tinkling of glass aroused even more attention from the patrons in the tavern, who spilled out onto the cobblestones in front of the establishment, holding mugs of ale and chattering as if they were watching no more than their favorite cricket teams compete against each other.

And then a noise erupted that Belle couldn't have predicted: a gunshot. But the runners didn't have pistols in their hands when they came out of the Horse and Groom, did they? She supposed it was impossible to tell. She regretted that she hadn't thought to bring one of her own pistols with her, although she could have had no idea the evening would come to this.

Dear God, please let Wesley be unharmed.

A hulking figure crawled out a side window and dropped down to the ground, unnoticed by anyone other than Belle. It was Arthur Thistlewood. He waved to someone else on the upper floor, and three more men promptly slid down to the ground. The last man down lay on the ground, clutching one knee. The others lifted him up, with two of them slinging the injured man's arms around their shoulders and half dragging him along.

The group of escapees started running to the back of the building, but something stopped them and they turned back to run toward the front. Directly toward Belle's hiding place across the street.

Were they fools? They thought they could get past the constables fanned along the street?

She opened her mouth to shout to the runners, but realized that the injured man was Wesley. Not that the constables needed her help, anyway. One of them noticed the set of men, hampered as they were by their injured member, and called out to the others.

Realizing that the authorities had seen them, the two men carrying Wesley dropped him unceremoniously to the ground, and took off with Thistlewood, who was running full tilt back toward John Street.

Wesley fell with a thud, and howled in pain. He was struggling up again when a runner got to him and kicked him in his ribs. Wesley fell again, his face landing in a carriage wheel rut full of water. The runner dragged him out of the water by his hair. "Can't have you dead yet, son, that'll come soon enough."

But Wesley's limp form was just a feint. For even in the dim light provided by a single gas streetlight and the lamps still burning in the tavern, she saw the glint of steel as Wesley pulled a knife from his waistband, and thrust it at the runner who was still pulling him through the street.

The knife made contact with the man's arm, and he howled in outrage as he let go of his prey. "Insolent puppy! I'll shoot you now, trial be damned!"

He fumbled with a pistol at his waist.

No, Belle thought. *No, no, no, no. That's my brother!*

From the corner of her eye, she saw another, vaguely familiar, woman rushing from the tavern into the street. Her screaming was discernible only by her white-eyed stare and open mouth, but Belle couldn't hear her over the general chaos.

Without pausing to think any further over her profound and immobilizing fear, Belle ran out from the corner of the building, intending to throw herself over Wesley's body. Surely they wouldn't shoot an innocent woman.

She heard herself shouting as she ran toward the runner and Wesley, but at a distance, as if it were someone else screaming like a banshee. The runner looked up, startled, and out of habit pointed his pistol directly at her.

She heard another gunshot, felt something heavy slam against her shoulder, and was aware of a peculiar drifting sensation as she, like Wesley, fell helplessly to the ground, her arm stretched out as though pointing to her brother. Her last thought was of outrage that someone was lifting her out of the street. But the resulting pain was so shockingly exquisite that she retreated into the bliss of unconsciousness.

A young woman was peering into Belle's face, her eyes open wide in surprise. The woman opened her mouth as though to shout, but all Belle heard was an agonized bark and then the woman was gone.

Am I still unconscious? Is this a macabre dream?

But the cup of water being pressed to her lips was real enough, as was a man's voice somewhere close by.

"Thank you, Frances. You've been so kind to my guest. Miss Stirling? Belle? Can you hear me?"

Put's face hovered over hers.

"Where am I?" Her voice sounded like little more than a frog's croak. Lord, but her head clanged, as if a smithy were pounding out a blade on it.

"My home. After I got you out of the scuffle last night, I brought you here to recover. You're badly bruised, but you should be fine."

Belle wrinkled her nose. So many questions formed in her mind. She wasn't sure which to ask first, so naturally she went for the most foolish one. "Were we alone here together?"

"Don't worry, as soon I settled you down, I sent for my cousin. I didn't want any improprieties, either. But Frances has been most devoted to you."

The young woman moved into her view again, this time with a wet cloth in her hands. She used it to wipe Belle's face, neck, and hands. It was refreshing, Belle realized, given how feverish she felt.

"Your house is unfathomably hot."

"Ah, that's probably all of the blankets we put on you. Just to be sure, you were warm." He gestured at his cousin while speaking his next words. "Frances, you should probably help Miss Stirling into a more, ah, comfortable state. I'll return shortly."

Using a variety of facial expressions and hand signals to indicate what she was doing, Put's cousin put Belle into a seated position, with a bolster of pillows behind her, and removed a couple of blankets. Belle saw that she had been divested of her own clothes and now wore a nightgown, and blushed to think how she might have gotten into it. She prayed it was by the woman helping her now.

Frances undid whatever remaining pins Belle had in her mess of curls, and sat down to brush it out in long waves, running the brush gently over what Belle now realized was a very large protrusion.

Belle couldn't remember the last person who had done this for her. Perhaps her mother, when Belle was around ten years old?

She wept from the sweet attention, and the uncertainty of her and Wesley's futures.

Put's cousin sat in a chair next to the bed, pointed to the brush, and shook her head.

You don't want me to do this?

Belle smiled, nodded, and pointed back to her head. Frances resumed brushing. After Belle's hair was tangle free and spread softly around her shoulders, Frances poured her another cup of water.

"Thank you, Frances."

Put's cousin motioned for her to drink. Belle did, then Frances fussed over her, retying the laces of her robe, giving her mint to chew to sweeten her breath, and pinching her cheeks to bring color into them. Frances stepped back and looked at her, as if judging her masterpiece. Nodding, she held up a finger and left the room.

She returned moments later with Put, and winked at Belle as she quietly made her exit again.

Put sat in the chair his cousin had just vacated. "You look well for having been caught in the violent dispersion of a conspiracy."

"It would seem you've become my hero, Mr. Boyce."

"You're lying in my bed after I carried you dozens of blocks to my residence, and now my cousin has been tending you for a day. I believe we can dispense with the formalities, can we not... Belle?"

"I suppose I can't argue with you. Very well, Put-rhymes-with-shut, tell me, where is my brother? Is he safe? His so-called friends abandoned him. And how did you happen to be there?" She reached up to her shoulder. "I don't feel a bandage here, although the pain is considerable. Did the bullet pass through me?"

"You weren't shot."

"I wasn't? Impossible! I saw the runner point his pistol at me, and heard it fire."

"He pointed it at you, but the gunshot you heard was elsewhere, and killed one of the conspirators. You were struck by a rock thrown by one of the runners that unbalanced you, and your head made regrettably good contact with the ground."

"And what of Wesley? Is he safe?"

Put cleared his throat. "I'm sorry, but your brother is sitting in Newgate Prison. He and about a dozen other men are all awaiting trial."

"But the king should be able to intervene. After all, they were doing work for him. Although I hardly understand why it required so many men to manufacture false evidence against the queen."

"Pardon? What are you talking about?"

"The conspiracy my brother was involved in. It was to help the king bring false evidence of treason against his wife."

Put shook his head sadly at her. "Belle, Wesley wasn't doing any such thing. He was following a radical named Arthur Thistlewood, who imagined he could bring the violence of the French Revolution to England's shores. Thistlewood has already confessed everything. His plan was to invade a cabinet dinner in Grosvenor Square and kill as many members as possible, then set up a temporary headquarters at Mansion House, directing the country's revolution from there.

"Unfortunately for Thistlewood, the newspaper advertisement for the cabinet dinner was a fake, planted by Parliament when they realized he intended sedition. They knew the lure of so many members in one place would be too attractive for him to resist."

"But how did they learn about him?"

"Thistlewood has been followed on a regular basis since his involvement in the Spa Field Riots of four years ago. They had a man named George Edwards pretend to be a radical and join Thistlewood's group, called the Spencean Philanthropists. Edwards pointed out the cabinet dinner notice to Thistlewood, and was able to relay the group's movements to Parliament. Do you want to read more in the paper? I have it downstairs."

"No, no, I couldn't bear it. I'd rather hear it from you."

"Right. Well, Thistlewood promised most of his followers plum positions in the new government that would be created once Parliament was decimated. I suspect Wesley had one of these assurances."

"But what about the king? He would have still been in charge even if they murdered all of Parliament."

"They had some sort of idea of capturing him and holding him as a hostage. Utterly bumbling beyond all reckoning."

Belle digested what Put told her. "So what did the secretary have to do with anything?"

"I don't know. It's not mentioned in the newspapers."

"I see. What are the charges being brought against the conspirators?"

"High treason. And Thistlewood has the added charge of murder, because he stabbed one of the constables who entered the hayloft."

High treason. An offense punishable by hanging until dead, and posthumous beheading and quartering.

It couldn't be. It just couldn't. At least England had abolished partial hanging and disemboweling its half-dead subjects. Wesley wouldn't like that. She heard cackling laughter in the distance.

"Belle?" Put leaned forward and took both her hands in his.

And she realized that it was her own half-mad hysteria filling the room.

"Is there anything I can do for you?" he asked, his gentle voice calming her.

Save my brother. Remove yesterday's events from my mind. Make me sleep for another month.

"I suppose not. I think I just need to sleep."

Belle turned her head to one side to let tears fall unchecked against her face. Put quietly departed, leaving her alone with her troubling thoughts.

She awoke the next morning to the smell of sausages, which Frances delivered to her on a tray with toast and tea. Belle ate ravenously, and as she licked gooseberry conserve from her fingers she looked up to find Frances watching her, hands folded at her waist.

"My apologies," Belle said. Put's cousin shook her head—*It's nothing*—took away the tray, and offered Belle a wet cloth to wipe her hands.

"I'm going to visit my brother today."

Frances cocked her head to one side and shook her head again, pointing to her lips. *Say it again. I didn't see your mouth when you said that.*

But this time Belle smiled and shook her head. No need to alarm Frances, who would run and tell Put, and heaven knew what he would do to prevent Belle from going to Newgate.

"He's in one of the wards in the chapel yard, 'less you plan to pay for more comfortable accommodation?" The man talking to her seemed to be no more than a prisoner himself.

Belle replied carefully, hoping he couldn't see, nor hear, the bulge of coins she'd sewn into her dress. Over her arm she carried her St. Bart's basket, this time full of food as well as blankets. "I am, of course, concerned for my brother's welfare."

The man shrugged and led her through dank, stinking hallways, poorly lit by inadequate gas lighting. They stepped through a courtyard, where a line of about thirty men, all chained together at the ankles, walked in a ragged circle. They made a motley group, some dressed comfortably in beaver hats and well-cut coats, while others were in threadbare tatters.

Her escort turned to see why she'd stopped. "Exercise," he said. "Now, c'mon."

Belle clutched her cloak tightly around her. She saw one of the men pointing at her basket as she hurried by.

Her escort stopped at a forbidding iron door set in an endless row of such doors, studded with nails and with only tiny square openings in it for air and light. The man unlocked the door and it swung open, screeching on its hinges.

Was that a rat she saw shuffling in the matted straw covering the floor?

The cell was a large, open space surrounded by stone walls that were once whitewashed but now just oozed trails of moisture and slime. Along the edges of the walls were wooden bunks, some completely bare except for prisoners sitting on them or curled into balls, asleep. Other bunks were decently covered with blankets and pillows.

The smell in the room was a noxious blend of excrement and

unwashed bodies, but the prisoners, who sat or paced listlessly, didn't seem to notice. Or care. Even the chilled air seemed stifling to everyone subjected to it.

Some of the fortunate ones, if there was such a thing in this devil's hold, were visited by wives and their crying children. She spotted Wesley huddled on the floor in front of a bunk, stripped to only his trousers and shivering.

"Knock when you're ready to be let out," her escort told her, pulling the door shut behind her. She rushed to Wesley's side and knelt before him.

"Belle?" he asked, lifting his head and sitting up. His eyes were unnaturally bright and his lips were cracked.

He eyed her basket. "Is there something in there for me?"

She sat in front of him, placed the basket between them, lifted the lid, and removed a wool blanket, draping it over his shoulders. He pawed in the basket himself, chewing hungrily on cheese, bread, and smoked fish.

"Here," Belle said, removing and uncapping the jar of water. He downed it in two gulps.

"Wesley, what happened to your clothes? Your shoes?"

"I had to sell them for garnish."

"You had to sell your own clothing in order to be permitted into this filthy place?"

"It's how they do it. Did you bring me anything else? My pipe?" He dug around further in her basket.

"I'm sorry, no. I stayed out of your room, although now I see that I needed to bring you some shirts."

"Yes, I need clothes and a blanket. And I need my pipe. Bring the entire pipe box." Wesley grabbed Belle's wrist, sending shooting pains into her injured shoulder. "Bring my pipe soon. I need it. I need money, too, so I can purchase ale in the taproom."

"There's a tavern inside this fetid place?" She gently disengaged her wrist from his hand.

"Yes, some inmates started a trade in spirits. I need money for that and for bribes. They won't let me keep what you bring me unless I can continue paying for them. I also need to pay for exercise time."

Dear God.

"What else can I bring you? Do you want a Bible?"

He shrugged. "If you wish. But anything else would be stolen." Averting his eyes from her face, he added, "This is no fit place for a man, Sister."

"I know." She reached out a hand to stroke his cheek, but he jerked away from her.

"I guess you know everything by now," he said, face down as he picked at the skin around his fingernails.

"Except for why you involved yourself with a radical like Arthur Thistlewood in the first place."

Wesley stopped playing with his hands and offered her the most honest and direct answer she thought she'd heard from him in years. "Because I wanted to prove myself to you, Belle. There was someone, a friend, who convinced me that I could make a mark in the world by becoming Mr. Thistlewood's confidant. Fat lot of good that did me.

"I hear he's in one of the better cells and only has to share with a couple of other prisoners. Keep telling myself that's because they want him to stay healthy so they can be sure to watch him swing. Me they probably don't care about, so I'm stuck here with the other rabble. But maybe it means they'll let me go."

"Perhaps you're right, Brother. There's something else I'm wondering about." She selected her next words warily. "I understand from Mr. Boyce that you asked him to build a secretary for me, but then you had him deliver it to Cato Street. What was the real purpose of it?"

"Mr. Thistlewood wanted it."

"But *why?*"

Wesley was working something over in his head, she knew it. He opened his mouth to speak, then snapped it shut.

"Wesley?"

"It was important to the cause."

How exasperating her brother could be, even when in a dire situation like this. "Where is the secretary now?"

"It's safe."

"Why won't you tell me where it is?"

"Because it contains damning information."

"How could it possibly be more damaging than your possible conviction of high treason?"

"It's not me I'm worried about." Wesley folded his arms in front of him, signaling the end of that line of questioning.

Belle sighed. "Do you know when you'll go to trial?"

"No. Perhaps in a couple of weeks."

"Well, I can't sit by and watch this happen to you. I'm going to do something."

"What can you possibly do?"

"I'm going to try and see the king, and beg him to bring his influence to bear. And if begging doesn't work, I'll demand it."

A shadow of a smile flitted across Wesley's face. "You've always been part dragon. I've had dreams about dragons. Except in my dreams the fire-breather has been Alice Treadle. Do you remember Alice?"

"The girl from the Pack Horse Inn who went to India with you."

He nodded. "She haunts me, Belle. I have waking nightmares of her. They stopped for a while, after I met Dar—I mean, after I met Mr. Thistlewood. But now they're back." He clutched Belle's wrist again. "Lord, Belle, what if it's Alice who drives me into the grave, instead of my jailers?"

She winced at the sharp pain, but allowed him to hold on to her this time. "Let's hush this talk of you going into the grave, Brother. I'll return tomorrow with the things you want, then I'll see the king and get things straightened out for you."

He released her, like a child who has been promised a toy he has been pleading for.

Belle picked at the secret pouch she'd sewn into her cloak and pulled out a drawstring pouch full of coins. She pressed it into Wesley's hand. "I'll be back as soon as I can."

And as she went to the cell's door to knock, she heard Wesley's voice float across the stench and the crying and the misery: "Don't forget, I need my pipe."

And as the door clanged shut again behind her, she realized that Wesley had not apologized to her, nor had he thanked her for her visit.

March 1820
Brighton

Belle waited for the king once again, this time in one of the re-furbished drawing rooms. Only this time, it wasn't just a draper and an architect in the vast room waiting upon a prince. There were numerous courtiers and government officials who had fol-lowed the king to Brighton, milling around, hoping for an audi-ence, too.

A liveried servant entered and everyone stilled. "His Majesty will now see Lord Crugg."

The rest of the room groaned in disappointment as Lord Crugg strode proudly to the door, to be led by the servant to the king's presence.

Looking at the number of people in the room, Belle suspected this could take all night.

She found an empty bench under a window and sat down. Oth-ers eyed her suspiciously, most likely because women weren't granted private audiences with the king. Unless they were his mis-tresses, that is.

Let them think what they want. My reputation is nothing as compared to Wesley's life.

She surreptitiously rubbed her shoulder. It was still sore, al-though thankfully her headache was gone. In her haste to see the king, she'd ignored her own pain.

After visiting Wesley at Newgate, she'd returned to Put's home, where he and his cousin waited anxiously for her. Assuring them both that she was perfectly well now—a lie; her head still throbbed and her shoulder was in greater pain after Wesley's pulls on her arm—she told them that she planned a trip to see the king to ask for his intervention on Wesley's behalf.

She still fumed, remembering Put's look of pity and his obser-vation that little could be done for Wesley. "He's cooked his own goose." Still, he offered to accompany her and, when she refused, asked her to at least bring along Frances for company. She turned that down, as well.

Better to be alone with anxious thoughts, to plan what she would say to the king.

Belle returned once again to Newgate before boarding the coach to Brighton, bringing Wesley clothing, more money, bedding, and his beloved pipe box. Putting everything else to one side, Wesley slid the top off his pipe box, pulled out the wooden stem, and caressed it. "Belle, you've made my intolerable situation just a bit more bearable."

"I'm glad. I'll be back after I see the king. He's fled to Brighton because of your . . . well, because of the disturbance."

"Will he actually give you an audience, now that he's king?"

"I don't know. But I have to try. I'll do everything I can, Wesley."

He wagged the pipe at her. "See that you do, Sister. I believe I am out of other options."

She shook clear the thought that, once again, Wesley was less than grateful for her assistance. She had to free the thought from her mind, lest she turn herself over to anger over his stupid, spoilt behavior, not only with Arthur Thistlewood but in everything Wesley had ever done.

Belle also didn't want to think about why his pipe had become his most prized possession. The contemplation of what he might be smoking in it was too much to bear. She shouldn't even have brought it to him, but what use was it to castigate a man whose life as he knew it was no more?

No, if she remained a loving sister and they could get this all behind them, perhaps they could regain a warm relationship again.

Although that did leave the problem of Mr. Putnam Boyce, didn't it? What would her relationship be with him once this was all over?

"His Majesty will now see Miss Annabelle Stirling."

She jumped, surprised that she was actually going to be granted an audience, much less that it would be so soon. She squared her shoulders with a wince, determined not to leave Brighton without the king's commitment to help free Wesley.

After a long day of meeting with petition seekers, the king shut the door to his bedchamber and turned to the plump woman in his black and gold canopied bed. "My dear, you have no idea how exhausting it is to run a country with as much care as I do. And sometimes I'm visited by the oddest creatures with the most unusual requests."

The woman lay on her side, propped up on her elbow. The diaphanous gown did little to hide her ample hips. She patted the bed next to her. "Did you have an odd creature today, Your Majesty?"

She sat up against the pillows as the king sat down heavily before her, lifting his arms so she could undress him. She was never quite sure if she had mastered the fine techniques of seductive undress, and made up for it by leaning forward and rubbing her bosom against him while she struggled to divest him of his clothes. The woman wondered if Lady Conyngham had this much trouble being a temptress.

"I did. Mr. Nash's assistant, or I suppose now she's Mr. Crace's assistant, I can't remember. Her name is Annabelle Stirling. She thought I would be fool enough to intervene for her brother, who rots appropriately enough in Newgate."

Displaying no reaction at all to this news, she pushed his waistcoat back over his shoulders as gently as she could, pretending that it was a simple task and that he wasn't a mountain of flesh that made her own figure look willowy. "What is his crime?"

"He was one of the Cato Street conspirators. As though any clemency should be shown to that group of radicals. Why, they planned to kidnap me! Me, their sovereign king. Damned good riddance to the lot of them. No, she'll see no quarter from me. And certainly not from Liverpool, I'll wager. Scratch my back right there, would you, sweetheart? Ah, excellent. You give me great comfort."

Although the story of Miss Stirling and her unfortunate brother was of great interest to her personally, she lost her curiosity as her mind wandered on to whether the king would continue to see to her comfort, and that of her children, as payment for the great sacrifice she'd made for him in his chambers.

*   *   *

April 1820
London

Darcey stamped her foot prettily. "Father, I tell you, it's true."

Mr. White sighed as he put down his magnifying glass. What a plague his wife and daughters were. He just wanted to spend some time alone with his insect collection. He'd just received a rainbow scarab, and was admiring its metallic blue-green and copper colors and the long, curved horn extending from its head that marked it as a male.

Fascinating creatures, dung beetles. The adult male and female worked together, as equals, to dig beneath the excrement they treasured as a food source for their young.

If only he could make his family understand that Parliament was their dung heap and Mrs. White needed to work with him to ensure they could roll it and mold it into a perfect circle to benefit them.

And their daughters, well, what an impossible pair of harpies they were turning out to be. And not even in their twentieth years yet, either of them, every day resembling their mother more and more. Just constant carping about the decisions he was making for their own good.

And did Darcey think he was blind to her constant escapes and lies about attending to her great-aunt Lydia? A man like Julian White did not manage to enter Parliament without having a modicum of wits about him. Darcey's long fabrication about spending a few weeks with her aunt so she could sit by the old woman's bedside and read to her was a bigger ball of excrement than any beetle could ever hope to roll up. The girl had been running wild for months and reeking of pub fumes, but he had little energy to spare for wondering about it, much less chasing her down and disciplining her.

And here she was, confessing her own sins with her ridiculous story that one of the conspirators was misled into his role by his sister and a cabinetmaker in Shoreditch. What the hell was she talking about?

Yes, Darcey complained bitterly that she was a caged bird, but she was more like a wild raven, dark eyes flashing amid her squawking and screeching. He could practically see her wings flapping as she spoke now.

"They conspired, Father, to force Wesley—I mean, Mr. Stirling—into participating with that Mr. Thistlewood. He was duped into thinking he was doing something noble for Parliament, no, for the king. He is innocent of his charges. You must help him, Father. Do something before he's sent to trial and convicted. They'll hang him!"

"Darcey, you're raving. George Edwards was the informant inside that group. He kept Parliament well aware in advance of how the conspiracy was formed, and there was no cabinetmaker or lady draper involved. Besides, Thistlewood has acknowledged everything. You're babbling nonsense. And what's your interest in this Stirling fellow, anyway?"

"I met him . . . a few times . . . at the hospital, when I took Aunt Lydia for cures. Mr. Stirling was . . . a gentleman who . . . who was there caring for his dying wife. She had a wasting illness and was bedded next to Aunt Lydia. And he told me . . . he told me that his sister, Annabelle Stirling, had practically blackmailed him into helping her and her . . . her paramour, Mr. Putnam Boyce, into serving the conspiracy against Parliament."

"Blackmailed him *how*, exactly?"

"They told him that . . . that . . . they would invent a story about his . . . honestly, Father, I can't quite remember what they threatened him with, but it was perfectly awful. As a member, you have the power to help him, don't you? Speak to Mr. Abbot or Lord Liverpool, can't you? He was innocent in the whole affair."

Darcey clutched her hands tightly before her as she glanced nervously around the room. She was sweating, as well. What was the matter with the girl? Had she gone completely off her nut?

"It's becoming clear to me, Daughter, that I should have married you off to Mr. Fretwell's son when he proposed a match between our families, rather than letting you pout and sulk your way out of it, for if I'd done so, I'd not be listening to this gibberish right now. Instead, you'd be bound to your husband and unleashing your vitriol on him. The biggest mistake I ever made was not seeing you into that marriage. Who knows when a willing soul will come along again?"

A willing soul who wouldn't send her packing back to her father after her first shrewish rant.

"Darcey, I always thought that between you and your sister, you were the one with sense, but I can see now how utterly incorrect I was in this assumption. You have no understanding of the events of Cato Street. I have no idea why you're defending some random conspirator, but I'll have no more of this. Here." He fished around inside a bowl on his collection table and pulled out several coins. "Go purchase a pair of gloves or something. Forget about all of this fee-faw-fum."

She shook her head. "Really, Father? Well, if you won't act on the information I'm giving you, I can see I'll have to do something myself."

Darcey stamped her silk-encased foot once again and fled to her room to hide her tearstained face, but not before reaching out to grab the money her father had dropped on the table.

"Humph," Mr. White said, sitting down to resume admiration of his scarab collection.

Lord Liverpool had never actually been to Lord Harrowby's home in Grosvenor Square before, despite all of the planning and secret meetings that had occurred to secure the surprise capture of the Cato Street conspirators based on the supposed dinner scheduled at this address.

But this evening the two men sat together in Harrowby's study, smoking cigars to congratulate themselves on their successful infiltration of the plot.

Liverpool leaned back in the leather chair to enjoy the aroma. "Excellent, Harrowby. Quite smooth."

"Glad you like it. I imported a box from Jamaica. Lady Harrowby hates the smell, so undoubtedly the room will be subjected to an army of servants airing and beating and scrubbing the soul out of it tomorrow."

Liverpool laughed politely. "It's proving to be a good year thus far, isn't it? We've got the Peterloo conspirator trials under way in

York, and next month the Cato Street boys will experience English justice."

"What were the conspirators at Peterloo eventually charged with?" Harrowby asked.

"I believe it was 'assembling with unlawful banners at an unlawful meeting for the purpose of exciting discontent.' Doesn't get more unlawful than that."

"Ha! True. I imagine, though, that they'll get light sentences. At least, I hope so. Too many women were killed for the government to take too hard a stand against them. And there's no real proof that they intended treason, much as I hate their radical agitating. Unlike with our Cato Street situation, where it's obvious to even the most dull-witted street urchin that they planned the overthrow of the government."

"Well, the passage of the Six Acts back in December will seal the Peterloo rioters' fates, and was fortuitous in helping our own cause with the Cato Street conspirators, eh?"

Harrowby spat away a bit of cigar leaf that was stuck on his lower lip. "Indeed. Although I'm worried that the specific measure prohibiting public meetings of more than fifty people without permission may work against us. After all, there were only about a dozen of them, meaning their meetings were not illegal, per se."

Liverpool shook his head. "Not to worry. The Cato Street brutes will certainly be found guilty of gathering for the purpose of training for a radical act. I just wish we'd been able to make that punishable by death instead of just seven years' transportation. Although the government will present such a terrifying case of what the no-good knaves were up to that there won't be any doubt as to the trial's outcome."

"So, your prediction is . . . ?"

"My prediction is that the scaffoldmaker will be a very busy man next month. Which reminds me, I had a visit from one of the conspirators' family members, a young woman, begging for the life of her brother. Sad, really. She'd been to see the king, who of course paid her no attention. I sent her on her way, too. I see no reason to show a traitor mercy just because he has a beautiful sister, do you?"

Harrowby sat up straight in his chair. "Was her name Annabelle Stirling, by chance?"

Liverpool frowned. "Why yes, I think it was."

"Do you know the woman visited me, as well? She must be making the rounds on Parliament, trying to find a sympathetic member. A fruitless effort, poor girl. Although I wouldn't use the word 'beg' to describe her visit. Miss Stirling was quite ferocious about her brother's release. Said he was her only family left in the world. I had to explain to her that justice doesn't make decisions by counting siblings. Honestly, I had a moment where I thought the woman planned to tear out my eyes. I'd hate to be married to such a she-wolf."

"Why? For fear she would make you give up cigar smoking altogether?"

"Ah, you're a scoundrel, Liverpool. But that reminds me, I need to dash off a note to my valet to send off for another box of Jamaicans. The Spaniards produce some decent cigars, too, and I hear that veterans of the wars are trying their hand at growing tobacco. I doubt anything will beat my Jamaicans, though."

Lord Harrowby opened the slant front of his new secretary, and pulled up a chair in front of it. "You know this is the desk they sent over in their obvious attempt to get the layout of my home?"

"Is it? Exquisite work. You profited handsomely by allowing them into your home."

Harrowby smiled. "I deserved no less. Imagine the risk I ran of the constables not breaking them up when they did, and instead having criminals arrive on my doorstep with torches and pitchforks."

"Yes, the gossip would have been unbearable, I'm sure. It seems a heavy expense for the group, don't you think? It must have cost them easily quite a few quid."

"Perhaps they had a wealthy financier. Or Thistlewood had a rich widow in the background."

"Possibly. Still, it strikes me as an odd 'gift' to present you just to gain access to the home. Surely they could have found something more reasonably sized. What did you find inside it?"

"Nothing. It was brand-new. Still smelled of staining oils."

"Then why—just a minute!" Liverpool jumped up from his chair. "Aren't these things sometimes made with secret drawers and hidden nooks and such?"

"I suppose. But why would they want to give me a desk with secret compartments?"

"I don't know. Why would they want to kill everyone in Parliament? Move aside, Harrowby, let's have a look."

Lord Liverpool pushed the slant front closed, and pulled out the drawers that lay beneath it, handing them to Harrowby, who looked over each one for false bottoms before setting it on the floor. Liverpool dropped to his knees and felt around inside the carcass of the desk, seeking springs, knobs, or anything else that might suggest a hiding place.

Nothing.

He stood and opened the two doors on the top of the desk, admiring the fine marquetry that displayed a scene of female Greek statues swathed in gently draped fabrics. He could find nothing inside here, either. Perhaps it was just a foolish notion on his part.

"Harrowby, do you mind if I look in the slant-front section, as well? Anything personal of yours in it?"

"Go ahead. I've hardly used the desk at all yet. I'm interested now myself in what you might find."

So Lord Liverpool pulled the heavy wood front down again, and started anew the process of pulling out the myriad of drawers, this time miniature in size. One drawer rattled.

"What's this? A pin. It must have a use. I seriously doubt the craftsman who made this piece would have been careless enough to leave a pin in it."

Liverpool probed the slots and drawer openings with his fingers and the pin. He was about to admit defeat and apologize for tearing the secretary apart when he felt a tiny click as he ran the pin along a drawer wall. He repeated the action slowly. There. The pin connected with a small depression in the wood. He pressed harder against the indentation, and a decorative column popped away from the front of the interior, revealing a long slot behind it.

"Well, what do we have here? A secret compartment, stuffed full of papers." Liverpool turned it over, scattering its contents on the desk. "Receipts, bills, a map of Grosvenor Square. Harrowby, I do believe we've found documents of utmost interest to the Cato Street trial. God has smiled upon us tonight, my friend. I'll carry them to court myself first thing in the morning."

"Wait a minute. Something is coming to me. I recall someone— a fellow member?—mentioning a cabinetmaker. Something about the fellow being falsely associated with the conspiracy. Or was he a conspirator who got lost in the melee? Hmm. Wonder if it deserves an investigation."

Liverpool clapped him on the shoulder. "Up to you, although if it was a false accusation, it might make fragments of the pie, eh? Perhaps it's best to stick with the ingredients we know won't crumble our case."

"You're right. I just wish I could remember what it was I heard, and from whom. It nags at the back of my mind."

"Harrowby, you are your own worst nag. How about breaking open that bottle of port I see on the sideboard? Damned selfish of you to taunt me with it all evening."

And so the two men celebrated victory for a second time that evening.

❧ 13 ❧

Forgiveness spares the expense of anger, the cost of hatred, the waste of spirits.

—Hannah More, English writer, 1745–1833

April 1820

Belle sat in the gallery of the courtroom, watching in dread as the inevitable played out before her. Her brother was shuffled in each day with the rest of the conspirators, chained and unwashed, as evidence was presented and arguments made.

The court was startled by last-minute evidence provided by Lord Liverpool in the form of documents seized from Lord Harrowby's home. The documents were discovered inside a secretary that the conspirators had given the earl as a supposed anniversary gift in order to have a look inside his home.

A secretary! Belle spun her head to look at Wesley, who, for the first time, looked nervous instead of expressionless. He fidgeted in his chains while the contents found in the desk were enumerated, but visibly settled down when the itemization was complete.

Why? Did Wesley know about the documents stored in the desk? Was there something specific he thought troubling?

Would she not ever understand her brother?

Her subsequent visits to Wesley since trying to find a sympathetic ear to his plight had been less than successful. His body was more emaciated, and his eyes more vacant. He took little interest in the food offerings she brought him, nor in any of the shop gossip about some of his favorite patrons.

He was fading away, dying in a surer way than any hangman could impose.

A woman seated next to her leaned over and whispered, "Looks like they's just presented the length of rope, hasn't they? There hasn't been a public hanging in London in some time. It'll be a lesson to other radicals, won't it?"

Belle stared straight ahead without replying, willing herself not to cry. Or slap the woman.

The trial had thus far revealed the infiltration of a George Edwards into the Thistlewood group. Edwards helped the conspirators form the plan to invade Lord Harrowby's home and kill as many members of Parliament as possible.

Edwards revealed that the conspirators' most brutal act would be to cut off the heads of at least two members and spirit them off to Westminster Bridge, putting them on pikes as a broad announcement of their accomplishment and as a warning to others.

Belle was even more aghast to learn that the conspirators intended to fire a rocket from Lord Harrowby's home to signal to other Spenceans in the city that the deed was done, followed by setting fire to a nearby oil shop to add to the confusion and attract a mob. They then planned to attack a bank and throw open the gates of Newgate to thoroughly paralyze the city and enable their escape.

Although the conspirators had posted a couple of watchers outside Harrowby's residence the day of the supposed dinner party to ensure all was going as planned, they were duped by a real dinner party being hosted by the Archbishop of York, who lived next door. So the parade of carriages lining the street assured them that all was well, and they reported it as such to Thistlewood. Hence the Bow Street Runners were able to intercept the conspirators before they ever left their secret meeting place.

One of the runners provided damning testimony about their watch on the Cato Street hayloft from the upper story of the Horse and Groom. From their perch, they were able to witness far more about the proceedings than Belle, and offered significant detail as to how the conspirators were heavily arming themselves inside the hayloft. The constable also gave gruesome details of Thistlewood's murder of the Bow Street leader, a man named Smithers, who was one of the first to climb up into the hayloft.

After Thistlewood's drop from the window, he made a temporary escape to a house in Little Moorfields, but was apprehended the next morning, wearing a military sash and breeches full of pistol cartridges. His flight only added to the list of that man's crimes.

Thistlewood made a long, rambling speech, primarily slandering the informer, George Edwards, who he suggested was the greatest villain of them all for having joined "the reformers" under false pretenses and continued to encourage them in their vital work without confessing to his immoral workings against the group.

Other conspirators attempted the same line of attack, only to be greeted with scorn. Wesley remained silent throughout the proceedings.

The mulatto William Davidson presented his own eloquent defense, telling the jury, "You may suppose that because I am a man of color I am without any understanding or feeling and would act the brute. I am not one of that sort. When not employed in my business in Birmingham, I have employed myself wisely and conscientiously as a teacher of a Sunday school. "

But the presiding judge responded, "You may rest most perfectly assured that with respect to the color of your countenance, no prejudice either has or will exist in any part of this court against you. A man of color is entitled to British justice as much as the fairest British subject."

Belle had hoped British justice would mean mercy for her brother, but her hope was fading like the embers of a kitchen hearth, long after the family meal has been cooked and eaten, nor did anyone much care whether her hope flickered out.

The court recessed for the day, and she hurried home to pack a basket of foodstuffs to take to her brother. She dreaded having to trudge back to court again tomorrow, after enduring yet another sleepless night, to hear verdicts.

Shame on you, Belle Stirling. How sleepless do you think it will be for Wesley?

She'd tried so hard to find someone who would intercede for her brother, but it was no use. The king, Lord Liverpool, Lord Harrowby, and a half-dozen other members of both the House of Lords and the House of Commons completely ignored her, if they didn't outright laugh at her.

Mr. Nash was sympathetic to the situation, but only offered her the same sad shake of the head to tell her she was on a fool's errand.

Amid the years of famine, unrest, and rioting, England sought a way to put a final ending on the turmoil. This trial was the government's statement that it was quelling all insurrection in the country.

Wesley accepted the food with perfunctory thanks, although it didn't look as though he was eating anything she brought him. Of more concern to him was money to purchase ale and "other supplies" as he could find in the prison.

Belle dropped another pouch into his outstretched hand.

She arrived at court as early the next day as possible, to ensure a seat along the banister overlooking the trial. It went much as she expected, with a supreme look of satisfaction as the same judgment was rendered on all of the suspects.

Guilty.

Except that justice was parceled out differently to the various conspirators, according to their roles in the plot. Thistlewood, of course, had the harshest sentence brought against him: to be hung by the neck until dead, then beheaded.

Perhaps his head would be posted where he once intended the members of Parliament's heads to be staked.

The Jamaican-born Davidson and three others were also found guilty of high treason, and sentenced to hanging and beheading. But the embers of hope were stoked again in Belle when several other men were found guilty, but because of their lesser roles in the conspiracy, they were sentenced to deportation for life.

Deportation! Was it possible that Wesley could find mercy by deportation to Australia or America? Belle was mentally calculating what would have to be done in order to close down the London shop to start anew in one of those countries, but was diverted by the judge, who placed a black cap on his own head before pronouncing Wesley's fate.

Guilty of high treason, with a sentence of hanging by the neck until dead, followed by ceremonial beheading, outside Newgate Prison two days hence.

Belle heard no more, for the world collapsed around her in a violent torrent of blood rushing in her ears, blocking out the clinking of chains as the prisoners were filed out of the courtroom for the final time.

The king and Privy Council met, as was the custom in death sentences, to determine whether some of the conspirators should be offered a reprieve. To no one's surprise, all of the sentences were upheld, yet Belle held out hope that the king would extend mercy to her brother at the last minute, if for no reason other than the fact that he was brother to the Pavilion's draper.

She paid her final visit to Wesley in Newgate. He had been moved into a condemned cell, which had the ironic benefit of larger, more private quarters, with a better bed and more windows, although here the thick walls were covered with nail-studded planks.

But a condemned man spent his last hours alone, without the chaotic company of dozens of other prisoners around him. Belle would have thought all of those other people might be of comfort at such a time, but prison officials apparently thought otherwise.

Wesley's mood was strangely calm as he sat on the edge of his bed with Belle next to him.

"You don't understand, Belle. They want us to make peace with God, without distractions. I suspect that's entirely too late for me, don't you?" His upper lip cracked from dryness as he smiled, sending a small rivulet of blood into the corner of his mouth.

She took his hands. They were damp and sticky, in sharp contrast to the dryness of his mouth, and giving the lie to his placid demeanor. Her brother was as terrified as she was. "I am so sorry, Wesley, truly I am. I tried everything I could. No one would pay me any mind."

He shook his head. "No, I didn't think anyone would."

"I still think a pardon could come at the last moment. It's happened before."

"I doubt it. Others have also tried to help me, with little result. I seem to have made one bad decision after another. At least I'll die knowing that I prevented taking anyone else with me."

Belle was moved by his concern for her. "I wish I could take this punishment for you, Wesley. How preferable it would be to end my own life than to see yours gone."

"Don't be ridiculous, Belle. You warned me not to involve myself in anything illegal. But I had my own selfish goals, and here we see the outcome. I just wish I weren't shaming our family name."

"I'll never be ashamed of you. You made a mistake, is all." She lifted one of his clammy hands to her face, but he pulled it away.

"A mistake? A mistake is ordering cotton when you intended to order velvet. A mistake is cutting three yards when you mean three and a half. What I did was make a colossal blunder. The Duke of Monmouth couldn't have been more foolish when he tried to take the throne of England."

But what difference did the level of Wesley's crime make now? "I can't believe it's all come to this. How will I live without you, Brother?"

"More nonsense. You'll be much better off without me, I think. You should marry Mr. Boyce. He's fond of you. You should have seen the secretary he made, thinking it was for you. He'll take care of you, Belle."

"I don't require anyone's assistance."

"Sister, he's not like me or Clive. I admit now that my intention was to take the business from you. And Clive wanted you to abandon it altogether. But I don't think Mr. Boyce has that kind of design on you. Think how complementary his cabinetmaking shop would be to our—your—draper shop."

Belle laughed uneasily. Hadn't Put said much the same thing to her? "This is hardly the topic of conversation for such a moment. We should be discussing what else I can do for you."

Wesley disengaged his hands and turned away from her. Placing his elbows on his knees, he leaned forward and rested his chin in his palms. "There's nothing else that can be done for me, Belle. Lord, how I wish I hadn't listened to Dar—others. If I'd paid the slightest attention to you, I wouldn't be sitting in this rathole today."

He put both hands to his neck. "What do you imagine it feels like, Belle? The rough rope around your neck, slowly choking you to death? Do you think you black out quickly? That you're in blissful unconsciousness before you actually die?"

No, she didn't think that. Although the hangman's noose was intended to quickly break a man's neck and prevent suffering, many a man had struggled mightily against the rope, sometimes for up to a half hour. The heavier a man, the more forceful his drop, and the more likely that he would die quickly. But Wesley, poor Wesley, was so thin and gaunt now that he would probably flutter in the breeze endlessly. Belle shuddered. No, no, she couldn't let that happen.

She spoke quietly, hardly believing her own words. "Brother, there is one last service I can provide you. I can pay to have someone posted underneath the gallows, to pull on your legs when you drop. So that the end is more . . . immediate. Do you want me to do this?"

He sat straight again to face her. A single tear coursed down his face. "Yes, Sister. I deserve no mercy from you, but if you will grant me such a favor, I will be eternally grateful. Eternally grateful, ha! Grateful in hell."

"I only wish I could do more."

"Tell me, will you be there tomorrow?"

She'd dreaded this question. How was she ever going to manage watching her brother executed before her very eyes? She swallowed the sob that so desperately wanted to escape her throat.

"Of course," she whispered. "I will be your rock and your fortress. Just look for me."

"You can depend upon it."

Belle spent the remainder of her time with Wesley giving what meager comfort she could. Eventually he told her to go, that he wanted to rest and prepare himself for the ordeal the next day. She clutched his pitiful frame, as much to comfort herself as to soothe him.

As she left the prison, she passed another woman being led in by one of the prisoner-wardens. The well-dressed woman was sobbing uncontrollably into a handkerchief as she was led to the row of condemned cells.

Poor thing, Belle thought. *Must be one of the conspirators' wives. How much more horrible to be one of these men's wives than his sister?*

Put handed the newspaper to his cousin, pointing to the article he'd just read regarding the trial. Every detail had been noted by a journalist sitting in the gallery. Put was purchasing every paper he could find, trying to figure out what role his secretary played in the conspiracy.

He'd finally found it. The conspirators gave the secretary to Lord Harrowby and his wife as an anniversary present in order to gain access to his home. By all accounts, it appeared that the secretary was still inside the earl's home.

Fine recompense for knowingly opening your home to murderers.

Lord Liverpool boasted that he'd discovered the desk's secret compartment and that it held the damaging evidence they needed to prove that Thistlewood's plans were far more devious than originally thought, for it showed that his ultimate plans to bring down the government went back *years,* not mere months.

The newspaper account mentioned just the one compartment had been found, and surely it was Wesley who put those papers in there, since he was the only one who knew about it. Yet Put had shown him a second hidden compartment below the first.

I wonder . . .

Frances read the article, looked up at him, and shrugged. *What does it mean to you?*

Put started to explain, but stopped. Perhaps it was better if he kept his thoughts to himself for now.

* * *

May 1, 1820
London

Wesley's execution day was sunny and warm, and the fragrance of profusely blooming violets everywhere mocked Belle as she walked back to Newgate for the last time. Their sweet, unmistakable scent reminded passersby of the everlasting cycle of plant life every growing season, life that brought sustenance to all and was so easily reborn by the scattering of seeds.

But of all the seeds Belle had scattered to save Wesley, none had taken root. Except the one she planted to serve his last request. She just hoped now that the man would hold to his promise and hadn't just taken her money and ambled off to the nearest tavern. She also hoped that her description of Wesley's worn and scuffed shoes was enough for the man to recognize her brother as he fell through the trapdoor.

She brushed the thought from her mind. There was still time. The king may have reconsidered and was sending a messenger even as she approached the prison. Or perhaps Lord Liverpool and the other members of Parliament had considered her request and were meeting with the court right this very minute to bring a special judgment of mercy on Wesley.

A small flicker of hope rose in her once again. They might still decide to deport Wesley. She would go anywhere with him. America, Australia, a pestilence-ridden island in the middle of the ocean, anywhere. If only *someone* in authority would grant Wesley one more chance.

Was there anyone she'd missed in her pleas for clemency? She didn't think so. Dozens of doors had slammed in her face, dozens more faces had either scowled or laughed at her.

A crowd was already gathering around the gallows, rolled out of storage and brought out for today's event. As she drew closer, her heart nearly stopped to see that in addition to the set of five nooses, five coffins were laid open on the platform, a structure at least twelve feet high and completely enclosed underneath.

Several more coffins were stacked up on the ground next to the scaffold to await the second batch of prisoners.

Belle bristled. What purpose did this serve? Why must the condemned men's final resting places be evident to them as they ascended the tall platform? Must they be tortured even further in their final moments of life?

Stop it. Salvation is at hand, you know it is.

Several constables on foot, plus one on horseback, meandered through the crowd to maintain order, occasionally shouting at a spectator or brandishing a stick. The people were mostly peaceful, though, and laughed good-naturedly at the pompous officers.

Yes, everyone seemed downright exultant about the proceedings, much to Belle's disgust. Everyone except for a woman about thirty feet away. She already wore a dress of black bombazine—a sign of the poor woman's deep distress—wait, that was the same woman she'd seen leaving the prison last night. The woman's face was swollen from crying, and she scanned the gallows furtively, waiting for her loved one to emerge from the prison.

Overwhelmed by sympathy, Belle went over to her, to comfort her in some way. But before Belle could reach her, the woman turned and locked gazes with her. To Belle's shock, the woman's eyes changed from deep sorrow to a murderous rage and she snarled, "Stay away from me!" at Belle before melting away into the crowd.

Belle froze in place. Did the woman have her confused with someone else?

She was interrupted from her thoughts by a hand on her back. She turned to find Put standing next to her, his eyes not hate filled at all, but dark with worry and concern.

"I wasn't sure I'd be able to find you here," he said. "Thought you could use some company at this moment."

"I'm fine. Wesley is at peace, I think, and if he is, why then, so am I. Besides, there could still be a reprieve."

Put nodded, unconvinced. "Nonetheless, I'll stay here with you if you don't mind."

"I don't mind at all." Belle turned back to the gallows so he wouldn't see the tears of gratitude forming in her eyes for the presence of the man who had been right all along about Wesley, and whom Wesley had deemed a good choice of a suitor.

The first group of prisoners was brought out, unchained but with their hands bound in front of them. The crowd reaction was a combination of boos, taunts, and cheers. As they ascended the platform, Belle could see that Wesley was among them.

He was in the same clothing he wore last night. The lines of dissatisfaction and pain were erased from around his eyes. As she told Put, he was at peace.

He must also sense that a reprieve is on its way.

Belle fought her way forward in the crowd, and Put stayed with her. Finally she was close enough that if Wesley would just look her way, he'd see her.

Please, Wesley, over here. I want you to know I'm here.

But her brother stared resolutely ahead, through the opening of the noose that dangled in front of his face. What was wrong? He said he would look for her. Belle waved a hand, but Wesley was oblivious to his surroundings, as though he'd already departed the scene.

A man pushed his way through the crowd, brandishing a newspaper. "Buy an execution special! Read their confessions and last words! Only a penny!"

Belle gasped as the man waved the broadsheet in front of her. "How about you, mistress? Care to read about the prisoners' last moments?"

"How could you possibly know what they—" she started, but stopped when Put grabbed the man and threw him bodily off to the side, warning him loudly, "Don't let me hear your hawking again, do you hear me? Else you'll find yourself in bad circumstances with my temper."

The man scurried away with his stack of broadsheets. Belle opened her mouth to thank Put, but he shook his head to let her know it wasn't necessary. She was openly trembling now, between the seller's audacity and her concern that the moment of execution was coming without any sign of a messenger from the king or anyone else.

After some nattering about justice served and the saving of His Majesty's kingdom, the presiding official asked if any of the men had last words. The mulatto, Davidson, was in deep conversation with a chaplain and completely ignored him. The man Belle recognized as Thistlewood nodded his head, and he was allowed to address the crowd from the edge of the platform. Incredibly, he pulled an orange from his pocket and began sucking on it casually as he spoke. But his words were those of a crazed, delirious madman consumed with his own sense of greatness, and he was soon booed by the crowd and forced to terminate his speech to return to face his noose.

Thistlewood smiled his contempt at the crowd and roared out snatches of a song about Death or Liberty. After running out of lyrics, he turned to the executioner, nodded, and said, "Do it tidy."

How had Wesley ever fallen under the spell of such a man?

Yet he seemed confident. Maybe he knew for certain that this was not going to be a day of hanging.

Hope pushed its eternal way back into her heart again.

The other prisoners declined an opportunity to speak, and the nooses were thrown about their necks. A drummer began the steady staccato beat that would overpower the sound of the men dropping to their deaths.

Where was the messenger? Was he delayed? Did the executioner not realize there was to be a reprieve?

Was she deluded in thinking there would even be a reprieve?

Dread recklessly shoved hope out of the way.

Belle trembled. Her resolute determination to stay focused on Wesley through everything was wavering, especially since her brother hadn't thus far noticed her in the crowd.

Her mind's effort to maintain sanity turned to practical matters. Was the man she paid perched now under the gallows, waiting for Wesley's poorly shod feet to appear?

Her breath caught in her throat and her heart pounded with the ferocity of one of Put's wooden mallets. In all of her frantic plans to save Wesley, she'd forgotten to plan for his burial in the event that he was not rescued. What would happen to his body? What would they do with the coffin set aside for him? Would he be thrown into some unidentified mass grave with the others?

Lord, why me? Why Wesley?

She turned her face to the sky to glare at the brightly smiling sun, its rays a mockery of the tragedy being played out before her. She looked back at her brother, who finally turned her way. She once again lifted a hand in greeting. Wesley's eyes shifted as he took in the fact that she waited there with Put.

He smiled as though in approval, and resumed staring straight ahead.

She wasn't sure whether to be happy that his suffering was ending sooner or to lament the fact that he didn't have just a few more precious minutes to enjoy the warm day and breathe deeply of the abundant purple violets.

And still there was no man dramatically rushing up offering a stay of execution. Her efforts had been for nothing. Her brother, her flesh and blood, was about to be dispatched like a lamb at Easter, with ruthless efficiency.

As the official opened his mouth to shout the execution order, Put's hand came around the side of her face, and he pulled her to his shoulder. She struggled only a moment, for she really didn't want to see. The command to drop the doors sounded like a gunshot in her ears, and it was instantly followed by a cacophony of wood squeaking and splintering as five trapdoors opened simultaneously and five bodies rushed violently downward, pulling down with great cruelty on the hanging beam above them.

At least they were concealed by the enclosure beneath the platform.

Belle only became aware of her own sobbing as she realized that Put was stroking her hair and mumbling words of comfort in her ear. She knew she mustn't let him do this, but it did feel soothing, almost like being a child again and having her father console her over the loss of her little striped kitten that had mindlessly run out in front of a horse one day.

Except that Put wasn't her father. She hadn't permitted him to be anything, for fear that, like Clive, he would turn into something unexpected and take away her livelihood.

Oh, honestly, Belle, came her brother's voice unbidden in her mind. *Who gives two shakes if Put shares your interest in the shop? He's a decent man, not an ogre. Be done with your precious sense of self-importance.*

And she found herself wrapping her arms around Put's neck, clinging tightly to him for strength. No one noticed their embrace in the crush of activity surrounding the executions. Belle listened unwillingly as the crowd first cheered, then sighed disappointedly in the quick dispatch of all five men.

Chattering resumed as the dead men were pulled back up through the trapdoors and their nooses removed. Then a terrible *whump* sounded as an ax presumably cut through Thistlewood's neck and connected with the block. The crowd rejoiced again, most likely in response to the barbaric practice of waving the freshly decapitated head for approval from the bystanders. She was quaking uncontrollably now, despite Put's firm grasp on her. If not for him, she would have already collapsed, unconscious, and been trampled to death by the energized bystanders.

Belle blocked her ears against the remaining beheadings and wavings, burrowing her face in Put's neck. Put kept her tightly turned toward him, never telling her when it was Wesley's turn at the block. A deafening clamor ensued as all of the bodies were tossed into their respective coffins. Belle shook her head.

I can bear no more of this.

Put led her away before the next group of conspirators was brought out to meet their demise. He had to push their way through the roaring crowd, whose appetite had only been whetted by the first executions of the day.

They didn't speak the entire way back to her lodgings, as she fought to maintain control.

I shouldn't be returning home yet. I need to obtain possession of Wesley's coffin. I must bury him myself. I need a priest. I need—

"Here you are. May I send my cousin to stay with you? To at least visit you? She would be very happy to do so." Put opened the door to let her inside the lodging house, but made no attempt to follow her in.

"No, thank you. I'm tired, and believe I need to sleep for several days. Although that won't be possible, for my customers will wonder where I am. If I'm not ruined by all of this. Actually, I'm not sure I care if I've lost all of my customers. Perhaps I should return to Yorkshire."

"Surely you don't mean that, Belle. Your presence would be sorely missed. By all of London. Not just your customers, I mean."

She smiled tiredly at him. "Thank you, Put. I do appreciate what you and Frances have done for me. But I really just need to be alone for a while."

"As you wish. But Belle"—Put lifted her hand and pressed his lips to her wrist before gently releasing it—"you can rely on me for any assistance whatsoever."

She nodded her thanks and retreated up to her own room. What assistance could she possibly need now? She required help while Wesley was still alive, while he still had a chance to be free.

The only assistance that would be of any help would be a potent sleeping draught.

Drat Wesley for leaving his pipe to his sister. And what had he left Darcey? Nothing, absolutely nothing. Except for unfinished plans and dreams. And what could she possibly do with the tatters of hope she had once held in him?

Darcey had never been so furious at a dead man before. Her last visit with him in his condemned cell was one of heated embraces and rushed pleasure, followed by a most unsatisfactory discussion, since all Wesley wanted to do was talk about Belle and how guilty he felt for bringing such hardship upon her.

Despite it being his last night on earth anyway, Darcey was consumed with the thought of personally choking him to death. It was his dear sister's fault that he was sitting in a condemned cell to begin with. Honestly, how blind was he? If Belle had been any sort of decent, gracious sister, she would have shared the spoils of her shop with her brother.

"Wesley Stirling, every time I think I've educated you about your sister, you revert back to a subservient toad. Belle mangled your life, don't you understand that? If it weren't for her, you'd be your own man, proprietor of a successful shop, with me as your helpmeet. Instead . . ." She waved her hand around the cell.

As if to further infuriate her, Wesley just smiled sadly at her and shook his head. "No matter, Darcey. What's done is done. As I told Belle, I need some time alone."

"You mean you don't want me to stay here with you all night?"

"No, I think it's best if you go back to your parents' house, where you belong. Obey your father, and marry whomever he picks out for you."

"I can't believe you're saying this. You and I were meant to be together. For eternity. You talk as though you don't care what happens to me now."

"I nearly destroyed you in this, but in the end, they found nothing significant and I can die knowing you're safe."

Nearly destroyed her? She was utterly ruined! Cracked. Damaged. Useless. What did he mean that nothing significant was found? Found where?

But before she could protest further, he stood up, signaling the end of their conversation, and called for the jailer to escort Miss White out.

"Wait!" Darcey clung to Wesley, desperate for more moments with him. "Have you nothing to leave me? A memento of our love?"

He laid his hands on her shoulders and looked around the room. "I own nothing except the bedding."

"What of your pipe, our pipe?"

"I gave it to Belle as a remembrance. After all, she purchased it in the first place."

I didn't know that.

Her fury over the pipe having been a gift from Belle replaced every other emotion. It pooled with anger at her father, Wesley's execution, and her failed dreams, surging together in a scarlet, boiling wave that crashed repeatedly inside her skull. She pressed a hand against her forehead to stem the crashing. It was too much to bear.

"Darcey?" Wesley's voice echoed relentlessly against the walls in the room. She clapped her hands over her ears to block it out.

What was happening to her?

Something flashed in her mind at that moment, and the pain brought her gasping to her knees. The agony was replaced by a tranquil, whispering voice, urging her as to what she must do next.

Ah, the voice was a calming sensation, replacing her turbulent anger with a serene peace.

All was clear to Darcey now.

She stalked out of Wesley's cell without looking back at his puzzled expression.

No, there would be no more tears for Darcey White. She'd entered the prison nearly blinded by her own crying, but that was over.

It should have been obvious before that Darcey would have to handle matters on her own. Her final tribute to Wesley would be permanently fixing the situation with Belle. He couldn't do so during his own life, but Darcey certainly would now.

And then Belle Stirling would suffer the same fate as Wesley.

❧14❧

The heart will break, but broken live on.

—Lord George Gordon Byron, British poet, 1788–1824

April 1820

Put carted over a new coffin the next day, confessing that he built it once the trial started, in anticipation of an unhappy outcome. He obtained Wesley's body and transferred him to the mahogany box, the top of which was intricately decorated with inlaid swirls and acanthus leaves.

Belle's throat nearly closed in gratitude. She knew coffins were typically a good source of income for cabinetmakers, since there was always a steady stream of customers for them, but they were usually hastily constructed of cheap pine, and not always even painted, much less oil-rubbed and embellished as this one was.

Along with Frances and a local priest, they buried Wesley, and Belle entered the drudgery of daily life without her brother. She stumbled through the next few weeks in a murky fog. Her feet carried her automatically to the shop every day, where a series of curiosity seekers and gossips stopped in to ask her about Wesley's role in the conspiracy. She responded to everyone with as much politeness as she could muster. She would have felt more gracious if these nosey rumormongers were actually interested in purchasing some fabric.

Her customers who normally made regular purchases were giving the shop a wide berth. A few of them even sent notes, explaining that continued patronage of her shop would be simply impossible, what with her brother's unfortunate demise.

She cast all of the unwanted correspondence into the parlor fireplace, watching with satisfaction as it turned to ash in dark, withering curls.

Even worse was when she visited Lady Derby in Grosvenor Square to check up on whether the countess needed further help with her bedchamber. Belle swallowed her fear and disgust of nearby Number 39, Lord Harrowby's home, yet was rewarded with a curt "We no longer need the services of a traitor's sister, thank you" by Lady Derby's housekeeper and a slammed door in her face.

Perhaps I really will *be driven to leave London.*

She gratefully accepted Frances's invitation to sup with her and Put, realizing now that the Boyces might be her only friends left in London. Put and his cousin studiously avoided any discussion about the conspiracy, even though it continued to be a topic of great interest in the newspapers, and instead chatted about mundane items, such as the weather and a neighbor's child who had a chronic cough. Their suppers together became a regular occurrence, and Belle learned how to communicate with Frances through a series of hand gestures and explicit pronunciation while directly facing her. It was hard to believe she'd once viewed this lovely girl as an enemy.

Especially now that Belle was surrounded on all sides by enemies.

One evening at the dining table, Put wordlessly handed her a newspaper. She scanned it, immediately finding the article he wanted her to see, which read like a hysterical clamoring for witchcraft trials.

> . . . and having ferreted out this latest of
> insurrections against king and country, it makes
> every thinking man realize that for every
> radical who is caught in his misdeed, there are
> three, four, nay, five more in his shadow, waiting

for an opportunity to step into the gas lamp's
light and take his brother's place.

And should not all concerned men consider
this in a literal sense? Are not the most likely
candidates to emerge from a radical's shadow
his own relatives? That they would embrace
such unwise actions before a man's friends and
acquaintances? Good sense requires that we
examine a man's brothers, his father, his
uncles. Yes, even his female relatives, for are
they not the weaker sex and therefore even
more prone to accepting foolish notions?

All of the king's subjects would be well-
advised to serve him by keeping watch for
suspicious behavior by the relatives of these
convicted miscreants.

She handed it back to Put. "What drivel. Just because one man
is a fool doesn't mean his entire family is equally muttonheaded."

"No, but it does mean you might be in danger from those who
take the newspaper seriously. I think you should stay here while
tensions are high in the city. I know Frances would be pleased to
have you here, and it would make us both rest easier to know
you're safe."

"Thank you, but no. I don't think anyone would seek out a
mere draper. And Wesley's role was insignificant in the conspiracy.
They've more prominent relations to seek out. Those of Thistlewood's, for instance."

Put slammed the paper down on the dining table. "Belle, you
couldn't be more wrong. First, Wesley's participation was not that
of some innocent dupe. He knew full well what he was doing. He
was Thistlewood's trusted agent. Second, a populace frightened
by a perceived radical movement isn't going to empathize with a
'mere draper,' as you say. You'll join the list of possible suspects.
And that places your life at risk. You shake your head no, but I tell
you, the threat to your person is real."

Deep concern was etched in his face, and Frances grasped both of Belle's hands in her own, as if by doing so she could pass a secret message to her.

"Thank you both for your concern," Belle said. "I have to think on things."

How easy it would be to become part of this family. To be Put's wife and embrace Frances as a sister. Put's home on the edge of Shoreditch was simple but clean, and a house any merchant's wife would be proud to own. Belle respected his woodworking talents—there were few shops that produced furniture as well built as his. He was strong, kind, and fiercely loyal.

If only she didn't worry so much about losing her livelihood to a husband. She'd been her own woman ever since she could remember, and couldn't stop now.

Well, what she *could* do was stop dwelling on it. Her primary concern was combating attacks on her reputation. She'd kept quiet about the ongoing decline in her shop's business, but it took enormous will not to share with Put the letter she received from John Nash, temporarily severing their relationship and informing her that the king would not require her services, saying that ". . . in light of the current circumstances, His Majesty deems it best that a connection to the name 'Stirling' be put in abeyance until the agitation over recent events has settled down."

Belle knew full well that this suspension on her services extended to Mr. Crace, so there was no point in trying to seek business from him or anyone else connected to Brighton.

What was she to do? Her reputation and business were collapsing around her like a hailstorm.

There was more disaster to come.

Arriving early at her shop one morning, she found the words "A Traitor Lived Here" painted across the panes on her front window. Anger replaced her grief and fear. How dare some busybody deface her property like that? She scrubbed away the paint until the glass sparkled anew, but there was more in store for her.

Days later, she sat behind her counter, going through her account books once again to see how much longer she'd last at her declining rate of sales, especially with losing the king's custom.

Her situation was grim.

No matter, Belle would survive it. She'd move back to York-shire; she'd start a cloth-finishing factory; she'd raise chickens and sell eggs if necessary. She stretched her arms and picked her pen up again. Maybe she could find a miscalculation somewhere that might prove to be in her favor.

The crash of glass startled Belle from her computations. She looked up to realize that a small, jagged rock had been thrown through her clean window and now rested innocently in the mid-dle of the shop's floor. Two more stone missiles soon joined it, each one breaking a different section of the front glass.

Now what? Was someone planning to charge into her shop? Set it afire? She drew a deep breath. Perhaps Put was right about the menace she was facing.

Ignoring her nerves, Belle pulled one of her pistols from its hid-ing place behind the counter. Hiding the unloaded weapon be-hind her back, she darted to the front door, flinging it open violently and shouting, "What do you want here?"

A pair of teenage boys stood in the middle of Oxford Street, making obscene gestures and laughing at her.

Boys. Mere boys. Thinking they could ill-treat an innocent shopkeeper. She felt rage creeping up her spine, white-hot and scorching. This was just like the invasion of her family's shop back in Leeds.

"So, my little friends, you thought you'd have a little fun with my shop, did you?"

"We didn't mean nuthin'! We were just having fun. Besides, we were told that you were easy pickings."

"Is that so? How about if I pick your little ears off the sides of your heads?"

A wagon rolled to a stop behind the boys, and a burly laborer jumped down.

"Something wrong here?" he asked.

Thank goodness, help had arrived to serve justice to these two street rats.

"Yes, sir," said the taller of the two boys. He pointed at Belle. "She's been threatening us, and all we were doing was tossing a ball out here."

What?

The laborer frowned at her. "Aren't you a relative of one of them radicals? A niece or something?"

Belle lifted her chin. "My brother was convicted in the Cato Street Conspiracy, yes. What of it?" She pointed her chin to the window. "What's that to do with my window, broken by these two little scoundrels?"

The man rubbed his unshaven face. "Not really a crime if you're a secret radical, is it?"

"Not a crime? Do I really look like a radical to you?" She glanced down at her simple dress and back up at the man.

"I guess I don't know what a lady radical looks like. But your brother was one, and I hear as they've been poisoning all of their relations with crazy thoughts. So you just might look like a radical."

A few people were gathering to watch their exchange. By this point, the boys had skittered away.

Belle clutched the pistol firmly behind her back. She wished she'd loaded it before bringing it outside, but it took so long to complete the steps.

She spoke up loudly, so that everyone around could hear. "The idea that because my brother was convicted of a crime that I am necessarily guilty of the same is completely absurd. I've been operating my shop on this street for nearly eight years. In fact, many of you have patronized me. At least, you used to patronize me, until you started believing lies. Surely over the years you've learned far better about me."

The watchers shrugged and moved on, with one muttering, "She's doing no harm."

"Seems to me you're the one with the learning to do, miss." The man walked close enough to her that she could smell his foul breath. He could grab her if he wanted; everyone else was too far away and too disinterested to care.

"Step away from me, if you please." Did her voice falter?

"I don't think you should be quite so high-and-mighty, miss. You might be a traitor."

Now, Belle.

She pulled the pistol out from behind her back, holding it level with the man's expanding belly. She prayed he wouldn't notice its unloaded state.

"Sir, I'm going to suggest once more that you step away from me, lest in my high-and-mighty state I accidentally pull this trigger and send you to the place where all radicals end up."

The man licked his lips. "There's no need to be angry about it. I was just trying to protect those boys."

"I'm sure you were. Please don't darken my doorstep ever again."

Belle held the pistol steady as the man backed away from her and ran back to his wagon, lumbering up onto the seat and whipping his nag unnecessarily to move her forward. As he rumbled out of sight, Belle leaned against the shop's door in exhaustion.

She'd prevented any real violence today, but could she continue to do so? What if rioters showed up while she wasn't here? What then?

She went back inside and turned the sign to read "Closed." She stood in the middle of the shop, hands on her hips as she contemplated the damage. Further compounding her problems was that her window was irreparably shattered. With what money would she replace it?

The dollmaker from next door paid a visit the next day.

"I saw your bold defense of this shop yesterday," Lady Greycliffe said. "I confess I was watching from my own window and was planning to intervene, but then I saw you brandishing the most marvelous brass-handled pistol. I assumed then that you had the situation well in hand. *Vous êtes très brave.*"

Belle blushed. "Hardly, madam. I was merely doing what any tradeswoman who is frightened out of her wits would do. Actually, I'm not sure I could have actually shot someone, no matter how threatened I was."

Lady Greycliffe's laughter resonated inside the shop. "And we have all had our frightened moments, have we not? I came to say that I am sorry for the loss of your brother, Miss Stirling. Also, I heard of your, shall we say, persecutions, since the trial. It is unconscionable. I myself have also had my shop attacked. In fact, it was once nearly destroyed by some rioters."

Lady Greycliffe's eyes clouded over at some memory, and she shook her head. "And so we must each be *un protecteur* for our livelihoods every day, no? But I have another purpose in my visit."

The dollmaker pointed up to a large roll of fabric. "I'm planning my most ambitious set of dolls ever, a complete set of the queens of England. *Remarquable*, no? I believe I will need copious amounts of different-colored velvets. I'll also need some silks. I don't see anything resembling sixteenth-century cloth of gold here. Can you find something less expensive and order it for me? And I'll certainly need dozens of pearl buttons, small as you can obtain, ribbons, and leather for shoes."

Belle searched out paper to write down Lady Greycliffe's considerable order, and promised to have everything in two weeks' time. The two women shook hands, and Lady Greycliffe laid a gloved hand on Belle's cheek. "All will be well, my dear."

After Lady Greycliffe's departure, Belle reviewed the woman's order. As she calculated it out, she realized that the dollmaker had just rescued her from going under.

At least for the moment.

Darcey White stood in the middle of her parents' ballroom. The rich green wallpaper with its trompe l'oeil landscape pattern was a vivid contrast to the fringed draperies of mauve and gold stripes. The chandeliers and sconces gleamed brightly, as though issuing a welcoming smile to all who entered. All of her mother's hand-selected furniture pieces were arranged just so in anticipation of a multitude of guests.

Now, why had she come in here?

Oh, of course, she'd left her guest list on the settee in here. The one specially placed to enable her to look out over the back gardens. She spent many hours here, either sitting or standing up before the window, gazing down at the Whites' neatly planted rows of flowers and shrubs. Sometimes it was just so nice to sit and relax from all of her myriad of responsibilities.

She sat down and picked up her list of guests for the engagement party her parents planned to host for her and Wesley. The tattered piece of parchment was full of scribbles and cross-marks through names. Really, she should just start over. Coming up with the proper mix of guests for her grand ball had proven entirely too difficult. After all, only the right sorts of people, amusing and witty, could be invited, and she wanted everything to be perfect for Wesley.

Yes, finalizing the list was a grueling challenge, but Darcey White wouldn't relax until she'd done her best.

She spent several minutes adding more names and crossing off others, then picked up a small bell from the floor next to the settee and gave it several vigorous shakes. A maid appeared and stood between Darcey and the window.

"Maggie, it took you entirely too long to tend to me. I expect promptness from the staff here." There. It was always wise to occasionally put servants in their places.

"Yes, miss." Maggie's face was blank.

"Has my father returned home from his club?" Darcey asked. "I need to go over my revised guest list for my engagement party."

"No, miss, Mr. White isn't here."

"Of course not. He and Mother completely ignore me these days. There's so much work to be done before a ball, and my parents just don't seem to care."

"Yes, miss."

Darcey allowed her gaze to wander off from the maid. Yes, her parents were proving very selfish lately, but wasn't Wesley, as well? He hadn't come to see her at the Horse and Groom in quite some time. Presumably he wasn't wasting time slavishly following his cow of a sister around.

How dare Belle Stirling think she had the right to influence her Wesley?

Soon they would be married, and would take a cottage somewhere far away from her parents and his sister. Maybe they could return to Yorkshire where he'd grown up. No one would follow them there.

She'd talk to Wesley about it straightaway.

But then, Wesley never listened to her anymore. Why was that?

Wait, wasn't Wesley sick in the hospital? A breathing problem? Or had he perhaps died? No, that couldn't be right. It was so hard to remember every little detail of life these days.

She turned her attention back to the maid.

"Well, then, send Jane to me. I want her to copy this list over. It will be good practice of her penmanship."

"Yes, miss. Can I get you some tea and a novel while you wait?"

What was that foolish look on the girl's face? How dare she look pained! "No, I do not want tea. Why is everyone constantly offering me tea, biscuits, a cold compress, or an escort to my room for a nap? Doesn't anyone realize how much work I have to do? Time is running short."

"Yes, miss."

"And I noticed a fine layer of dust on the mantelpieces. I want them cleaned immediately." She hadn't really noticed the fireplaces, but it was also desirable that one exhibit as much power as possible. Wesley's friend, Mr. Thistlewood, had shown her that.

The maid bobbed a curtsy and turned to leave.

"Don't forget to send Jane to me," Darcey called out after Maggie, who didn't bother to acknowledge the instruction. Insolent girl.

Darcey stood and went to the window. Too many blooms were shriveling and in need of clipping. She turned away from the window. My, but the bamboo chairs in this room were stunning. Perfect accoutrements for her party. She imagined the perfumed and graceful young ladies sitting in them along the walls, waiting for their opportunities to dance with Wesley, practically choking with jealousy to know that he belonged to Darcey and was completely off the marriage market.

Yet something niggled at the back of Darcey's mind. Something about Wesley and his future. It was important. She felt her stomach turn one revolution as she struggled to recall what it was. She turned back to the window and touched her forehead to the glass.

Ah yes, Wesley had accidentally thrown a vase out of the Cato Street window and broken it. Quite a mess it was. And a ridiculous fuss made over it by the authorities. Although they finally declared that it was Wesley's fault.

As though *fault* could be assigned in something that was so clearly an accident. A mistake.

Then the lawyers and courts had swept in with sheaves of papers to be read aloud and signed and folded back up for safe-keeping. Very pompous and self-important they were. She recalled one solicitor having a tinny, high-pitched voice that cracked as he read his documents. So many people watching the proceedings, too. Much ado over a bit of nonsense.

Darcey laughed, a sharp noise in the stillness of the ballroom. She made a mental note to mention it to Wesley when he returned that evening. He would surely enjoy remembering it over a smoke.

Now, why had she come in here?

Belle accepted Put's invitation to visit Madame Tussaud's wax exhibition, which had again returned to London for a limited engagement in anticipation of the king's coronation. The exhibit was as fresh and engaging as it was when Belle had toured it four years ago, and just as crowded with eager patrons.

Belle reached up to touch Queen Elizabeth's wax face. Here was a woman accused of heresy by her sister and who nearly lost her life as a result. A monarch who rose from the ashes to become great and successful.

Like the owner of the waxworks.

"Madame Tussaud nearly had to start over at one time, didn't she?" Belle asked.

"Yes," Put replied. "She's undergone exhibition losses more than once because of tragedies from riots to shipwrecks. She always rebuilds with remarkable speed and efficiency."

"But she must be quite old. Hasn't she been traveling with her exhibition for nearly twenty years now?"

"I'd say she's nearly sixty. She and her son have been touring Great Britain since 1802."

Belle was quiet as they passed through the other tableaux in the exhibition. Other women before her had risen above their terrible circumstances, why not her? And both the illustrious queen and Tussaud had done so almost completely on their own, without husbands or brothers to help them.

Lady Greycliffe's purchase was an excellent start to her own recovery. Perhaps there was hope that Belle could also revive her business and be stronger than ever.

Perhaps there was much to be learned from a proprietress like Madame Tussaud.

Put offered to introduce Belle to the great lady, but she was away on a buying trip on the Continent, although Belle had the opportunity to meet her twenty-year-old son, Joseph, a solemn man who became animated when honoring Belle's request to tour the young sculptor's own favorite pieces in the collection.

After the waxworks, Belle and Put walked to a nearby coffee shop for cups of chocolate, and by the end of the day she was feeling cheered about her future. She found herself conversing happily about what she could do to expand her shop and revive interest in her goods. Put smiled indulgently at her endless chattering during their walk back.

Her enthusiasm broke off in a gasp as they neared the shop. The scene before her was horrifyingly unreal.

"Good Lord, what happened here?" Put said.

Strewn in front of the Stirling Drapers shop was a heaping, stinking pile of trash. Food scraps, small animal carcasses, and other debris had been amassed at the front door.

And was that . . . ?

Belle disengaged her hand from Put's arm and ran to her newly repaired window. The stench was nauseating. She looked back to Put. "Excrement. Someone has flung feces at my shop. At *my* shop. First those boys, now this."

Atop the refuse mound was a crudely painted sign:

ALL CONSPIRATORS WILL BE FOUND.
NONE WILL ESCAPE PUNISHMENT.

Under that was a drawing of a gallows, with a woman in the noose.

If anyone expected that Belle would cry or tremble uncontrollably, he was wrong. She was beyond any sense of fear or outrage.

No, this didn't compare to a shipwreck. Or imprisonment in the Tower by a fanatical sister.

Belle Stirling planned to fight whatever forces were ranged against her. And they would sorely rue raising hands against her.

Put set down the jack plane he was using on some freshly delivered satinwood intended for a cradle he'd specially designed for a customer's set of twins.

"Good Lord," he said, and realized that he was saying it more and more often these days. From Belle's ferocity in reestablishing her ground again in her business, to the ongoing swirl of political chaos in England, to the rumor Gill had just brought him, well, there was much about which to be concerned.

Telling his other workers that he'd be back shortly, he slipped into the streets and nearby taverns to see what else he could learn.

What he discovered was disturbing. Yet it was clear what he had to do next.

He hurried to his house to talk to his cousin, who by now had simply moved in with him permanently. Put liked her company, and felt it provided respectability to Belle's visits.

Not to mention that deafness had little impact on Frances's ability to make succulent roasted duck.

"Frances," he said, speaking directly to her. "I think there may be some trouble for me."

She nodded and raised a palm. *What can I do?*

"Someone is bruiting it about that a cabinetmaker was actively involved in the Cato Street Conspiracy."

Frances pointed at him.

"Yes, that's what's swirling around. Now, we may know that Belle's brother hoodwinked me into making that secretary, but that doesn't mean the public will believe it to be so. Belle is already so very close to the conspiracy because of her brother, and my continued association with her will only bring more suspicion on us."

Frances frowned and shook her head. He knew this would be her reaction.

"And so"—he took both his cousin's hands in his and kissed

them—"my responsibility is to you and the shop. I'm going to break it off with Belle. If we're fortunate, she won't come after us, brandishing a pitchfork."

Frances laughed despite herself. It came out in its usual strangled way.

Put smiled as his cousin put a sympathetic hand to his face and gave him a quizzical look.

"No, it's better that I remove myself from her completely until the public's interest in the conspirators completely dies down."

She nodded. Removing her hand from his cheek, Frances made a scooping hand toward her mouth.

"Dear cousin, I would love a slice of your pork pie. Afterwards, we'll discuss what to do to ensure no further trouble visits our door."

Belle held the two letters in her hand. What was happening here?

First was the short missive from Put, informing her that due to unforeseen circumstances, he would be unable to see her for some time.

No explanation accompanied his curt declaration. What had caused him to do this? Was he angry with her for some reason? Was he tired of waiting for her to come round on their relationship? Admittedly, she'd never let the conversation return to anything near marriage. Or even courtship. But that was no reason to abandon her company entirely.

Even more disturbing was a note from a Darcey Whitecastle, who claimed she was once a patron in Belle's shop.

Except the woman claimed she was no longer Miss Whitecastle. She was Mrs. Stirling.

The letter rambled at great, confusing length about how Miss Whitecastle and Wesley were married some weeks prior to the Cato Street debacle. They'd kept it a secret by fleeing to the Scottish border town of Gretna Green to get married, where they could avoid the English requirement of having banns read.

Impossible. Wesley had never been out of her sight long enough to make a trip to Gretna Green.

Had he?

He never mentioned any specific woman in all the time they'd been in London. Of course, Wesley was so full of secrets and silence toward the end that it was difficult to know what he might have been doing.

Oh, Wesley, I wish I could have known the true state of your mind. I wish I had been a better sister to you, but you always wanted the one thing I couldn't give you. And nothing else would satisfy you.

The letter went on to inform Belle that the new Mrs. Stirling intended *"to make my rights on Wesley's inheritance known."* The woman claimed that Stirling Drapers actually belonged to her as Wesley's wife, and that Belle would be brought to justice for having stolen the shop from her husband.

What a ridiculous claim. Whoever this woman was, whether or not she had actually married Wesley—a highly dubious claim in Belle's mind—she certainly was in no position to make claim to her cloth shop. These were the ravings of a madwoman.

Probably some lunatic who had followed the trial and sought to profit from it. Belle crumpled up "Mrs. Stirling's" letter and tossed it aside for discard.

It was Put's letter that disturbed her more. Reading it again, she came to a different conclusion than what he himself stated.

> *. . . I must apologize in advance that I risk your*
> *displeasure—and perhaps the loss of your affection—by*
> *withdrawing my attentions until certain of my own*
> *private concerns are resolved. Yours & etc., Put*

What circumstances were these? She doubted seriously that the cabinetmaker was in frightful circumstances. And why didn't he speak plainly to her? Hadn't she had enough intrigue with Wesley?

Her conclusion over Put's flowery, nonsensical words—most unusual in a tradesman, too—angered her more than all of the glass breaking and excrement throwing in the world.

Put is forsaking me, from fear for his own safety, out of cowardice, and because he is afraid to stand with me. So be it, Mr. Boyce. I've no need for your protection. I'll manage the Miss Whitecastles of the world on my own.

❧ 15 ❧

Most gracious queen, we thee implore
To go away and sin no more;
Or if that effort be too great,
To go away at any rate.

—Anonymous pamphleteer, on the occasion
of Queen Caroline's trial for adultery, 1820

June 1820
Carlton House

George IV paraded up and down the length of the Blue Velvet Room. "That cow has made me look a fool from Lake Como to Jericho, and in every city in between where she's been parading her lover, Pergami. She thinks she has me cornered like a flea-bitten rat, but the two bags of incriminating documents I've delivered to Parliament will leave them no choice but to grant me a divorce. What I truly want is a bill of attainder, to enable me to have her stripped of every title, confiscate her undeserved property, and put her in my complete power. Then we'll see who the cat is and who is the rodent, eh? Ha! We need another Cato Street hanging and beheading."

The king was in his most exquisite form today: the outraged, deceived husband. It was also when he was at his most tiresome, Lady Elizabeth Conyngham thought, as she nibbled on some sugared orange slices from her recamier sofa. She nodded to encourage George in his tirade.

"I told Liverpool in no uncertain terms that I demand a trial for that harpy. Anyone who says she should have been the man, and I the woman, in our marriage has no rights in *my* kingdom. I want her publicly discredited before my coronation next month."

Flecks of foam flew from George's mouth as he paced back and forth, stopping only to spin a globe or clean his fingernails with a letter opener. Not that she could blame her lover, even though he railed exhaustingly about his wife. Lady Elizabeth had seen for herself that Caroline talked too much, dressed like a common trollop, had little moral sense, and had even less common sense.

But for heaven's sake, all of England knew of Caroline's shortcomings, and George had already subjected the woman to an investigation fifteen years ago. The "Delicate Investigation" resulted in a royal reprimand for Caroline, but the primary consequence was George's own waning popularity, and Caroline's increasing one. Even so, in 1814 she'd had the decency to leave the country, claiming that since the English court would not give her the honors due to a Princess of Wales, she was content to travel the Continent as just plain Caroline, "a happy, merry soul."

Why couldn't he be content with that?

Lady Elizabeth supposed she should be happy that today he was vitriolic, instead of glum and morose, a far more difficult mood to break in him.

Personally, her only concern upon hearing that the queen consort had arrived in Dover in early June, and progressed her way to London to the accompaniment of wildly cheering crowds at Westminster Bridge and even as she passed Carlton House, was what it might mean for her own position. The people's madness for their queen might translate into hatred for the king's mistress.

It had already translated into loathing for the king himself.

Of course, the king was far too devoted to Lady Elizabeth, and certainly wouldn't give her up, no matter how vociferously the public might acclaim their queen. But he might make concessions, and it was what form those concessions might take that bothered her.

She wasn't about to move out of either Carlton House or the Pavilion. Especially the Pavilion. Her apartment there was being tastefully decorated in exquisite wallpapers and luxurious fabrics that begged to be stroked every time she entered her rooms.

As the king progressed further into his lather, Lady Elizabeth reflected on how amazing it was that George, the rightful ruler through either regency or legitimate inheritance of the throne, was made to be a pariah, whereas a screeching baboon like Caroline had been able to win the people's hearts and slavish devotion. You'd think she'd fought and won more battles than Wellington, instead of having made a ridiculous exhibition of herself by living with Bartolomeo Pergami, an Italian Lothario, in an openly lascivious relationship.

It was grating, when one considered that Lady Elizabeth had enjoyed the same sort of liaison with the tsarevitch of Russia a few years ago and had been branded "vulgar." Of course, Lady Elizabeth had never faced a trial, had she?

Yet the whole affair nagged at her. For certain the king wouldn't win his subjects' love by his relentless persecution of his wife, especially now that she was rightfully queen. No, George must be distracted by another path, one that would earn Britain's respect and set him apart from Caroline.

Lady Elizabeth downed the last orange segment. Maybe it was time she brought a more pious tone to George's life. It wouldn't hurt for the people to see their monarch consulting theological tomes and consulting with a priest or two.

She licked the sticky juices from her fingers. Yes, she would help recover the king's reputation and, in so doing, recover her own.

Lord Liverpool normally loved spending hours inside his library at Fife House, but not tonight. He shut the law book with a sigh and rubbed his temples.

"Did you find something, Robert?" asked his wife, Louisa, who sat nearby with one of her endless canvasses and a bottomless basket of threads.

"Fortunately, yes. Or, rather, unfortunately. It's an old and dubious process, far outside the legal system, but it might work."

"What is it?"

"A bill of pains and penalties. Under it, if the king proves his case of her treasonous activities to a special session of the legislature, she would forfeit her rights as queen and be divorced by the king. It's intended for offenses of high treason, but does not allow for death as a punishment."

Louisa put the embroidery down in her lap. "Are you saying the queen would not be permitted a trial?"

"She would be granted an irregular one, yes. We would try her in private in the House of Lords, then submit our findings to the Commons."

"So the queen would not even be allowed a solicitor?"

"She would, although I have no idea what good it would do, given the foregone conclusion. But it gives the king what he wants—a divorce—yet doesn't go so far as to introduce a bill of attainder. He will undoubtedly be pleased."

Louisa shook her head and returned to her embroidery.

"Truly, Wife, it goes against my conscience to persecute this woman, debauched as she is, when her husband has been the most notorious, dissolute rake of our time." He sat back in his favorite leather chair. "But we examined the contents of the bags the king provided, and they really are of a scandalous nature."

He shook his head and sighed once more. "And yet, I fear it's all going to be one long, embarrassing episode of nincompoopery."

From her bedroom, Darcey breathed a sigh of relief as she heard the door shut behind her parents, sister, and servants, as they departed on the household's twice-yearly visit to church, once to celebrate the Resurrection and once to commemorate the death of her brother, who'd died as an infant so many years ago that it was impossible to understand why the family still made such a fuss over him.

It had been no easy feat convincing not only her parents but that old buzzard Mrs. Fraser that she was sick and needed to stay back.

Mrs. Fraser had been the housekeeper for as long as anyone could remember. Little got past her, and she was never one for missing an opportunity to report on the White children's bad behavior.

Mother and Father always listened to whatever Mrs. Fraser had to say. It was so unfair. After all, Darcey was an adult and quite capable of making her own decisions.

She just had to make them in secret.

Darcey shook her head. If she'd learned anything over the past year, it was to work like an angel and play like the devil himself, and this motto had thus far served her well. And today she'd seized an opportunity to cavort with the devil. Just this morning she'd developed the perfect idea for incriminating Belle Stirling in the Cato Street Conspiracy, thus vindicating her Wesley and ensuring that nasty drab lost everything she owned.

Which of course Darcey would swoop in to take for herself, as her due.

Then she got the news that her parents wanted to cart the entire household to church. Church! To listen to some popinjay thunder and roar about everyone else's sins when he was probably cavorting about with half the congregation's wives?

Darcey wasn't going, not if she could help it.

She complained of a sore throat and bodily aches, conditions not easily disproven, and asked her father prettily if she might have the privilege of reading from the Scriptures in her room, disappointed as she was not to be in a state to sit in the pew. As an added measure, she volunteered to pray for dearly departed whatever-the-babe's-name-was.

With only minimal eye rolling, her father acquiesced.

She waited in her room a full half hour after the carriages pulled away before executing her plan. She figured the household should be gone at least two hours, giving her plenty of time to complete her mission.

She laid open her Bible onto her bed, just in case they should come back early. She could then claim she'd been praying and reading, but her condition had worsened so she'd gone off to find some throat drops at the chemist's shop.

The Bible flipped open to the book of Proverbs. She glanced down at the words, and read:

> These six things doth the LORD hate
> yea, seven are an abomination unto him:

A proud look, a lying tongue,
and hands that shed innocent blood,
An heart that deviseth wicked imaginations,
feet that be swift in running to mischief,
A false witness that speaketh lies
and he that soweth discord among brethren.

Darcey grinned. Well, she was safe then, wasn't she? For she wasn't any of those things. And her feet might be making haste now, but not to anything evil. To the contrary, she was bringing about justice, for it was Belle whom the Lord chastised.

Wesley will be so proud of me when I tell him.

She crept down the stairs and into the streets of London, where she made her way to Grosvenor Square to wait, hoping that Lord Harrowby was a devout man.

She was quickly rewarded by the sight of a well-dressed man and woman leaving number 39. She darted out from behind shrubbery in the park across from his residence.

"My lord! Lord Harrowby!" Darcey called, running out in front of a carriage that had to swerve to avoid running her down. "I must speak with you!"

Lord Harrowby looked entirely too stricken by her appearance, even as he kept walking. She must learn to present herself calmly.

"Lord Harrowby, forgive me for intruding on you." She curtseyed quickly to the earl and countess. "I have something of utmost importance to tell you. It's critical to the safety of the country."

Lord Harrowby stepped in front of his wife so that Darcey couldn't see her. He brandished his cane at Darcey.

"Who are you, Miss—?"

Best not to tell him her name, lest he connect her to her father.

"Who I am is not important, my lord. What is important is the secret information I have for you. About the Cato Street Conspiracy. There are others involved that you don't know about, others that still plan to attack the government. To attack you, Lord Harrowby."

He lowered his cane. "I don't believe you. We thoroughly

rooted out that affair and everyone was brought to justice. There couldn't possibly be any radicals remaining."

Darcey sensed his indecision.

"But there are, there are. I know firsthand that one of the conspirators was deceived into the plot by his sister, who today remains free. And she's still plotting with other radicals to overthrow the government. In fact, she's leading them. Yes, she holds secret meetings. I can take you to her."

The earl pursed his lips. "How would a street person such as you have access to such information?"

Darcey looked down at herself. Perhaps she should have changed into something she hadn't worn continuously the past five days.

The earl's crested carriage pulled around and stopped to pick up its passengers. The driver jumped down and held open the door. Darcey only had seconds left. Her words tumbled out in a rush.

"Her name is Annabelle Stirling. Wesley Stirling was her brother. He was implicated in the secretary that was brought to your home, my lord. But it was all Miss Stirling's idea. She goaded him. Shouldn't justice be served on her?"

Harrowby again put out his walking stick to block Darcey as he helped his wife into the carriage. "My dear, I don't know who you are, but you are obviously very troubled. I recommend that you return home to your husband or family and cease your fantasies."

He stepped up into the carriage behind his wife. The driver shut the door and climbed up to his post.

Darcey pressed her face to the carriage's window. "My lord, please, you must listen to me. London needs to see one more criminal swing. I can prove to you—"

The earl completely ignored her. He tapped his cane on the ceiling of the carriage and it started off with a lurch. Darcey jumped back to avoid being run over by the carriage wheels.

Incensed, she stomped off for home, plans for newspaper gossip and letters to radical men churning in her mind. If Lord Harrowby intended to ignore her, she still had many more ideas to pursue.

Something the earl said, though, lingered. He'd told her to get home to her husband. She'd nearly forgotten that part of things.

Hmmm.

That afternoon, over a beneficial helping of opium behind one of the Grosvenor Square mews, Darcey developed her best idea of all.

Imagine how proud Wesley will be when he visits next and I share this inspiration with him.

Belle's anger at Put continued unabated. He had abandoned her at a great precipice, and she was slowly being dragged to the edge, despite her great efforts to recoup her business and her reputation.

A longtime customer, Mrs. Finch, who had adored Wesley, simpering and cooing at anything he said as he convinced her to buy bundles of fabrics to cover her ample frame, arrived one morning. What a relief to have a friendly face show up in her shop.

"Mrs. Finch, welcome. Can I interest you in this beautiful Egyptian print? It just came in yesterday. The mechanical finishing processes have become quite good, as I'm sure you'll see—"

"I didn't actually come to purchase anything."

"No? Then how may I help you?"

"Several of us were wondering—and I was the only one brave enough to come down and speak to you directly, you understand— several of us have heard the most scandalous tales about you and wanted to know if they're true."

"I see. Tell me, Mrs. Finch, what salacious gossip you've heard."

"Well! Mrs. Lloyd heard it from Mrs. Purcell, whose housekeeper is sisters with Lady Derby's over in Grosvenor Square, that you've been more than just a sister to Mr. Stirling."

"Pardon me?"

"Yes, we hear that you've picked up his torch, so to speak, and are heavily involved with radicals. Is it true? Are you planning to blow up Parliament or something? Imagine having two Guy Fawkes Days each year to celebrate. And that I would be acquainted not only with a Cato Street conspirator, but another radical in the form of his sister."

"Lady Derby said this?"

"Not exactly. It was her housekeeper."

"I see. And on the word of someone who has never met me, you've run all the way over here with this succulent bone in your mouth, hoping to confirm its truth, so that you can be the luminary at your next evening of cards."

"Hardly! I was just concerned for you. You know how much we all simply worshipped poor Mr. Stirling before the, er, unfortunate events of a few months ago. He was so kind and entertaining, and had a very talented eye for selecting ball gown fabrics."

"Indeed. Although I don't recall you extending a single word of condolence following Wesley's death. Nor have you returned until this day to patronize the shop."

"Of course not. That would have been unseemly, what with the Stirling name in tatters. But your brother's messiness is behind us, and the idea that his prim and demure *sister* might harbor militant notions, well, that required an investigation, didn't it?"

Belle blinked. This woman's audacity was beyond her capacity to form a response.

"Now, please be assured, Miss Stirling, we all sympathize with your situation. Our interest in you is merely wonder, not malice."

"Get out."

"Sorry?"

"Get. Out. Of my shop. Immediately, Mrs. Finch. I'll not have my inventory tainted by your poison."

"Miss Stirling, you misunderstand me. I'm not against you, I'm just curious—"

"I understand exactly what you're about, Mrs. Finch. Good day to you." Belle strode to the door and flung it open.

Mrs. Finch sniffed in annoyance, and left Belle with parting words: "You'd do well to cultivate what friends you have left, Miss Stirling."

"I'll do exactly that." Belle knew it was childish to slam the door, but was nonetheless gratified to watch Mrs. Finch jump at the rattling of the door's panes as it banged shut behind her.

Belle was certain she was the invisible but much gossiped about guest at Mrs. Finch's next card party, for all of that lady's friends sent along rude notes. Really, was it necessary for them to send letters informing her that their business would go elsewhere and that they were telling their seamstresses to shun Belle? Could they not merely stay away?

After that, she avoided even glancing at the newspaper, for fear of seeing her name emblazoned across it or of accidentally reading some juicy bit of gossip snaking its way through its pages.

Her fears increased with the feeling that someone was following her. She never saw anyone in particular, but she couldn't shake the eerie feeling that someone was tracking her movements to and from the shop.

I'm becoming unhinged. I see ghosts and spirits where there are none.

Thank God for Lady Greycliffe, who made frequent visits to the shop for purchases and invited her next door routinely for tea. Belle suspected her neighbor was also encouraging some of her own friends to place orders with the Stirling Drapers shop, too.

Belle's worst day was when three men, dressed in the homespun of tradesmen, entered the shop. Lowly dressed men were not a frequent sight in a draper's shop. Belle was instinctively glad she stood behind the counter, near her pistols.

"You're Miss Stirling?" asked one of the men without preamble.

"I am. And who are you, Mr.—?"

"Garret. John Garret. My friends and I hear that you're one of us."

"One of you?"

"Come, don't be coy." The man winked at her, a little too lasciviously for Belle's comfort.

"Pray, sir, please tell me what it means to be one of you." She quietly slid open the cabinet door under the counter that hid her pistol box.

"We hear you're interested in seeing change come to England, by whatever means it takes. That you might not be afraid of London's streets getting a bit bloody in the process."

Belle sighed. "Dare I ask where you might have heard this?"

He shrugged. "Here and there. We hear tell you're looking to avenge your brother's death. You managed to escape taint in the Cato Street affair, didn't you?"

"Not particularly."

Garret made an appraising glance around the shop, at the shelves groaning under the weight of unsold fabrics. "Looks like you must have plenty of money. You could help finance us. We were thinking of kidnapping the king to raise money for our real goals, but if you were to help us, we could avoid touching His Royal Pigginess."

The other men laughed at the insult.

"Are you deranged? What fool insinuated that I was unbalanced enough to immerse myself in some idiotic plan to subvert the government?" Actually, who *didn't* share this opinion? "Hasn't there been enough trouble already, Mr. Garret?"

"We have it on pretty good say-so that you were as revolutionary as your brother. Even more so, tho' he was the one the judge chose to dangle from the three-legged mare."

"Your information sources consist of rogues, villains, and miscreants, Mr. Garret. I had nothing to do with my brother's activities, and have no intention of involving myself in radical activities. I do, however, intend to protect my livelihood."

She lifted the lid to her pistol box and pulled out the nearest one, pointing it directly at Mr. Garret's chest. Completely unloaded, of course.

Mr. Garret's good humor disappeared. "Now let's not be aiming your barking iron at me, miss. I came here in good faith."

"I'm going to assume, then—*in good faith*—that you plan to leave quietly before I have to shoot you. I have a shop to run, gentlemen, and I intend to do so, without the interference of wandering mischief-makers. Now, out with the lot of you!"

Maybe she should consider locking the shop and evaluating patrons through the window before permitting them in.

With grumbles of "Not our fault" and "Don't need to work with a shrew," the men hurried out of the building.

She sat down, numb. Would this tiresome parade of half-wits never end? Where were all of these rumors originating? What if they traveled as far as Parliament and someone there took them seriously?

And who was following her? Her sense that she was being silently pursued was unshakable.

* * *

Put climbed the steps of Lord Burdett's home in St. James's Place, wearing his uncomfortable day clothes and carrying both a small tool chest and an awkward sack. The baronet had sent a carriage around to pick up Put so that he could repair his old walnut desk, which had a broken leg. Put wasn't used to such finery for himself, feeling almost embarrassed as his workers watched him enter the black-lacquered coach with its fancy trims.

The young maid who answered the door showed him to Lord Burdett's private bedroom, where the desk sat at the foot of the baronet's bed. She continued to flutter around him while he worked.

"May I get you some tea to drink?"

"No, thank you."

He opened his burlap sack full of walnut leg parts that he had brought along, matching them up until he found a style that was close to what the original cabinetmaker had used. It would only require a little carving and shaving to create a match.

"Do you require more light? Here, let me draw back the draperies for you."

"Thank you."

The leg was damaged beyond repair. Put removed the straps from his portable tool chest and searched for his file and several carving tools. He poised the leg over the burlap bag, made some minor modifications to the shape of the leg, then filed it until it was smooth. Going back into his tool chest, he rooted around until he found a brush and his jar of boiled linseed oil. He quickly brushed oil on the entire leg with long, smooth strokes to prevent any drip marks, then rested it across two other legs to let it dry for a few minutes, then applied a second coat.

Now to remove the old leg from the desk.

The maid was now standing over him, wide-eyed and breathless.

"It's amazing work you're doing, Mr. Boyce."

"Thank you."

"I imagine your wife really appreciates such talent."

"I'm not married."

"Really?" Her eyes grew wider.

"I'm not married *yet*."

"Oh. Right. Well, I must be off to my dusting. Pull the rope next to the bed if you require anything."

Finally left alone to concentrate on his work, Put started by emptying the desk of its contents, so he could flip the piece over to figure out how the leg was attached and remove it. He carefully removed each drawer and set it on the floor so that he could remember the exact order in which they fit back into the desk.

The baronet's desk contained all of the usual things aristocrats maintained in drawers. A silver pocket watch, pens, pots of ink, parchment paper, a blotter, a personal journal tied with twine, a small pouch of tobacco, and a couple of sovereigns.

Put shook his head. Funny how wealthy men zealously guarded their homes with armies of servants but left small, valuable goods lying about in an unlocked desk where anyone could find them.

He carefully rolled the desk on its back, then upside down so he could carefully saw off the old leg. He planed down the place where the old leg was attached to the body of the desk, to provide a smooth, even location to place the new one. He then chiseled out a mortise, so that he could glue in the replacement leg's matching tenon for a strong joint between the pieces.

He touched the recently varnished leg. Dry enough to work with. Using a combination of horsehide glue and nails, he added the new leg to the desk, and left it sitting upside down to partially set while he cleaned up his tools and sack of parts.

Shavings were scattered on the rug where he'd been working. Well, he'd wait until he was ready to leave before calling anyone to come in and sweep, lest the maid return right away.

Satisfied that the leg was sufficiently dry to sustain the weight of the desk, he went through the process of rolling the desk over again and setting it upright. He surveyed his work.

"It'll do," he said aloud.

His only remaining task was to put away the drawers. He gently pushed back in the wood boxes containing the watch, writing materials, journal, tobacco—

Wait a moment.

This reminded Put of something, something very important. What was it? He closed his eyes, trying to remember, but it was lying just out of reach.

Put finished replacing the drawers and decided to unstrap his tool chest again for a fine-bristled goat's-hair brush to dust inside the fine crevices of all the desk's carvings. Perhaps Lord Burdett would appreciate Put's attention to detail.

Like as not, he wouldn't even notice. But it gave Put time to think.

The man had his personal diary lying in his desk.

A desk. A diary.

"Good Lord," Put said, as he scrambled up quickly, pulled the bell rope, and shouted out to anyone who would listen that Lord Burdett's rug needed cleaning. He clattered down the stairs with his belongings and rushed out to the street.

He had to get to Grosvenor Square as quickly as possible.

Belle spent the morning looking at potential new lodgings. She could no longer bear her current place, where Wesley's room had been taken over by new tenants, a nice young couple who were nonetheless a reminder to Belle that her brother had not only ceased to exist but now had every last vestige of his life stripped from the earth.

She'd stowed the crate of his belongings in her own room, and would take it to her new lodgings, wherever they might be.

After purchasing a spiced meat pasty from a street vendor, she stopped to visit Lady Greycliffe, but a sign in the door indicated that the dollmaker's shop was closed that day. Disappointed to miss her new friend, Belle returned to the shop for what would surely be a long afternoon.

Put paced back and forth under gathering clouds outside the servants' entrance to the Grosvenor Square residence. *What can I possibly say to the worker who opens the door that will permit me entry?* *"Your master has a desk with a secret drawer he doesn't know about?"* *"I'm a man under suspicion by His Majesty's government, and the only way to clear my name is to suspiciously burrow through Lord Harrowby's desk?"*

Think, Boyce, think.

After several minutes of deliberation, he decided on his course. It was weak, and probably wouldn't fool an infant, but it was all he could think of on such short notice. At least he still had his tools with him to lend his story credence.

To his great surprise, it worked. The elderly housekeeper who opened the door believed his inane account of Lord Harrowby's new desk having been varnished with potentially poisonous shellac. Put embellished the story by saying that he'd already been to several other distinguished homes in the area to cover up the old shellac with a new, non-poisonous coating. It was vital that he inspect the earl's secretary immediately to ensure it had not received the lethal covering.

What nonsense. Anyone even vaguely familiar with wood finishes would know that any sort of poisonous vapor would be long gone from a piece that was finished months ago. Unless the owner decided to make kindling of the desk and release noxious fumes in the air, an unlikely occurrence in Lord Harrowby's case.

But providence was with him. Lord Harrowby wasn't home, nor was his wife, and the nervous servant didn't want to be blamed later for turning away rescue of life-threatening furniture. So she admitted Put inside and led him to her employer's study.

The secretary stood magnificently against one wall of the room, across from the fireplace and two comfortable leather chairs.

He turned back to the servant, who looked uncertainly between him and the piece of furniture. He said to her, "Perhaps you should close the door and leave me here alone, so as not to let the bad air into the rest of the house."

"Yes, a most advisable idea. Not meaning you any harm, of course."

"No, of course not."

Miraculously, he was alone with the secretary.

"Mr. Bloom," the housekeeper said, trying to keep her lips from quivering. "I might have done something wrong. I let a cabinetmaker into the master's study. He says he made the new desk, and that it might be poisonous and he has to fix it. Mr. Bloom, he was talking about the desk that was part of that Cato Street business."

"How can a desk be poisonous?" the butler asked.

"Well, I'm not sure, but he explained it right well. Now I'm thinking he's up to something. What if he's another one of them radicals? Oh dear, what have I done?" She rubbed her veined hands together.

"I'll see him myself."

"No, I don't think that's a good idea. Do you know where the master is? I think he'll want to see this man himself."

"He went to his club. I'll fetch him."

Belle climbed down from the ladder and brushed her hands together to release the dust from them.

I really do need to clean those shelves, she thought. *I can't show customers dusty merchandise.*

She patted down some loose hairs. *Presuming I ever have a full complement of customers again.*

Belle pulled some spools of ribbon out of her storage closet to cut pieces of them for her ribbon rack that dangled over the far end of the counter. Small clips held individual strips of ribbon, which Belle cut in the most highly desired lengths for tying bonnets and lacing handkerchiefs. The ribbon display helped the shop look cheerful and interesting, with its waterfall of brightly colored trims fluttering down, begging to be touched.

So engrossed was Belle in measuring, cutting, and artfully hanging the ribbon, she hardly noticed her next customer's arrival. Had the doorbell even rung as the woman entered?

She was unsettlingly familiar, despite her bedraggled appearance. The woman smelled to high heaven and wore a long, narrow pouch at her waist, tied on with a length of filthy rope.

Perfect. Another vagabond come to ask if Belle was a radical or wanted to join an extremist cause.

Belle put down the rose-colored ribbon she was about to clip to the rack. "Welcome to Stirling Drapers. How may I help you, madam?"

The woman didn't respond, but merely glared at her through glassy eyes.

Where had she seen her before?

Oh! Belle knew her now. It was the woman from Wesley's execution who had stared at her so malevolently. What was she doing here now?

"Madam," Belle said carefully, a prickle of unease creeping up her neck. "Do I know you?"

The woman nodded with eerie slowness, as though she were a puppet being gently maneuvered from above. "Yes, you know me. You just don't know how."

"I believe I do. I remember you from the day my brother was— from the regrettable day in front of Newgate."

That sluggish nodding again. "Yes, you'd surely remember me from there. But I've been here before. I promised I'd be back."

More recognition dawned in Belle's mind. "You're Miss Whitecastle. You asked me questions about my shop's ownership."

"Except I'm not really Miss Whitecastle. I'm Miss Darcey White. Perhaps you remember my name?" The woman patted the pouch at her waist, as though to assure herself it was still there.

Belle was more disturbed by this waif than by any other peculiar customer who had ever walked through the door. Miss Whitecastle was not altogether sound. She was here for some wicked purpose, for certain, but it was impossible to know what that purpose was.

How is it that I can still be surprised at people's ill intentions toward me?

The past months had seen all manner of curiosity seeker, fanatic, and fortune hunter hound her for vile reasons.

Fortune hunters! Wait, wasn't it a Miss Whitecastle who sent her that incoherent note, claiming to now be Mrs. Stirling? Surely Wesley hadn't married this unpleasant creature.

"Would you be the same Miss Whitecastle who sent me a letter recently?"

A smile spread across Miss Whitecastle's face in her lingering style. "The same. Except, as I said, I'm not really Miss Whitecastle. Or even Miss White. I'm Mrs. Stirling, your dead brother's wife, and you never bothered to respond to my letter. Today, though, we're going to discuss it."

The woman went back to the front door, made sure it was firmly shut, threw the bolt, and turned the window sign to read "Closed." Turning back to Belle, she said sweetly, "Ready for a chat, dearest sister-in-law?"

The woman pulled a knife from the pouch at her side.

Put paused only for a moment, wishing that he'd never built the damned secretary. He'd so wanted to believe it was for Belle that he hadn't spent enough time questioning Wesley about it. He should have been more suspicious about the boy's desire to give Belle such an extravagant gift.

No matter, no matter. If the desk was hiding what Put thought it might be, all would be made clear and the rumors would stop. He pulled the slanted front down, and removed the usual desk items that were blocking the secret compartment, placing them carefully on a nearby sideboard already cluttered with bottles full of amber- and burgundy-colored liquids.

He opened the drawer next to the secret one and pulled it out. Where was the pin? There was nothing in here but a couple of letters. Put set the drawer down on the floor and withdrew another one, then another, looking for the opening pin. Ah, here it was.

He inserted the pin in its slot, and felt the compartment release gently into his hand. Dread shot through his spine as he slowly pulled it out. What if nothing remained in the secret compartment beyond what was presented at trial? What if he was utterly, completely mistaken in his belief? How could he then exonerate Belle—

"What in the name of St. Peter are you doing here?" thundered a voice from behind him.

"I don't believe you. Do you have a marriage certificate?" The longer Belle listened to this woman, the more she was convinced she was an escaped lunatic.

"You'll not ask any more questions. I'll ask them. First, where is my pipe? I need it."

"Your pipe? You mean Wesley's pipe?"

"No, it's rightfully mine. He and I shared it and he meant to leave it for me. He'll be furious when I tell him I don't have it."

What was she talking about?

"I have it at my lodgings. I can pick it up and bring it back here to you tomorrow morning," Belle said.

"Oh yes, you believe you're very clever, don't you, Miss Stirling? You'll dash out of here, never to return, and because Darcey White is just a simple, stupid member's daughter, who will believe any outrageous lie fed to her, she'll go along with it. Is that what you think? Is it?"

"Miss White, I—"

"I'm not Miss White! I'm Mrs. Stirling! Wesley's beloved."

Doubtful. "My apologies, Mrs. Stirling. What would you like me to do?"

"I'd like you to shut your gob. I said *I* would be asking the questions. Don't interrupt me. Be quiet so I can think."

Darcey's eyes rolled back in her head as she rubbed her temples.

Belle looked down the length of the counter. Could she reach the other end and open her pistol box before Darcey realized what was happening? The girl was crazed, but didn't seem dangerous. At least not yet. But Belle had enough experience to know that the sight of a revolver in her hand calmed the barmiest opponent. So far, she'd had no cause to actually fire it at anyone.

Of further concern were Darcey's glazed eyes, reminding Belle of Wesley's glassy looks that accompanied his periodic outbursts.

The slow smile returned. Darcey was calm again. "You do know your man is probably in Newgate by now, don't you?"

"My man?"

"Putnam Boyce. He made the secretary that was delivered to Lord Harrowby."

"Yes, but Mr. Boyce had nothing to do with the conspiracy."

"What difference does that make? I'm a parliamentarian's daughter. Do you think I don't know how to make political gain? To twist things to my own purposes? A word in the ear of a tavern owner, a whisper to a newspaper owner, and soon we have scandal that benefits me immensely."

"Miss Wh—Mrs. Stirling, how could a scandal involving Mr. Boyce possibly benefit you? Presumably you don't even know him."

"No, but I did know you. And I knew from Wesley that you were squiring about with him. He was with you at my Wesley's end, wasn't he? So to ruin him would be to ruin you, a most agreeable outcome. Combined with my other actions against you, well, something was sure to work and lead to your arrest."

"My arrest for *what?*"

"Why, for your involvement in the Cato Street Conspiracy. What the authorities didn't understand is that you pushed Wesley into it, and allowed him to take the blame for *your* activities."

"What you're saying is completely false. I knew nothing of Wesley's involvement with Arthur Thistlewood."

Darcey lifted a shoulder. "No matter. I just needed others to know the truth of the matter. Although thus far nothing has worked properly. Which is why I had to come visit you myself."

"I don't understand. Why did you need me wrongly implicated in the Cato Street affair?"

"Wrongly, dear sister-in-law?" Darcey's smile was that of a demon. "My life was ruined when Wesley went to jail. I wanted you to hang, so that you would have the justice you deserve for throwing Wesley to the hounds and not bringing your supposed influence to bear in getting him released from Newgate."

Belle was speechless.

Darcey's voice dropped to nearly a whisper. "Not only that, I am laying claim to this lovely shop for myself as the nearest Stirling kin. A suitable inheritance, since Wesley didn't see fit to leave me his pipe. I must speak to him about his oversight when I meet him later for supper." She sighed. "But as I was saying, others have refused to take the action I have been calling for. You aren't arrested, you aren't on trial, and you most definitely are not hanged. And I intend to correct matters. Now."

Belle changed her mind.

This woman was dangerous.
And no one in the world knows that I'm trapped in here with her.

Put turned, the long compartment still in his hand.

Lord Harrowby. Couldn't the man have stayed away just ten more minutes?

"I asked, who are you, and what the devil are you doing in my home? Quickly, before I have you arrested."

"I'm Putnam Boyce, sir. I'm the cabinetmaker who was contracted to build this secretary."

"What of it? How dare you skulk your way into my home and paw through my desk. You'll be fortunate if you're not on the gallows by morning."

"Yes, sir. I'll be on the gallows anyway if I don't clear my name of the Cato Street Conspiracy. I made the secret compartment of this desk and I simply need to check it to ensure there aren't any secret documents in it that might exonerate me."

"Lord Liverpool and I have already thoroughly searched out the desk, and found the compartment you're holding. Look inside, you'll see that it's empty. All the documents held in the desk were presented as evidence in court."

Put looked down. The main opening was, indeed, cleared of its contents.

"Yes, sir. However—"

"I can't understand why everyone is still so blasted concerned about Cato Street. First that street woman, now you."

"What street woman?"

"Some vagrant. Never gave me her name, but made reference to one of the conspirators. Let's see, which one was it? Shipley? Sparling? No, Stirling, it was Stirling. Now I remember. She said that Stirling was actually an innocent, having been goaded into the conspiracy by his sister. I rightfully dismissed the woman as being mentally unsound. She insisted on this sister's guilt, though. You say you were the cabinetmaker Stirling contracted to make the secretary. Do you know this sister?"

"I do."

"Could she be guilty?"

"No, my lord. It is impossible that Annabelle Stirling be guilty of anything."

"Is that so? And you claim innocence for yourself, as well? Very convenient for a man who has used subterfuge to enter my home. Poisonous varnish, wasn't it?"

Put sensed that this board could warp in either direction. It was up to him to make sure it lay even. Calm and steady pressure was required.

"My apologies, Lord Harrowby, for my intrusion. However, I ask your indulgence. If you would kindly extend me just one more moment of grace while I examine the rest of the secret compartment, assuredly I can put your mind at rest."

"But I've already told you, Lord Liverpool and I emptied the compartment. It's empty."

"If I may?"

Harrowby nodded at him impatiently.

Put held up the box and slid up the secret back panel that revealed the long, narrow space beneath the emptied section. Harrowby gasped. "It would seem I was mistaken."

The closest Put would get to an apology from an aristocrat.

Inside was a sheaf of tightly rolled paper. Put fished it out, struggling to work his large index finger into the narrow space. He finally got a corner pulled out, and the rest followed easily.

Placing the secret compartment on the floor, he unrolled the papers out on the desk, holding them flat with his hands. "My lord, this is what I was hoping for: Wesley Stirling's journal. Shall we read together?"

"Yes, yes, of course. Let me light a lamp."

The cabinetmaker and the earl stood shoulder to shoulder and read Wesley Stirling's final writings.

It was a long chronicle detailing Wesley's struggles, disappointments, fall into opium addiction, his love affair with a woman named Darcey White, and his ultimate entanglement with Arthur Thistlewood at Miss White's behest.

But it was the end of the journal that concerned Put the most.

> *. . . D——— is consumed with the notion that Belle is the source of my difficulties. When we are together after indulging ourselves with opium, I can believe it to be true. But when I separate myself from D———, I wonder if, in fact, my sister isn't necessarily the harpy D——— envisions her to be.*
>
> *It is very confusing sometimes.*
>
> *My great hope is that Mr. Thistlewood's plan succeeds, and that a new government is formed in which I will be his trusted advisor. I will finally be my own man, and perhaps D——— will be content to stop her persecutions of my sister. Only then will I decide if I can live with her as man and wife.*
>
> *If our plan fails, and I hesitate to look into my future if it does, I worry that D——— will attempt something vindictive against B———. Yet I cannot warn B——— now, lest I place D——— in trouble.*
>
> *D——— has been to the shop to covertly visit Belle. I'm not sure I approve of D——— inspecting my sister without her knowledge. D——— is capable of great hostility, I believe, and I dread to think of what she might do under failed circumstances—*

"Good Lord," Put said. "This woman is unhinged. She must be the source of all the rumors. Miss Stirling might be in grave danger at this very moment."

"I'm afraid it's going to be of no concern to the government, Boyce. We achieved our aim of destroying the conspiracy, and no one will take up the cause of a quarrel between a conspirator's doxy and his sister."

So that was how the board was warping. Very well. When could a peer be trusted either for payment or for justice?

To his credit, Harrowby flinched under Put's hard stare. He held up his hands. "I can't help you, Boyce. My regrets."

Put got up wordlessly, folded the papers, and pressed them into Harrowby's hand. "Have my tools sent back to my shop on Curtain Road," he barked at the Earl of Harrowby, who meekly nodded.

Once again, Put fled into the streets of London, where it was now raining with malicious force. Ignoring the soaking downpour, he ran like an overflowing river, jumping over and around anything in his path on his way to Oxford Street.

Darcey could hardly believe her moment had come. The flicker of fear in Annabelle Stirling's eyes was a glorious sight to behold.

"What do you want from me?" Belle asked.

Yes, there was fear in her eyes, but not enough of it to suit Darcey. Wesley's sister had always been too uppity, too sure of herself. She had to be brought to her knees first.

"I want you to beg for your life before I kill you."

Belle's gaze shifted to the other end of the counter and back to Darcey. This wouldn't do at all. Belle Stirling wasn't nearly frightened enough.

"I'll not beg anything from you," Wesley's sister said. Spat, was more like it. It was time to get this arrogant biddy under control.

"You'll do as I say. Everyone always does, eventually."

"I've never paid attention to foolishness, and I don't intend to start today."

How dare she accuse Darcey of being a fool. "Do you think I'm not intelligent enough to bring you grief? Who do you think left that stinking pile of garbage in front of the shop, and hired those boys to smash your windows? Who would have suggested that you be recruited by other groups wanting to overthrow the government? They were all my brilliant ideas, you know."

"You're insane."

"I'm as sound as anyone, and certainly more so than a feather-brain who couldn't figure out how to save her brother." Ha, what a fine dig at Wesley's sister.

"You know nothing of my relationship with Wesley. And I prefer to know nothing of yours."

"Then perhaps I should give you deep, intimate detail. About our long nights together at the Horse and Groom. And how I had him completely at my mercy. He did whatever I told him to do."

"Stop this, now."

"In fact, no act was too dangerous for my Wesley when it came to my desires. I held complete power over his weak mind."

"Don't you dare speak ill of my brother."

At the loud crack that rang in her ears, Darcey stopped, stunned. It was unbelievable. Wesley's sister had just struck her in the mouth with her fist.

Darcey put a hand to her lips and looked at her fingers, which came away bloody. "How dare you! You nasty little drab. Killing you will be my greatest happiness."

"This will not be my last day on the Lord's earth."

"That's a lot of bluster from someone who isn't the one holding this." Darcey held up the blade and pointed it at Belle, smiling.

Belle took a step backward. Much better.

"I'm going to slice out your guts and feed them to my dog. I'm going to cut off your head and carry it through London on a pike. I'm going to—"

Darcey was so busy enumerating her planned acts of humiliation for Belle's dead body that she didn't notice the draper pick up a large wood spindle from the counter until it was too late. Belle swung it at her, but missed, and it fell to the ground.

How dare this twit attempt to strike Darcey White, twice?

Darcey shoved the knife back into its pouch. Why hurry things?

She picked the spindle up. "Your aim is off." She swung it herself, with much better accuracy. Belle's head hit the counter with a satisfying crack before she crumpled to the floor.

But before Darcey could finish her off with the knife she intended to plunge as far into Belle's heart as she could, she was distracted by a terrible clamoring at the door behind her.

Go away, she thought. *The Stirling Drapers shop is not open for business.*

But the banging went on endlessly, distracting her from her important task with the prone figure before her.

She tucked the knife back in its pouch once again and turned to see who was creating so much fuss. At that moment, the door crashed open and a thoroughly soaked man came barreling inside.

She could hardly believe her eyes.

"Wesley, sweetheart! I didn't expect you to meet me here. I'm almost finished with matters here, and then we can sup together."

Wesley looked at Belle's fallen form, then back to Darcey. She smiled and held out her arms. How proud he must be of what she'd accomplished here thus far.

"Kiss me, love. Ignore that little bit of nastiness on my mouth. Your sister here"—she nudged Belle with her foot—"was a little spirited and thought she could best me. But we see who is more powerful now, don't we?"

She walked to Wesley, expecting his arms to open and enfold her. What was wrong with him? As he approached her, his eyes, they were so . . . heated. But not in the lustful way she was used to seeing. Had she made a mistake? Did he expect to see more blood? Easily fixed. She withdrew the knife from her pouch again and held it up for him to examine.

The sight of it froze him in place and he locked gazes with Darcey once again.

From behind her, Darcey heard faint movement, a reminder that she must return to the business at hand—

"Drop that knife or I'll strangle you myself." Wesley's voice boomed inside the shop. Whatever was the matter with him? Her Wesley would never treat her so roughly.

Why, this wasn't Wesley at all. Who was it? She needed time to think.

But the man refused to give her time to deliberate on what was happening. He grabbed her wrist and shook it to dislodge the knife, which clattered to the floor.

She reached out her free hand and scratched him, as deeply as she could manage, across the face. The man yelped in pain and released her. Darcey searched the floor for the knife. Ah, there it was. She bent down just as the man swiped at the air to grab her again, while clutching his other hand to his cheek.

May you suffer for eternity, she thought, *for daring to impersonate my Wesley.*

The knife's leather handle felt warm and comfortable in her palm, like the touch of an old friend. She should have stolen it from her father's collection long ago.

The man reached for her again, but this time he made contact with her neck. So her attacker thought he might choke her, did he?

Darcey brought the blade up in the air, intending to thrust it into the man's neck, but he released her neck and stepped back from her, and she cut through air.

And thus her dance with the man continued relentlessly, he trying to divest her of her weapon, Darcey slicing through the air at him, the man dodging her lunges.

Dodging all of them, damn him.

But she still held the knife firmly in her grasp, and he would eventually tire. She would stab him, then return to Belle and slice her heart open, as well. And Wesley would be impressed by the quick dispatch of her two enemies.

"Darcey." She heard her name spoken in a flat tone, and turned toward the sound of it.

She saw the cloud of smoke and flash of fire from behind the shop's counter just before the deafening bang that followed it. What was this? As if in a dream, she felt herself slowly falling backward, down, down—ah! Such exquisite pain as her head struck the floor. All was eerily silent in her murky dream. She turned her head in time to witness her knife dropping down beside her.

She tried to focus on the movements surrounding her. Familiar faces hovered above her own. Wesley? No, it was that other man. Why was he poking about her bodice? And why was Belle there? She should be dead, killed by Darcey's own hand. No, wait, she hadn't had an opportunity to stab her yet.

Darcey felt around blindly for her knife. Her entire upper body felt like it was weighted down and completely unmovable, preventing her from turning her head to one side and looking for it. Where was it? Gone, it was gone. How could she kill Belle now, and wipe that idiotic look of concern from her face?

What was that moaning? It sounded as if it were coming from beneath her. How irritating. It prevented Darcey from concentrating. So much to concentrate on. Her breathing, for instance. It was so difficult to take in air while lying on the floor like this. She really must sit up. If only everyone would get out of her way.

And now there was another figure in the room, dressed in a

black hood and floating patiently behind the others. Ah, to be able to suspend oneself in the air, as graceful as the autumn leaves as they are carried on cool breezes in pleasing flashes of gold and scarlet. Darcey wished she were floating.

Suddenly, the black-hooded figure swept over her, and she was, indeed, suspended in the air. The figure whispered where he was taking her, and Darcey suddenly wished very much that she could instead remain on the floor, where it was so much safer than where she was headed.

Belle dropped to her knees next to Darcey and held the girl's hand, while Put investigated her bloody chest for signs of life.

Finally he sat back. "She's gone, Belle."

Belle gazed down sadly at Darcey's body. "This was my brother's wife. Or so she claimed. I can't believe I killed my own sister-in-law."

"She was no relation of yours. Wesley never married her. We can be thankful to him for that and more."

"I think I owe you a debt of gratitude. How did you manage to show up at the right moment?"

"That's why I'm thankful to your brother. In that blasted secretary he left behind notes that condemned Darcey and exonerated you. For whatever he was while alive, Belle, he atoned for it all from the grave. We have much to discuss about it, but first, let me see that nasty wound on your head." He offered her a hand up, and ran his fingers gingerly over the spot where Belle's head struck the counter he made. She winced, but didn't cry out.

"I'm fine, truly I am," she said. "I just need sleep." But she knew she was trembling. "I believe Darcey may have been following me for quite some time. I never saw her, but I knew someone was watching me."

"Oh." Put looked at her sheepishly. "Perhaps I am not a particularly good shadow. After I sent you that note—which I did to protect you from rumors swirling around me—I couldn't allow you to run around with no one to keep an eye on you, so I attempted to watch over you in the background. Rather unsuccessfully, I guess. It doesn't matter now, you're safe."

Put pulled her close, planting kisses all over her face, neck, and hands. "Good Lord, what if I'd lost you?" he murmured over and over.

Belle threw her arms around his neck, clutching him to hear his heartbeat and feel the warmth of his damp skin. Clive, Amelia, Jane, Wesley, and now Darcey White, all gone. She'd had enough of death. She wanted life. Even if she had to find it in this most macabre of moments.

Put pulled back just enough to look at her. "Would this be an improper moment to tell you I love you and would like to skip all of the courtship fripperies and go straight to marriage?"

Belle smiled. "On one condition."

"Name it."

"You really must let me pick out some fabrics for a new wardrobe for you. You must be the most uncomfortably dressed man in England."

"Granted."

"And no more fights with tigresses." She reached up to touch the scratch marks embedded on his cheek.

"Thy will be done, Annabelle Stirling."

"Why then, Put-rhymes-with-shut, I accept your gallant offer."

To Lord Harrowby's credit, he came through for the couple, presenting Wesley's diary to the authorities and ensuring the investigation of Darcey's death was wrapped up quietly with haste. Darcey's father, a member of Parliament, stayed out of the way, issuing a statement that his daughter was disturbed as of recently.

Lady Greycliffe fluttered around the shop upon her return, all hugs and kisses and the constant "*Je suis désolée* that I was away during your hour of need."

To repent of her own perceived sin, the dollmaker sent some of her own maids to the shop to scrub the wood floors of blood and to remove any evidence of the altercation.

Belle and Put had banns read as quickly as possible, and were married privately by the same priest who helped them bury Wesley, Frances serving as their only, silent witness. The three supped together quietly afterwards at a nearby inn.

Frances put them through a mock bedding ceremony that evening. She dressed Belle privately in the bedroom, slipping a fine lawn nightgown trimmed in dark green ribbon over her head and dabbing lavender-scented water behind Belle's ears, wrists, and knees. After brushing Belle's hair out, she helped her into a seated position under the covers of the four-poster bed, which were also fragranced with lavender. Frances arranged Belle's hair around her shoulders and nodded.

I must look acceptable.

Frances slipped out the door, and came back several minutes later, holding Put's hand. He, too, had been dressed for the occasion, in a nightshirt. Frances was now nodding vigorously and pointing back and forth at them. With two great claps of her hands, she laughed in her barking way, and left.

Even in the darkness, lit only by a few candles, Belle could see Put reddening in embarrassment, the color completely concealing the fading scratch marks on his face.

He came around to her side of the bed.

She wasn't frightened, only worried that she would disappoint her husband.

He picked up a lock of hair from her shoulders and kissed it. "I have to tell you, Belle, this is exceedingly distressful for me."

"You've not been married before, and now you have to share your room with me."

"No, that's not what I mean. It's that I'm not used to these infernal nightshirts. What was my cousin thinking?" He pulled it off as though it were one of the stiff collars or fancy vests that he hated wearing.

Belle smiled at her new husband's irritation. Even the nightshirt couldn't hide the fact that years of working with saws, mallets, and heavy planks of wood had honed Putnam Boyce into a solid, finely crafted piece that would surely endure for decades.

Put relaxed at seeing Belle's amusement. He sat down on the bed next to her and kissed her, very gently at first, then with increasing intensity. His urgency transferred itself to her and she found herself gasping with need of him.

He put his hands to her cheeks and kissed her forehead. "And will you promise to come to bed every night of our lives just as God made you, Wife?"

"I will, but you may have to help me divest myself of my finery."

"Gladly, woman." And with an exaggerated bear growl, Put picked her up, set her feet on the floor, and proceeded to lovingly remove her simple nightgown.

No, she wasn't frightened at all.

Later, as the newly married couple lay ensconced in bed, Belle's head on Put's shoulder, she held out her hand to examine the gold band encircling her finger.

"You realize I'm now fully obligated to enter into an affair with the king?"

"Hmm?" Put asked drowsily, pulling her closer against him.

"Never mind. Just an old memory from an old life. Good night, Husband."

November 10, 1820
Carlton House

"Ingrates! Fools! Whelps that should have all been drowned at birth!" The king was nearly howling in his rage, but not howling nearly as deafeningly as the public had after Lord Liverpool introduced the Bill of Pains and Penalties.

Liverpool discreetly added a few drops of laudanum to his glass of brandy. His physician had recommended it for demanding, tiresome occasions. The night might prove to be long and taxing indeed. He glanced over at Lady Conyngham, who was ostensibly tranquil, stretched out on a Grecian sofa the king had moved into his private rooms for her.

She nodded at Liverpool, a simple gesture full of her shared impatience at the king's temper tantrum.

"I blame you, Liverpool. You should have worked harder at convincing the Lords to move forward with it." The king stopped his heavy clumping back and forth long enough to point a chubby, beringed finger at him.

The queen's trial had been lengthy and appalling, starting in August and limping to finality just today. The salacious details of her affair with Bartolomeo Pergami were read aloud, to the great amusement of all in attendance. A parade of witnesses gave testimony as to Caroline's unseemly familiarity with Pergami, while the queen sat through it all, unperturbed.

She remained unmoved by the effort to damage her, because more than eight hundred petitions and nearly a million signatures were sent in favoring her case. Talk of revolution in the queen's name reached Liverpool's ears, an unsettling thought after having just ferreted out the Cato Street Conspiracy—an episode that was still ringing in the country's ears.

The queen claimed to have committed adultery only once, and that with the husband of Mrs. Fitzherbert, the king. Londoners loved the joke and it endeared their queen to them more than ever.

Highly troubled by the entire proceedings even after the Lords passed the bill, Liverpool addressed the House and declared that since public tensions were so high, the government would withdraw the bill.

"Your Majesty, the people's outcry scared Parliament more than anything I could have done. There was little chance that the Commons would have passed it."

"The people! As though they have any sympathy for me and my sorrows. Have I not been the most patriotic of men? The most solicitous of rulers? I am wounded—*humiliated*—at such disregard by my subjects. And plain incensed by Parliament's weak-kneed response. Very well, that voracious monster called my wife will herself be humiliated for all of England to witness. Get that rat cartoonist, Cruikshank, to do some satire on her."

"Your Majesty, we just gave the cartoonist a handsome financial settlement in return for his pledge *not* to print any further caricatures of you."

"I don't want him to satirize *me*, but to skewer my wife. See to it!"

Liverpool drained his glass. The king was working himself into a state of apoplexy, for certain.

Mercifully, Lady Conyngham interjected an opinion, deflecting the king's poisonous attentions away from the prime minister.

"Dearest Majesty, you are rightfully angry about the wrong done to you, but I wonder if you might benefit, both in your person and in public opinion, by incorporating a spiritual aspect to your daily life. Might I suggest that we invite a priest to attend to your royal needs? He might be able to offer comfort in these trying times, and the people would view such an act as one of great devotion to the good of the nation."

"Are you mad, dear lady? I am the king, not a penitent. It is Parliament that requires forgiveness and solace, not I."

Lady Congynham's face was a bland mask, but Liverpool noted hints of wearied irritation around her eyes. The look was gone in an instant as she replaced the mask with a cheerful, toothy smile. "No, of course you aren't, Your Majesty. You must forgive the dithering of someone who merely adores you above all others and is stretching her simple, yet devoted, mind to its limits to find ways to comfort you."

The king's disposition altered as swiftly as his mistress changed facial expressions. "And this you do quite admirably. I need no man of the cloth to attend to me, I just need my dear Lady Conyngham."

Lady Conyngham artfully simpered and bent her head in modesty.

Lord Liverpool had to give the woman credit. She was a master politician, and better able to placate the king's irrational moods than any of his advisors. Himself included.

If only the whole nasty business could be concluded. But there was one more issue to be addressed.

"Ahem, Your Majesty, I took the queen aside and informed her that under no circumstances should she attend your coronation services, that she would be neither welcome nor permitted inside Westminster Abbey."

"Quite right she won't be allowed in. In fact, I want pugilists to stand guard outside and forcibly remove her if she dares present herself. If that woman defies me over my coronation, I'll . . . I'll . . .

I'll see that she pays for it in the most hideous way possible, Parliament be damned."

"Yes, Your Majesty."

"On the other hand, there are certain people I must have in my presence during my coronation. I believe I've already mentioned to you that Lady Conyngham must have a place of honor."

"Yes, but, Your Majesty, the people might—"

"If they think I'll give up my sweet and precious heart at my coronation, well, they have something to learn about their sovereign. I must have her nearby, else I can't possibly be happy for this most momentous course of events. You'll see to it, won't you, Liverpool?"

"Of course, Your Majesty."

Liverpool simply wanted this tiresome meeting done. But Lady Conyngham had one more card to play.

"I can hardly think how grand Your Majesty's ceremony will be, and how gracious he is to include me. And although my family is the unworthy recipient of so many of your favors, may I recommend that my son, Francis, already a groom of the bedchamber, be permitted some role in Your Majesty's august day?"

The favor was bestowed without a second thought. "Of course, my lady. Hmm, how about if I make him master of the robes for the day? He can oversee the pages who carry my robe, and I'll see to it that he has specially marked vestments to set him apart."

Lady Conyngham's face changed again, into a melting gleam of self-satisfaction.

Because society loves a scandal, Belle was once again the focus of attention following Darcey's death. Belle and Put were completely exonerated, not only officially but in the court of public opinion. In fact, the public was once again fascinated with the draper turned conspirator turned draper once again. Even Lady Derby sent a servant to express great desire to have the first look at next season's newest fabrics.

Belle's infamy as the sister of a Cato Street conspirator was now tempered by her newfound fame as the survivor of an attempted murder—by a parliamentarian's daughter, no less.

The newspapers reported accounts from Lord Harrowby, reprinted articles from the Cato Street Conspiracy, and wrote their own dramatic versions of what happened that day inside the Stirling Drapers shop. They also lurked around Mr. White's home for several weeks, hoping for more gossip, but the grieving family shut itself completely away, and eventually the reporters grew bored with them.

Belle was inundated with a constant stream of visitors, who were only too disappointed to learn that the floors had been scrubbed clean by Lady Greycliffe's staff, then revarnished by Putnam Boyce. Nevertheless, it became fashionable to order fabrics from the lady shopkeeper who actually dispatched a crazed female assassin.

As the orders continued to pour in, Belle realized she needed to hire someone to help her. She asked Lady Greycliffe for advice, and the dollmaker recommended one of her own household staff's daughter, who didn't want to follow her mother into service but wanted to learn a trade. Molly proved to be capable and enthusiastic, and once more Belle was grateful for Lady Greycliffe's friendship.

Even more gratifying was the letter Belle received from John Nash, congratulating her on her marriage and achieving such great fame. The letter went on to tell her that the king once again viewed her favorably, and asked that she consider returning to work on the Pavilion.

She discussed it with Put and together they decided that however badly the king had treated her, it was, after all, his prerogative as king and there was great benefit to be had in working on a royal palace.

Besides, the official plans for the king's coronation were announced for July, improving Belle's fortunes as never before, so in an odd way she had King George IV to thank for her revival. A steady stream of customers and seamstresses trailed in and out of her shop each day, with extensive lists of velvets, furs, silks, tassels, and gold trims that they needed for robes and other vestments worthy of attendance at the king's coronation.

July 19, 1821
London

The king's coronation was rumored to be costing more than a hundred thousand pounds from the treasury. If the canopied walking platforms stretching from Carlton House to Westminster Abbey, specially erected just for the coronation procession, were any indication of the great lengths the Crown was going to for its new king, Belle figured the estimates were probably true.

Brimming with curiosity over what a coronation ceremony was like, she insisted that Put and Frances join her in attendance. Although regular citizens wouldn't be permitted inside Westminster Abbey for the actual crowning, they could line up anywhere along the route to watch the new monarch pass by.

It was a blistering hot day. Belle wore her best gown of creamy white Indian sari silk, shot through with a gold-thread pattern, thankful that she'd chosen something light and weightless for the day. How the king and his attendants would manage in their robes was beyond imagination.

Rather than trying to join the crowds along the long parade route, Belle determined that they should purchase seats on a platform next to the west door of Westminster Abbey, thinking they'd be among the first of London's citizens to see the king emerge in his crown. Rumor had it that the king had acquired a large blue diamond looted from the French crown jewels during the Revolution and had it set in the crown. Would she be able to see it twinkling in the sun, even at this distance?

The press of people on the tiered seating platform, as well as on the ground as far as the eye could see, made the day even more oppressive. At least everyone was good-natured about it. Thus far.

The roars and cheers of spectators far off announced the king's impending arrival, and from her place Belle caught a glimpse of his procession as it arrived, led by the king's herb woman and six young attendants dressed in white strewing the way with herbs and flowers. The entourage entered the abbey, finely dressed in Tudor-inspired breeches, neck ruffs, and crimson robes.

Too bad Belle's regained favor with the Crown had not extended to the provision of cloth for the coronation itself.

As the great doors to the old Gothic cathedral slammed shut behind the procession, a group of burly liveried men spread themselves out in the street across from the entry, as though daring anyone else to approach.

Yet someone did approach. A finely wrought closed carriage pulled by two magnificent plumed horses came barreling down the street to the abbey, its driver shouting at dawdling spectators to remove themselves. He pulled up in front of the guard line, and the carriage had barely stopped rolling when the door facing the crowds was flung open from the inside. The driver and a footman scrambled down to assist the occupant out, but a corpulent woman in a feathered headdress, her face mottled scarlet, stumbled out on her own.

Caroline, the queen.

As if just now realizing that she was on a parade route, the woman looked up at the spectators in the stands. She waved a pudgy hand at the Londoners, who were too shocked to do anything other than collectively gasp. Everyone knew about the queen's show trial, and although she had enjoyed immense popularity throughout it all, the people had since grown weary of the queen's antics. Parliament had agreed to pay her a fifty-thousand-pound annuity if she would simply go away. She'd agreed to it, but here she was today.

Belle looked at Put, who shook his head in amazement.

"She shouldn't be here," Belle whispered.

"No, and this might prove her undoing. The people want to witness a coronation, not a fishwife's waspish demands."

"But she *is* still the queen."

"Only in her own mind."

What became clear was that Caroline was out of her mind.

After waving and blowing kisses to the crowd, she lifted her skirts and ran on her stocky, jiggling legs past the ferocious-looking guards, who were initially too shocked to react. She spoke to the liveried man posted in front of the door, gesticulating wildly.

He shook his head at her.

Caroline waved even more passionately and shouted incoherently.

The man put his hand on his sword hilt.

She shoved the man aside and began beating on the abbey's door, screaming volubly so that London's citizens were treated to an unexpected circus event.

"Let me in! I am the queen! Open this door immediately!"

Everyone outside was hushed as Caroline continued her rampage.

Thump! Thump! Thump! She beat her fists repeatedly against the door.

"I will be permitted entrance! I am the queen! I will be crowned today, too! I am Her Majesty, Queen Caroline!"

Thump! Thump! Thump!

"I demand that the king open this door to his wife!"

By now, the guards had sufficiently recovered their wits to surround Caroline and nudge her away from the door. She struggled against them, shrieking about her right to be part of the coronation ceremony. But the burly men encircled her and led her back to the carriage, unceremoniously pushing her back inside.

Even where Belle sat, she could see that the driver and footman were white as sheets and anxious to be gone. The moment the door was shut again, the driver snapped his whip and the carriage drove off wildly, with the queen's voice still at an ear-shattering volume, screeching about her rights and privileges as Queen of England.

When the king himself reappeared later after his ceremony for the walk to his coronation banquet at nearby Westminster Hall, the crowds had sufficiently recovered themselves to remember to cheer for their newly crowned monarch.

"God save the king!"

"God save me from that woman! May He strike her dead!"

Lady Elizabeth Conyngham murmured soothingly as she cut a piece of bread and held it between her fingers, "May He indeed, Your Majesty."

"I tell you, dearest lady, I tolerated much from her, when I was in no manner obligated to do so. So many arrows have I had in my quiver, and so few have I let fly."

"Of course, my love, of course. You must try this cheese brioche." She popped it in his mouth, and allowed him to nibble the crumbs from her hand.

"Yes, most excellent. Where was I?"

"Your full quiver."

"Yes. And Liverpool warned her that she wouldn't be welcome at my coronation, yet she defied me again. Again! At least she wasn't able to interfere with my dearest Lady Elizabeth's presence inside the abbey, but no matter, no matter.

"I am a patient, tolerant man, full of love and goodwill for my subjects, as you well know, but I have finished with her, Lady Elizabeth. She is done in my kingdom forever."

Something in his tone caused Lady Conyngham to put down the serving knife she was using to cut another piece.

"What do you mean, Your Majesty?"

"As I said, my quiver is not nearly empty, and my bow begs for one more shot. Let's have done with the sweets, dearest. I have other delicacies in mind that you'll want to enjoy with your newly crowned sovereign."

She rose and made preparations to join the king in his chamber. A mistress's work was never done.

July 21, 1821
Brighton

Knowing the king would be busy in London immediately following his coronation, Belle left the shop in Molly's good hands and returned to Brighton, traveling together with Put for the first time, so she could introduce him to Mr. Nash and the dour Mr. Crace, and to view progress on the palace.

So many rooms were finished now: the Entrance Hall, the Great Corridor, the Music Room, the Banqueting Room, and the Great Kitchen were all finished to Nash's and the artist-designers' exacting standards.

The North Drawing Room would be finished soon, as would the Saloon. The new stucco-and-stone exterior had about a year until completion, but workers swarmed all over it to ensure it was finished at the earliest possible date.

To think that I've been a part of it all. It was too much to contemplate.

It was marvelous to immerse herself back in the heady world of the Pavilion once again, especially with Put at her side.

A piece of bad news fluttered down to Brighton while they were there. Queen Caroline was ill and had taken to her bed. The Boyces and the Nashes expressed best wishes for the queen's health, assuming she was merely tired from the turmoil surrounding the trial and her resulting disappointment at the coronation.

A few days later, on August 7, the queen was dead.

August 14, 1821
On the road from Hammersmith to Harwich

The funeral procession had been stopped for nearly a half hour. Lady Anne Hamilton, Caroline's most devoted lady-in-waiting, leaned out the open window of her mourning carriage, one in a train of ten behind the queen's glass coffin hearse. One of the five hundred mounted soldiers assigned to attend the cavalcade was coming down the procession line, and stopped next to the polished black carriage draped in matching bunting to acknowledge her.

"Why have we been at a standstill for so long?" she asked. "We're hardly out of Hammersmith. Isn't that Kensington Church up in front of us?"

"Yes, Your Ladyship. There's just a small disturbance ahead. Some carts placed in our path. It's just a few drunkards and rovers trying to divert the train back into the city instead of letting us proceed north toward Islington. Nothing to worry about; we'll have them dispersed shortly."

"Divert the train? Why? Have they no respect for their queen?"

And had they no respect for how unbearably hot it was in a closed carriage with no air moving around them?

As if in response to her complaint, rain began misting over the area. She quickly tucked her head back inside, where Lady Jane Hood was clucking her tongue at the news.

The soldier made no reaction to the rain. "That's just it, madam. The people want to pay their respects. They think the king is sending her off too mysteriously."

Lady Anne nodded in understanding, and the soldier moved on. She turned to Lady Jane. "Even the common people understand what a jackanapes he is."

"A final humiliation is what it is." Lady Jane followed up her noises of disapproval with a resounding sniff.

"I shouldn't wonder that the king would be avoiding any inquiry by the public."

"So you still think the queen's death was unnatural?"

"Come, Jane, you were with me at her bedside. You saw how quickly her body swelled and turned black."

"Within just a couple of hours. It certainly was suggestive of a poison, wasn't it?"

"Yes, and the king showed not a whit of regret at her passing. As though he expected it."

"It's treason what we're suggesting." Lady Jane's voice implied that she wasn't sure if she was more fearful of being caught or thrilled to be gossiping in such a manner.

"I know. We dare not speak of it outside this carriage."

"Do you think there might be another investigation? Just imagine the king on trial this time!"

Lady Anne smiled at the other woman's thought, but knew better than to think it could be reality. "Place not your trust in princes," she murmured.

She leaned against the plush, tufted-leather seat and stared up at the mythological scene painted on the ceiling. At least they were given a fine carriage with good springs for the seventy-five-mile journey that lay ahead of them. There were planned stops in Chelmsford and Colchester, then their queen would be taken aboard a ship in Harwich and from there sail back to Brunswick.

Queen Caroline had specifically stated that she wanted to be buried in her homeland, and government officials had been so fearful of demonstrations in London that they'd concocted this convoluted plan of overland travel with her body from her home in Hammersmith to the Harwich launch point in Essex.

And although Lady Anne had packed enough trunks to support a sea voyage, she still hadn't made up her mind whether to accompany her mistress all the way back to Brunswick.

The carriage started off again with a lurch. Finally they were to make some progress. But they'd not gotten as far as Hyde Park Corner when the two women saw members of the Life Guard galloping past them, pistols drawn, toward the front of the procession.

And they halted once again.

"What has happened now?" Lady Anne asked.

"More troublemakers, I'm sure. If they respect Queen Caroline, they should let us pass freely."

And the carriage lurched forward once again, amid distant shouting and the crashes of overturned carts. Lady Anne stuck her head out the window to ascertain what mishaps lay ahead. The rain had stopped, but the sky was still dark and gloomy. Ideal, really, for the funeral of the queen she'd loved so well.

Their carriage passed the gates into Hyde Park and picked up a reckless amount of speed, careening past others as their driver cracked his whip violently overhead. The dignified funeral procession was now a stampeding commotion. Dirty, angry faces were now pressing forward, trying to reach the procession. Shouts of "Give us our queen!" and "Only a murdered queen would be taken out in secret! Let us see her!" Protestors at the back of the crowd were hurling bricks and stones at the soldiers, who were trying their best to reorganize the procession and quell the disturbance.

Lady Anne quickly retreated back inside the carriage and turned to Lady Jane. "Jane, if you are the praying type, this might be an opportune moment to employ your skills."

Her last words were cut off as shots rang out, followed by the noises of outrage in the crowd. A soldier galloped past her, his pistol still smoking. "Got one!" she heard him shout as he passed.

But it had the desired effect of quelling the crowd, and the carriages slowed back to their decorous pace. As they passed back out of Hyde Park, she witnessed Sir Robert Baker atop his horse, reading the Riot Act of 1715 to the assembled crowd.

" *'Our Sovereign Lord the King chargeth and commandeth all persons, being assembled, immediately to disperse themselves, and peaceably to depart to their habitations, or to their lawful business, upon the pains contained in the act made in the first year of King George, for preventing tumults and riotous assemblies.'* "

Sir Robert folded up his copy of the law. "God save the king!" he added, as the crowd, mindful of the severe penalties to be suffered for disobedience after being delivered this formal warning, melted away.

Lady Anne believed the fracas to finally be over, but she was wrong. For although the cortege was finally put on the road to Islington, yet another mass of carriages and carts were chained together at Tottenham Court Road, forcing them back again. Another soldier came by to inform them that the procession would indeed be returning to the city for a slow walk through the streets before going on its originally planned route.

"The people are such brutes. If they don't get this mob under control, we'll be as harassed and persecuted as Marie Antoinette on the road back from Varennes," complained Lady Jane. "And it will take us days to reach Harwich at this rate. Our queen deserves burial."

But for all of her fear of the demonstrators, Lady Anne was secretly pleased. In the end, the people loved their queen, despite her imperfections, and were willing to go to great lengths to pay their last respects. Yes, she deserved burial, but she deserved the accolades more. After the great final injustice that Lady Anne suspected had been heaped upon Queen Caroline, the very least the queen's devoted lady-in-waiting could do was suffer the long journey to Harwich in silence.

And Lady Anne right then made up her mind. She would accompany the queen's body back to Brunswick from Harwich. For if her devotion to Caroline was greater than anyone else's, how could she do less? If only there were other subjects as suspicious of the queen's death as she was.

Belle and Put stood at a distance under an umbrella, somberly watching the queen's funeral cortege struggle to make its way through the crowds.

"The Riot Act? The king is using the Riot Act? I can't believe this, Put. Why is he treating his people so dreadfully?"

Put draped his arm around her shoulder and kissed the top of her head. "He's certainly aware of his own unpopularity. Perhaps he suspected the people might riot over their queen's loss."

"But that's just it. The people were generally tired of her conduct and not as likely to cheer her on. But we've always paid our respects to our dead monarchs, openly and together. What's the purpose of this secret run to the coast to deposit her body on a barge? What is he hiding?"

"What are you suggesting?"

Belle didn't answer, instead asking more questions. "How could the queen have died so suddenly? We just saw her at the king's coronation, and she was certainly in fine form then."

"People get sick and die, sweetheart."

She dropped her voice. "Do you remember when I told you that I thought Wesley was involved in a plot to discredit the queen?"

"Yes. You thought he was helping the king manufacture evidence against her, evidence we know was produced for her trial, but that Wesley had no real hand in."

"But what if the Cato Street Conspiracy wasn't what it seemed? What if it really was about the king's desire to discredit the queen—or even to concoct a way to kill her—and the conspirators involved thought they were accomplishing their goals when really they were just providing cover to His Majesty's plans?"

"Belle, you're talking nonsense."

She rushed on as though she hadn't heard him. "The Cato Street Conspiracy occupied the public for months, during which the king was gathering, or manufacturing, evidence against his wife. What if he was doing even more beyond anyone's notice? He knew the public's opinion of his wife and that he couldn't rationally compete with her in that department. For heaven's sake, Put, maybe even the trial was intended for show while the king followed through on plans to poison the queen."

"If the king planned such a thing, surely it would have been impossible to carry through with it. He had no direct access to her, and no one would have been party to such a scheme."

Belle's fears were not assuaged.

She was even more concerned to read that on August 17, just three days after the queen's funeral debacle, the king had decided to still take his planned trip to Dublin so his Irish subjects could lay eyes on their monarch and he was now happily touring and receiving their accolades.

"It's terribly convenient that the king had this trip planned on the heels of the queen's death, isn't it?" Belle asked as she passed the newspaper article to Put over the breakfast they shared with Frances. He quickly scanned it.

"I'm worried," she said. "I think the king may have gotten away with murdering his wife, and this trip distracts the public from what he's done."

"Annabelle Boyce, why all of this obsession about the king? Caroline is dead and buried back in Brunswick. What is the point of gnawing on this soup bone?" He handed the newspaper back to her. "Involving us in a scandal like this would only serve to ruin our lives again, and we've been close enough to the edge as it is."

She sighed. "You must think I've gone totty."

Frances shook her head. *You aren't crazy.*

"More totty than when you refused my sincere and gentleman-like advances?" Put asked.

"Even more than that. But shouldn't even a king be called to account for murdering his wife?"

"Belle, it's not our place to be the king's conscience, nor his trial judge."

"No, no, of course you're right." She sighed. "These biscuits are truly heavenly, Frances. I'll be a stout old fishwife in no time by living with you."

Frances beamed.

Yet the situation continued eating away at Belle. When Nash

summoned her again to Brighton to reveal the finish of the North Drawing Room, she went alone. Easily enough managed, since Put and his workers were furiously trying to finish an entire houseful of furniture for a newly married woman given free rein by her husband to refurbish the family home.

Her first stop, though, was a visit with the charming Maria Fitzherbert, who welcomed her with genuine delight. It was difficult not to adore the effervescent Mrs. Fitzherbert, and to feel a tad sorry for the rotten way in which the king had treated her.

Although, in looking at Mrs. Fitzherbert's lovely surroundings, one saw she certainly had not suffered financially through the king's parting from her.

"I'm so happy to see you again, Miss Stirling," Maria said over iced lemon cakes and tea.

"Actually, I'm Mrs. Boyce now. I was recently married."

"Indeed? Tell me all about your new husband. Is he here in Brighton with you?"

Belle sketched out quickly for Mrs. Fitzherbert all that had happened to her, from Wesley's involvement in the Cato Street Conspiracy to Darcey's attempted assassination and her own marriage to Put.

Mrs. Fitzherbert gasped and leaned forward across the tea table in her parlor. "Remarkable! And you say you shot your brother's lover? You are a playwright's dream. We should plan a closet drama here at Steine House based on your adventures. How amusing it would be."

"I hardly think I am the stuff of dramatic theatre, Mrs. Fitzherbert."

The older woman laughed in her merry, infectious way. "My dear Mrs. Boyce, you hardly know how you've livened up my quiet days. What a joy to have you here."

"I've come to be in attendance on the king when he views the opening of his new North Drawing Room. He has high expectations for it, and I believe Mr. Nash and Mr. Crace have succeeded well."

"I'm sure you've provided well for it, too."

Belle reddened under Maria's praise. "Thank you, but my part is so small compared to theirs."

"Nonsense. No one's part is small when it comes to serving the king. Everyone does his part. Which reminds me, how is Mary Ann Nash these days?"

"I'm sorry? Mary Ann Nash reminds you of serving the king?"

"Hmm, perhaps I said too much. I just assumed that since you were friends with the Nashes and worked so closely with Mr. Nash, that . . ." Maria sipped her tea to avoid completing her thought.

"Does Mrs. Nash serve His Majesty in some particular way?"

"Well, perhaps 'serve' is not the correct term. The two have been . . . special friends for many years."

Belle nearly dropped her cup. "Pardon me? Are you disclosing that Mrs. Nash is the king's mistress? Behind my patron's back?"

Mrs. Fitzherbert laughed, an incongruously happy sound against such horrifying news. "Mrs. Boyce, you hardly understand the situation. The three of them are great friends."

"What do you mean?"

"The king and the Nashes have had an arrangement for years. All of her children are actually the king's. His Majesty, in his kind effort to take care of her, recommended Mr. Nash as a good protector, and so he has proven to be one. In return, the king has granted Mrs. Nash's husband considerable architectural patronage. They are all quite happy in their business arrangement."

"So Mr. Nash is a cuckold."

"Not at all. The three of them have agreed to the situation, as it benefits them all in different ways. The king can visit his dear Mrs. Nash as he pleases, Mrs. Nash knows her children are taken care of, and Mr. Nash is successful beyond his wildest dreams."

Belle was stunned. This was incomprehensible.

"Mrs. Fitzherbert, are you saying they are just a merry band of players together?"

Maria smiled. "You might say so, yes."

Belle could hardly believe what she was hearing. Mr. Nash was an agreeable participant in this charade with the king in order to advance his career? Mary Ann Nash willingly watched the king flaunt his official mistresses around for the crumbs he threw her? King George IV happily ensconced his mistress and children with another man in order to openly pursue other women?

Really, why am I surprised about this in a man who secretly married one woman, then married another?

"But what of the king's other . . . attachments?"

She lifted a shoulder. "He is the king and therefore privileged. Remember, there is great reward in always serving your monarch well. I, too, have served my king in the ways he needed. You, Mrs. Boyce, are just as indebted to the king for your livelihood as I am for my own circumstances, as well as that of my children."

"Your children? I didn't know you had any."

"I am a babbling brook of secrets today. Yes, the king and I have two daughters together, Mary Ann and Mary Georgina. Alas, the king desired that I send them out to be raised by others, so I did. They hardly know me now, and I don't intrude on their lives."

For heaven's sake, was there nothing this king was incapable of? How many children had he farmed out to others?

Mrs. Fitzherbert laughed at her discomfort. "Come, come, no need to look so troubled. You've been let in on a great secret today, a great honor for you. Let it be. After all, didn't the great bard warn us that 'discretion is the better part of valor'?"

Belle was still speechless. And in sudden need of a thorough scrubbing.

When she spoke again, it was slowly, as if in a murky fog of deception. "You once told me that the king could hardly stand his own daughter. I suppose you meant his acknowledged daughter."

"I do try to honor the king's wishes in all things by not mentioning his other children."

"I see. So what the king does not like gets put away, much as a toy that a child has outgrown." Belle put down her plate. She'd lost all appetite for food.

"Mrs. Boyce, it's not quite that severe. I—"

"And we know that the person the king was most tired of in this world was his wife, Caroline. His wife who is now dead. Who fell ill the very night of her husband's coronation, and was dead three weeks later, swelled up mysteriously into a bloated, black corpse. Do you not find that just a little odd, Mrs. Fitzherbert?"

"If you are suggesting that the king—"

Belle sighed. "I suppose I'm not suggesting anything. How could it be proven? Even if I could, of what value is the opinion of an Oxford Street draper whose brother was hung for plotting against Parliament, and who herself recently killed an intruder in her store?"

Maria put down her own plate. "You did a courageous thing against your intruder. Your concern now is perhaps a little less . . . wise."

Perhaps that is so, but can I live with a soiled conscience? How have you done so all these years?

"It seems to me that aristocrats and royalty are a world unto themselves, are they not? We lesser mortals are not to question their actions or intentions. If we fly too close, we risk getting singed by the flame, or being swept into their virtueless world."

Maria spread her hands. "All I can say is that you simply don't understand the intricacies of the king's life."

Belle stood. "Mrs. Fitzherbert, I must leave before I become ill from this conversation. You have been very gracious to me, and I thank you, but I believe this is all just too much for me to grasp. I need to walk and clear the cobwebs from my mind."

She left after a flurry of kisses and embraces from the king's previous wife and mistress. Escaping into the open air along the Steine, she paced back and forth along the fence for an hour, yet still had no solution to her quandary.

It was time to attend to the king inside the Pavilion to reveal the North Drawing Room to him. Steeling herself for what was to come, she walked over to the palace, and found that the Nashes, Mr. Crace, and the king's other designer, Mr. Robert Jones, were already assembled to welcome the king. She made the barest polite acknowledgments of the others while they waited for His Majesty to arrive in his opulently furnished and decorated room. It carried the same busy and colorful chinoiserie flavor as incorporated in many other rooms. Immense columns down the center of the room contained a vibrant pattern of Chinese dragons in vibrant reds and blues. Another sumptuous room in a breathtaking palace.

The king was jovial and puffed out to twice his normal personality today as he entered, flush from the success of his trip to Ireland. "And what a pleasing vision this all is. How distressing that our dear friend, Lady Conyngham, couldn't be here to see it, but she was unwell and wanted to rest at her town house."

The king's architect and designers offered their regrets that dear Lady Conyngham couldn't be present for the occasion.

Belle glanced at Mary Ann Nash's calm composure. Was there a flicker of jealousy in her eyes at the mention of the king's mistress?

"Felicitations are due to you on your happy occasion, is that not so, Mrs. Boyce, I believe it is?"

Belle curtseyed. "Yes, Your Majesty. My husband greatly regrets that he couldn't accompany me to Brighton."

"Pity. We would like to meet the man who tamed you."

"Tamed, Your Majesty? I don't believe my husband would think he accomplished such a feat."

The king laughed, his eyes disappearing into slits. "Your husband is a wise man. For what bold and brazen woman can be tempered by her husband, eh?"

It depends on whether your husband is the king.

"Indeed not, Your Majesty."

"Take my friends, Mr. and Mrs. Nash here. I daresay Mr. Nash has never quite mastered his wife's spirit."

"No, sir."

Belle's stomach churned at all of their duplicity. How they must laugh behind cupped hands whenever Belle left the room, amused at her rustic naiveté over the ways of her betters.

She took in John Nash, plump and aging but always smiling. He'd profited greatly by taking in the king's mistress all those years ago. He lived nearly like a prince himself, and didn't seem to mind that he was rearing his patron's children.

And what of Mary Ann Nash? For years raising the king's children while playacting as Nash's wife. Sitting on the sidelines while the king carried on with his public mistresses. What was it like to live year in and year out, watching your children grow up without knowledge of their real father? To know that his interest in them was no more than handing over a purse of gold to your caretaker, while you were still expected to bring him pleasure when he demanded it?

She didn't know Mr. Jones, but Frederick Crace was no more than a fellow tradesman who had somehow developed airs of grandeur from working on the palace, as though it were his own residence. Did Mr. Crace believe that as an artist-designer he somehow had more knowledge of his craft than she had of hers as a draper?

She looked at the king, the very center of all of the deceit and effrontery. He was a glutton for food, attention, and women, and expected all those in his orbit to satisfy those needs. And they did. Everyone in this room had sold his soul for the favor of the king.

I won't do it.

She needed to escape it all, but how?

The king had a surprise for her. "My dear Mrs. Boyce, you have so spectacularly assisted us on our beloved Pavilion that we have decided to grant you the royal warrant for provision of cloth to the Crown."

Belle held her breath. The royal warrant! Her shop would be secure forever. It would be a worthy establishment to pass to her children one day. She self-consciously placed a hand on her midsection at the thought.

Does the royal warrant equate to giving up my own spirit and moral fiber?

"But more important, Mrs. Boyce, in light of my great respect for your downright pluck in the face of many prospects of ruination, I've decided to release you from your obligation to me that came due upon your marriage." The king winked at her exaggeratedly. "You thought I might have forgotten our delectable arrangement, eh? But how could I, now that I am a happy bachelor once again?"

The room went silent at the crass reference to Caroline.

Then the king's laughter rent the air. "Ahaha. I played a little joke on you, didn't I, Mrs. Boyce? I quite enjoy seeing your shocked face."

The room visibly relaxed.

Belle's mind worked furiously. This was all that was wrong with tying one's future with princes. She despised the thought of forever nodding and smiling in the face of the king's cruelties and peccadilloes. And at any moment he might decide that he really did want an affair with her, and would hold the royal warrant as hostage.

The Nashes might have sold their souls to this devil, but she never would.

Belle stood, trembling, but determined to have her say.

Careful, don't let your uncontrollable tongue ruin your life.

"I'm sorry, Your Majesty, but as great as the honor is, I'm afraid I can't accept it."

The king was no longer laughing. "Pardon me, Mrs. Boyce? Did I hear you aright? Did you just refuse the royal warrant?"

"I regret that I must."

"You would be the first tradesman in all of English history to turn it down. Is there something about you that is unsuitable for such an honor?"

Mr. Crace jumped in. "Yes, Your Majesty, it has been my experience that she is utterly unsuitable for work on an important project like the Pavilion. Too outspoken and vulgar."

"This is none of your concern, Mr. Crace," Belle said. "Kindly conduct yourself accordingly."

Crace gaped at her.

"As I was saying, Your Majesty, I regret that I cannot accept this singularly distinctive honor. For you see, I plan to join my husband in his cabinetmaking shop. I will no longer be a draper."

"Ah," Nash said. "So does this mean your shop will be available for purchase?"

Wesley's voice reached out to her from the past. *Has it ever occurred to you that Mr. Nash wants to take possession of your shop?*

"No, Mr. Nash, it does not. I will use my existing inventory for covering furniture in my husband's shop and then shutter my own shop entirely."

Nash's face fell, but only for a moment before radiating sunshine again. "It was worth asking. Pity, though. Such a profitable enterprise."

"Your appreciation for my success is overwhelming, sir."

The king was frowning, his mind working furiously behind his eyes. "Mrs. Boyce, I believe we have a problem here. You are turning down the royal warrant, yet I cannot be known as a king whose generous offer was refused."

"No, Your Majesty."

"Therefore, our trade with you must cease immediately. You can no longer consult with Messrs. Nash or Crace."

Crace was practically bouncing in joy.

"Of course, sir, I understand."

Belle knew she was saying good-bye to the Pavilion forever.

Belle bathed to remove all of the road dust and grime and changed into her nightgown. She typically loved this exact moment every evening, when Put slid into bed next to her, and they murmured quietly together as the candle burned down and sleep overcame them.

Tonight, though, she needed to tell him what happened with the king.

He went right to it. "How was everything in Brighton?"

"I suppose that depends on what sort of outcome we were hoping for."

"I see. Do you plan to confess your sins to me?"

"Suffice to say that for one brief moment I held the royal warrant for the provision of cloth, but refused it because of what may have been either the smartest or stupidest decision I have ever made. Actually, I managed to lose my work on the Pavilion entirely."

He kissed her. "So you were quite reckless in your decision?"

"Mmm, I would say resolved."

"Yes, you are that. Well, I'm not surprised. So now what?"

"I was thinking . . ." She entwined her fingers with his and put her head on his chest. "I was thinking that perhaps running a draper's shop isn't the most profitable use of my time."

"And what would be a better use of Mrs. Boyce's time?"

"I thought perhaps a certain cabinetmaker could use his wife's talent for picking out fabrics for furniture and covering them. I'm imagining copying some of the fantastical pieces in the Pavilion for sale to London's elite."

"But you know nothing about upholstery."

She shrugged. "I knew nothing about cloth until my father showed me. I knew nothing about interiors until Mr. Nash taught me. I can learn upholstery."

"What about your shop?"

"Molly is learning quickly. I'll sell it to her, and she can run it under another name. She can order whatever fabrics I need to cover the exotic pieces that the Boyce Cabinetmakers shop will produce."

"Boyce and Sons sounds better."

She squeezed his hand. "One thing at a time, husband. What do you think of my idea?"

"A fine solution to losing the king's work, I think."

"I think so, too."

As she closed her eyes, she sent up a little prayer of apology to her father for walking away from the business he'd worked so hard to pass on to her. She sensed Fafa would understand her desire to renew her life.

Just as sleep was about to overtake her, Belle realized that she still didn't know whether the king was guilty or innocent in his wife's death. With her dismissal from the Pavilion, she might never know the truth.

Nor would the world.

AUTHOR'S NOTE

George Hanover, the **Prince Regent** and later **King George IV** (1762–1830), was one of the more unloved monarchs of British history. Unquestionably a self-absorbed, hedonistic, gluttonous spendthrift, he was also a great patron of the arts, and was largely instrumental in the foundation of the National Gallery in London, as well as King's College.

His father, George III, who would eventually die after years of suffering from porphyria, had little use for the young George, and therefore gave him few duties and responsibilities, yet expected the young prince to behave in a . . . well . . . princely manner. It was an impossibly conflicting goal, and George misspent his youth. The young George thwarted his father in everything, from illegally marrying the Catholic Maria Fitzherbert to running up debts to the tune of over £600,000 (nearly $80 million in today's money). The London *Times* once wrote that he would always prefer "a girl and a bottle to politics and a sermon."

After his father's death in 1820, George ascended the throne as George IV, and his personal antics continued to swell in direct relationship to his waistline as he unsuccessfully attempted a divorce from his legal wife, the Princess Caroline of Brunswick. This very public affair soured whatever popularity he may have had with the public.

His extravagant coronation can be marked by his coronation crown, which was adorned with 12,314 hired diamonds. The new king acquired the large blue diamond that would become known as the Hope Diamond. It had been looted from the French crown jewels in 1792. The gem turned up in England as a recut stone, after the statute of limitations had run out in 1812, in the possession of a diamond merchant. George IV purchased the stone in 1820.

On George's death in 1830, the London *Times* editorialized that "there never was an individual less regretted by his fellow creatures than this deceased king." An interesting and telling commentary regarding a monarch who had effectively been on the throne for nearly twenty years.

There are numerous statues of the self-indulgent George IV, many of which were erected during his reign, including a bronze statue of him on horseback in Trafalgar Square, London, and another outside the Royal Pavilion in Brighton.

Although the series of kings named George have a style named after them, it is interesting to note that one of those kings, who ruled in his own right a mere nine years, had an entire style—in both architecture and fashion—attributed to his tastes. Regency architectural style is marked by residences typically built as terraces or crescents, with multiple homes joined together to resemble one great mansion. Elegant wrought-iron balconies and bow windows came into fashion during this period. Regency interiors were typically filled with exceedingly elegant furniture, vertically striped wallpaper, painted decorative effects such as marbling or stenciling, lavish draperies covering both windows and walls, and indoor potted plants.

Regency clothing for men was typified by the famous dandy Beau Brummell and his simple—but always elegant and perfect!—clothing. The empire silhouette reigned for women's gowns.

George IV may have lacked morals, manners, and restraint, but he certainly had style.

The ongoing scandal of George IV's treatment of his wife, **Caroline of Brunswick** (1768–1821), Princess of Wales and later Queen Caroline, was more than equaled by Caroline's own peccadilloes. George's complaints of her personal hygiene seem to have been justified, yet she was also a kind woman, adopting and fostering out nearly a dozen children and engendering loyalty and devotion from people in many quarters.

Her rapid decline over the course of two weeks in July–August 1821, combined with the fact that her body swelled grotesquely and turned black within two hours of death, led many to conclude that Caroline had in fact been poisoned to death. Her physicians speculated that she may have had an intestinal obstruction. Modern medical opinion concludes that she likely died of natural causes, possibly a tumor with the complication of a blood infection, which would account for the blackening of her body, but the exact cause of her death remains unknown.

In any case, a poison rumor creates great fiction, and I chose to use it in my story.

The Prince Regent may have cast aside **Maria Fitzherbert** (1756–1837) to disastrously marry his cousin, but it was Fitzherbert who won in the end. Their on-again, off-again relationship lasted for more than twenty years, and she did indeed take up residence in a house merely a stone's throw from the Royal Pavilion. After their final break in 1811, she retired into private life with a £6,000 annuity (worth around $6 million in today's money, not shabby). Interestingly, Maria remained greatly respected by society and other members of the royal family for the rest of her life. In her will, Maria outlined her two principal beneficiaries, Mary Ann Stafford-Jerningham and Mary Georgina Emma Dawson-Damer, who were nominally the daughters of other people but to whom Maria wrote that she had "loved them both with the . . . affection any mother could do, and I have done the utmost in my power for their interests and comfort." Presumably, these were George's children, since there is no evidence of children from either of her first two marriages.

Lady Isabella Hertford (1759–1834) was the Prince Regent's mistress from 1807 to 1819. The Prince Regent really did give her a Gainsborough portrait of his youthful mistress Maria Robinson as a gift. The painting now resides in the Hertfords' London home, now known as the Wallace Collection museum.

Lady Elizabeth Conyngham (1769–1861) picked up where Lady Isabella left off, serving as the king's mistress from 1819 until his death in 1830. Both she and Lady Hertford shared the same appreciation for money, rank, and favors. Both women also had compliant husbands, who seemed to not mind their wives' activities if it meant furthering the family's social position. Especially in the case of Lady Conyngham, who had multiple love affairs even prior to that with the king, including Lord Ponsonby and the future Tsar Nicholas I of Russia. George gave Lady Elizabeth expensive clothes and jewels, and her husband successive titles.

Lord Conyngham rose from viscount to earl to marquess in only twenty years. In return, Lady Elizabeth kept the aging king amused. She did attempt to instill more spirituality in her sovereign. After the king's sudden death in 1830, Lady Conyngham fled to Paris for a time, then returned to England. She died near Canterbury in 1861, at the ripe old age of ninety-two.

John Nash (1752–1835), born rather inconspicuously to a millwright, had a rather lackluster career before coming to the notice of the Prince Regent. Although Nash had a distinguished schooling under the eminent Palladian architect Sir Robert Taylor, he was never a learned student of the Classical Orders and rebelled against them, preferring his own version of the Picturesque style. His early career was marked by scattered commissions all across England, Wales, and Ireland, as well as by a financial calamity when he tried his hand at London real estate speculation.

Although Nash designed so many country houses, cathedrals, and castles that his entire body of work is still not documented, it is his skill as a city planner where his talent truly shone. With the Prince Regent's passionate support, Nash created a master plan to develop Marylebone Park, an area that stretched from St. James's northwards, and included Regent Street, Regent's Park, and all of the surrounding streets, terraces, and homes.

Although named for him, Regent Street was in no way the Prince Regent's idea. However, he did give it enthusiastic support, viewing it as an achievement that would "quite eclipse Napoleon," a sentiment that would have garnered popular support of the time. Ironically, Regent Street was designed from the beginning to be not only a direct connection from Carlton House to a royal park, as well as a convenient route for inhabitants of the West End to reach the Houses of Parliament and the social whirl of St. James, but also as a pleasurable shopping district for the *ton* members of society, and was therefore an accurate reflection of the prince's character.

Although Regent Street is still a famous shopping district, most of Nash's buildings have since been replaced, except for All Souls Church. This early nineteenth-century church stands oddly against the backdrop of the very modern BBC Broadcasting House.

Nash was also a director of the Regent Canal Company, established in 1812, to provide a canal link from west London to the Thames River in the east. Other notable commissions included a remodeling of Buckingham House (later Buckingham Palace), the Marble Arch, Trafalgar Square, St. James's Park, Haymarket Theatre, Carlton House Terrace, and All Souls Church, Langham Place.

But Nash's lasting achievement was his work on the Royal Pavilion, the Prince Regent's extravagant palace in the seaside resort town of Brighton, East Sussex.

Nash wasn't given the work of transforming the Royal Pavilion until 1815, although it better suited my story for it to start three years earlier. Henry Holland redesigned the existing farmhouse into the first incarnation of a "pavilion" for the Prince Regent in 1787, and the nucleus of that building still remains today. Nash's expensive and extravagant additions and renovations would last until 1823. The king confessed that he cried for joy when he contemplated the Pavilion's splendors. Interestingly, George IV only made two subsequent visits to the palace, in 1824 and 1827.

John Nash was well-known as very good-natured and civil to all around him. Although he was characterized as having "a face like a monkey's," he was also clever and amusing, as well as self-deprecating. He also completely disregarded social barriers and assumed he would be welcome at all levels of society. He usually was, attracting work from both landed aristocrats with inherited fortunes and the nouveau-riche.

After George IV's death in 1830, Nash was dismissed on grounds of profligacy from his work on remodeling Buckingham House. The pain of this public humiliation was too much for him. He suffered a stroke, and retreated to his favorite home, East Cowes Castle, on the Isle of Wight, where he never really recovered, dying bedridden at the age of eighty-three in 1835.

Although England had guilds for nearly every profession under the sun, there was no guild for architects and they were not formally licensed to do business. Nor was there any formal training or schools dedicated to the study of architecture. Someone simply studied under a respected architect long enough until he was able to secure his own commissions. Nash studied for ten years under Robert Taylor.

Mary Ann Bradley (1773–1851) was, by all accounts, a vivacious and beautiful woman when Nash married her and took her five children under his wing in 1798. All of her papers were later burned, but there is evidence—including a plethora of later political cartoons showing a corpulent prince and his equally corpulent mistress, Mrs. Nash—to suggest that she was indeed the Prince Regent's mistress for many years and that all of her children were actually his. Did Nash and George IV have an agreement whereby Nash would house Mary Ann and her children in exchange for preferential building contracts?

Regardless, Nash's household and way of life demonstrated inexplicable affluence from 1798 on, and he did become the prince's favorite architect.

After her husband's death in 1835, Mary Ann Nash moved permanently to Hampstead, where she lived with her daughter, Anne, until her own death in 1851.

Frederick Crace (1779–1859) and **Robert Jones** (about whom little is known) were artist-designers heavily involved in Nash's rebuilding of the Marine Pavilion into the Royal Pavilion, with Crace beginning work in 1815 and Jones joining the project in 1817. Most of the major rooms (the Banqueting Room, the Saloon, the Red Drawing Room, and the King's Apartments) were designed by Jones, while Crace undertook the Music Room and the Banqueting Room Galleries. Both men were in complete sync with Nash's and the prince's desire to create a magnificent setting for the man who became George IV. My portrayal of Crace's personality is a complete invention.

The Prince Regent greatly admired **Jane Austen** (1775–1817) and kept a set of her books at each residence. The admiration was not mutual. In fact, in once referring to Princess Caroline, Jane said, "I hate her husband," and, "I am resolved at least always to think that she would have been respectable, if the Prince had behaved tolerably by her at first." But in November 1815 (I pushed the date up to May to better suit my story), George's librarian, **James Stanier Clarke** (1766–1834), invited Jane to visit the prince's London residence, Carlton House, and hinted very directly that Jane should dedicate her forthcoming novel, *Emma*, to the prince. How could she refuse?

Later, Clarke sent Jane a letter thanking her on behalf of the Regent for his copy of *Emma* and also providing suggestions as to what European royal houses she might want to dedicate future novels, as well as what topics she should pursue in her writing. Jane later wrote *Plan of a Novel, according to Hints from Various Quarters*, a satire on how to outline the "perfect" novel, based on Clarke's many suggestions.

For the purposes of my own novel, which was fortunately not under the influence of someone like the Prince Regent's librarian, I chose to let Clarke press Jane to dedicate *Emma* to the Prince Regent, as well as make his infamous "recommendations" to her, all in one sitting.

Jane never viewed her novels as romances, as we do today. Rather she saw them as contemporary commentary on the values and social customs of nineteenth-century English country families. In other words, she wrote what she knew.

The second **Lady Derby, née Elizabeth Farren** (c. 1759–1829), was a stage actress who caught the eye of the rather squat and unattractive Derby. He married her with indecent haste after the death of his first wife, also Elizabeth, who left him for John Frederick Sackville, the Duke of Dorset, after many years of a miserable marriage. Derby was besotted with his second Elizabeth, though, and together they had four children.

Lord and Lady Derby did indeed reside at number 23 Grosvenor Square, that square being one of the most fashionable locations in London. The earliest, seventeenth-century, houses there were built as three main stories plus an attic, but most were rebuilt in the eighteenth and nineteenth centuries, generally acquiring an extra story. Robert Adam rebuilt the Earl of Derby's home, and it is regarded as one of the architect's finest works.

On a personal note, I was in London on September 11th and attended a memorial service three days later at Grosvenor Square, where the U.S. Embassy is now located. As of this writing, it has been ten years since that event, and I am still deeply grateful to the British for their outpouring of kindness and love to a pair of stranded Americans in their city. The memorial service was very moving, especially coupled with the great respect the people of London showed by silencing their cars at noon in a show of sympathy. I shall never forget it.

The Regency era, for all of its fancy balls and elegant manners, was a time of great social unrest in Britain, marked by periods of famine, chronic unemployment, and parliamentary abuses. The economic depression was especially felt in the cloth industry, among textile weavers and spinners, who saw their wages plummet by nearly 70 percent.

Cloth manufacture remained an extremely laborious, time-intensive process until the advent of early nineteenth-century machinery. Merely turning the flax plant into linen involved over twenty different steps, which I simplified for the purposes of this book. It is interesting to note that today's political term of "heckling" is derived from this industry. The flax hecklers of Dundee, Scotland, established a reputation as radical agitators. The heckling shops were places of ferocious debate over the day's news while working. Eventually, the hecklers moved their arguments from their shop floors to public meetings, where they would bait politicians with questions to comb out truths that might otherwise be concealed; hence the activity became known as heckling.

The Luddites were British textile craftsmen who created a social movement to protest the changes produced by the Industrial Revolution, which they felt was destroying their way of life and leaving them without work. These protests frequently took the form of smashing the new, automated machinery used in cloth finishing but occasionally became more violent. The Luddites took their name from Ned Ludd, a weaver who is presumed to be responsible for breaking two knitting frames in a fit of rage in the late 1700s. The new movement in 1812 adopted Ned Ludd as their mythical leader. The term "Luddite" has come to be synonymous with anyone who opposes, or fears, the advancement of technology.

George Mellor was one of many men nicknamed "King Ludd."

His attack on Cartwright's mill was indeed greeted by the mill owner's men pouring acid containers from the roof.

The 1815 passage of the Corn Laws, which covered not only corn but various grains and cereal crops, placed an import tariff on foreign crops. Prices had dropped dramatically following the end of the Napoleonic Wars, and the intent was to protect the profits of British farmers. The result, however, was disastrous, since it prevented any foreign grains from being imported until the domestic price reached a certain level, resulting in grain shortages and, consequently, rioting and strikes.

Matters were further worsened by the dreadful harvest in 1816, following the eruption of Mount Tambora in 1815, which resulted in the "year without a summer." People were especially hard hit in the north and places like Wales, and refugees poured into London, looking for relief.

There was great opportunity in times of such uneasiness for extremists like **Arthur Thistlewood** (1774–1820) and **Henry Hunt** (1773–1835). Thistlewood spent time in France during that revolution and sought to import those radical ideas into Britain. His goal was an immediate, bloody overthrow of the government. His claims of great genius are true, and my description of him on the scaffold chewing an orange, singing, and telling the hangman to "do it tidy" is also accurate. Thistlewood was the mastermind behind the violent, but ultimately harebrained, Cato Street Conspiracy, through which he took many others to the gallows with him.

Hunt was a charismatic speaker and agitator who advocated parliamentary reform and repeal of the Corn Laws. He was at the forefront of many events like the Spa Field Riots.

The Peterloo Massacre was an unfortunate event in British history. An assembly of about sixty thousand people was formed at St. Peter's Field in Manchester to demand parliamentary reform. Unlike many other protests, the organizers were determined that this would be a peaceable gathering, and this was reflected in its attendance by a large number of women and children. Unfortunately, the local magistrates assumed the worst, which was not completely unreasonable based on other rioting going on around the country, and called in the military. A detachment of horse artillery attempted to calmly disperse the crowd, but the horses became frightened, and chaos ensued. When it was over, eighteen people had been killed and around five hundred were wounded, many of them women. Journalists on the scene were quick to publish stories about the carnage, with James Wroe of the *Manchester Observer* nicknaming the event Peterloo, a cross between "St. Peter's Field" and "Waterloo."

Tragically, Peterloo's immediate effect was a governmental crackdown on any reform, with the passage of what became known as the Six Acts, a series of laws designed to suppress radical meetings and publications. By the end of 1820, nearly every significant reformer—including Mr. Wroe—was in jail and civil liberties had been curtailed to pre-Peterloo levels.

Other historical people in the novel include **Lord Spencer Perceval**, who was indeed assassinated by **John Bellingham** inside the House of Commons, although I moved the date from May 1812 to June 1812, to better suit my story's time line. This murder was the only successful assassination of a British prime minister, although other attempts have been made throughout history. Other real people who make brief appearances are **Lord Liverpool**, Speaker of the House **George Abbot**, **Lord Harrowby**, **Lady Anne Hamilton**, **Lady Jane Hood**, **Thomas Spence**, the spy **George Edwards**, and conspirators **John Brunt**, **William Davidson**, **John Harrison**, **James Ings**, and **Richard Tidd**.

The illegal opium trade of the nineteenth century was just coming into vogue in the time period of this story, spurred on by trading activities of the East India Company. The "opium dens" sensationalized by nineteenth-century novels were far more prevalent in cities like San Francisco and New York than in London. The English consumption of opiates was typically in the form of laudanum, sleeping draughts, poppy tea, and other legal, widely available "remedies."

Furniture makers, more aptly termed cabinetmakers, of the period not only built traditional furniture but were also responsible for picture frames, musical instruments, wall sconces, mirrors, and even coffins. Coffin-building was a profitable sideline during slow periods, since there were always new customers needing them!

Whereas the furniture of the late eighteenth century trended toward a delicate, spindly look, the Regency brought about a more opulent style, still Classical in inspiration but with more ornamentation.

It can be difficult to attribute pieces to specific cabinetmakers of the time, because most British cabinetmakers didn't sign their products. Hence we see terms like "Hepplewhite-style" to refer to pieces that could have either come from that workshop or been directly copied by other artisans.

As with architects, there was no formal cabinetmakers guild. This is ironic, since there were guilds for just about every other aspect of woodworking: The joiners, carpenters, carvers, and turners all had their own guilds.

There were generally three levels of cabinetmaker: apprentice, journeyman, and master cabinetmaker. An apprentice usually started around the age of fourteen, and would be selected by the master based upon strength, a necessary attribute for working with wood. An apprenticeship lasted seven years, meaning he could achieve journeyman level by the age of twenty-one. An apprentice received room and board but no pay, whereas a journeyman was paid and received nothing else.

The master cabinetmaker usually owned the shop and would always be the one to greet customers and discuss commissions.

Those who have read my previous two books, *The Queen's Dollmaker* and *A Royal Likeness*, will perhaps forgive an author's fancy in bringing back the great Madame Tussaud for one final mention, as the provider of Put's glass eye. Her traveling wax exhibition did actually pass through London in 1812, although she probably wouldn't have been handing out replacement parts to her visitors. It would be twenty-three more years before Tussaud settled down into a permanent location on Baker Street in 1835, later moved to nearby Marylebone Road.

Christine Trent
NOVEMBER 2011

SELECTED BIBLIOGRAPHY

Beard, Geoffrey. *The National Trust Book of English Furniture*. Harmondsworth, Middlesex: Viking, 1985.

Black, Maggie, and Deirdre Le Faye. *The Jane Austen Cookbook*. Toronto: McClelland and Steward, 1995.

Carroll, Leslie. *Notorious Royal Marriages: A Juicy Journey through Nine Centuries of Dynasty, Destiny, and Desire*. New York: New American Library, 2010.

———. *Royal Affairs: A Lusty Romp Through the Extramarital Adventures That Rocked the British Monarchy*. New York: New American Library, 2008.

Chippendale, Thomas. *The Gentleman & Cabinetmaker's Director: Reprint of the Third Edition with a Biographical Sketch with Photographic Supplement of Chippendale-Type Furniture*, New York: Dover Publications, 1966.

Davis, Terence. *The Architecture of John Nash*. London: Studio Books, 1960.

———. *John Nash: The Prince Regent's Architect*. Cranbury, NJ: A.S. Barnes and Co., 1966.

Fraser, Flora. *The Unruly Queen: The Life of Queen Caroline*. Berkeley: University of California Press, 1996.

Gaynor, James M., and Nancy L. Hagedorn. *Tools: Working Wood in Eighteenth-Century America*. Williamsburg: The Colonial Williamsburg Foundation, 1993.

Griffiths, Arthur. *The Chronicles of Newgate*. New York: Dorset Press, 1987.

Hobhouse, Hermione. *A History of Regent Street*. London: Macdonald and Jane's, 1975.

Hughes, Kristine. *Everyday Life in Regency and Victorian England, from 1811–1901*. Cincinnati: Writer's Digest Books, 1998.

Lewis, Ethel. *The Romance of Textiles*. New York: Macmillan and Company, 1937.

Mansbridge, Michael. *John Nash: A Complete Catalogue.* New York: Rizzoli International Publications, 1991.

Nash, John. *Views of the Royal Pavilion.* Introduction by Gervase Jackson-Stops. New York: Abbeville Press, 1991.

Nylander, Jane C. *Fabrics for Historic Buildings.* Washington, DC: The Preservation Press, 1990.

Parissien, Steven. *George IV: Inspiration of the Regency.* New York: St. Martin's Press, 2001.

———. *Regency Style.* London: Phaidon Press, 1992.

Priestley, J. B. *The Prince of Pleasure and His Regency.* New York: Harper & Row, 1969.

Service, Alastair. *The Architects of London and Their Buildings from 1066 to the Present Day.* London: The Architectural Press, 1979.

Watson, Sir Francis. *The History of Furniture.* London: Orbis Publishing, 1976.

Yorke, Trevor. *Georgian & Regency Houses Explained.* Berkshire: Countryside Books, 2007.

INTERNET REFERENCES

The Georgian Index
www.georgianindex.net

Royal Pavilion, Museums & Libraries
www.brighton-hove-rpml.org.uk

Spartacus International
www.spartacus.schoolnet.co.uk

DISCUSSION QUESTIONS

1. What was it about architecture that made it primarily a man's domain? After all, there were noted women artists of the time and architecture is certainly an art form. What made people view this business in an entirely different way than mere art?

2. How were city planning projects in early nineteenth-century Great Britain different from, say, twentieth-century United States projects? Think in terms of financing, authority, and concepts like "eminent domain."

3. Would it be difficult in the Regency period for a woman to carry on her father's trade as a draper? How were women's roles in society changing by this point?

4. Do you think Wesley Stirling's troubles were caused by his sister, were a result of his opium addiction, or were caused by some blend of the two? How might one have fed off the other? What do you think made opium a particularly attractive substance at the time?

5. The Industrial Revolution was in its bare infancy in 1815, therefore we must assume that most of the furniture and decoration made for the Royal Pavilion was crafted by skilled artisans of the time, and not produced in a factory. Although some limited pieces might be available for purchase from the cabinetmaker's showroom floor, most likely the buyer would order furniture and wait months to receive it. How might the furniture-buying habits of a homeowner in the early nineteenth century be different from today?

6. The Cato Street Conspiracy, which was modeled on the plans of the French Revolution, was obviously a miserable failure. Why do you think that such schemes tend to go awry? Compare and contrast leaders like Arthur Thistlewood and Maximilien Robespierre.

7. Given that he received money based on a strict annual allowance from Parliament, how was the Prince Regent able to initiate such grand schemes as Carlton House and the Royal Pavilion? How could he assure creditors they would be paid?

8. Do you think it's likely that John Nash married Mary Ann Bradley as a favor to the Prince Regent? If so, does it change your view of Nash? Your opinion of the Prince Regent? What does such a marriage suggest about Mary Ann's role in society?

9. The Prince Regent secretly married the Catholic widow Maria Fitzherbert in 1785. He did this in express defiance of both the 1701 Act of Settlement, which prevented any royal from marrying a Catholic, and the Royal Marriages Act of 1772, which prevented a royal marriage from taking place without the express consent of the monarch. So, in your opinion, what took precedence: a marriage performed by a clergyman or the rules established by the Crown? Was George in fact married to two women at once?

10. Do you think the poisoning rumors that circulated after Queen Caroline's death were just wild speculation, or was there sufficient reason at the time to think they might be true?